The Songbird's Way

Jennifer Barrett

POOLBEG

Published 2014
by Poolbeg Press Ltd.
123 Grange Hill, Baldoyle,
Dublin 13, Ireland
Email: poolbeg@poolbeg.com

A catalogue record for this book is available from the British Library.

ISBN 978178199-9936

Printed and bound by CPI Group (UK) Ltd, Croydon, CR0 4YY
Bird illustrations by Maureen Barrett

www.poolbeg.com

About the Author

Jennifer Barrett is a writer, and chief executive of a
developing world charity.
She was born just outside of London and has lived most
of her life in Dublin, Ireland.
The Songbird's Way is Jennifer's second novel. Her first,
Look into the Eye, was published in 2013.

Follow Jennifer on:
www.jennifer-barrett.com
Facebook *(JenniferBarrettAuthor)*
Twitter *(@JenBarrettEye)*

Acknowledgements

Family is a central theme in this story, and *The Songbird's Way* is dedicated to my parents John and Maureen, and also to my grandparents and our extended family. I am so grateful to you all for giving me my roots and a sense of belonging to so many great places. Dublin is the city I call home, but Kerry, London and Kent are all a part of me too and it was very special to revisit these second homes with my folks while I researched and wrote this book.

Lots of terribly clever, interesting people helped me in my research for *The Songbird's Way* – I am so grateful to you all. Any inaccuracies or errors in these pages are entirely my own. Thanks so much to John Collins for driving us all over the Kent countryside in search of nightingales, to David Lee for sharing your local Dingle knowledge and to Helen Kelly for helping me to get to grips with the teacher-training system in England. Thanks also to Brother Denis Gleeson for enlightening me on the Enneagram and aspects of Jungian psychology, and to my green-fingered friends, Kara Flannery and Denise Hope – thanks for the suggestions for some of the featured 'flora'. And as for the 'fauna', mahooooosive thanks to Sheila O'Driscoll – my amazing birding guru. Thank you, Sheila, for sharing your in-depth bird knowledge with me – as you can see, your passion for our feathered friends has rubbed off!

To Fiona Clinton and Lawrence Mitchell, thanks for your hospitality and patience as I combined book edits with my visit to you in New York, and to you and Kerri Grimshaw for feeding and entertaining me during writing breaks in Martha's Vineyard – best BBQs ever! To Jessica Kavanagh, thank you for the much-welcome retreat to Wicklow, the stay that helped me make it across the finishing line with this book. And back at the starting line, much of the initial plotting and planning was done on a cycling holiday along by the canals and through the villages of Burgundy. Thanks so much, Caitríona Ní Liatháin for waiting patiently for me to jot down my notes when we stopped for those much-needed breaks along the way!

Thank you to my talented mother, Maureen Barrett, for the wonderful bird sketches – I love them so. To Lisa Byrne, thank you so much for picking the perfect name for the character of Ethan Harding. Thanks also to other Facebook friends for all the great suggestions, and of course for responding to my random research questions along the way – you never fail me, guys! To Helen Coughlan, many thanks for your valuable feedback on the draft of some of the early chapters. And to Aiveen Mullally, who once encouraged me to 'use my voice' – little did you know that you were inspiring the next novel, eh?! Thanks so much for the advice and inspiration, Aiveen.

I've found one of the most unexpected and loveliest things about having my books published to be the overwhelming outpouring of good wishes and support from family and friends – old and new. Space precludes me from naming everyone individually here, but thank you all so, so much for your incredible support over the past couple of crazy years – it means so much to me. I do have to say a special thank-you to my gorgeous nieces and nephews, Daniel, Isabel, Rachel, Liam, Laura, Marianne and Lochlann – I've been so touched by your genuine enthusiasm and interest in your nutty auntie's writing. Love you, guys!

Music, and especially singing, is a great passion of mine and I have to admit to shamelessly indulging said passion in these pages. I'm hoping, dear readers, that if you listen very carefully you might even be able to *hear*, as well as read, this book! A very special thank-you to Caoimhe O'Neill and to Sian Sharkey, Maddy Ryan, Fiona Quinn and all the awesome Choir Club Singers. Being back singing with you all has been such a joy, and no minor source of inspiration to the musical storyline of this book.

To Poolbeg Press, thank you so much for believing in me and for all that you do to ensure new Irish writers are published and read. Special thanks to Paula Campbell for all your support, encouragement and words of wisdom. Thanks also to Ailbhe Hennigan, David Prendergast and all the Poolbeg team for everything you do. And to my editor, Gaye Shortland – thank you, Gaye, for always challenging me to go one step further with my writing and for casting that eagle eye of yours over my words. Not to mention, O Grammar Guru Gaye, for enlightening me as to the existence of all those obscure grammar rules. I love working with you all.

And of course to you, kind Readers, thank you, thank you, THANK YOU! You are the reason I write, and I appreciate your support and interest more than words can express. To the fantastic booksellers, bloggers and reviewers who help to keep this world of printed words alive and kicking, thanks for your kindness and generosity to this newbie writer. And to the amazing group of talented, witty, clever, endlessly supportive writers I have been so fortunate to have got to know – thank you for the lunches, the advice, laughs, encouragement and moral support. You're the best!

And so to Africa. Over the years, I've had the privilege of working with so many inspiring people whose work with the poor and vulnerable of the developing world has been very humbling to witness. These extraordinary men and women give their time and in many cases their entire lives in service to other people and I am constantly in awe of their energy, and of their selfless commitment to the communities they work with. Thank you to those in Africa and at home who helped in my research for this book. And to all at Edmund Rice Development and throughout the Edmund Rice network around the globe, thank you all so much for your support. I really do appreciate it.

And finally, thanks to my mother's cousin and our dear friend, Michael Collins. When last I met Michael he quoted a few lines from a George Pope Morris poem in reference to his beloved home in Garfinny in Dingle. I had never heard the poem before, but thought the words a perfect fit for Mrs Thorpe's story and asked if I could use them in this book. Thank you so much for sharing these touching lines with us, Michael. May you rest in peace, gentle man.

Woodman, spare that tree!

Touch not a single bough!

In youth it sheltered me,

And I'll protect it now.

From 'Woodman, Spare that Tree'
by George Pope Morris

For Maureen and John,
and for the Collins, Dowds, Barretts and McCarthys,
with all my love
xxx

Part one

The Nightingale

Chapter 1

They say parents should give their children roots and wings. I'm not sure about roots, but mine certainly gave me wings . . . and wheels. One of the few things I had left to remember them by was a much-loved, old, blue bicycle.

My father bought the sturdy second-hand Raleigh from the woman who ran the stall next to him in London's Greenwich market. He fixed the bike up himself, sprayed it a light-blue colour and delighted my mother with it on the morning of her thirtieth birthday. He said the colour was to remind her that, no matter where in the world her work as a travel-writer took her, all three of us would always share the same blue sky above. My mother named the bike Sky and from that day forward they were rarely apart: Kenya, Tanzania, South Africa, Zambia, France, Holland, Portugal, Spain . . . she travelled through them all on Sky's two wheels, becoming something of an authority on travel by bike.

I was eight years old on the day of her thirtieth birthday. It was twenty-two years ago, and my mother had already been at home with my father and me in our

3

small two-bedroomed garden flat in Greenwich for almost two weeks. I loved when the three of us were back together and I was very happy to snuggle up in bed beside her that morning after my father went to work in the market. I glanced over her shoulder at the birthday cards from her family in Ireland that she was reading, then I opened up my *Famous Five* book. I rested it on top of the blankets over my chest, preparing to settle in for a leisurely morning – but I should have known that my mother wouldn't stay still too long.

As soon as she'd finished reading them, my mother put the cards on the bedside table, threw back the bed covers and leapt out.

"All right, Chip, let's get moving," she said.

Everyone else called me Chrissie, short for Christine – I was named after Christine McVie from my parents' favourite band, Fleetwood Mac. As I got older though my parents had both started to call me 'Chip' – something about being a 'chip off the old block' . . . or blocks. They reckoned I was just like both of them, though how one person could be like two, I never quite understood at the time.

"Aw, can we not stay here a little longer?" I rested the book flat on my chest. "Daddy won't be finished work for hours yet."

My mother went to where Sky was propped up against the end of the bed and held the handles. She pulled her long, red hair back from her face. It spilled in waves down the back of my father's old, greying Fleetwood Mac T-shirt which looked like a flowing nightdress on my slender mother. She looked lost in thought for a minute, then she pulled the T-shirt off over her head and shouted back to me as she headed to the bathroom: "No more lying about,

Chip! Come on, the sun is splitting the stones out there. We can't lie around and wait for life to come to us – today's a day for adventure."

That got me. I jumped out of bed and tore my own nightdress off as I ran down to my room to find something to wear.

"Can we bring Elvis?" I shouted into the bathroom as I passed. Elvis was my beloved black Scottish terrier – his name had been my father's idea.

"No, not this time, love," my mother shouted back out to me. "We're going to be taking the bikes – I want to try Sky out." She popped her head out around the door. "We'll leave lots of food and water for him though and I'll ask your Uncle Donal to feed and walk him tonight."

I stopped in my tracks, just outside my bedroom. "Ooh, are we going away for the night then?"

"You'll see!" My mother always loved to build suspense.

Elvis was sitting in his usual spot on top of his kennel outside my bedroom window. I opened the window and patted his head. "Sorry we can't take you today, boy." He wagged his little tail furiously as if I'd just told him he was having steak for dinner. "If it was up to me, you'd be coming, but Mummy says you have to stay here and Daddy said she's the boss when she's home."

My parents had met nine years earlier, when my young mother bought a cassette from my father's market stall. A native of Dingle on the southwest coast of Ireland, she was in London for a week, staying in Charlton with her brother Donal and Gemma, his then-girlfriend, now wife. My mother was travelling on from London to Madrid to start touring Spain for her new job with the *Small World*

5

travel guide company. It was the Fleetwood Mac cassette *Rumours* that she bought from my father's stall. He loved the album too and they got chatting about it. His favourite song was 'Songbird', but my mother preferred 'Go Your Own Way' and they enjoyed an animated discussion about the album and about music in general.

My father asked her out there and then and they spent most of the remaining five days that my mother was in London together. My father showed her all around his adopted town of Greenwich and neighbouring Blackheath, and he scraped his pennies together to take her to London to watch the West End musical, *Cats*. He told me that she even held the umbrella while he busked outside the Leicester Square half-price ticket booth on a rainy afternoon in May to get the last of the money together for the show tickets – that's when he knew she was a keeper. My mother loved the show and by all accounts over the course of those five days they fell madly in love. They promised to meet again as soon as my mother's trip was over and wrote to each other regularly while she travelled – proper, mushy old love letters and postcards. Five months later, she stopped off in London to see my father on her way home to Ireland from Spain and it was on that visit that I came into being. I believe I was a big surprise to my mother and the very big, very Catholic Devlin family, not to mention to my father and the staunch Presbyterian Coles.

Just over nine months later, I was born in Tralee Hospital in Kerry. I spent my first year living with my mother, my grandma and several of my mother's younger siblings at their home in Dingle. My father stayed with us for a short time at the beginning too, but the cottage was overcrowded and the arrangement didn't work so well.

Daddy went back to London when I was just a couple of months old, coming back to visit whenever he could afford it. My grandma has since told me that that period wasn't a good time for my mother. She missed my father and she struggled to deal with a young baby on her own, and of course she desperately missed her life on the road. She couldn't accept that, at just twenty-two years of age, her dream of travelling the world was over. At least that was how my grandma explained my mother's decision to go back to work when I was just a year old. The plan was to leave me with Grandma just for a few weeks while my mother travelled to Spain again to finish off her guide. But when she told my father the plan, he came straight over to Ireland and brought me back to London to live with him. I think my mother preferred that arrangement anyway and Daddy quickly got used to being full-time father to a young baby. My mother's travels went on longer than a few weeks though – they went on for the rest of her life in fact. She stayed with us between trips or when she was writing up a travel guide, coming home for anything between three weeks and three months at a time. Those were my favourite times.

My father was my rock, the solid, dependable force in my life, whilst my mother brought adventure and was always fun to be around. We both missed her desperately when she was travelling, but she would return with the most incredible stories and presents from far-flung places that made me the envy of all my school friends. At the time, I didn't mind the arrangement too much – it was the only life I knew.

Half an hour after getting up on the morning of her thirtieth birthday, my mother and I were cycling in the sunshine from our flat on the outskirts of the town down the busy main street towards the centre of Greenwich, a big rucksack on my mother's back. I was very excited at the prospect of the surprise trip and pedalled hard to keep up with her.

Before long we were locking our bicycles around the corner from Greenwich tourist office. My mother pored over maps and looked through pamphlets and brochures with the woman behind the desk for what felt like hours, but was probably only a few minutes. I kneeled up on one of the chairs and stared out the window at the people walking past.

Eventually she called me over to the counter. "Right then, we have it down to two options. Which would you prefer: a magical, enchanted forest or a haunted stately home?"

"Magical, enchanted forest! Definitely the forest!" I leaned up on my toes to try to see over the counter – half hoping to see a few goblins and fairies on the other side.

My mother just nodded to the lady behind the desk who smiled at me, then started tapping away at the computer.

After the tourist office, my mother bought us two tubs of vanilla ice cream in the corner shop and we pushed our bikes down to the Thames, past the *Cutty Sark,* to eat them. I gazed up at the masts of the huge old clipper ship in its dry dock as we passed by, and I imagined the adventures she must have had carrying her cargoes of tea through the Suez Canal and her shipments of wool from Australia all those years ago.

My mother found us a free bench by the riverside and we rested our bikes against the back of it then sat down and ate creamy mouthfuls of delicious ice cream from small wooden spoons. We watched people walk past on the footpath in front of us and the riverboats sail slowly by on the Thames, the dark blue water twinkling in the June sunshine. We made up stories about the passers-by, who quickly became double agents, private investigators and celebrities in disguise, while the passengers on the river boats became pirates, smugglers and galley-slaves. I loved playing make-believe with my mother – she made up the best stories and was enormous fun.

At noon we went down to the market to meet my father – he was closing up the stall early that day so we could all spend the afternoon of my mother's birthday together. He was busy loading a crate into another stallholder's van where he stored his stock – the crate must have been very heavy because he seemed to be struggling to lift it. My mother leaned Sky against a wall and went over to help him. I followed her, still holding onto my bike.

"Hey, what are you two doing here?" he said as they slid the crate into the back of the van together. "I was expecting to pick you up back at the flat." He gave my mother a kiss, then rubbed my head.

I peered inside the crate – it was full of second-hand paperbacks, vinyl records and music cassettes. It may have been 1991, but my father resolutely refused to stock CD's. It had taken him a long time to acquiesce to stocking cassettes – his heart belonged to vinyl – "the only way to listen to music," he always said.

"It was such a beautiful day we decided to get out and about," my mother said, holding Sky to one side. "And I thought I'd give my lovely new bike a test run." She rubbed her hand over the shiny handlebars.

Daddy slipped one arm around her waist. "I should have known Nuala Devlin wouldn't have been able to sit still for too long."

He gave her a long, slurpy kiss. And I didn't even mind. My best friend from school, Rachel Howard, said she hated when her parents kissed in public, that it was so embarrassing. But I didn't mind mine kissing, not one bit, I was so happy to see them together.

My father looked around at me when they finished. "Right, I'll just finish packing up here, Chip, then how about we go up to the park?"

"Ah sure, we can go to the park any time," my mother said. "We've been working on a surprise for you."

I was about to burst with anticipation. I couldn't wait for Daddy to hear what we'd been planning.

"Oh yes?" he said.

My mother turned around to show my father the large rucksack on her back. "I have clean underwear and pyjamas in here for us all, and enough food for an army. We're stealing you away for an adventure, my darling." She winked at me, and I beamed back at her.

"Emm . . . all right," said my father. "I am quite tired though, Nuala. Must be because we were so busy this morning. I hope this surprise won't be too far away or too energetic? I know you have energy to burn, but . . ."

"Ah, go away out of that with your *tired*!" said my mother. "You've been saying that since I got home. A bit of country air in those polluted city lungs of yours will do you the world of good. Come on! Chip and I will help you finish packing up the van, then you can grab your bike and we can get on the road while the sun's still shining."

My father looked at me and raised his eyebrows. "Bossy woman, your mother, eh?"

I laughed, then hurried to lean my bike up against the wall so that I could help pack up the stall.

Chapter 2

I spent most of the short train ride to Chatham with my nose glued to the window, gazing out at the passing scenery. I didn't want to miss a thing. My parents chatted and cuddled in the seat opposite me and it wasn't long before we'd arrived at Chatham Station.

We collected the bikes from the luggage carriage then wheeled them outside the station into the sunshine. It was the perfect day for a cycle – warm, with a slight breeze. For almost an hour we cycled up and down hills, through small towns and villages, past the imposing Rochester Cathedral, over the Medway River and along by the railway lane until we were deep into the Kent countryside.

It felt like we'd been cycling forever by the time we got to Harkston. We passed through the small, quaint village and, about a mile outside it, turned left off the country road to cycle up a long avenue of tall elm trees. At the top of the avenue we stopped to look up at the old Tudor-style inn facing us. It was painted a bright white colour and the facade was criss-crossed with a black wooden pattern. A sign saying *The Three Songbirds Inn* swung from a long post above the open old wooden door. There were quite a few cars parked in the car park in front and a group of people had just arrived ahead of us. The inn looked very welcoming and I hoped we might go inside for a cool drink – I was quite tired from the cycle, and my father looked exhausted. My mother however was bounding with energy – she jumped off her bike and wheeled it over to a fence in front of the car park. She left us to lock the bikes there and walked up to the inn, stopping to touch the bark of a beautiful old oak tree that stood in the centre of the car park across from the front door. Then she passed the inn and walked right over to the map on the board to the side.

"So how did the new bike go for you, Nuala?" Daddy asked when we joined her at the map.

She turned around to him. "Oh, it was wonderful! I love her. Sky moves like she has wings." And she must have been right because even though my mother insisted on carrying the big rucksack herself, she'd been way ahead of my father and me all the way.

My father smiled. "Ah, that's great." He took my hand then and we peered up at the map she'd been studying. "All right then – where are you taking us, Nuala?"

My mother tapped a spot on the map. "Right here. We just need to walk up through Collinswood behind the inn to the clearing at the top where the woman in the tourist office said we'd have the most marvellous view of the Kent countryside. That –" she pointed up at the trees, "will be our picnic spot." And without another word she strode off in the direction of the woods behind the inn.

My father raised his eyebrows at me. "Right then, we'd better follow her or we'll get no food."

I laughed and ran to catch up with my mother.

We had to wade through long grass at the back of the inn to get over to the entrance of Collinswood. It didn't look like too many people had been through there in quite some time – the track through the woods was very overgrown. It was a relief to be out of the sun for a time though. I was quite hot from the cycle and the cool air of the woods was very welcome. The sun twinkled through the gaps in the tall trees and I skipped along in front of my parents, stopping every now and then to pick foxgloves and put the flowers on the tips of my fingers as though they were pretty pink thimbles.

Eventually we came to the top of the path and the trees gave way to a wide-open clearing.

"Aha!" My mother arrived behind me. "This looks like our picnic spot." She looked around and pointed a short distance away from us to a sun-drenched fallen tree trunk – it was lying just at the edge of the woods, surrounded by tall, bright-green grass. My mother took the big rucksack off her back and strode over towards it.

It wasn't a moment too soon – my father, who followed behind her, looked worn out. I'd noticed that he'd been walking particularly slowly towards the end.

My mother had noticed too. "Bobby, are you okay? You really do seem tired, love," she said as she put the bag down by the tree trunk.

"I'm fine and dandy," my father said, straightening up and giving her a huge smile. "Starved though. Chip, get over here and help me shake out the rug."

We were soon sitting on our old scratchy tartan picnic rug, drinking milky tea and devouring corn-beef sandwiches. They were the nicest I'd ever tasted – picnic sandwiches are always the best, as if they get sprinkled with some magical seasoning that can only be tasted outdoors in the sunshine. I'd taken off my trainers and socks and was wiggling my bare toes in the hot summer sun as I ate. I couldn't have been happier at that moment.

"Sing us a song, Chip," my father said as he picked another sandwich out of the Tupperware box.

I shook my head and looked down at my now-still toes.

"Come on, you have a lovely voice," he said. "How about we sing one together for Mummy?"

"No, Daddy, I can't."

"Nonsense – I heard you singing along quietly behind me at our band rehearsal last week. You thought I couldn't hear you, didn't you?" He looked at my mother then. "I took her along to rehearsals in Bill's flat the other day. Honestly, Nuala, you wouldn't believe it – our Chip has a beautiful voice – sweet and clear with great pitch and tone. I don't know how we haven't heard her sing before." He turned to me. "You should use your voice, love. Sing up so people can hear you."

I put my head down and just stared at my sandwich without eating another bite.

I often sang quietly to myself in my little bedroom at home. I'd listen to my father play his records and practise his guitar in the living room at night and I would sing along quietly in bed. I loved all of his music – the ballads, pop songs, old folk tunes – his band had a wide repertoire. He wrote his own songs too and I particularly loved those – he was very talented. But much as I loved the music, I couldn't imagine singing for anyone else – not even my parents – the thought filled me with abject terror. I

14

couldn't believe my father had heard me singing at his rehearsal. I couldn't help but sing along to the beautiful new song he'd written but I'd thought I was being too quiet to be heard by anyone, least of all my father.

"Leave her, Bobby," my mother said. "She's eating. And she doesn't want –"

"Wait!" My father cut my mother off. "Listen to that, girls." He stood up, tilted his head sideways and put his hand behind his ear.

I stood up too. "What, Daddy? What are we meant to be listening to?"

"Shhh! We've got be very quiet." He held one finger up to his lip and the palm of the other hand out to stop me talking. "Yes! It's definitely a nightingale. What a treat – you rarely get to hear them nowadays."

My mother stood up too, and that's when we all heard the song of the nightingale together. It was impressive – a fast succession of very rich high and low notes – there were trills, tweets and gurgles, each call ending in a loud whistling crescendo.

"Beautiful, eh?" My father looked directly at me. "He's not afraid to sing out loud, Chip. And he's only a tiny little thing."

"He can sing like that because he's hidden in the bushes." I went back over to the rug and put my half-eaten sandwich back in the container. "It's easier to sing when no-one's looking at you."

But my father didn't seem to be listening to me. By then both my parents appeared entranced by the bird's song. My mother had moved over closer to my father so that she stood right in front of him, leaning backwards against his chest.

"The songbirds know," my father whispered to my mother.

I took a step back over to them. "Know what, Daddy? What do the songbirds know?"

He glanced around at me. "They know when to be heard."

I didn't really understand what he meant but I didn't ask any more questions. Daddy had turned back to my mother. He gently kissed the top of her head and squeezed her in tighter to him. Then, very softly, he started to sing "Songbird".

As well as being my father's favourite song, the Fleetwood Mac ballad had become mine too. Daddy always sang it alone when his band were rehearsing – it was his solo piece and always came at the end of their set. The others would sit back and we would all just listen to him singing the soothing words as he picked out the delicate, comforting tune on his guitar. And every time he sang that song, no matter who else was there, it felt like he was singing it just for me.

I felt the cool grass between my bare toes and, as I listened to him sing, the simple words of love and comfort began to enchant me once again. Each syllable, every phrase served to make me feel safe and secure as they eased away my childhood fears. Whenever I heard my father sing "Songbird" I was reminded of how much he loved me, and I knew that he would always be there for me. His voice melted into soulful harmony with the nightingale as he sang that day, and I closed my eyes to let the soft, sweet melody of their music wash over me. Listening to my father serenading my mother made me feel happy and all the more protected by the certainty of his love for her too. In that moment with both my parents, I belonged – together we were a family, united by love, protected by an unbreakable bond.

I stood up on my tip-toes and mouthed along to the last few lines of the song, wishing it would never end.

"That was really lovely, Bobby," my mother said when Daddy had finished singing.

He turned her around until their eyes were locked together.

"I love you, Nuala." He smiled after he said the words but he seemed almost nervous.

My mother smiled back at him. "I love you too, Bobby – more than ever." She leaned up to wrap her arms around his neck and they kissed for a very long time. There was nobody else around, but this time it went on so long that I felt my cheeks redden a bit. I wasn't sure whether it was from embarrassment or from joy at witnessing my parents' love for each other.

When they finally stopped kissing my father held on to my mother's arms and looked down at her. "I wish you were always here, Nuala. Chip and I miss you so much when you're on the road. Let's get married, have more kids. I'll give up the band and get rid of the stall. I'll get a proper job instead . . . maybe take up teaching. I've been thinking about all this a lot lately. I could teach English . . . History too maybe." He laughed. "My parents would love that. I'd finally have one of those respectable careers they're always banging on about, and you wouldn't have to travel any more. We could have daytrips like this every weekend. Come on, Nuala. Let's do it – marry me. What do you say?"

My mother pulled back, a look of deep shock on her

face. "I'd never ask you to give up your music, Bobby. Or the stall. You love them both."

She tried to smile then but I knew from her face that it wasn't going to end well.

She took his hand. "Someday, I will marry you, my love, just not yet. When I do settle down I want it to be for the right reasons."

I went and sat down on the rug. I could hardly bear to listen any more.

My father nodded over at me. "Isn't Chip reason enough?"

"That's not fair, Bobby. We need the money from my job for Chip's future." She sighed and squeezed his hand. "I've never misled you, have I? I told you from day one that I wouldn't be getting married before I was at least thirty-five. So I still have another five years to go. I haven't even nearly done everything I want to do before I settle down."

My father closed his eyes and rubbed his eyebrow with his left hand.

She took him by the arms then. "Bobby, I hate leaving you two behind every time I go away, but I think about you all the time – and we make it work, don't we? I know it's not conventional, but we always said we wouldn't do things just because that's the way everybody else did them, didn't we?" She tried to tickle him but he pulled out of her way in time.

"Sure you'd hate me if I didn't work anyway," she went on. "I'd be just another boring, miserable housewife, giving out to you for making so much noise with that band of yours."

My father nodded. "You gotta 'go your own way', eh, Nuala? Like the song says."

She took his arm, rubbed it and smiled sadly. "Just for now, love, but it won't be forever. Tell me you understand?"

My father took a few steps away from her, then looked down at me. "It was worth a try, eh, Chip?" He sat down on the rug beside me then, seeming beaten.

I hated seeing him like that – especially when we'd been having such a lovely day until then. I desperately wanted my mother at home all the time too so I opened my mouth to speak.

I wanted to say something like: 'You couldn't ever be boring, Mummy. And you'd love it here with us. You could take me to school all the time like the other mummies do – they're all such good friends – some of them work but they also have coffee mornings and go for walks together in the evenings and afternoons. And . . . you could come to look at the stars in the Observatory in Greenwich Park with me and Daddy on the weekends, and bring Sky for bicycle rides to see if we can see the red squirrels. Daddy says they're dying out, but I've seen them in the park loads of times, I'm sure of it. Oh, and you could help us feed the ducks there. Daddy always forgets the bread, but you wouldn't – you would remember, wouldn't you? You always remember things like that.'

But I didn't have the nerve to say the words. I didn't want to stir things up any more. So instead I closed my mouth again and said nothing, attempting a smile for my father's sake.

My mother glanced at my father, then sat down on the rug beside him.

A minute or so later she leaned over and gave me a nudge. "I have to go to France next week, Chip. I'm researching a new guide about cycling in Burgundy. When your summer holidays come . . ." She looked at my father. He nodded, but didn't fully look round at her. "When the holidays come," she went on, "you're going to come over and join me in France. Daddy and you are going to come over on the ferry. You can bring your bike – we'll be cycling everywhere – all along by the canal. It's so flat and the canal-paths are so pretty, and the weather will be lovely and warm. The canals are full of otters if you look hard for them. You'll love it."

My eyes widened at the prospect of such an adventure. My mother had always promised I could come with her on one of her trips when I was old enough and I was thrilled to hear that the day had finally arrived – it made me feel like an instant grown-up. I looked over at my father for verification. He smiled at me and nodded, but he didn't look happy – he just seemed really tired and beaten.

"What about Elvis?" I asked him. "Can we take him with us?"

Daddy shook his head. "Your Uncle Donal and Auntie Gem will mind him while I'm gone. I'll have to come back after a few days to run the stall anyway. Not to mention play our Saturday-night gigs – can't let the guys in the band down."

I thought about that for a few seconds – I knew I would miss Elvis and Daddy but the arrangements seemed perfectly acceptable to me. "Wow! France!" I leaned over my father to give my mother a hug, then I sat back and looked at him. "I can really go?"

"Yes, you can really come," my mother answered quickly for him, seeming a little irritated.

My father looked at his watch. "It's getting late, guys. Nuala, this has been lovely – thank you for the surprise but I must admit I'm pretty whacked."

She looked at him for a few seconds. "I wonder are you coming down with something." She put her hand on his forehead to feel his temperature. "You don't feel feverish."

My father stood up and started packing the things away. "I'll be fine, but we'd better get going – it's getting late."

My mother had booked us a room in the old inn and my father went for a lie-down as soon as we checked in. My mother and I went out to the beer garden behind the inn while he rested – it was a lovely shaded spot with a few picnic tables and lots of poppies growing in the tall grass beside the old stone wall enclosing the woods. My mother bought me a red lemonade while she had a glass of white wine and we sat at one of the tables looking over at the trees that were swaying in the gentle evening breeze. She told me all about France and about what we should expect to see there.

My father joined us a few hours later for dinner.

But Daddy wasn't just tired from the market, or from the long cycle, or even just deflated from his failed marriage proposal . . . I found out later that, by the time of my mother's birthday, he'd already been feeling tired and lethargic for months. He hadn't wanted to worry me or make too much of a fuss about it, but my mother had noticed. She thought he was just a bit under the weather and hoped the day trip might give him a lift. But a few days after our night away, when he didn't seem to be getting any better, she insisted he make an appointment to see the doctor.

It's hard to believe what a difference a week can make.

One Saturday evening I was sitting in the evening sun at The Three Songbirds eating fish and chips with my parents, and by the following Saturday everything and everyone around me had changed.

Cancer . . .

Aggressive . . .

Primary source unknown . . .

Body riddled with it . . .

Six months . . .

They were all whispered phrases that swirled around in the air above me and Elvis as the adults talked, then tried to explain the worst news possible to a terrified eight-year-old child.

He lived for another seven months as it happened. Seven very special months. We never did go to France – instead my mother stayed by his side every day of that time. She had to fight hard with his mother to do so though. My grandmother wanted to take her only son back to live with her and my grandfather in their huge, scary mansion in Hampstead. She could hire a nurse to give him round-the-clock care, she'd said. But my mother refused, insisting we all stay together in our flat. They had a huge fight about it. Things were tense between the two of them before my father got sick, but after that they never spoke again – not one single word – and I didn't see my grandparents again for many years.

When my father got sick, my mother bought a small second-hand Mini Cooper to drive him to all his hospital appointments. I got to know the corridors and the doctors and nurses of the hospital very well. And even though we were desperately scared and sad, we were also, strangely, very happy. In fact, I remember that time as one of the happiest of my life. My overriding memories are of my parents and me laughing together, eating together, going to the hospital together, crying together . . . We shared every experience and felt every emotion, good and bad – all together.

One Saturday morning, my mother came into my bedroom to wake me up. She'd told me the day before that she and Daddy had a big surprise planned for that day, but wouldn't tell me what it was. I jumped up out of bed, but almost dived back in under the covers when I saw what dress she'd pulled out of the wardrobe – it was a frilly, pink dress with a scratchy lace collar that Auntie Gem had bought me for my birthday the year before – I hated it and had never worn it. I didn't complain though, just took it from my mother and slowly got dressed.

She wore a new blue knee-length chiffon dress she'd bought from the market. It was the same colour blue as Sky and she looked more beautiful than I'd ever seen her look. She wore a single white carnation in her long red hair to match the one in the button-hole of my father's only suit jacket. He was lost inside the now seemingly very big suit. My mother and I had had to scour the flat that morning to find enough safety pins to take the trousers in at the back so they would stay up.

And though my mother was not yet thirty-five, they got married that day at the Royal Greenwich registry office. Uncle Donal and Auntie Gem were witnesses, and I was the flower girl. I had a bunch of white carnations to hold. My parents looked so happy as they stood shoulder to shoulder in front of the fireplace of the cosy registry office, repeating their vows to the Registrar. I knew it took all of my father's strength to stay standing beside my mother throughout the twenty-minute ceremony, but anyone who didn't know us would have thought them just another young couple about to begin the rest of their lives together. As I stood beside them and watched my parents marry, I felt the happiest and the saddest I've ever felt in my life – all at the same time.

We went for dinner at the Clarendon Hotel in Blackheath after the registry office. My parents both seemed so happy but I watched my father push his food around his plate throughout the meal, barely able to eat a thing. We didn't stay for dessert. When we got home I sat with my father as he settled in bed and my mother went out to make him a cup of camomile tea. I pulled Daddy's blankets up for him and, once he got comfortable, he patted the bed beside him. We often read together before bedtime so I turned from him to pick up my book from the nightstand.

But this night was different. "No, don't worry about that, Chip. I want to talk to you," he said.

He eased himself slowly up further on the pillows but it seemed to take all his strength. My once broad, strong father had grown so thin and weak. The day had been very special but it seemed to have taken a lot out of him.

I climbed up and sat beside him on the bed.

"Are you okay, Daddy?" I asked. "Will I get you something?"

He just shook his head, leaned over to the nightstand and picked up a small brown-paper bag.

"Open that, love." He handed me the bag, then put his frail arm around me.

I snuggled in to him, then opened up the bag and took out a small brown-and-grey china bird. It was sitting on a low perch, its beak wide open. My father held out the palm of his very pale, thin hand and I put the bird down on it.

"It's a nightingale," he said. "I found it in the market many months ago but with everything that's happened since, I almost forgot to give it to you. I bought it just after that day in the woods, the day we heard the nightingale sing. Do you remember it, Chip?"

I nodded. "Of course I remember, Daddy."

"They're such shy little birds,' he went on. "They hide out in the trees and bushes and they don't like to stand out too much. But boy oh boy, can they can sing! Such beautiful songs – they bring such joy through their music."

He squeezed me a little tighter beside him as we both looked at the little bird in his palm.

After a moment he said: "Turn it over there."

I picked the bird up out of my father's hand and looked underneath. There were just three words written on the base: *Use Your Voice*.

"Don't you realise that you've been given such a valuable, beautiful gift, my little nightingale?" he said. "It makes me sad that you're too shy to use it. Will you sing for me today? It's such a happy day and I'd so love to hear your voice in song."

I stared at the three words written in my father's handwriting. Then I looked up to see my mother standing behind the bedroom door. I saw a single tear roll down her cheek before she could wipe it away.

I smiled at her, then I took a long, deep breath in. I inched myself off the bed and turned to stand and face my father. I felt the small china bird in my hand, took another long, deep breath then tilted my head back and began to sing 'Songbird' – the song I'd heard Daddy sing so many times himself.

I sang it quietly, shakily, at first, surprised and nervous to hear my own voice out loud. But by the time I'd got to the first line of the chorus, every note, every word emerged in magically sweet, flowing tones. They came from a place I'd never discovered before, from somewhere deep inside me. And I realised that singing the song aloud made me feel good – alive, free and fearless. With my parents together with me I felt as if I could do anything.

My mother came into the room and sat beside my father on the bed. "The best wedding present ever," I heard her whisper to him. They smiled at each other and kissed gently, before cuddling up and listening to me . . . together . . . just as they'd listened to the nightingale sing that day in the woods.

After 'Songbird' I sang song after song until my father drifted off to sleep, his bride in his arms.

A few weeks later my dear daddy . . . my rock . . . my heart . . . flew away and left us for the last time. I still think of him whenever I gaze up at the blue sky above.

Chapter 3

A permanent position, she'd said.

As I approached my own thirtieth birthday, I couldn't decide whether I was interested in the regular income or daunted at the prospect of my life finally approaching something along the lines of conventional. I'd been working at Park View Grammar School for Girls in Blackheath for almost six months when the headmistress, Ms Delamere, asked to meet me in her office after the final bell. I hadn't had too much to do with her since I'd taken up my contract as a teacher's assistant, but we were only four weeks from the end of term and the end of my contract so I imagined it must be something of an exit interview. I certainly hadn't expected her to be keeping me in mind for a permanent position.

Ms Delamere explained that they'd been very happy with my year-long placement and were keen for me to go on to do my teacher training with a view to coming back as a permanent teacher. I began to lose track of what she was saying though as she went on about all the benefits of a career in teaching. My eyes roamed to the large window behind her wide, varnished, walnut desk. The sun was pelting through the gaps in the metal venetian blinds and I could just about make out the huge sycamore trees swaying in the warm June breeze outside. It was late Friday afternoon and the school was already freakishly quiet – most of the teachers and pupils had scattered as soon as the bell had rung to enjoy the beautiful weather. I could just about make out the birds singing outside over Ms Delamere's soliloquy– it sounded like two blackbirds calling to each other – a sweet, melodious, low-pitched warble.

I tried hard to focus back on Ms Delamere's pale, thin face, making sure to nod occasionally as she spoke. I took in her greying hair tied back in a neat chignon – every day the same hairstyle, never a hair out of place. She wore her own uniform every day too regardless of the weather. She must have had a wardrobe full of fitted tweed suits that she alternated – each one a matching, short box jacket and long pencil skirt worn over a high-collared, white blouse. She teamed the suits with sensible, low-heeled, black court shoes and flesh-coloured tights, and always completed the look with pearl earrings and a small gold cross-and-chain around her neck.

She was sitting forward in her chair, intermittently tapping the document on the desk in front of her as she spoke. "Feedback from our parents has been extremely positive," she was saying. "Of course your teaching methods can be a little unusual at times – using a drum to teach the girls poetry is not something I've ever seen before in all my years of teaching."

I wanted to tell her that the drum I used to teach the children about poetic rhythm was actually called a bodhrán – a traditional Irish percussion instrument made of stretched goat-skin. My own bodhrán had been specially made for me near my mother's home in Dingle. I wanted to clarify this, but I didn't like to interrupt her flow.

"Your methods may be a little unorthodox," she was saying, "but you seem to be getting the results and the children certainly respond well to you." She picked up the document from her desk and handed it to me.

I was almost afraid to handle it in case it meant there would be no going back, but I took it from her and leafed through it to keep up appearances.

"As you may know, Mrs Hunt will be retiring next year. That is an outline of her job specification – it's essentially an English teaching position, with some extra-curricular responsibilities. So if you were to complete your teacher's placements here at Park View next year while studying for your teaching qualification," she leaned forward over her desk and looked directly at me, "I think you would be top of the list for the permanent post in a year's time. No guarantees of course, but we like to look after our own." She smiled. "And we do consider you to be one of our own now, Chrissie."

I was surprised on a number of levels, not least because it was the first time Ms Delamere had ever used my first name – I was usually 'Miss Devlin-Cole' when I met her in the corridors or in the staff room – but also because she considered me 'one of our own'. It was nice to hear, but I wasn't sure I was ready for all of the implications.

Ms Delamere pointed to the job specification in my hands. "We will be hoping the successful candidate will also be able to take on Mrs Hunt's running of the debating society which has been doing so well of late. We were all delighted when they won the –"

But I was only half listening. Whilst I had enjoyed teaching over the year, I wasn't one-hundred-per-cent sure Park View was the school for me. Worse than that, though, I wasn't even sure whether teaching was for me. I'd almost fallen into it as it seemed a logical progression after my degree. The problem was, in recent months I'd begun to think more and more about travelling, maybe working somewhere else for a while. It was an inconvenient, unsettling feeling, and not one I'd hoped to be entertaining at the time.

I didn't say anything about my doubts though, just nodded at the requisite moments.

"There is just one thing." Ms Delamere shuffled in her seat and began to look a little uneasy. "Some of the mothers have a concern. They have noted that you run a stall in Greenwich market on Saturdays and they don't think it the right image for a top London grammar school to have one of its teachers . . . eh . . . working on a market stall."

She said the last few words as if they were dirty, which really irritated me. I loved the market and had been running my father's stall since I'd reopened it four years earlier, not long after I'd moved back to London.

Until then I'd been a singer with *Celtic Wings*, the hugely successful Irish music and dance show based on the legend in which the children of Lir, the High King of Ireland, are turned into swans by their father's new wife. I was only eighteen when I joined the show. Living in hotels and tour buses quickly became the reality of my adult life and, though I was a somewhat reluctant performer, I settled into my role as a singer in the chorus very quickly. I found touring very exciting and for years I loved my life on the road, making some very good friends in the cast, and meeting so many interesting people along the way. We visited so many amazing places too, performing in almost all the big-city concert halls of America, Europe, Australia and New Zealand. We'd even played some special concerts in Beijing, Hong Kong, Tokyo and Singapore.

As time went on though, the lead singers left the show for other gigs or solo careers and my name started to be mentioned as a potential stand-in for the lead female singing role of Fionnuala. I only once had to sing the part at a show in Singapore. I just about got by, possibly even enjoyed it a little, but I was so nervous that I was physically ill beforehand. I was never comfortable alone in the spotlight and I knew it would only become harder and harder to avoid if I stayed with the show much longer.

Also, as time went on, I grew tired of all of the internal wrangles and dramas of a close-knit touring group – there were more reported affairs and break-ups amongst the singers, dancers and crew of *Celtic Wings* each week than there could have been in any celebrity gossip column.

So – at the ripe old age of twenty-five and feeling especially disillusioned after my own failed relationship with one of the other singers, I finally decided to leave my musical career behind. I wanted to try to put down some roots so I moved back to London and with my *Celtic Wings* savings put a down-payment on a small flat a stone's throw away from the market in Greenwich. I signed up to study for a BA degree in English at the University of London with money my mother had saved and put aside for my education and I fitted the market stall in around my lectures, using the money to pay for my bills and spending money.

It was around that time also that I started seeing Tim, my cousin's best friend.

As I sat there, watching Ms Delamere's lips move, I thought about all I had yet to do to pack up my flat. I was due to move in with Tim that weekend. He'd always been especially keen on me settling down and I knew he'd be delighted at the prospect of me taking a permanent job at Park View. He was the one who'd suggested I consider teaching after my degree and he'd encouraged me to take the contract at Park View. It had been an enjoyable enough year, though I'd had to cut down to just Saturdays on the stall which had been difficult because I loved the market and the freedom it gave me to be my own boss.

"Just something for you to bear in mind, Chrissie," Ms Delamere was saying. "You wouldn't be able to keep the market stall going anyway when you're doing your teacher training, would you? You'll need all your spare time to study when you're not working on your placements here."

I responded to her raised questioning eyebrows with a thin smile. "Thank you for letting me know about the position, Ms Delamere." I picked up my backpack, unzipped one of the pockets, then folded the job specification to put it in.

Ms Delamere gave a little cough, covering her mouth with her small, loosely clenched fist as she did. "There is just one other small matter I have to mention, Chrissie."

The over-use of my first name was making me feel increasingly uneasy. I wondered if I should call her by *her*

32

first name too, but damned if I could think what it was. Penelope? Pauline? I rested my backpack down beside my chair and chose to say nothing – safer that way.

"You may find you would do better with the interview panel were you to consider a slightly more . . . eh . . . *conservative* wardrobe? Something more befitting a grammar-school teacher?"

She scanned me from head to foot, drawing my own eyes down to my clothes. I had on my loose, dark-brown, cotton maxi dress with string straps that I'd bought in a market in Beijing years earlier, and I was wearing a long, lime-green chiffon scarf in my waist-length hair. I kept my hair dyed a dark shade of brown so I thought the dress went well, suited me even. I knew I was no great shakes in the looks department but, as my Irish grandma always told me: "Yerra, sure you'll always get by, girl – with a bit of make-up and a comb for your hair."

I hated the thought of not fitting in though. I could see my chocolate-painted toes poking out of the top of my flat, tan-coloured sandals and suddenly felt quite embarrassed by Ms Delamere's words. I uncrossed my legs and pulled my dress down to cover my feet.

"We expect very high standards from our teachers here at Park View Grammar, Chrissie. Perhaps you might consider covering your shoulders, and wearing something a little less bohemian – something more fitted perhaps? Shorter . . . but not too short!" Ms Delamere seemed to find herself amusing. "The Good Lord knows, we have some young teachers here who wear their skirts much too short – not a good example for the girls. I must talk to them too before the end of term." She wrote something down on the notebook on her desk then looked back up

Jennifer Barrett

at me. "Do let me know if you need any help applying for your teacher training, Chrissie." She nodded towards the door then. "You might be so kind as to close the door on your way out?"

I was very relieved to finally be outside in the glorious sunshine. I unlocked my mother's bike from its schoolyard shackles, put my backpack on my back, then hitched my dress up and wrapped it tightly around my thighs. Poor old Sky started to rattle as I rode her out of the yard, making me feel quite guilty. I'd heard something rattling in her back-wheel area a few days earlier but kept forgetting to take a look at it.

Thinking about the conversation with Ms Delamere distracted me again. Of course I knew that Park View was a great school – the pupils had so many incredible opportunities to explore their interests while I had such mixed feelings about my own early schooldays at the nearby Charlton Preparatory School. I'd got mercilessly teased for the Irish looks I'd inherited from my mother and could only ever have imagined going to such a school as Park View. With its top academic record, school orchestra, annual school musical, debating society, mini-companies, choice of three hockey pitches, swimming pool and multiple tennis courts, Park View really had it all.

I cycled past the ivy-covered granite walls of the main school building. I guess I'd be crazy not to go for the job, I thought as I freewheeled down the hill past the sycamore trees that lined the avenue to the main road. Just a few metres from the school gates I had to hit the brakes hard to avoid a grey squirrel that ran across my path. The leafy school grounds were full of squirrels who loved to play chicken with cars and bicycles on the avenue, often losing their lives for the cause. I managed to stay upright, but stopped for a second as I watched the little guy scamper up one of the trees – probably to high-five his bushy-tailed buddies who'd been watching his daring feat from their VIP seats in the top branches.

I tried to put all thoughts of the job out of my mind then as I got going again. And that's when I noticed the rattle again. I wasn't sure if I was imagining it, but it seemed to be getting louder. I resolved to look at it when I got home, then I edged out onto the main road and cycled on by the wide-open, sun-kissed grassy heath, feeling better by the minute. I hummed to myself as I followed the bicycle path on the side of the road right up to Greenwich Park.

The entrance to the park was already busy with office workers and families escaping into the outdoors to enjoy the gorgeous summer evening. I could feel the sun beating down on my bare shoulders as I cycled through the gates and then, rather annoyingly, Park View popped back into my head again. I thought about the other permanent teachers there – many had been working at the school for twenty, some even for thirty-plus years. I was suddenly gripped by a crippling fear as I thought of my thirtieth birthday approaching in two weeks' time. If I did do my teacher training and got the job next year . . . gave up the stall . . . changed the way I dressed . . . might I eventually turn into one of those Park View Lifers? Would I too become predictable, sensible . . . *permanent*?

I shook my head and shoulders to try to get the whole thing out of my mind once and for all. It was Friday after all, the weekend had just begun.

I had to dodge the cars and hordes of people along the main avenue of the park. A couple of them gave me funny looks which I assumed was because of the now quite loud clanking noise Sky was making, so I cycled on quickly past them. At the end of the main avenue I veered left to turn onto the path which circled behind the Royal Greenwich Observatory. Just before I turned onto it I stole a glimpse at the view down over Greenwich, out across the Thames River and all the way down to the Millennium Dome. That was my favourite part of my daily cycle – the feeling of space and the brief glimpse of London followed by the long, steep hill down to Greenwich on the other side of the park.

When I got to the top of the hill I rested my feet on Sky's pedals and let go. Within seconds Sky had picked up speed and we were flying down past sauntering tourists and mothers with pushchairs. I threw my head back and enjoyed the feel of the warm air rushing past and my hair billowing behind me.

Then, just as I passed by the back of the Observatory, I heard a loud bang, and before I knew what was happening poor Sky had skidded to the ground and I'd fallen off sideways, landing in a crumpled heap a few metres away. I tried to get up to check on Sky but my legs were so shaky that I couldn't stand up properly. I sat back down and looked at my hand – it was badly grazed. I wiped away a few loose pieces of gravel, then noticed the rip on my dress and blood on my knee.

"Oh my goodness, are you okay?" A woman leaned over me. "That was a nasty fall. Let me take a look at you."

I looked up at a couple of blurry shapes. "I'm fine. Is

my bike all right? Please tell me my bicycle is okay? It's very important."

"Yes, the bicycle is fine," a man's voice said. "Don't worry – we'll get you both fixed up."

Sky escaped the tumble in the Park relatively unscathed. Apparently her back carrier had been very loose and it had finally fallen off, getting caught in the back wheel as I cycled down the hill. My new friend, Isaac, fixed her up using nothing but his penknife, while his wife Joan cleaned and bandaged my cuts and scrapes in the café beside the park gates just down the hill from where I'd fallen. Isaac and Joan had taken me there to recover.

We got chatting and I soon became fascinated by their story. Both now in their fifties, Isaac was an engineer who came from a very poor, small village about two hours south of Lusaka in Zambia. He'd got a chance to go to a missionary school there when he was young, did well, and then got a scholarship to go on to university in England. Joan was a nurse from Lewisham in London. They'd met when, in their thirties, they were volunteering at the same time in Isaac's village. I was fully captivated by the story of their romance and lapped up all of the details of their life in Zambia.

"So we both live here in London now – mainly for work reasons." Joan squinted against the sun, across the table from me. "We have a lovely lifestyle." She squeezed Isaac's hand and he smiled at her. "Life has been good to us, but I think it's fair to say that our hearts are in Zambia."

Isaac nodded. "Oh yes. We go back quite regularly to volunteer in my home village – we don't have a family of our own so we can continue to care for other people. I have helped to install water pumps and boreholes for fresh water supplies and my wife works in the local clinic and teaches English at my old school."

I listened to them, my head resting in the palm of my hand. They seemed so content, so happy, so in love. We sat in the sunshine at the picnic table outside the café for hours – chatting and telling each other our stories. All too soon though the café wanted to close up and Isaac and Joan had to get going.

"Make sure to go to my home town if ever you are in Zambia." Isaac wrote the name of the town on the back of his business card then handed it to me. "They can always use good teachers if ever you wanted to go for longer to volunteer. I've written down the name of the volunteer agency we use there too – the Christian African Legion."

"Thanks." I looked at the card. "I'm not all that religious, really."

"Oh, don't worry about any of that," said Joan. "It's a great volunteer agency and open to all."

I smiled. "Well, you've give me real food for thought, you two." I hugged my new friends then let them get back to their Friday evening.

Chapter 4

I hummed to myself as I unlocked my front door and wheeled Sky inside my flat. It was really little more than a few rooms above a vintage clothes shop on the corner of the busy Creek Road, but it was mine and I loved it. I had my own front door, a small kitchen-cum-living-room, separate bedroom and bathroom and a handy area just inside the front door where I could store my crates for the market and keep Sky locked up safely overnight. But best of all was my lovely Zen roof garden which gave me a bird's-eye view of the busy streets of Greenwich below.

"You'll live to ride another day, my friend." I unwrapped Sky's lock from her frame. "I really do think you must be invincible." I smiled and patted the saddle.

"There you are!"

I jumped, then looked up to see Tim standing at the top of the stairs, peering down.

"Gosh, you frightened the life out of me!" I said, hand on my chest.

Tim sat down on the top step. "Sorry! I just popped in before my run, to drop off those boxes and newspapers

39

for your packing." He nodded sideways at the inner door of my flat.

"Oh great, thanks, love." I finished locking Sky, then walked up the stairs. "Sorry, I'm late back." I gave him a kiss on the cheek when I reached him at the top.

"No bother. Everything okay?" Tim followed me into the flat.

"Yes, everything's fine. Isn't it such a glorious evening?" I looked around at the living room. There were piles of newspapers on the coffee table and empty boxes almost filled the entire area. I turned back to Tim. "Lot of boxes here, aren't there, Tim? Exactly how much stuff do you think I have?"

"Better to be safe than sorry." He shut the flat door then went into the kitchen and poured a glass of water from the tap.

I took my backpack off and dropped it on the floor beside the kitchen table, then sat down and hitched my dress up over my knee to inspect my injuries. I glanced up and smiled as Tim put the glass of water down in front of me. "Thanks, love."

He sat down in the chair beside me then and watched me peek underneath the Band-Aid. "Hey, are you okay?" He flinched as he saw the cut underneath, which thankfully had stopped bleeding by then. "That looks nasty, Chrissie – and you've torn your dress too. What happened?"

I pressed the Band-Aid gently back in place. "It's nothing really – looks worse than it is. I fell off Sky in the park earlier."

"Did you hurt yourself anywhere else?"

"No, no. I'm fine. Nothing more than a cut knee and a graze on my hand." I held up the palm of my hand. "I'll live." I picked up the glass and took a long drink of the cool water. I was parched and quickly emptied the glass.

Tim frowned and sighed. "That bloomin' bike. How old is it now?" He pushed his small frameless glasses up his nose. "It's always breaking down – maybe the time has come to replace it altogether? Upgrade to a car perhaps?"

"No!" I said, a little louder than I'd meant to.

"All right." He leant back.

I put the glass down. "Sorry, I didn't mean to shout." I put my hand over his on the table. "It's just that Sky means a lot to me, that's all."

"Yes, I know it does, and of course I understand why. But sometimes I think you care more about that old bike of your mother's than you do about your boyfriend." He made a fake sad face. I smiled and rolled my eyes. "It's like that television advert – you know, the one where the car gets more love than . . ."

But when Tim started comparing our lives to television commercials, I usually tuned out. I rarely watched television, so I never recognised any of the advertisements he quoted. Tim was a successful advertisement executive, a good one. He'd established his own agency with two friends from college and had done very well over the years. He was a creative guy which was one of the things I loved most about him – he always made me funny, romantic cards for my birthday and for Valentine's Day, and he loved to organise different ways of celebrating special occasions. He'd been planning my thirtieth birthday party for months – we were having a pig-on-a-spit in his back garden in a couple of weeks' time. It wouldn't necessarily have been my choice, but Tim had done so much work to organise it all – he'd invited everyone we knew and had even hired a huge pagoda in case it rained – he always thought of everything.

"Sorry, I haven't seen the advert." I patted his hand. "But you can rest assured that I do not think more of my bicycle than I do of my boyfriend." I leaned in and kissed him on the cheek.

"Hmm, well, I should hope not." He smiled.

Tim looked cute when he smiled. While he probably couldn't ever be described as good-looking exactly, I loved the way he always tilted his head to one side and scrunched up his nose when he smiled. Tim was a few inches shorter than me but, given that I stood at just under six foot, so were a lot of men. He still had all of his own fair hair though – an added bonus. I looked him over as he ran through the comparisons between my bicycle and the family car in the advert. He was wearing a running vest, loose tracksuit bottoms and trainers – all ready for his run. Even though he was eight years older than me, he put me to shame running the London City Marathon every year and taking part in triathlons and various fitness challenges around the country on a regular basis. I loved that Tim was so active and that he was lean and fit. He was one of the most motivated people I knew – if Tim set his mind on doing something, he always did it. He was good for me in that way – left to my own devices I'd never get anything done.

When he'd finally finished talking about the car commercial, he leaned over and gently touched the side of my knee. "So how did you get the Band-Aid?"

"Joan put it on for me. She said she always carries a small first-aid kit in her handbag. Isn't that such a good idea? Actually, I think I'm going to do that." I jumped up and wrote 'small first-aid kit' in chalk on the blackboard stuck to my fridge.

"Joan?" said Tim, leaning back in his seat.

I leaned back against the counter. "Oh yes, sorry. Joan, of 'Isaac and Joan'. They're such a lovely couple. You'd love them. Joan's a nurse from Lewisham and Isaac's an engineer, originally from Zambia. They met when they were volunteering at the same time together in Isaac's village in Zambia. Isn't that so romantic?"

"Ah, so you've been picking up strangers again?"

I smiled and came back over to sit on his lap. Tim put one arm around my waist, the other on my ungrazed knee.

"You should have called me," he said. "I would have come to pick you up."

"I was fine. I so enjoyed chatting with Isaac and learning about what it was like for him arriving in London as a teenage student. While he was fixing Sky up Joan told me all about how they'd met on the volunteer programme in Zambia – they have such an interesting story. And you should see them – you'd never have put them together. She's tiny – not much more than five foot – if even. She has blonde hair and is a little plump. Isaac is the complete opposite – tall and thin with the whitest teeth you could ever imagine. I'm not sure if they just looked whiter against his black skin or if he'd had them whitened. I bought them a coffee while they fixed both me and Sky up." I laughed. "Mind you, that only took a few minutes – we must have been there for almost two more hours, chatting."

"I see." Tim tapped my good knee and I got up so he could stand himself. He took the empty glass from the table and put it by the sink.

I sat down on the chair, I could tell that he was a little put out but wasn't entirely sure why.

He turned back to face me. "Chrissie, I wish you would let me take care of you more, not try and do everything yourself, or pick up random strangers for the job. I'm your boyfriend – *I* should be the one fixing your bike, the one looking after your cuts and scrapes."

I burst out laughing. "You make me sound like a five-year-old."

Tim tried to stay annoyed but after a few seconds he had to laugh too. "Come here, you." He pulled me up from the chair and into his arms. "I'm serious, Chrissie. We're about to move in together – we need to be more of a unit. Sometimes you can be infuriatingly independent, girl."

I knew my independent streak bothered Tim. In almost all other aspects of his life, he was self-assured and confident, just not always about me. I was always trying to reassure him that I was happy to be with him and, for the most part, I was. Tim made me feel loved, he gave me a sense of place, a sense of belonging. He'd been trying for years to persuade me to move in with him, and though I did like my independence and I loved my little flat, as I approached my thirtieth birthday I'd finally given in. I knew it made sense on so many levels, but I was dreading getting strangers in to rent out my beloved flat, and I couldn't imagine what it would be like rattling around in Tim's huge four-storeyed house in Blackheath. I felt like I was in a luxury hotel any time I stayed there – almost embarrassed by all the unnecessary space. I was very excited about having a dog again though. Tim had the most gorgeous red setter, Jasper, who I adored.

I put my arms around Tim's waist and pressed myself against him. "We're a unit now?"

He kissed me and squeezed me in close to him – Tim gave the best cuddles. We had a long kiss before eventually he patted my back gently to break the hug. He kissed the top of my nose then walked over to the coffee table in the living area, stepping over the boxes as he went.

I followed him, hoping for more snuggles, but he picked up a magazine from the top of the newspaper pile.

"I was thinking we might take a bit of a break – when you finish school for the summer."

I took the magazine he was holding out, then realised that it was actually a travel brochure. I moved a couple of boxes off my armchair, put them on top of a bigger box on the floor and sat down.

"We'd need to get something booked soon before the flights fill up," Tim said, leaning back against the bookshelf to watch me flick through the brochure. "I was thinking maybe late next month?"

I glanced at the pictures but I couldn't think about holidays on top of everything else. At least not the type of holidays Tim had in mind – the type that could be laid out in a glossy brochure. I threw it down on the coffee table, leaned forward and picked up one of the newspapers from the top of the pile.

"One thing at a time." I held up the newspaper. "I can't move house *and* plan a holiday."

But Tim wasn't letting me off the hook that easily. "Don't worry – I'll sort the holiday booking." He came over and squashed in beside me on my cuddle chair. I called it that because it was semicircular-shaped and almost hugged you when you sat into it. I would have liked to have just snuggled up on it with Tim for the evening and relaxed, but he seemed to be on one of his organising streaks – he was all business.

He picked the brochure back up and flicked through it until he got the page he wanted. "Remember that place I took you for your birthday on our first holiday together three years ago? The four-star place in Malaga – The Hotel Mariba? Well, if you thought that was good, check this place out." He folded back the pages of the brochure and handed it to me. "They've just opened a new five-star place next door – The *Royal* Hotel Mariba. It looks incredible, doesn't it?"

I smiled and nodded along as Tim pointed out all of the facilities at the plush hotel. Memories of the trip to Malaga came to mind. It hadn't been the worst holiday – I'd had plenty of time to catch up on my reading and rest after the stress of the previous months. It just wasn't really somewhere I would have chosen to return to. My mother flashed into my mind then – unless she had to for work, she would never visit the same place twice – "Life is too short, and the world's too big," she'd say. And I agreed – apart from repeat trips back to visit family in Ireland and also to New York, San Francisco and Sydney with *Celtic Wings*, I'd never travelled to the same place twice. The only thing worse than a package holiday to Malaga in my mind, was *two* package holidays to Malaga.

"I'm not sure, Tim." I handed him back the brochure. "Now that my Park View contract is finishing up and I've saved a little bit of money, I was half-thinking of perhaps going somewhere a bit more long-haul. I'd love to really see Africa for example. I was meant to meet my mother for the last part of her Tanzania trip there a few years ago, but then . . . well, y'know . . . she had the accident . . . It wasn't quite how I expected to see Zanzibar." I took a deep breath. "Anyway, I'd love to travel in Africa someday – to really see Tanzania, also Kenya, maybe even Zambia. I loved Mum's Zambian travel memoir, and talking to Isaac and Joan today has got me thinking about it all again."

"Zambia?" Tim screwed up his nose. "There'd be insects as big as rodents there. Do they have any decent hotels even?"

I shuddered internally at the mention of the insects but didn't want Tim to see me weaken. "Yes, I'm sure they have some excellent hotels there," I said, sitting up straighter. "But to be honest that's not the kind of trip I had in mind, Tim. I'd like to really see and experience the country – stay in the villages, eat the local food, meet the Zambian people, see the sights. Isaac was saying that the Victoria Falls are incredible during the rainy season – like nothing you've ever seen. He said there could be so much water falling and hitting the ground at such force that it feels like you're in a rainstorm – you get soaked through in seconds." I sighed. "I'd so love to experience that. It must be amazing."

Tim looked unsure. "How long would we need for a trip like that?"

I looked at him in surprise. I hadn't even considered that Tim might come. True, we hadn't travelled separately since we'd got together, apart from a few of my trips back to Kerry to see my grandma. But other than the few package holidays and city breaks we'd taken together, I hadn't really done much travel at all over the past four years. I'd been studying so hard for my degree and any spare time I'd had was spent working on the stall. I'd imagined my first big trip back on the road would be a solo trip. But Tim and I were a couple – it was probably quite reasonable to expect we should go places together.

I looked down and started to unstrap my sandals. "A few months . . . three maybe? No more than six anyway." I kicked off the sandals without looking up.

Tim laughed. "Well, that's that then. Not a hope! There's no way I could take more than a couple of weeks away from the business at a time." He stood up and looked at his watch. "Right, I've got fifteen kilometres to run before dinner to keep on track with my marathon training schedule. We can decide on the holiday later, look at some other locations and dates over dinner. What do you fancy tonight?"

"Hmm?" I was looking at him but my mind had started to drift. I was wondering what you'd need to wear to look at the Victoria Falls in the rainy season. Poncho? Rain gear? Swimming togs even? You'd certainly need a good waterproof bag for camera equipment . . .

Tim clicked his fingers to bring me back.

"Oh sorry, love. I was miles away."

"So? Will we order in?"

"Mmm . . . sure."

"What do you fancy?"

"I don't mind." I stood up. "Whatever you like."

"What about a couple of Mario's gourmet burgers and some of those garlic fries he does? Bit unhealthy, I know, but I'll have earned it after my run."

I nodded. "Sure. That sounds fine." I walked over to the window and leaned on the wall beside it, looking out for a moment. Then I turned back around. Tim was rolling down his tracksuit bottoms. He pulled them off over his trainers and threw them on the cuddle chair so that he was just in his running shorts and singlet. Then he bounded over to the door.

"See you later!" he shouted back.

I heard him thump down the stairs before the door to the street banged shut.

I watched him run down the street from the window – he had to zig-zag to avoid the shoppers and commuters emerging from the Docklands Light Rail station across the road.

I went to the kitchen to make myself a cheese sandwich then brought it back into the living room. I wasn't really a big meat eater but I knew if I didn't finish my burger Tim would devour what was left, he'd be so hungry after his run, so it wouldn't go to waste. I went over to the full-length window and opened it into the room. Tucking the newspaper I'd been waving about at Tim earlier under my arm, I picked up my sandwich and stepped out onto the narrow walled ledge outside the window. I held the sandwich on its plate out to my side and climbed the small three-stepped ladder up to my rooftop. I put the sandwich and newspaper down on the wall that enclosed my little rooftop haven, then leaned over it to gaze out at the flowing Thames in the distance. Then I looked down at the people milling about on the street just below. Across from my flat, amid an arched arcade of shops and cafés was the entrance to the station. It was busy with lots of commuters coming home from work and tourists arriving to Greenwich to enjoy a bright summer's evening by the riverside. The traffic below was heavy and loud – a couple of cars honked their horns aggressively, clearly frustrated by their lack of progress. I shook my head – I just never could understand why people chose to drive around London – I couldn't bear sitting in such heavy traffic when I could cycle by unhindered by the congestion.

I looked over the rooftops again and, as I stared at the tip of the *Cutty Sark's* masts, I thought of my mother and the day of her thirtieth birthday all those years ago. I remembered sitting down on the bench close to the ship that day, eating vanilla ice cream and making up stories about the passers-by. How simple life had seemed to me back then, and yet it hadn't been simple for my mother. On the one hand she had my father and me here in London, desperately wanting her to settle down and be with us full-time, whilst on the other the whole world lay out there waiting for her to explore and report back on. She'd been very clear about her decision that day anyway. She wasn't prepared to give up her life on the road for us – not until she had to at least, when Daddy got sick.

I sighed and closed my eyes.

I often wondered what might have happened to us if my father hadn't got sick and died. Would my mother ever have settled down? Or would she have carried on just as she was – cycling around the world on her own, her loved ones always left behind waiting for her? I couldn't help but question whether it was fair to have children when you couldn't give them roots. And if my mother had settled down and given me the solid roots I so craved, could she have been happy?

I turned around from the view and leaned back against the rooftop wall. The wooden wind chime my mother had brought me back from Kenya was picking up a good breeze from its wall hanging – it was tinkling and clanking away above the seedlings I was growing in pots below. There were a couple of blue tits picking at the bird feeder that I kept tied to the tall potted bay tree in the corner of the roof garden. I watched them perched on the feeder, greedily eating their fill.

And at that moment I felt a familiar pang and so wished my mother was still alive – barely a day went by when I didn't curse the ferry accident in Zanzibar where she disappeared, presumed drowned. As I approached my own thirtieth birthday, I wanted to talk to her more than ever. I wanted to ask her questions, to get her advice. Especially to ask her to help me work out if I was right to be settling down. Tim was a good man who could offer me stability, a good home, a place to finally put down roots. It was exactly what I'd thought I needed a few years ago after my mother died and I'd left *Celtic Wings*. I was in a bad way then. As time had gone on, though, I wasn't so sure about settling down any more.

I sighed – long and hard. Then I gazed around my small but beautiful Zen garden. I knew I was really going to miss my little flat and especially this rooftop haven.

Just then, one of the blue tits made a bid for my cheese sandwich – I'd left the plate resting on the wall. "Hey, you! That's mine!" As he swooped in, I dived to grab the plate. I laughed as both birds flew away, then I sat down on my blue-and-white-striped deckchair, plate in hands. I leaned back, closed my eyes and held my face up to the sun. The warmth felt so lovely against my skin and I just sat like that for a few minutes. I heard a bird tweeting then and noticed the blue tits had come back to the bay tree, the suet balls and seed feeder too much of a temptation to resist for very long. I smiled. "I'd better eat this before you pair get hold of it." I took a bite out of one of the sandwich halves then put the plate down on my white metal circular garden table.

As I ate, I reached over to the wall for the newspaper, which had begun to flap in the warm breeze. It was only a day old so I glanced through the headlines on the front page. I turned the page then reached for the second half of my sandwich, but as I did the headline of a small article in the bottom right-hand corner caught my eye: '**Musical Memorial for Composer and Activist, Christine**'

It was the name 'Christine' that caught my eye first. I put down the sandwich and sat forward to read about my namesake. Then I noticed a reference in the article to The Three Songbirds – the place where my parents and I had stayed on my mother's thirtieth birthday. Until then I hadn't even realised that it was still open, I hadn't been out that way in years, not since that day. I folded the paper over in quarters so I could read the short article properly.

Christine Thorpe died peacefully in her sleep at her home in Kent yesterday, aged 89. A well-known composer, filmmaker and conservationist, she is perhaps best known for the time when, aged sixty-eight, she and her husband Harvey Thorpe protested against the demolition of Collinswood in Kent. Their action sparked a nationwide campaign, successfully ensuring the conservation of forestry in that part of Kent and the protection of wildlife in the area.

Committed world travellers, the Thorpes divided most of their time between the UK and

Africa, where Mr Thorpe's charitable foundation, The Tuskhorn Trust, operates. The Thorpes were avid cyclists and founded the Kent Cycle Club, which runs weekly leisure cycles in the UK countryside and regular cycle tours abroad.

Mrs Thorpe's work as a composer of film scores and as a music producer earned her international acclaim and it is expected that a wide range of international musicians will perform at a special memorial service for her on Sunday 14th July at The Three Songbirds just outside Harkston in Kent.

I rested the paper on my lap and sat back. "Christine Thorpe . . ." I said her name out loud.

From the short piece, it sounded like she'd led such an interesting life. To have travelled, enjoyed a successful career in music and have been brave enough to stand up for what she believed in – I was impressed. I loved the idea of a memorial service filled with music, and at The Three Songbirds too – it sounded magical.

But my regard for Mrs Thorpe just made me feel worse about myself. I sighed, then put the paper on the table, got up and looked over the wall at the tip of the *Cutty Sark* again.

Christine Thorpe and I might have shared the same first name and an interest in music, but that was where the similarities between us ended. I considered what an article about my own passing might read when my time eventually came:

Chrissie Rogers, former singer, former market

retailer and one-time world traveller, died at home in her sprawling Blackheath mansion. She had just returned from her annual holiday to the exact same resort in Malaga, having recently retired from her job as English teacher at Park View Grammar School for Girls where she taught for thirty-three years. She is survived by her husband Tim Rogers and their four children, none of whom were at home when she died – they had all taken their mother's advice and were off having adventures somewhere much more interesting.

I smiled for a second. But my amusement quickly faded – it was all a little too close to reality to be amusing.

I heaved a deep sigh and closed my eyes. I tried to imagine what Christine Thorpe might have looked like and wished I hadn't left my laptop in school. I would have liked to have looked her up, to have learned more about her.

I turned around then and leaned back against the wall. I wondered if this Mrs Thorpe had been happy. Like my mother, she'd clearly lived her life her own way – she was married but it sounded like she'd still managed to be her own woman, to pursue her interests and live all over the world. Was that what I needed to be doing? To build a life with Tim but also follow my dream to travel more? Or had Mrs Thorpe actually been happiest when she'd settled down?

I thought about my mother again. Would she have been happy if she'd settled down? If my father had lived? They could have travelled together maybe when I was older – like the Thorpes had – they could have wintered in Africa, or wherever.

So many questions and thoughts were spiralling around and around in my head, my mind was whirling from them all. I shook my head to try to clear it. Then I had an idea: maybe I should go to Mrs Thorpe's memorial service. There's no better way to learn about a person's life than to be present as they leave it. I went over and picked the paper back up to check the article. The date of the memorial was Sunday week – the day after my thirtieth birthday party.

That could be tricky to get to, I thought. Not impossible though. I tore out the page with the article then jumped as I heard the flat door slam downstairs.

"Are you on the roof?" Tim called up to me.

I put the article into my pocket, put the newspaper under my arm and leaned over the wall. Tim was below me, leaning out the long window. His face was glistening with sweat, but he didn't look at all flushed.

"Hey there. Yes, I'm just wrapping some of my pots and ornaments up here." I waved the newspaper at him.

"Good stuff!" He held up his wallet. "I got halfway up to the Observatory and realised I'd left it here, so I doubled back to collect it. There'd be no dinner otherwise, eh?"

I smiled. "No, indeed. Good save."

"So the packing's going well?"

"Yes, getting there." I crossed my fingers behind my back.

"Great. Keep it up! Only another eight kilometres until burger time." He went back in through the window. "You might stick a couple of beers in the fridge?" I could just about hear him shout before the flat door slammed.

I nodded to myself, then turned around and looked at

the animal garden ornaments that I'd collected from the market over the last few years. They now littered my rooftop, as did the many clay pots and plant boxes. I sighed. "All right, can't avoid this any longer, I guess." I shook out the newspaper and got started.

Chapter 5

English summers can be very cruel – they lull you into a misplaced sense of secure gaiety at the arrival of the good weather; then, just as you're getting used to basking in the glorious sunshine, the rain arrives . . . The following weekend wasn't just wet, it was pure dank misery.

I finished packing up the last crate of books and records from my stall, then took off my money belt and put it into my backpack. I stood back then and listened to the rain pelting down on the market's steel roof while I waited for Abigail to close up. The rain had built up so much during the day that water was dribbling down onto the cobblestones through a couple of leaky holes at the side of the roof. I pulled the small children's blanket around my shoulders, rubbed my hands together and jumped up and down to try to stay warm. It had been a busy Saturday on the stall and there were still a couple of bedraggled tourists sheltering from the downpour in the market but by then most of the stallholders had started to close up.

"The blankie looks good on you," Abigail said as she

collected up the finger puppets that had been displayed on a mobile at the front of her stall.

I smiled at my friend and wrapped the blanket tighter around myself. "This has been a lifesaver today – thanks so much for the loan of it. Trust me to come out this morning in only light clothes." I looked down at my loose long dark-grey skirt and pulled the blanket tighter around my white string top and bare shoulders.

Abigail smiled. "You're more than welcome. I'm only sorry I had no cardigans with me to give you. One of the older children's ones might have fitted."

Abigail and I had run our businesses side by side since I first reopened Daddy's stall a few years earlier. I missed seeing so much of her when I'd taken the teachers' assistant job with Park View and had to cut back to just Saturdays. We generally had so much to catch up on by the time Saturday came that the customers almost got in the way. An avid knitter, Abigail had been creating her gorgeous knitted products for years – and she was good, very good. While the rest of us struggled with our 'knit one, purl one' technique at school, Abigail said she'd already been experimenting with what would come to be her own unique style. She used bright, primary colours to make children's toys and clothes and sold everything from cardigans, jumpers and hats to finger puppets and bags – and, thankfully, blankets too.

Abigail put the rest of the finger puppets into the top of her packing crate. "Right, that's it. Let's get this stuff out to the van – I'm dying for the grand tour of your new place."

I turned to push my trolley. "Thanks so much for giving me a lift, Abigail. I really appreciate it." I sighed –

I really hated having to rely on people for lifts but Tim hadn't been sure he'd be back from the triathlon in Oxford in time to pick me up so I'd had to ask Abigail to drop me home. "It was so handy living across the road from the market before – I'm really missing my little flat already."

Abigail laughed as she started pushing her own trolley. "My heart bleeds for you, Chrissie. Such a hardship having to live in that beautiful mansion with your charming boyfriend. It's a tough life you have."

I stuck my tongue out at her and we both laughed as we pushed our trolleys as fast as possible to her van through the rain.

It felt so strange coming home from the market to Tim's house. I'd been living there just under a week at that stage. The new tenants for my flat – a young Polish couple – had already moved in. There really was no going back.

Thankfully it had stopped raining by the time we got to the house. I put down the crate of books I was carrying to open the front door.

Abigail, who was following behind with one of my crates of records, stopped halfway up the steps. "Wow – this place really is huge! It didn't look as big from the road but when you stand here you really get a sense of the full scale."

"I know." I opened the door and was immediately almost knocked over by Tim's dog, Jasper.

"Back, boy!" I managed to say as I regained my balance and held him back from the open door with one leg. He obeyed me and stayed inside the house but continued to jump about and bark in excitement – having been home alone all day he was particularly lively.

Abigail came in behind me and I closed the door quickly.

"I'll grab the other couple of crates out of the van when you're going," I said to her, putting the crate of books down in the small cloakroom by the front door and leaning down to give my favourite pooch some attention.

Abigail struggled to fit the other crate into the cloakroom with mine.

"Ah, sorry about that," I said, getting up to move a sports bag off the floor to make room. "Tim was going to clear this place out this morning to make space to store my stock but he mustn't have had enough time before he left." I looked at my watch. "He should be back soon though." I stood up. "Right – which would you like to do first? Grab a cuppa or take a quick look around?"

"Oh, I'd love to see round the place." Abigail patted Jasper who looked like he was about to jump up on her, but changed his mind when he saw my frown. "I might have to pass on the cuppa though." She looked at her watch. "Penny will kill me if I'm too late back. It's Saturday Date Night – as soon we get the kids to bed, the red wine will be opened and after dinner we'll put on a DVD – the perfect night in."

I laughed. "Sounds thrilling indeed!"

Abigail nodded and smiled as Jasper and I began to lead her on a whistle-stop tour of Tim's house. When he'd bought the place six years earlier, Tim had hired an interior designer to decorate and every room was finished off beautifully, in muted tones, with just the right balance of furniture, artwork, storage and soft furnishings. I showed Abigail the spacious kitchen and living areas downstairs, the wine cellar and games room in the basement and the office overlooking the leafy garden – the walls of the office were covered with dozens of framed posters of Tim's company's successful print advertisements which Abigail politely admired. We went upstairs then and I showed her the main bathroom, the master bedroom and the biggest guestroom – all of which she raved about. And finally we moved on to the smaller guestrooms up on the next floor.

"Gosh, you really are so lucky to have all these bedrooms, Chrissie." Abigail stopped to take a breath at the top of the stairs, allowing Jasper to bound ahead of us.

We followed him into Tim's third spare room.

"Our two little monkeys will be sharing for the foreseeable future the way our finances are looking," said Abigail, who was admiring the huge built-in wardrobes. "I'd love all this space for Molly and Matthew." She closed the wardrobe door and turned back to me. "You and Tim are going to have some very lucky children."

Her words stopped me in my tracks. I'd never really talked to anyone about my feelings on children before but it was something that had been on my mind quite a bit recently. Perhaps it was something to do with being on the verge of turning thirty, or it could have been because I'd moved in with Tim – it was reasonable for people to expect it to be the first step toward us settling down together and starting a family. It all made me very uneasy, but I'd successfully avoided discussing the topic out loud with anyone until then. I knew it was something that I'd have to face sooner or later though and I trusted Abigail.

I sat down on one of the twin beds and Jasper leapt up beside me.

"Down!" I pointed to the floor.

Jasper jumped back down but sat staring up at me, his long tail beating off the floor.

I glanced back up at Abigail. "I'm not entirely sure I want to start having babies to be honest."

"Well, that's okay," said Abigail. "You're only thirty – you've lots of time yet."

"Mmm, it's just . . ." I hesitated. "I'm not entirely sure I want to have children myself at all."

"Really?" She sat down on the other bed opposite me. "I thought you loved kids? You're great with ours and I know you love teaching children. Why wouldn't you want your own, Chrissie?"

Jasper rested his snout on my knee and gazed up at me. I smiled at him and rubbed his head. "I just can't imagine it really," I said to her. "I do love children, but babies don't do so much for me."

Abigail took a theatrical loud breath in. "How can you say such a thing?"

I smiled. "I know. I'm sorry! It's just that there are so many other things I'd like to do. I want to travel more, see the world. And I don't think you can do that and have children. I know some people do, but I don't think I could ever do that to a child."

Abigail raised her eyebrows. "What other things would you do? Where would you go?"

"I don't know. I haven't figured it all out yet." I sat forward. "I read this article in the newspaper though. It was about an almost ninety-year-old woman who died recently. It was a very short article but it sounded like she'd led such an interesting life. She'd travelled and lived all over the world and had been a composer, a cycling enthusiast and a conservationist." I looked at Jasper. "Isn't that good, boy?" He wagged his tail, then stood up expecting some activity.

"She does sound interesting," said Abigail.

"Yes." I stroked Jasper's head and sighed. "The only problem is that Tim is baby-mad. As long as I've known him, he's always said that he wants at least three, if not four, kids. But I'm not sure. On the one hand, I just can't get excited at the idea at all and on the other I'm afraid that if I don't settle down and have them with Tim, that I'll regret it some day."

Abigail got up from the other bed and came over to sit beside me. "If that's how you feel, Chrissie, you have to tell him. Tim's a good guy, he wouldn't pressure you to do anything you don't want to do, but if he does want children some day and you're not sure . . . well, you need to be honest with him. It's too big an issue to ignore."

I turned to face her. Jasper gave up on us then and wandered over to lie on the floor by the door. He let out a deep sigh but kept one eye trained on us just in case.

I nodded. "It's just that . . . because I don't really know what I want – not with any great degree of certainty anyway – I can't start the conversation with Tim. I'm afraid of upsetting him."

Abigail raised her eyebrows. "But you *have* to speak up, Chrissie. Even if it does mean upsetting him or a bit of conflict. Tim can't read your mind."

I knew she was right, but I also knew how hard it would be. "I just wish I could be more like you, Abigail – more self-aware. I wish I knew what I wanted . . . then I might at least be able to express it better."

I really did admire my friend. It hadn't been easy for

her to come out to her friends, family and especially her former colleagues in the magazine all those years ago. But Abigail never thought too long about what anyone else thought of her – she seemed to have a way of just getting on with things, of doing what she set out to do. She and Penny had started seeing each other six years earlier when Abigail was thirty-two. After their first year together as a couple they decided to try for children, found a donor agency and were thrilled when Abigail very quickly became pregnant with Molly. A year and a half after Molly was born, she had Matthew – both children had the same donor father so that they were full siblings by birth. Abigail and Penny were one of the best couples I knew – they were clearly so happy together and utterly devoted to their kids. When Abigail had been pregnant with Molly she decided she'd had enough of the fast-paced life of a London magazine staff-writer and chose to turn what up until then had been her hobby into a business. Penny, who had a very secure solicitor's job, fully supported her partner's dream which gave Abigail the confidence she needed to take the risk. So she set up a website for her knitted creations, promoted it through her magazine contacts and had done very well selling her quirky designs and knitted items to the yummy mummies of South West London. The stall was just a small part of her ever-growing empire – as she said, "a chance to interface with my customers in person".

Abigail put her hand on my back. "Are you okay, Chrissie? Is this all just about children or is there something else bothering you?"

I looked at her. "I don't know. I guess life just feels like it's moving very fast at the moment. I mean, on the face of

64

things everything's great . . . fantastic even. I have everything I should want – a great boyfriend, good career prospects . . ." I looked around the room, "and a beautiful home."

I stood up and walked over to the window. Jasper jumped up and came over to me. He looked expectant for a moment then flopped down at my feet again when he realised there was nothing much happening.

"When I was in *Celtic Wings*, especially after Mum died, I was dying to finally settle down in one place. So why aren't I happy now, Abigail? Isn't this what everyone wants?"

"Ah yes, I see the problem," said Abigail. "You're going through an early thrisis."

"A what?" I looked around at her.

"A *thrisis*. I wrote an article about this not long after I turned thirty myself. Just before I decided to come out. A thrisis is a thirty-something crisis as opposed to a *mid*-life crisis. They're all the rage at the moment."

I looked down at the dog. "What is my daft friend talking about, Jasper?" He just wagged his tail, then stood up and offered me his paw. I bent down to pet him.

Abigail sat forward on the bed. "No, I'm serious. If we think of life as three stages – the first from childhood up to your thirties, the second up to your sixties, and the third age up to the end – well, the thrisis now happens to a lot of people at the end of the first stage, in their thirties. In this part of the world anyway, by that stage many people have achieved a lot of what they were led to believe they needed to be happy in life: the successful career – the comfortable house – the devoted partner. But more and more of these people are feeling unfulfilled and having a crisis of a different kind to the better-known mid-life crisis. Rather than looking *back* on their lives and acting out by buying fast cars, having affairs or the like, our disenchanted thirty-somethings today are looking *ahead* and worrying about what will happen with the rest of their life. Having moved at full speed through adolescence and early adulthood to get to where they are, they can have become so goal-oriented that often they arrive in their thirties without knowing what really makes them tick. They get there and realise that the things they've been striving for don't necessarily make them happy at all."

I came over and sat back down on the bed beside her, followed by my canine shadow. "This is interesting. Go on."

"Well, it's all about our decisions really," said Abigail. "Whether we realise it or not, we've been making decisions all our life. Think of it: the decision to live in a certain place, the decision to date a certain person or to do a certain job."

I nodded. "Yes, that's true."

"Well, we almost have to *remake* those decisions at regular intervals in life – and either decide to carry on, or to make some quite radical changes. Those are the two most likely outcomes of the thrisis – people generally either make the decision to just get on with things or they decide to give their lives a complete overhaul. Either one can be a very brave way to go. It's not an easy choice and of the people I interviewed, the one thing they kept saying was that the most difficult part of their own thrisis was getting the people around them to understand why they weren't satisfied with their seemingly perfect life."

I raised my eyebrows. "I can't imagine Tim understanding, that's for sure." I sighed and leaned back on my hands. "You know, I was encouraged to go for a job in Park View College last week."

Abigail tilted her head sideways. "But you're already working there, aren't you?"

"Yes, on contract, and that's almost up. But this would be a permanent job as a teacher. It starts there in just over a year. I'd have to get my teaching qualification first though – that'd be another year in college."

"*Eeeshh!*" Abigail sucked in her breath. "A permanent job? Chrissie Devlin-Cole, you really are being tested with this thrisis, eh? Mind you, the permanent job would make Tim happy, I expect? What does he think about it?"

"I haven't told him." I saw her frown and felt bad. "It's just that I *know* what he'll think, Abigail. He'll think it's great and in no time at all he'll be researching training colleges, filling in the application forms for me and making my packed lunch and a good luck card for my first day. *Och!*" I threw my hands in the air. Abigail smiled. "Maybe I *am* going through a thrisis?" I sighed. "I just can't get my head around this permanent job idea. I'd have to give up the market, y'know? *And* get a whole new wardrobe."

"What?" Abigail scrunched up her nose.

"Don't ask!" I shook my head then heaved a deep sigh. "I just keep wondering what my mother would think of it all." I looked around the room. "She'd probably turn in her grave at the idea of me living in such a lavish mansion."

"I'm sure she'd be happy knowing you were safe and well." She touched my arm. "Anyway, it's not your mother you need to think about, Chrissie. You have to work out what it is *you* want, and it sounds like you have

67

to do it kinda fast. Whether he realises it or not, Tim is calling all the shots at the moment. If you're not careful you'll wind up in this permanent job, not to mention married, perhaps even pregnant in no time at all. Which would all be wonderful, if that's what you want, but disastrous if it isn't. Tim's a good guy, but you can't mess him around. If you don't want all those things, you have to tell him."

I nodded. "I would if I knew what I wanted, but . . ."

Jasper let out a whimper and clawed at my foot. He was clearly getting very bored with the conversation and lack of action.

"You'll work it out, Chrissie," Abigail said.

I nodded. "I know. Thanks." I wasn't so sure, but I put my hand on her arm to thank her for listening, then I stood up. "All right, we'd better finish this tour before Penny sends out a search party for you, and this guy," I patted Jasper's head, "dies of boredom."

Just then I heard Tim's car pulling up in the driveway. Jasper heard it too and bounded down the stairs to sit by the front door, giving us a few minutes' peace to see the last of the bedrooms.

We walked down the corridor to the smallest bedroom of the house.

"Tim's been very sweet," I said as I opened the door. "He said I should take one of the guest rooms for my boxes and stuff, so this is the one I've chosen."

Abigail followed me in. The bedroom at the front of the house had a single bed and double built-in wardrobes. Like the rest of the house the walls were painted an off-white colour but three framed vintage motorcycle prints and avocado-green curtains added some colour.

"It's nice," said Abigail, "but how come you chose the smallest room? The one we were just in is so much bigger."

I'd gone over to the window to see Tim but he'd already come inside. I could just about hear the commotion downstairs as hound greeted master. I turned back to Abigail then. "I just love the view," I said. "Look – we're level with the tops of those evergreen Leylandii trees in the garden. We've got a couple of wood pigeons nesting in one of them."

Abigail came over and looked out the window beside me.

I opened it up. "If we were here long enough we'd see them," I said. "Or even hear them cooing gently to each other – it's very calming."

"Well, I can't see any birds, but the view over the heath is really lovely," said Abigail. "I still think I'd pick a bigger room though – you'll need it for your books alone."

"I keep telling her that."

We both turned around to see Tim come into the room followed by a very excited Jasper who was leaping around and trying very hard to resist the temptation to leap up on his master – an act that he knew would mean instant banishment to the garden.

Tim was wearing his mucky tracksuit and was in his stocking feet. He came over and slipped his arm around my waist. "Hey, you. Welcome home!" He gave me a kiss on the cheek.

"Hi there." I kissed him back. "So how did the race go?"

"Superb! I beat my personal best and Conor's too."

Tim grinned, clearly delighted with himself. "He was sick about it – he'd been lording his last blasted half-marathon victory over me for months."

I rolled my eyes. "You and my cousin are way too competitive for your own good." I looked over at my friend. "I was just showing Abigail around your house. Hope that's okay?"

Tim looked slightly offended. "Yeah, of course – this is *our* house now, Chrissie. You can have friends around any time – the more the merrier." He poked Abigail in the side and she giggled. "Especially the wacky ones. So how are the kids, Abs? Last time I saw you, you were pregnant. Still think it was a good idea to go again?"

She smiled. "Absolutely! Best thing we ever did. Mattie is a dote – he's actually been a very easy baby. It's Molly who's turned into a monster overnight. Talk about the Terrible Two's! We just got through those – now we're on to the Torturous Three's!"

Tim laughed. "That reminds me of an advert we did for toddler's training pants last year. You might have seen it? You know the one where –"

"All right, love." I put my arm around his waist and gave him a squeeze. "Abigail needs to get home at *some* point tonight."

Tim put his arm around my shoulder. "Chrissie, I sometimes think my talents are wasted on you." He squeezed me closer to him.

I raised my eyebrows and smiled.

"So did you show Abs the garden?" Tim looked back at Abigail. "We're putting up a bouncy castle next week for this one's big birthday. The kids will love it – but, more importantly, it should occupy them for long enough for the adults to enjoy the party too." He gave my shoulder another squeeze and I dutifully smiled.

"Sounds great!' said Abigail. "Molly will love that."

"Oh, while I think of it, Chrissie," Tim started rooting in his pockets, "I found something on the floor of my jeep today." He pulled a small object out of his tracksuit pocket. "I wasn't sure what it was, but didn't want to throw it out in case it was important? It could be a piece of one of your ornaments. It must have fallen out of one of your boxes when we were moving you in last week. I found it under the seat when I dropped my water bottle."

I recognised it immediately. "Oh my goodness, yes!" I grabbed it from him. "How stupid of me not to pack it in better! Thank you so much for finding it, love." I gave him a kiss on the cheek.

"No problem." He put his hands on his hips. "Right, best go shower and tidy myself up. You girls make yourself at home."

I sat down on the small single bed when Tim left the room and turned the piece of brown china around in my fingers.

Abigail held her hand out. "What is it?"

I handed it to her. "It's the wing of a small china nightingale figurine. The rest of it should be packed in one of those boxes." I nodded at the pile in the corner of the room. "My father gave it to me not long before he died. I love it. But it fell one day and the wing broke off. I keep meaning to glue it back together." I held out my hand and she dropped the fragment back into my palm. The whole wing was no bigger than half my thumb. "I can't believe how close I came to losing it – stupid."

"It must be quite special to you if it was from your

71

father?" said Abigail, sitting down beside me on the bed. "He died when you were quite young, didn't he? Was it very upsetting for you when it broke?"

I looked up at my friend, but almost didn't see her any more. My mind was distracted by the sudden rush of memories.

"Chrissie . . . Chrissie, are you okay?"

I focused back on Abigail. "Yes, I'm all right." I looked back at the broken wing. "It's just that nobody ever asked me what *I* wanted."

Chapter 6

Six months after my father died, we moved to Dingle, or 'home' as my mother kept calling it. Except that it wasn't home to me. In fact, after Daddy died, I had no idea where home was any more. I remember walking back into our flat in Greenwich the evening after he'd been taken to the funeral home, and just wanting to turn around and sprint back out. I could hardly bear the pain of being there without him. I clung on to Elvis, barely letting him leave my side for long enough to eat. My mother let him sleep on my bed for the first few nights which was a comfort. In the beginning it didn't seem real at all. If it hadn't been for the mark on the wall I might have thought it was all just a horrid dream. When my Uncle Donal and the five members of Daddy's band lifted the coffin out of the flat they'd banged it off the wall in the hallway – just beside the front door. They left a black mark on the white woodchip wallpaper and it caught my eye every time I walked past: a constant reminder that Daddy wasn't ever coming back.

We stayed in Greenwich for just six months after

Daddy died – until the school year was finished. Eventually, though, my mother ran out of money and had to go back to work. I was almost ten when we gave up the flat and moved to Dingle. I missed my father so much and I was crushed again when I was told we'd have to leave Elvis behind because Grandma already had another dog. Uncle Donal said they would take good care of him and my mother promised me we would go back to visit – it was small comfort, but even though I was very upset I didn't protest. For my first few months in Dingle I mourned Elvis in silence and if it hadn't been for Cara – Grandma's black-and-white, year-old sheepdog, I'm not sure how I would have coped. Thankfully Cara, whose name meant 'friend' in Irish, became just that to me – a sweet, gentle and much-loved best friend.

My grandma once told me that Dingle's rugged beauty and remoteness made her feel closer to God there than anywhere else. "Dingle is close to heaven and the people in heaven," she often said. It was a somewhat consoling thought when I was so far away from the place I had lived with my beloved father, and missing him every day.

Grandma's cottage was nestled high up on a hillside in Garfinny, just outside the town. Garfinny means 'rough ground' and it certainly was that – the fields surrounding the cottage were rugged and wild and many of the roads around the hills had grass growing in the middle of them. Grandma's cottage overlooked Dingle Bay in the distance below. It was such a beautiful setting when the sun shone over the bay but it got very bleak and wild in winter and was one of the windiest places I've ever known. As soon as you put your head outside the door on a windy day your hair usually stood on end and your eyes filled with tears. Not even the trees could escape the wind's force – the small hawthorns looked to be frozen in time, their branches all swept in one direction by the strong winds.

From the start I struggled to fit into my new life in Ireland – especially when it came to school. When I'd started school in London, I was the Irish-looking kid in the English school – then when I started in Kerry I was the English-sounding kid in the Irish school. To make matters worse, Dingle was a *Gaeltacht* area – the Irish language was spoken regularly throughout and was very important to the locals. Of course I didn't speak any Irish when I arrived but, as I was under eleven years of age, I had to learn it – that was the rule. It took the school several months to sort out extra lessons for me and even then I was always terrible at Irish. I hadn't been brought up in the staunch Catholic tradition either which caused more problems. Whilst I had been baptised in Dingle as a baby, I'd never made my First Communion. Neither of my parents had been that interested in religion, and before Daddy died it hadn't featured very much in my life at all. My grandma was, however, horrified to learn this, and promptly insisted on saving my soul. I never did quite understand what my 'soul' was – but it sounded serious and something worth saving so I went willingly to Mass with her every Sunday. I would sit beside her in the Chapel of the Sacred Heart beside our school, and I would stare up at the light shining through Harry's beautiful windows, captivated by their beauty and intricate detail. Later in life I learned that the famous stained-glass artist Harry Clarke had made the vibrant, colourful stained-glass windows for the chapel, but when Grandma told me the windows were Harry's, I just assumed he was one of the priests in the parish. To make matters worse, before I could be confirmed with my own class, I was told that I had to make my First Communion – so, at the age of twelve, I was made to take Communion lessons with the six and seven-year-olds in first class. I hated every minute of the whole thing and, even though I didn't have to wear the white dress, the few friends I had teased me mercilessly about it all.

All in all, I was destined to be different, and for a lot of my childhood I felt like I was on the outside of an inside joke.

It didn't help that Grandma was the local faith healer so we didn't have what you might call a traditional home life. A regular collection of local characters streamed through the cottage each week looking for a cure for their ugly warts, verrucae and eczema. Grandma was well known to everyone in the town as a likeable eccentric. She had an impressive success rate though and she was always happy to oblige a local by removing their unwanted growths in exchange for a fruit cake or box of biscuits. Grandma never accepted money – she said she couldn't take payment for her gift from God – that it was her duty to pass it on.

My granddad, a native of Dingle, had been a soldier in an Irish regiment of the British army – he'd died from a heart attack when my mother, her sister and three brothers were in their teens. The family didn't talk about him too much – I didn't quite understand it at the time but I know now that Grandma was worried about a potential backlash against his chosen career from some of the more nationalist locals.

My aunts and uncles had all left home by the time we

arrived on Grandma's doorstep so she was delighted to have the company and to have me come to stay. My mother wasn't quite so happy about it though – she'd always been more of a one-on-one type person and hated the constant flow of people through the house. She and Grandma just about tolerated each other really – I could tell they were both uneasy while my mother was home. "Why don't you rest a while, girl?" Grandma would say to her. "You're always on edge, always wanting to get going."

And of course Grandma was right. Less than four weeks after my mother took me to Dingle, she left for Africa to begin the Kenya travel guide that took her over three years to write. I was used to my mother leaving, but that time was different. To be left behind tragically by one parent's death was extremely painful, but to be consciously left behind by the other when she was alive, I now realise, was utterly devastating. Of course I said nothing at the time though – it didn't occur to me to protest, or to be upset or angry with my mother. I just retreated deep into myself. For months, I went to school, engaging as little as I possibly could with the other children or with those living near us in Garfinny. My only real friend during that time was Cara – she became my loyal shadow around the cottage and the hills of Garfinny.

After school I had the job of feeding Grandma's chickens, ducks and prize cock. Aside from my welcome home at the gate by Cara every day after school, feeding the poultry was my favourite part of the day. I loved watching them wander around the yard and I got to know each of their funny personalities well. After dinner and homework I would retreat into my small bedroom, Cara would curl up on my feet at the end of my bed and I would lie there and read until I fell asleep. And any time I felt scared, angry or sad, I would climb up Garfinny Hill at the back of the cottage and sit there cuddling Cara and looking up at the blue sky above. It was there that I felt closest to Daddy in heaven. With nobody around except me and the birds I had full-scale conversations with him about anything and nothing – just like we used to. I'd tell him about whatever was bothering me, and also about the ordinary things – like about what had happened in school that day or about the people who came to see Grandma and their horrid warts or about the postcards and letters I'd got from my mother. And when I couldn't think of anything to talk to him about, I sang. I'd start with 'Songbird', then I'd sing a few of his old band tunes or his own songs, but as time went on, Irish songs started to slip in – songs that I'd overheard at Grandma's regular music sessions.

On the last Saturday of every month, without fail, Grandma would host a music session at the cottage. A group of local musicians and singers would descend on the house for a night of music and drinking that always went on into the small hours. It reminded me a little of the nights when my father would rehearse with his band in our flat, or in their basements and garages. The music was the common magnet that brought the diverse group of people of all ages, abilities and backgrounds together. And when they were together, the laughter, chat and music always flowed. I stayed hidden in my bedroom for the first few sessions after I arrived but, as time went on I found myself listening in, even humming along to the music. Once I even caught my foot tapping in the air as I read my book on my bed.

In my fourth month in Grandma's, I'd just finished the last in the Enid Blyton *St Clare's* series and hadn't been to the library to get more books. The rain was pelting down and it was already dark outside – a bleak November evening in Kerry. As the musicians arrived for the monthly session, I stood by my open bedroom door to watch them. I could just about see the people in the open living room from my room. They seemed in good form and looked to be settling in for a good session as they shed their coats, hats and scarves, warmed themselves by the fire and shared the drinks around.

As I watched them, Grandma caught me peeking out. I pulled my head back inside my bedroom door, but it was too late.

"Get out here, Chrissie girl. Time we beat the Sasanach out of you!" she shouted down the hall to me. I had no idea what the *Sasanach* meant, but it didn't sound good. I ducked back inside my room, sat on my bed and grabbed the library book I'd just finished, pretending to read it.

Grandma appeared at my bedroom door. "Come on now, *a stóirín*. Why not put down the book and come join us?"

Grandma always called me '*a stóirín*'. She said it meant 'precious little one' which I liked a lot. But not enough to do as she asked. "No, thank you, Grandma. I'd like to finish this tonight."

She smiled. "Always so polite."

I looked back at my book, pretending to read it again, certainly not expecting what happened next. Grandma whipped the book out of my hands, threw it on the bed and grabbed my hand.

"By God, girl, I'll see a smile on that lovely face of

yours before the year is out, if it's the last thing I do! We've had more than enough blinkin' moping about for one lifetime. Come on now. I'm not taking no for an answer."

And she did. She pulled me by the hand from the bed. For an older woman she had surprising strength – I had no choice but to follow her out into the living room.

The usual group of locals were gathered and just settling down to get ready to play. A couple of the men had already claimed the best armchairs and were busy tuning up. I hovered close by them while Grandma's nearest neighbour, Seán Fada, tuned up his fiddle – *fada* meant 'long' and Sean was indeed the tallest, thinnest old man I'd ever seen. Beside him, Paddy Mac Donnell, or Paddy Mac as everyone called him, was trying out a few chords on his guitar. Eileen Dolan from the town sat on a kitchen chair, her accordion poised and ready for the first tune to start. Fergal, her middle-aged bachelor-farmer son, sat beside her, his bodhrán resting on his knee as he poured himself a glass of stout.

And then Brian Fallon, the one I had really been peeking around my bedroom door to try to see, pushed open the front door. He was with his father Dennis. The Fallons were close neighbours of Grandma's and father and son came to every session. Grandma told me once that Dennis Fallon had 'done a line' with my mother when they were younger, but that she'd soon got fed up of his drinking and they didn't last too long. Brian had his own mother Mary's sallow skin, black hair and dark-brown eyes – it made him look very exotic by Kerry standards and I thought him the most gorgeous boy I had ever set eyes on. Of course I knew he was way out of my league, something to be admired from afar. Regardless, I watched from a little closer than usual as he came in that evening, then took off his coat and made his way into the circle.

Aside from his good looks, one of the other things that made Brian so attractive to me was his singing. He almost always closed Grandma's music sessions. Long after his father would doze off, Brian would still be singing. I would hear his voice from my bedroom, always note-perfect, and he knew the words of all the old Irish tunes. I was a little in awe of him – at fourteen he was four years older than me and I'd never had the courage to so much as speak to him before.

I was so embarrassed when Grandma nudged me forward into the middle of the room. "Brian, why don't you show Chrissie how to play the bodhrán?" She pucked Paddy Mac then who looked very comfortable on the couch. "Shove up, Paddy, and let the young ones sit in there together. The girl needs to start learning our ways."

Paddy moved along to the end of the couch and Brian sat down on the other side. He took his bodhrán out of its bag and handed it and the stick to me as I stood before him. I couldn't even meet his eye, I was so nervous and embarrassed. I held the bodhrán by the wooden crossbar on the underside and studied its dark round wooden edging and off-white drum skin. I rubbed the flat of my right hand over the skin then and felt its coarseness.

"That's goatskin," said Brian, reaching out and tapping the skin with the tips of his fingers. "They stretch it tight to make the sound."

"Are ya going to learn to play it or make butter with it?" Grandma said to me. "Sit in there now beside Brian."

I squashed in on the couch between Brian and Paddy

as Seán Fada and Dennis Fallon smiled over at us. I blushed so red I thought I might combust.

"So you hold it like this." Brian placed the bodhrán on my lap so that it was leaning up sideways under my left arm, the skin facing out. "Hold on to the back wooden crossbar of the bodhrán, then hold the stick as though it was a pencil." Brian put his hand out and I handed him back the stick so he could show me. "Angle your hand back in like this – and tap on the centre of the bodhrán." He handed me back the stick, then leaned across me and held his hand over mine to tap out the beat. It was the closest I'd ever got to a boy.

"You need to make the first beat strong: AON – *dó* – *trí* – *ca'er* . . . AON – *dó* – *trí* – *ca'er*. We just roll *ceathar* into one syllable – *ca'er* – to fit the reel pattern." Brian tapped out the beat slowly a few more times and bit by bit I began to relax and both my face and the rest of me calmed down. I would have been quite happy for us just to have stayed playing like that all night – me holding the drum and Brian leaning over me and holding my hand to play it. All too soon though he took his hand away and sat back on the couch.

"What's Aindow Tree Ca-err?" I asked as I struggled to angle the stick in my hand by myself.

Brian laughed. "Ha! That's a good one!" He stopped then and pulled his head back. "Are you serious? *Aon – dó – trí – ceathar*? It's Irish. One – two – three – four?"

"Oh, okay." As usual I felt like the idiot outsider again. "I'm sorry – I haven't started learning Irish yet."

"Really?" Brian shrugged his shoulders. "Sorry, I shouldn't have laughed. Maybe forget about the numbers – what else do you know or like that would fit the beat?"

I thought about it for a minute. "I do really like that Ethan Harding song at the moment."

"Ethan Harding?" Brian screwed up his nose. "Is he that new English singer and songwriter?"

I nodded. "I think his name would fit the beat?"

Brian stuck out his bottom lip and rocked his head from side to side as he contemplated the matter. He took the bodhrán and stick from me. "All right so. We'll try it." He tapped out the beat slowly. Tilting his ear to the bodhrán, he tapped out the rhythm, repeating: "*ETH – an – har – ding . . . ETH – an – har – ding . . .*" He looked back at me and nodded. "Yeah, that'll work." He handed the bodhrán and stick back to me then. "Now you try it."

A few minutes later the session got underway in earnest. Seán Fada led off and the rest followed: Paddy Mac strummed, Dennis Fallon played the tin whistle, Eileen Dolan got a great sound from the accordion, Brian sang and Grandma kept beat with the tambourine and danced – first on her own, then as the drink started to get the better of him, with Dennis Fallon. I tried to copy what Fergal Dolan was doing with the bodhrán and I joined in very quietly here and there. He was very gracious though – both he and Brian taught me on the night, showing me where I was going wrong, correcting my rhythm. All in all, I quite surprised myself by how much I enjoyed the night and even found myself laughing at the jokes Brian made about his snoring father towards the end of the night.

When people were leaving I helped Grandma with the coats, grabbing Brian's before Grandma could get it.

"Thanks for teaching me tonight, Brian," I said as I handed it to him.

He took it with one hand, propping up his father with the other. "No problem, kiddo."

Kiddo? I flinched. I picked his bodhrán up off the side table then and tried to hand it to him too, but he shook his head.

"I've enough to carry tonight with this fella." He nodded sideways to his father who was holding on to the door handle while trying to sing his own confused, slurred version of 'Seven Drunken Nights'.

"You hold on to it for a while," Brian said to me, "so you can practise. I'll pop back for it if I need it before next month."

I held the drum to my chest. "Wow, thanks so much, Brian!"

As those first long, dark, grey winter months in Dingle passed, I became quite proficient on the bodhrán and I enjoyed squeezing in beside the other musicians on Grandma's couch at the last-Saturday session – especially when I got to sit beside Brian. Then one night in late February, we had a very heavy fall of snow. The roads were bad and only four people showed up for the session. Dennis and Brian managed to walk up from their farm, but Brian was recovering from a bad cold and sore throat and couldn't sing. My grandma hadn't a note in her head and the only other person there was Seán Fada who couldn't sing either.

After a few musical pieces, Dennis turned to me: "Have you a song for us yerself, Chrissie?"

"Ah Dennis, leave the girl alone." My grandma waved her hand at him. "Y'know well that we Devlins make the crows sound good."

"Yerra, don't mind her, girl," said Dennis, looking at me. "Go on, we don't mind how you sound. Sing us a song you learnt from school maybe?"

I bit my lip. The truth was, I'd actually been dying to sing for months. I'd listened avidly to Brian and the others, and had learned all the lyrics. I often hummed the tunes to myself and sang them to Daddy when the weather was good enough to go up on Garfinny Hill. I'd even started to write my own songs – they weren't much good, but I enjoyed playing around with different tunes and thinking up the stories and words for the lyrics. I'd always been too shy to come on out and sing with the group though.

Dennis had given up on me and had already tucked his fiddle back under his chin. He picked up his bow.

"Mind you, her father was a bit of a singer," Grandma said. "Wasn't he, *a stóirín*?"

I looked at her, surprised to hear Daddy mentioned. It had been less than a year since he'd died but sometimes, living in that remote corner of the world, it seemed as though he'd only ever existed in my memory and up in the clouds above Garfinny Hill. I missed him so much. I missed everything about him – telling him in person all about my day at school when I got home – watching his face as he practised the latest song he'd been working on, squeezing his eyes closed when he got to an emotional part of the song. I missed pretending to like the slightly burnt toast he always made with my beans and I longed for just one more of our walks in Greenwich Park with Elvis, or our red-squirrel hunts. Aside from Grandma, nobody in Dingle had really known my father – not well anyway – and since my mother had left I'd rarely even heard him mentioned, let alone talked to anyone about him.

"Did you ever sing together?" Brian asked me.

I looked over at him. "Not really, but I did sing for him a few times before he died."

"Just a few times?"

I nodded, tears welling up in my eyes. But in a strange way, they were good tears – painful yet pleasant at the same time. I wanted them there.

Grandma came over to sit down beside me. "I'm sure he loved to hear you sing, *a stóirín*. Your father adored his little girl." She put her hand on my arm. "Will you sing for him now?"

I closed my eyes for a moment and I was back in my father's bedroom in Greenwich, standing before his bed.

I heard him whisper to me: *Use your voice, Chrissie.*

I opened my eyes and looked at Grandma. Then I took a deep breath in, opened my mouth and, timidly at first, began to sing 'Songbird'.

Grandma leaned over and pucked Dennis in the upper arm. "Begad, our girl can sing!" I sang on as Grandma closed her eyes to listen to me. "Well, I'll be . . ." She shook her head, smiling.

When I finished the song, Dennis nodded his approval and Brian gave me a wink. I smiled at them, relieved to have finally had the courage to sing out loud again.

Grandma leaned over me then, took the bodhrán and stick out of my hands and handed them to Brian. "She won't be needing these any more." She looked around at the others. "Fellas, we have ourselves another singer."

The men mumbled their approval.

Grandma turned back to me and grinned. "Now let's see if we can't teach you a few daycent Irish songs."

Chapter 7

After that night I spent less time reading in my room, less time talking to Daddy up on Garfinny Hill and less time in the company of Cara and the chickens and ducks after school. I began to mix with the other children and made a few friends. And I did quite well in school, especially in English – even winning a county poetry competition in my first year of secondary school.

My mother visited me in Dingle when she wasn't travelling and as the years went on I spent my summer holidays either in London, visiting my family there, or joining my mother on the road. I travelled with her all over Europe, and I loved every minute of it.

My mother had worked solidly since my father's death and by the time I was eighteen she had got the money together to pay for me to attend university in Cork. I was due to go there to study English and History – that was until the *Celtic Wings* production team came to Killarney to hold auditions that autumn.

The show had been building up quite a following in Ireland and around Europe since it had been the central act in a televised variety concert in Dublin on Millennium Eve the previous year. The producers wanted to increase the scale of the show and to take it to America on tour so they were busy scouring the country for young singers and dancers to fill the new roles.

It wouldn't have even occurred to me to have gone to the auditions except that Brian was going. Brian had been working in O'Flaherty's Pub in Dingle since he'd finished school and he'd also followed in his father's footsteps by becoming one of their best customers. And even though he hadn't exactly set the world on fire, the passing years had only served to increase my crush on the boy next door. To my delight, not long before the auditions he'd broken up with Karen Kelly, his long-term girlfriend who had moved to Dublin to train as a nurse. After much soul-searching and encouragement from my friends who'd known for years about my crush, I plucked up the courage to invite the newly single Brian to my debutantes' ball that August. I was stunned when he accepted – just couldn't believe my luck – Brian Fallon was going out with *me*. I was absolutely thrilled. But I was alone in my glee – neither Grandma nor my mother seemed too thrilled at the prospect of me and Brian Fallon as an item. But I didn't care what they thought – Brian and I got together the night of my debs and had our first kiss outside the men's toilets at the Skelligs Hotel in Dingle – just a couple of weeks before the *Celtic Wings* auditions.

Brian didn't seem all that bothered whether I went to the auditions or not, but he was absolutely determined to get a place in the show himself. In all the years I'd known him I'd never seen him so motivated about anything. I helped him rehearse his audition piece over and over again until he was note-perfect. He sounded great and I was sure he would get the role. I practised hard for the auditions myself too even though I was very nervous at the thought of performing in front of the selection panel, let alone a packed auditorium if I got the part. Nonetheless, I made myself go through with it. The way I looked at it at the time – it had taken me eight years to get together with Brian Fallon, and there was no way I was letting him slip away with a company full of stunning female singers and dancers.

So on the day of the auditions I travelled to Killarney with Brian, who drove his mother's car. I practically shook from nerves all the way there but it was worth it for the chance to spend the whole day with my gorgeous new boyfriend.

I was right to have been nervous: the auditions alone terrified me. Lots of clipboard-holding people dressed in black milled around the lobby of the Gleneagle Hotel in Killarney – they talked into headsets and moved crowds of hopefuls along through the function room. There must have been hundreds of people there on the day and thousands more at the various auditions around the country. And though I was nervous, I was happy with my audition, but I still couldn't believe it when they picked me and Brian as two of the new show's group of sixteen backing singers.

My mother was furious that I was deferring college. We had a very strained conversation on the phone when I told her the news. She was speaking to me from some payphone in a hostel in Tanzania and I was talking on Grandma's phone at the cottage. I assured her I'd only do the show for the American tour, that I was just deferring my degree for a year. She remained unconvinced but she didn't stop me – my mother of all people could hardly argue against me wanting to see the world.

But nobody could have foreseen what a big hit *Celtic Wings* would become. The show was a massive success in the States. We got standing ovations every night and, as we were in New York on St Patrick's Day, we were asked to perform as the main act in *The Today Show*'s special St Patrick's Day concert outside the NBC headquarters at the Rockerfeller Centre. I was even interviewed by Katie Couric for the live show. It was an enormously exciting time and things went a bit nuts after that. The show's success spiralled and almost overnight *Celtic Wings* went global. I spent the next seven years touring the world as a cast member, and also as the second long-term girlfriend of heavy drinker and singer, Brian Fallon.

I saw less of my mother during that time – with both of us travelling the world our paths rarely crossed, aside from the odd Christmas in Dingle or cousin's wedding in England. She came to see the show a couple of times – once in Paris and the other time in London. She said she enjoyed it and that she was proud of me but I knew she was disappointed that I'd never gone to college – my mother didn't ever hide her feelings very well. That annoyed me. I thought her disappointment very hypocritical seeing as she'd chosen a life on the road herself. I never said anything to her about it though, and even though I was irritated by her disappointment, I suspect I was also actually a small bit disappointed about not going to college myself. As time went on, I began to think about studying more and more – especially as the cracks began to show in my relationship with Brian.

The after-show social life was pretty hectic on the *Celtic Wings* tour. We had a lot of fun in the early days and the cast and crew became almost like family to us. Brian, of course, was a heavy drinker. I enjoyed a drink myself, but I never overdid it. As a result I spent most of our days off touring the cities we visited on my own. I could usually be found on an open-top tourist bus or a rented bike while Brian slept off yet another hangover in a darkened hotel room.

Then there was his grand plan to produce his own production in competition with *Celtic Wings*. A year before I left the show, he started to work on the idea. He tried to persuade me to leave *Celtic Wings* to work with him on the project full-time, but even though I helped him to write some of the initial music, I wasn't sure I wanted to get involved in another show. Touring had been exciting at first, but I was getting tired of travelling, living out of a suitcase and moving from hotel to hotel. I'd left behind more books in more hotel rooms than I could recall and I'd begun to have dreams of my own – including a recurring one about owning my own bookshelf.

The strain on our relationship really began to show as Brian prepared to leave the show. We were giving a special homecoming performance at the INEC concert venue in Killarney just after Christmas. My mother and Grandma, and virtually the whole neighbouring town of Dingle, came to see us. Afterwards, Brian got very drunk in the hotel bar where the cast, crew and our friends and families had gathered after the show for a drink. I left him propping up the bar, drooling over Kate O'Donoghue, the show's latest star performer – who, I found out later, he'd been trying to tempt over to his new show too. Kate had been brought in to sing the lead female part of Fionnuala. I was used to Brian's drinking and flirting, but I was furious that he was ignoring me and spending all night latched onto Kate. I felt he'd let me down badly in front of my friends and family. So I decided to check out of our room at the hotel and go home to the cottage in Dingle with my mother and Grandma that night. Brian didn't even call me. I hadn't left him a message. He had no idea where I was, and, it seemed, he didn't care.

I stayed in bed in my old room in Grandma's cottage the next morning. My mother was heading back up to Dublin early to fly back to Tanzania after Christmas and I didn't want to face her. In recent years she'd been staying away on the road for longer periods at a time, graduating from travel guides to travel memoirs which took her even longer to write. I knew if I didn't see her that morning it would be months before our paths crossed again which, the way I felt that morning, was fine by me. I knew she'd have something to say about me and Brian and I didn't want to hear it.

I should have known I couldn't avoid her though – before she left that morning she knocked on my door. I tried to ignore it but she walked in anyway.

"Hey!" I sat up in bed.

"Sorry, love, I did knock." She came over and sat down on the bed beside me.

I stretched out my legs and arms and started a long yawn.

My mother came straight out with it: "Chip, love. I'm a bit worried after last night – are you really sure Brian is right for you?"

Her words stopped my yawn midway – ruining the effect. I frowned at her. "Yes, he's fine. He was just a bit drunk last night, that's all."

"Mmm, like the father. You've been together a long time now, though, haven't you? Is he ever going to change?"

I heaved a loud, irritated sigh. "Not now, Mum. I'm not in the mood for this." I nudged her off the bed so I could get up.

She stood up. "I'm sorry if the time doesn't suit you, Chip, but I need to talk to you on this subject –"

"Before you go." I finished her sentence for her. "Story of our lives eh? You leaving – you're always about to go somewhere."

If my mother was in any way fazed by my words or tone, she didn't show it – at first anyway.

"It's just that I wonder if the time hasn't come for you to move on from all this?" She sat back down on the edge of the bed and looked up at me. "The show was great last night, but it hasn't changed much in all these years, has it? You've been with it for seven years now, love. And you're so talented and intelligent – there must be other things you'd like to do?"

I'd started to get dressed. I knew what was coming next so I tried my best to ignore it.

"Perhaps you could do that degree you missed out on?"

I grunted as I pulled my jumper over my head. "I'd be ancient compared to the other students."

My mother pursed her lips. "Well, I've been thinking about this actually. You wouldn't have to do it in the university in Cork. I can understand you not wanting to be in class potentially with the younger brothers and sisters of your friends here. But what about London? We could find you a degree course for mature students there? You could stay with Donal and Gem." She paused for a moment. "And maybe you could look up that nice chap – Tim?"

I stopped buttoning up my jeans. "Who?"

"That friend of your cousin Conor's. Tim's been chasing you for years." She laughed. "How many shows of yours has he been to now?"

"Oh yeah, Tim." I smiled. Tim was a nice guy, and I knew he had a crush on me – he'd dragged poor Conor along to *Celtic Wings* shows all over Ireland and England. But I had no interest in Tim. I shook my head. "Mum, I'm with Brian. I know we're having some problems, but I still love him and I want to try to make it work." I said the words as much to convince myself as my mother.

"Mmm. Should it be so hard though?" My mother screwed up her nose. "I'm just saying that maybe it's time to think about the future. It sounds like Brian wants to continue touring, but is that what you want? I thought you might prefer to settle down a bit now? Decide where you want to live. Maybe think about kids?"

"Ha! You can talk!" I put my hands on my hips. "You, who's spent your whole life avoiding settling down."

"All right, Chip." My mother looked down at her hands for a few seconds before looking back up at me. "We're talking about your life now, not mine."

I had no idea what got into me then, but once I'd started I couldn't stop. "I'm well aware of that, Mum. And please don't call me Chip – nobody else calls me that. Whatever about Daddy, I am nothing like you." My mother tried to say something then but I held up my hand to stop her. "I have no intention of having children if I'm not going to be around to bring them up. I'm a singer – I spend my life on the road. I wouldn't leave a child behind with relatives. Have you any idea how traumatic that can be for a child?"

"I-I . . ." My mother looked shell-shocked. She stared up at me with her mouth open.

I just turned away from her and continued buttoning up my jeans.

After a few seconds she spoke again, her voice only just audible. "I never knew you felt like this, Chi– I mean, Chrissie. You never said anything before."

I spun around and glared down at her. "You never asked! Nobody ever asked me what I wanted. I went along with it all and said nothing. I didn't want to make a fuss, you see, didn't want to upset anyone. But I was nine years old. *Nine!*" I held up nine fingers to her to make my point. She closed her eyes and bent her head. "And you were my only surviving parent. How could you have uprooted me from the only home I ever knew? And then abandon me here? I didn't know who I was and where I belonged for most of my childhood – still don't if I'm honest. I grew up the eternal outsider."

My mother stood up to face me. "I didn't abandon you, Chrissie. I left you with Mam. I had to work. I had to make money for both of us."

"That's rubbish." There was no way I was letting her off the hook that easily. My mother had been using the same sorry excuse all my life. I'd heard her churn it out when my father was alive and I was still hearing it. I'd had enough. "It's not true, is it, Mum? That's not the reason you left me here after Daddy died, or why you left him and me in London all those times. You could have got a job here or in London." I took a step towards her and took her arm. "Admit it, you did it, you *do* it, for yourself."

My mother pursed her lips. I could see the tears hovering in her eyes but I couldn't stop. Years of suppressed anger, isolation and feelings of desertion had finally caught up with me.

"You have to understand, Chrissie. Travelling . . . writing . . . it's who I am. I can't change who I am. Believe me, there are times I wish I could."

"You could have if you'd wanted to." I let go of her arm. "Most people adapt their lifestyles when they have children."

"I did try a few times when you were two or three, but I was miserable. I ate too much, even started to drink – I got fat, bored, and cranky – I hated it. At the time, both your father and I agreed it would be better if I went back to work. He understood it was what I had to do. It was only as you got older that he started to reconsider, but by then I was very set in my ways. I did *try* to adapt though, Chrissie – believe me."

"Please." I turned my head to one side. "Having me had a minimal impact on your life – Daddy was always asking you to give up the travel but you wouldn't. I remember it clearly."

"Not at first, I tell you – in the beginning he supported it." My mother stared at me, then she just closed her eyes. "I know he did want me to stop as time went on. I'm sorry, Chrissie. I did the best I could."

But I couldn't let it go. "If that was your best, I'd really

96

hate to see your worst. Have you any idea what it was like to be left in a strange country without my parents, so soon after Daddy had died?"

My mother shook her head, tears falling freely from her eyes.

"I was devastated without him. I needed you, Mum." My own tears surprised me but I didn't wipe them away. After all the years I needed her to see my pain.

My mother stepped forward and rubbed my arm. "Chrissie, love – you're upset. You don't mean all these things you're say–"

"*Don't!*" I yanked my arm away from her and as I did she lost her balance and fell backwards against the bookshelf. As she tried to steady herself to get up, a couple of my childhood mementoes and ornaments fell off the shelf and hit off the side of the bed before they crashed down on to the floor.

"Daddy's nightingale!" I threw myself onto my knees to pick up the bird and its separate, broken wing.

My mother steadied herself against the bookshelf. "Oh Chrissie, I'm so sorry." She reached out to take the bird from me. "It should be easy enough to fix."

I snatched it away from her. "Don't touch it! Just leave it. Leave me." I stood up and pointed to the door. "Go on. I'm sure you're dying to get going again. So do it. Go! Leave! That's what you're best at, after all." I was shaking so much I thought I would fall over.

My mother could barely speak through her tears. "I'm not leaving you like this."

"Fine then. If you won't leave, I will." I dropped the ornament and the wing on my bed and stormed out.

Grandma was outside in the hall, her new collie pup,

Sam, in her arms. "Chrissie, *a stóirín*," she put her hand out to try to stop me, "are you all right?"

"I'm fine, Grandma." I grabbed my coat and hat from the coat-stand beside the front door then had to stop myself calling out to Cara who'd died of old age earlier that year. I went outside then and practically ran all the way up Garfinny Hill behind the cottage. I stayed up there for hours.

My mother had left by the time I got back.

Chapter 8

"That was the last time I saw my mother," I told Abigail as I stared at the broken wing in my hand. "We spoke on the phone a couple of times afterwards – she called me from London on her stopover, then a few times from Africa. And, thank God, I apologised for what I'd said. We were on okay terms, but I was looking forward to seeing her at the end of her trip and having a proper chat with her."

"I'm sure you were," said Abigail, putting a reassuring hand on my arm. "It's so sad that that was the last time you saw her."

I nodded. "I know but in some ways the argument was a good thing – it brought up so much that I'd been burying down inside me for years. It wasn't easy to deal with, but at least we were starting to deal with it." I wrapped the wing in both my hands and sighed. "It was five weeks after my mother left Dingle that she died in the ferry accident off Zanzibar. I never did get to have that final face-to-face conversation with her."

"Oh, that's terrible," said Abigail. "I knew she'd died

on her travels but you never mentioned before how it happened."

"I find it quite difficult to talk about really." I took a deep breath in.

"You don't need to say any more, Chrissie." Abigail put her hand on my arm. "I understand."

I smiled at her. "It's okay. It was a really awful time. I was with *Celtic Wings* in Berlin when I got the news." I sniffed. "Brian didn't even come to the memorial we had for my mother in Dingle. We'd been together over seven years at that stage and he couldn't be there for me."

Abigail sucked her breath in through her teeth.

"I know." I rolled my eyes and shook my head. "I should have ended it with him after that – stupid. In the end I waited until three months later when I found out that he'd been sleeping with bloody Kate O'Donohue for months." Abigail squeezed my arm. "I left *Celtic Wings* then and I haven't done any singing or writing since – just haven't had the heart for it really." I looked at the bedroom door. "Tim was amazing though. He came over to Dingle with Conor for my mother's memorial service – and was so sweet. They never found her body, so we couldn't have a proper funeral. One hundred and twenty-nine people disappeared in that accident and they only ever found a handful of bodies – it was an absolute disgrace. Then six weeks after the accident, Grandma got a call from the Irish Embassy. Apparently when they finally brought up the wreckage of the ferry they discovered something belonging to my mother – a bicycle. Her name was etched onto Sky's frame and they matched it to her from the ferry's ticketing records. So Conor came over to Zanzibar with me to collect a rusted, scratched-up bicycle and to see the place where my mother disappeared . . . where she died." I took a deep breath in, then smiled over at Abigail. "When we got back Tim had Sky fixed up for me so that she was almost as good as new. It was one of the nicest things anyone has ever done for me. We started dating soon after that."

Abigail took the wing out of my hands. "You've been through a lot, Chrissie, but you have a lovely partner and a beautiful home now. Your mother would be very proud of you."

"I know. I've been lucky I guess. It's just . . ."

"What is it, Chrissie?" Abigail looked at me.

"I just wish I could have had that one last conversation with her. I wish I could understand what she was trying to tell me that last time I saw her. I still can't understand how, if she really did love us enough, she could have left me and Daddy, time and time again. Why weren't we enough for her?"

But before Abigail could say anything, Tim walked back into the room. He was all cleaned up, wearing a fresh pair of knee-high chinos and a loose grey T-shirt.

"Fancy staying for dinner, Abigail?" he said. "It's really cleared up out there – I'm thinking of getting the barbeque going."

Abigail jumped up and looked at her watch. "Gosh no, I'd better get going. I'm dead late already. Penny will kill me."

I went into the kitchen after seeing Abigail out. Tim was out on the deck in the garden, taking the cover off the barbeque. I smiled as I watched him shake the rainwater off, carefully fold it over and put it on a chair. Jasper bounced about playfully beside him, delighted to be seeing some outdoor action after an afternoon indoors sheltering from the rain.

I went to the fridge and poured two glasses of white wine, then I went out to join my lovely boyfriend and my favourite four-legged friend on the deck.

Chapter 9

Tim was up before me the morning I turned thirty. Before I moved in with him, if I stayed over on Friday nights, I would kiss him goodbye in bed early on Saturday morning before cycling back to my flat to collect my stock and open the stall. In the past couple of weeks a lot had changed though. As I got up to take my shower I could hear him already clattering around in the kitchen downstairs. He'd insisted on getting up to make me a birthday breakfast.

I looked at my naked self in the en-suite mirror before I got in the shower. I didn't look any different – still my same skinny, lanky self. I certainly didn't feel thirty – I didn't feel any different at all in fact. I heaved a deep sigh and turned on the water in the shower. I knew that I needed to try to get excited about the whole birthday thing, but thirty just sounded so old. And even though I was looking forward to seeing our friends and family that afternoon, I would really have preferred a quiet dinner for two for Tim and me, rather than a bouncy castle full of screaming kids and a pig on a spit. I felt so sorry for the poor unfortunate pig.

"Hurry up, Chrissie," Tim called up the stairs. "Your bacon is cooked!"

"Coming!" I stepped into the shower.

"Happy birthday, gorgeous." Tim was wearing loose combat–type shorts with big pockets, a T-shirt and a pair of flip-flops. Spatula in hand, he had his *Will-Cook-For-Beer* apron dangling untied from his neck. He caught me as I went to pat Jasper who was wagging his tail furiously in his bed by the open patio doors.

Tim wrapped his arms around me and gave me a kiss. "Today's the big day," he said as he let me go. "I hope you're ready for some big-time spoiling!"

I smiled. "Born ready!" I looked out the doors and across the wooden deck. It was a beautiful summer's morning and I could hear the wood pigeons cooing their appreciation from the high trees. "You couldn't have asked for a better day for an outdoor party anyway."

"Not so far," said Tim. He grabbed a couple of slices of bread out of the packet on the counter.

I knelt down by Jasper's bed and gave him the attention he sought, patting his head and obliging him by rubbing his proffered belly.

Tim put the bread in the toaster then turned back to me. "The forecast predicts some pretty grim weather for later on though. Still, we have the pagoda for the food and drink, and I'm going to push back all the furniture in here in case we need to move the party indoors. We should be fine."

Jasper left me and went over to Tim to stand on guard for any morsels of falling food.

I stood up. "You missed your calling in life, love," I

said. "You should have been a party planner."

He laughed. "Yeah, that would've been good – I suspect it doesn't pay nearly as well as advertising though." He started to whistle while he put the oven gloves on. Then he took two plates out of the oven before standing by the hob and spooning scrambled egg out of the pot onto both plates. He went to pick up some bacon too but seemed to think twice. He looked over at me and raised his eyebrows to see if I wanted any.

"No, thanks. Just the eggs would be great."

"Righty-oh. More for me." Tim went back to whistling as he dished four slices of bacon out of the pan onto his own plate. He picked up both plates then and turned to me. "All right – if the birthday girl could take a seat, breakfast will be served."

I went over to the large round kitchen table beside the open doors. Tim had set it beautifully – white linen tablecloth, long-stem red rose in a frosted green vase, and matching green linen napkins in the silver napkin rings.

"This looks gorgeous, Tim." I sat down. "You shouldn't have gone to so much trouble."

He kissed me on the head as he put my plate down in front of me. "Nothing but the best for my girl."

I smiled at him as he sat down beside me. "Are you absolutely sure you can manage everything yourself for later on though? I feel bad leaving you to set it all up. I could close up the stall a bit before noon if you need me earlier?"

He took his apron off. "No, it's all under control – better you're out of the way for the morning. I've very little to do really. The caterers handle everything and the bouncy castle and pagoda people get here about ten, so there'll be plenty of time – the guests aren't due to arrive until two. Now eat up." He threw the apron on one of the other kitchen chairs and pulled his own chair in.

"Looks great, thanks, love." I picked up my fork.

"This is nice, isn't it?" Tim said a few minutes later as he wiped his plate clean with the last bit of his slice of toast. "Breakfast together in our own home."

"Mmm . . ." I smiled and put my hand over his, giving it a squeeze. "It's lovely. Such a treat. Thanks, love."

Tim frowned then. "Such a pity you're at the market every Saturday. Still, hopefully it won't be for too much longer."

I swallowed the bite of toast I'd just taken and looked at him. "What d'you mean?"

Tim pulled his hand away and sat back in his chair looking quite sheepish. "Well, you'll have to give up the stall when you start your teacher training, won't you? You wouldn't have time for it then, and you wouldn't want to jeopardise the permanent job in Park View, would you?"

"Permanent job? What makes you think I'm going to be made permanent?" Other than Abigail, I hadn't told anyone about my conversation with Ms Delamere.

Tim picked up his plate, stood up and started to walk to the dishwasher. "That full-time teaching job that will be going there next year sounds like it'd be perfect for you?"

I put my piece of toast down and spun around to look at him. "Where did you hear about that, Tim? It hasn't been made public at all."

"Hmm?" He glanced up at me from the dishwasher. "Did you not mention it somewhere along the line?"

"Nope."

106

"Hmm, funny. I was sure it was you." He stood up straight from the dishwasher and scratched his head. I always knew when Tim was bluffing – he was a terrible liar. I knew it, and he knew it. The look I gave him told him as much. He squinted as if trying to remember. "I guess it could have been Dave."

Dave was Tim's business partner.

"How on earth would *Dave* hear about it?" I stood up and went over to him, followed closely by Jasper who was still on crumb-watch. "I mean I know his kids are in the school, but the parents wouldn't know about it yet."

Tim moved away from the dishwasher and went to get the dog food out of the cupboard – his every move watched by Jasper who knew what was coming and gave a couple of excited yelps. "Dave's wife Rosalind is one of the governors at Park View – didn't I mention it before?"

I couldn't believe it. "No, you certainly did not mention it before."

"Didn't I?" Tim raised his eyebrows. "It's all good – I hear you're a big hit at the school."

Then a thought struck me. "Tim, you didn't have anything to do with me getting this teacher's assistant contract in the first place, did you?" I stared at him. "Now that I think of it, you were the one who showed me the advertisement for it."

I was almost afraid to hear his answer.

Tim had helped me in so many ways after my mother died and after the awful break-up with Brian. I needed him then – he was an amazing support – but over the last year or so I really thought I'd been beginning to stand on my own two feet again. I'd redecorated my own flat, done up the roof garden, built up a loyal customer base for the stall, got my degree and secured some temporary work. I thought I'd done it all myself and I liked the feeling of taking charge of my own life. The sudden question-mark over how I'd got the Park View contract was very unnerving.

Tim finished filling Jasper's bowl. He walked over to me then, put his hand on my arm and kissed my forehead. "Why would I need to get involved? Any school would be lucky to have you. Forget I said anything." He reached down into his shorts side pocket then and pulled out a small intricately wrapped box. "Time for presents! Happy birthday, my love."

I stood back from him. "Eh . . . thanks." I wasn't convinced at his answer, but I didn't want to ruin the moment. I took the box and went back over to the table. He followed me over and sat down beside me.

I looked up at him. "Beautiful wrapping."

He smiled. "Glad you approve."

I started to open the swirly gold ribbon and peeled back the thick, purple wrapping paper, my every move watched closely by Tim, who looked from the box to my face and back again – like Jasper did when he was waiting for one of us to feed him.

I opened the box and took out a black key. It was attached to a diamante key ring in the shape of the letter 'C'.

Tim had a massive grin on his face. "It's been tucked in the garage all weekend. I was terrified you might have seen it yesterday." He jumped up.

"Seen what?" I asked.

"Your new car!" He took the key from me and grabbed my hand.

"My new *what*?" I stared up at him in shock.

"Car!" He pulled me to my feet. "Come on – you're gonna love it, Chrissie."

I followed him almost in a daze. Jasper, who'd finished gobbling down his food, started to follow us, but Tim ducked back to close the kitchen door behind me to keep him in.

"I'll bring it round." Tim skipped ahead of me out into the hall and out the front door.

I stood at the top of the steps by the open front door and squinted in the early morning sunlight. Once I got used to the light I stared out at the hazy heath in front of the house, still in shock. I was a bike person – Sky was my mode of transport. I'd never wanted a car, couldn't afford to run a car, didn't need a car, could only just about drive a car . . . Tim knew all of this . . . Why the hell had he bought me a bloomin' *car* of all things?

I heard the sound of an engine revving, then Tim reversed out of the garage and manoeuvred the shiny, new, white Volkswagen jeep across the gravel driveway so that it was parked directly facing me at the bottom of the steps. It was enormous. I couldn't imagine ever driving such a car but I managed to plaster a smile on my face.

Tim jumped out, then stood with his elbow leaning on top of the open car door. He patted the roof then. "I know you said you didn't need a car, Chrissie. But I thought it was high time you had a run-around of your own. It'll be handy for getting to school and for visiting family. Come on down and take a look."

I dutifully walked down the steps and stood in front of the monstrosity. "Tim, this really is too much," I said, still somewhat dazed. "It must have cost you a fortune."

He came over, and stood behind me, his arms around my waist. "You're worth every penny," he said, leaning his chin on my shoulder.

We stood there like that for a few seconds just staring at the white tank, then Tim handed me the key and took my hand to lead me over to the driver's seat. He proceeded to point out every feature of the car while I tried my best to make all the right noises. I even sat at the wheel and indulged him by turning on the engine, then jumped when I heard a horn blow.

I looked in the rear-view mirror to see Abigail's little blue van drive up behind me.

I leaned over and gave Tim a kiss. "This is amazing, Tim. Thanks so much. Must dash now though."

"Why don't you drive yourself and Abigail to the market in your new car?" he said. "It's taxed and insured and has a full tank of petrol. And it's got a very big boot for your stock. You're good to go!"

I tried to hide my horror by looking away from him – Tim's house led right out onto the busy main road by the heath – it had heavy traffic at all times of the day and night. I wasn't a confident driver by any means, and the thought of driving out onto that road didn't appeal to me at all.

"Best not. Abigail's here now. Her stock will be all packed up in her van, and she's blocking us in. Sure I'll test-drive the car later – after the party."

"I'll hold you to that," Tim said. "I'll have it turned and facing out towards the gate, ready for you to pull out easily later on."

I made a big effort to smile. "Great. Thanks."

Abigail appeared at the open car door. "Is it yours?" she said to me as I got out.

Tim, who'd walked around to join her, said: "It certainly is. A birthday present for my favourite girl." He put his arm around my waist. "She hasn't been too keen on the idea of turning thirty, so I thought this might take the sting out of it."

"Yes, I expect it would help all right," Abigail said, laughing.

We both watched as she popped her head inside the car and looked around its interior.

"Wow, this is some motor!" she said, turning back to us. "So much space. I'd love something like this for the kids. Chrissie, you are one lucky lady. Are you thrilled?"

"Absolutely!" I looked at Tim, who thankfully seemed convinced by my forced enthusiasm. "I am quite embarrassed by all this fuss though. It's just my birthday – I haven't done anything to deserve it."

"This is just the beginning," Tim put his arm around my shoulder. "Wait until you see what I have planned for later."

I took a step back from him. "Oh Tim, tell me you haven't gone too mad. The party and the car is more than enough. I'd honestly have been just as happy with a picnic in the park."

"*Pfff!* For my girl's thirtieth birthday?" Tim made a grand sweeping gesture with his hand. "The sky's the limit."

Abigail raised her eyebrows at me.

"We'd better get going," I said to her. "I'll just go grab my stock."

Tim followed me into the house to help me and we left Abigail alone to *ooh* and *aah* over the car's features.

Chapter 10

Donal and Gem, my favourite uncle and aunt, were the first to arrive for the party. Since Uncle Donal had retired and sold his bakery in Charlton, he and Gemma were always the first to arrive for every occasion. Tim's lovely parents, Tony and Jane, weren't far behind them – they kept apologising about being early but Tim assured them that we were ready and delighted to see them. They were followed closely by Tim's younger sister Caroline, her husband John and their three children who ranged in age from seven to twelve. Two of my cousins, Peadar and Mick, Peadar's wife and kids and Mick's girlfriend Robyn arrived pretty much on time and within an hour or so most of the other guests were there too: Abigail and her family, Tim's colleagues and a bunch of other friends of ours. Thankfully, despite the forecast of rain, the weather had held and it was a gorgeous summer's afternoon – the sun beamed down on us and the pagoda on the lawn offered some welcome shelter from its rays. Tim had hired extra white PVC garden furniture which was just as well – the deck was full of people sitting or leaning against the railing drinking beer or Prosecco. The caterers had set up in the corner of the pagoda close to the deck and the poor glistening pig was turning on his spit. I felt sad every time I forgot to avoid looking over in that direction. Cling-film covered the bowls of salads that were laid out on long white linen-covered trestle tables. The bar was set up beside the food and the barman Tim had hired was already busy keeping the adults' glasses topped up and the children in fizzy drinks. And there were children everywhere – in reality about twenty or so in total, but it seemed like about two hundred they made so much noise as they bounced off the walls of the inflatable castle. Their laughter and shrieks of enjoyment were even drowning out the loud hum of the generator. It wasn't all fun and games though – every now and then there would be an incident caused by a bouncing collision or a hair-pulling episode, and a parent would very begrudgingly leave behind their drink to go play judge and jury. Ever the flawless party-organiser, Tim had thought of that and had also hired a jazz trio – three young local music students. The lively music of the double-bass, saxophone and keyboard somehow won out over the screeches of distressed children and the noisy chastising of stressed parents.

It was all a little chaotic and everyone was making quite a fuss of me. And while it was lovely to see all my friends and family and to enjoy the afternoon in the sunshine, I couldn't help but feel a bit embarrassed by it all, and quite uneasy at being the centre of attention. I tried to relax and enjoy it, but every time I sat down someone needed something or there was a new arrival to greet.

I was in the kitchen getting a cloth to mop up a spillage on the deck by one of Tim's colleague's children, when the doorbell rang again.

"I'll get it." Tim had just come into the kitchen from the den where he'd been checking on Jasper who was confined there. He doubled back out towards the front door.

I recognised my cousin's voice: "Alrigh', mate. Sorry we're late. Where's the birthday girl then?"

I put my head around the kitchen door. "I'm down here, Conor!" I turned and handed the cloth to the embarrassed mother of the child. "Sorry, Lydia, I'd better go and say hello to my cousin."

"Of course," she said. "Go on. I'll sort this."

I smiled at her and bounded up the hallway to greet Conor, his wife Rebecca and Patrick, their adorable but tyrannical handful of a three-year-old.

Conor was a big brute of a man. At six foot five, he towered above me, which was saying something – there were very few men I looked up to. I adored my cousin. The eldest of three brothers, he'd always looked out for me when I was growing up and he, Peadar and Mick were like brothers to me. Tim and Conor had been best friends since school and it was a rare weekend that they didn't hang out together, often meeting up during the week to train too.

"Happy birthday, cuz," Conor picked me up in his arms and twirled me around.

I laughed. "Hey, put me down! I'm far too old to be picked up now."

He did as he was told. "Ah, you're never too old for a Devlin birthday twirl."

I smiled and patted my dress back down into place. I was delighted with it – a darkish grey cotton material, it hung down off one shoulder and was quite loose and flowing with large feature pockets. I wore it over leggings of the same colour and, by that stage of the party, my old brown sandals. I'd bought a nice pair of white wedge-heeled sandals to go with it, but had already abandoned them for my most comfortable footwear.

Rebecca followed her husband in, restraining young Patrick by the hand – the child seemed very excited and eager to get to the action out the back. My cousin may have been a big man and owner of his own building business but the pretty, dainty Rebecca was very definitely the one in control of their household – until Patrick came along at least. Tim had told me that the choosing of Patrick's name had almost caused divorce. Conor had wanted the baby to have an Irish name in recognition of his Kerry roots, but Rebecca refused point-blank to call the baby Pádraig as he'd wanted. In the end they compromised on the name Patrick, with Rebecca being awarded full naming rights for baby number two. Said baby was scheduled to arrive any day and Rebecca looked stunning as always in a shocking red silk, bat-wing maternity dress and matching red mules. I got on reasonably well with Rebecca, but I found her a little intimidating. She was always so well put together and she chose her words so carefully that I was afraid of saying or doing the wrong thing around her. I also found her quite difficult to talk to – it was a struggle to think of what to say to her at all really. So much so that we usually only talked about things like the weather, or about what was going on in the news or the area. Tim was always on at me to try harder with her – I think he wanted the four of us to spend more time together as couples. I had nothing against the woman but I didn't feel fully comfortable around her and I didn't consider her so much a friend as Conor's wife – someone to say a few polite words to at family occasions.

She held the top of my arm and gave me a kiss on the cheek. "Happy bir–" But before she could get the words out, Patrick managed to wriggle out of her grasp and make a sudden dash for freedom. "Patrick!" Rebecca disappeared off down the hall, clutching her pregnant belly. "Come back here, young man, and wish Chrissie – *Patrick, put that down this instant!*"

"Take it easy, Becks!" Conor called after her. He looked back at us and shook his head. "That boy of ours is getting naughtier by the day. It's as if he knows his only-child status will be coming to an end soon and he's making the most of the time he has left. I hope you've secured all breakables."

There was a loud smash from the kitchen.

Conor nodded. "Yep, didn't take him long."

"*Patrick!*" came Rebecca's voice.

I laughed. "Let the destruction commence!"

Tim put one arm around Conor's back, the other around mine. "Sounds like you need a beer, mate. Wait until you see what we've done with the garden – the hog is almost ready and I'll bet Patrick will enjoy the bouncy castle."

We'd just begun to walk towards the kitchen when the doorbell rang again. Tim stopped to go back, but he'd been answering the door all afternoon. I wanted him to enjoy the day.

"No, it's okay," I said. "I'll go. You get Conor that beer."

The men went to join the party and I went back to open the front door.

There, looking nervous and almost surprised to see the door open, stood my father's parents, Nicholas and Susan Cole.

"Oh my goodness! You came! How wonderful! Come in, come in!" I held the door back, my mind already racing.

I'd invited my grandparents to the party but had never really expected them to come. Not long before my mother died, I'd decided to try to find them. I wasn't sure how receptive they'd be to the daughter of their errant dead son and his wilful Irish wife, but I'd thought and wondered about them so much over the years that, by the time I turned twenty-five, I finally decided to give it a go. My mother had always refused to so much as mention their names to me, but I found their details in her address book and, while I was in London with *Celtic Wings*, I decided to look them up. They were shocked when I appeared at the front door of their large home in Hampstead but, once the shock faded, they were warm in their welcome – well, as warm as the Coles could be – they were very reserved people. They were kind to me though, and once we got used to each other after a few visits Nicholas talked to me about what my father was like as a boy. And, though she rarely joined those conversations, Susan did show me a few of his childhood photographs. It was funny to see Daddy with such short hair – I'd only ever seen him wear it long and straggly. He was wearing his public-school uniform jacket in the photograph so he looked very posh but it was definitely him – I recognised his wide-eyed grin and the way he tilted his head slightly to the side in every photograph I'd ever seen of him.

I never told my mother that I'd got in touch with the Coles even though I'd met them four or five times before she died. I knew she'd hit the roof if she heard about it and I didn't want to deal with that. I felt guilty keeping the secret from her, but being with my grandparents made me feel closer to my father, so I kept seeing them. The only one who knew about it at all was Tim. It was he who suggested I invite them to the party. He'd said it was time.

"Hello, dear."

Susan held out her hand but I ignored it and drew her small, thin frame into a big hug. She didn't seem to know what to do – my grandmother still hadn't got used to my hugs. She stood there with her arms down by her sides for a moment, then she seemed to give in and returned the hug. Nicholas, who was tall and broad just like my father had been, followed his wife into the house. He tipped the beige trilby hat that he always wore and bowed his head at me. I gave him a big hug then too. As I drew back he took off his hat, then handed me a carrier bag. I looked inside to see a bottle of wine and a pot plant – a small pink miniature rose.

"Oh, it's beautiful – thank you both so much." I gave him a kiss on the cheek and he stood up straighter and smiled.

My grandfather was a retired academic, a psychology professor, and in his day head of department at Brunel University. He'd written several well-received books about Carl Jung and his theories of individuation and dream psychology and also one about Abraham Maslow and self-actualisation. His books weren't exactly an easy read, but they were interesting and my grandfather was a well-respected scholar in England. At eighty-one years of age, my grandmother should also have retired years earlier, but she'd refused to fully give up her work as editor with a large London publishing house and she still edited a few books a year. She specialised in academic texts and non-fiction books and had met my grandfather when she'd edited his first text over sixty years earlier.

"We can't stay long," Susan said, "but we couldn't let the day pass without seeing our granddaughter."

I smiled. "I'm delighted to see you – and, now you know where I live, you can come visit more often. Come on through – everyone's out in the garden."

I spotted their exchanged look of concern and, if truth be known, I was quite nervous myself. As we walked down to join the party I tried to reassure myself that everything would be fine, the old wounds would surely have healed by now.

I got my grandparents a couple of sparkling waters from the bar and a seat in the shade under the pagoda. Tim was busy showing Conor and Patrick the bouncy castle so I didn't get a chance to introduce them to him. Instead I sat and chatted with them by myself for a while. Nobody else paid us too much attention and I was trying to decide whether I should try to introduce them to some of my Devlin relations when I felt a tap on the shoulder from behind. I turned around to see Abigail standing there, a small gift bag in her hand.

"I'm so sorry to interrupt, Chrissie. I just wanted to grab you while I have five child-free minutes – Penny is supervising Molly and Matthew on the bouncy castle."

"Hey there!" I smiled at my friend. "Abigail, this is Susan and Nicholas – my father's parents."

"Wow, really? Lovely to meet you." Abigail smiled and shook their outstretched hands.

I pulled a seat out for her to sit on.

"I left your main present with the others in the kitchen," she said, sitting down, "but I wanted to make sure you opened this one now. It's just a little fragile."

"Aw, that's so sweet of you, but you really shouldn't be bringing me presents, Abigail." I took the little green bag from her and lifted the small bubble-wrapped object out. I peeled back the tape and pulled the bubble wrap away to reveal my now two-winged china nightingale figurine. "Oh my goodness, you fixed it!"

Abigail smiled. "Yes. I hope you don't mind but Tim smuggled it out for me during the week. I used this special glue I found for porcelain. It's supposed to minimise the look of the crack. I hope it's okay."

I tried to inspect the crack on the wing, but I could barely see anything through the tears that had welled up to blur my vision. I turned and threw my arms around my friend. "Thank you so much. It's the most wonderful, thoughtful present I've ever been given – twice!" I laughed, then sat back and turned the bird over to read my father's faded writing. "I absolutely love it." I looked back at her and reached out to squeeze her hand. "More than words can say."

She smiled at me.

"What is it?" asked Nicholas.

I handed him the china nightingale. "Daddy gave it to me before he died."

Nicholas took the ornament then glanced at Susan

who looked away. He turned the bird over in his hands to read the base. "*Use Your* . . . What's the last word?"

"Voice. It says *Use Your Voice*. Daddy was trying to encourage me to get over my nerves and sing." I felt a lump in my throat as I spoke, then coughed to cover it up.

Nicholas smiled sadly. I think he mumbled something then like 'That's my boy' to himself before Susan snatched the bird out of his hand and put it down on the table in front of me. I picked it up and wrapped it back up in the bubble wrap just as Tim came over to us. I put the small package into the deep side-pocket of my dress for safekeeping.

Tim smiled at Abigail and nodded to my grandparents. I was just about to introduce him to them when he said: "They're about to serve the food, Chrissie. Come on, we need the birthday girl to make the first carving in the hog."

I looked at Abigail. I didn't need to say anything – my friend was a vegetarian and I knew she would understand my horror.

She was about to say something when Nicholas spoke: "Pardon me, but I think it might be more traditional for the man of the house to carve the meat?"

Tim looked at him for a second, then nodded slowly. "Actually, I think you could be right, mate. Thanks for that."

"Tim, this is –" But before I could introduce him, Tim was striding over in the direction of the buffet table.

I looked back at Nicholas who gave me a wink and, whatever way he smiled at me, in that moment he reminded me so much of my father.

As people were finishing up the delicious strawberries and cream and cheesecake desserts, Uncle Donal, who had walked up on to the deck, clinked his spoon on his water glass. He seemed to be thoroughly enjoying the afternoon surrounded by his family and was standing beside the silenced jazz band, beaming around at the gathering on the grass below. As I looked at him standing there, I realised how old he was getting himself. Donal had been quite a strong, tall, red-haired Irishman in his day, but as the years had gone on he'd lost most of his hair and his muscles had disappeared to make way for his middle-aged spread. My once fit and sturdy uncle had turned into a cuddly teddy bear. He hadn't lost any of his spirit though – Uncle Donal still relished his role as head of the Devlin family and he enjoyed every opportunity he got to play the role to full effect.

"Your attention, please!" He clanked his spoon loudly on his glass again. People started to quieten down and look up in his direction. He put the glass and spoon down on the ledge of the deck beside him and leant down to speak into the microphone stand he'd taken from the band. "Is this working?" He tapped it a few times to reassure himself. "Right so. I'd like to get my niece up here now. Chrissie, where are you, girl?"

That was the part of the day I'd been most dreading. I looked around at all the expectant faces smiling over in my direction. There was no getting out of it – the sooner I got it over with, the better. I excused myself from the table I'd been sitting at with Conor, Rebecca, Mick, Robyn and Tim, and went over to join Uncle Donal. The others got up too and started to follow me over. I smiled at Nicholas as I passed his table. He and Susan had been sitting with Abigail and Penny for the lunch. He smiled back at me but Susan just squinted into the sun as she glanced up from her bowl of strawberries.

I climbed the couple of steps up from the grass to the deck. The sun had gone in by that stage and it had started to look a little darker, the clouds were beginning to hover threateningly above. They did nothing to dampen my uncle's spirits though – he was clearly enjoying himself.

"We'll have to get her to sing with you later, eh, lads?" he said to the band.

When I got up to him he put his arm around me and turned me out to face the crowd that had begun to gather around on the grass at the bottom of the steps to see the show. Even the children stopped bouncing, eating and dashing about to wander into the front of the semicircle. I could just about see Susan and Nicholas at the far edge of the group, now standing up beside their table.

"No singing today, Uncle Donal," I said with a smile. "I've retired from all that."

"Retired? At the grand old age of thirty?" Donal laughed and turned back to his audience. "We'll see about that, eh?" He winked at them. "Now where's the young man who made all this happen? Tim, my boy – are you out there?" He shaded his eyes and looked out at the tables on the grass.

Tim pushed his way up onto the deck through our friends and family, a big grin on his face.

"Go wan, my son!" shouted Conor as he passed him by.

Tim stood beside me, putting his arm around my waist. I smiled and leaned my head on his shoulder for a moment. My *Celtic Wings* training had taught me how important it was to give the audience what they expect. There was a communal "*Aww!*" from the crowd and, though I was quite embarrassed, I couldn't help but smile.

"And so I would like to propose a toast to this fine young couple on the occasion of my favourite niece's thirtieth birthday," said Uncle Donal, sounding very formal, making me feel even more nervous.

I just wanted the speeches to be over fast, so I could sit back down, out of the spotlight.

By then Rebecca and Conor were standing at the front of the group on the grass nearest to Tim and me.

"It's like a wedding," I heard Rebecca say to Conor.

He nodded and smiled at us. "That won't be long away, I'm sure."

I looked at Tim to see if he'd heard them. I wasn't sure if he had, but he gave me a squeeze without looking away from Donal.

"I think we would all agree that young Tim here has outdone himself today?" Donal walked around me to get to Tim.

I stood back when he grabbed him in a headlock and rubbed his head, messing up his hair. Everyone laughed, a few people clapped and there were a few cries of 'Good man, Tim!' and 'Hear hear!'.

When Donal finally released him, Tim stood back up straight and smoothed his hair down. He held up his hand to accept the appreciation. "All right, all right. Settle down, you lot!" He put his arm back around my waist and smiled at me.

"Our Chrissie certainly landed on her feet here, eh?" Uncle Donal laughed and patted me on the back.

I smiled and nodded along, all the while praying he would finish soon.

Donal went back over to the microphone stand. "All

jokes aside, the Devlins are very happy to see you with such a fine young man, Chrissie."

I smiled at Tim.

"Even if he is English," said Donal.

I rolled my eyes as everyone else laughed.

"Ah now, I'm only coddin' ye," said Uncle Donal, wiping the tears out of his eyes. He always cried when he laughed – as Conor always said about the Devlins, 'Our bladders are very close to our eyes.'

When he'd finished lapping up the appreciation, Uncle Donal finally carried on. "Despite our proud, Irish roots . . ."

My cousin Mick groaned from the left side of the group below. "Oh Jay-sus, here we go . . ."

"All right, that's it," said Tim in a mock-offended tone. "I'm off!" He leaned in to whisper to me. "I need to sort something out, Chrissie – be back in a second."

"No, don't leave me here –" I reached out to try to stop him.

"Back in a jiffy," he said back to me.

"He's off already! That didn't take long," said Uncle Donal. "No staying power, these English fellas."

Everybody laughed and Tim just lifted his hand and waved without turning around.

I felt even more exposed standing up there on my own with just Uncle Donal and the band.

"Anyway, *despite* our proud, Irish roots," my uncle repeated, "we Devlins have a tendency of merging with the English. And it seems our Chrissie is no exception. Neither your mother, nor meself, nor any of your cousins could resist their charm – we all ended up marrying a *Sásanach*. You'll do fine though, Chrissie – once you don't forget where you came from. As they say, you can take the girl out of Kerry, but you can't take the Kerry out of the –"

"She was actually brought up here!"

All heads turned to the back of the group on the grass where Susan was now standing next to Nicholas. She looked furious. Her white face had started to take on some colour and she was standing up poker straight. She handed her glass of water to Nicholas then walked forward, edging through the group of Tim's work colleagues and the row of children sitting cross-legged at the front of the group. She stood up on the lowest of the steps up to the deck, watched by everyone.

"Christine was brought up in England," she said, her steely eyes fixed firmly on Uncle Donal, her very refined, very English accent all the more apparent in the circumstances. "And she's a Devlin-*Cole*, not just a Devlin."

Donal took a step in closer to me. "Who the hell is she?"

I looked around at him, but I couldn't speak. I just wished I'd found the chance to introduce Susan and Nicholas to the Devlins earlier. In truth, there probably had been a few opportunities while lunch was being served, but I was so nervous about it I'd chickened out. I certainly hadn't meant it to happen like this – not in front of everyone. I'd hoped they might all get along – or at least pretend to for my sake.

"My husband and I are here to represent the Cole family today," said Susan. "And to wish our beloved granddaughter a happy birthday."

"Your beloved –" Uncle Donal, who had been

squinting at Susan to try to make out who she was, pulled his head back suddenly as he made the connection. He turned back to me. "What the bloody hell is she doing here? My sister couldn't stand that woman – she made her life a misery when Bobby was sick."

I didn't know what to say. I looked behind me for Tim. He'd know what to do. Where the hell had he gone?

"That is rubbish!" Susan stormed up the few steps to join us on the deck. She stood beside me. "I just wanted to provide the best care for my only child – but *she* wouldn't let me do that. Twenty-two years ago I allowed you Devlins to bad-mouth me and to steal away my only son, and in the process my granddaughter too. I'm not letting you do it again. Chrissie is as much a Cole, and as much an Englishwoman, as her father was an Englishman."

Uncle Donal's eyes were out on sticks. To claim me was one thing, to bring into question his niece's nationality was quite another. It may have been almost a century since Irish independence from the crown and my uncle may have married an Englishwoman himself but, right at that moment, none of that mattered. I knew by the look on his face that he was outraged – I could almost hear him spitting out the well-worn, out-dated 'six-hundred-years-of-oppression-by-the-English' argument he always used when he was trying to get the better of my long-suffering aunt. I looked down to Conor for support, but he was being held back by Rebecca himself. He looked like he was about to swoop in and carry me off on his shoulder – but for his wife's firm hand on his chest, he probably would have.

I was trying desperately to think of something to say

that might diffuse the situation when a voice sang out from the kitchen doors: "*Happy birthday to you! Happy . . .*"

We turned around and our small group at the top of the steps parted to let Tim and the huge white-and-pink cake covered with burning gold candles through. He was beaming from ear to ear, obviously completely oblivious to what had just happened.

I was never so glad to see him.

Bit by bit everybody else joined in with the singing, relieved that the tension had been dissolved.

Susan took a step back, then walked back down the steps and over to Nicholas. He looked as if he was annoyed with her but he said nothing.

I looked back at Tim as he held the cake up for me to blow out the candles.

I obliged him by blowing all but one candle out in one go. Everyone clapped, then Tim blew out the last candle and handed the cake to Donal. He turned back to me and took my hand, then looked out at the group below.

"I wanted to wish my favourite girl a very happy birthday today. And to welcome her to her thirties in style. She wasn't looking forward to turning thirty." He looked back at me and smiled. "But I hope I've shown you today, Chrissie, that it's not too bad really. In fact the thirties can be pretty awesome." He looked coy. "They've been pretty good to me and I feel like the luckiest man in the world to have you in my life." He smiled at me again. "I love you so much, Chrissie."

"*Awww!*" almost every person there said in unison.

I smiled at them and was about to give Tim a kiss when he seemed to disappear, dropping down on one knee. He took a small box out of his shirt top pocket, then opened it and presented it to me. Inside was a huge diamond solitaire ring. I stared at it. My heart was pounding inside my chest. I could barely breathe.

"Chrissie, will you marry me? Will you become my Mrs Rogers?"

I looked from the ring to Tim and just stared at him in pure shock.

In the space of a few short minutes, I'd been claimed by three families – the Devlins, the Coles and now the Rogers. I was losing track of who I was in the middle of it all. I looked around, wanting desperately to run away, far away – as fast as my legs would carry me. But Tim – lovely, kind, loyal Tim – was kneeling before me and holding up the ultimate symbol of love, offering me his heart in a small black box. And he was doing it in front of everyone we knew.

"Come on, cuz! Give the poor guy an answer," said Conor from below.

I turned around to look at him, then back to Tim who was starting to look uncomfortable. I looked around at the crowd, at Tim's lovely parents, Tony and Jane, who were standing shoulder to shoulder and beginning to look a little uneasy. I saw his sister Caroline who was hugging her youngest daughter. It felt like someone had pressed the pause button of life. Everyone was frozen to the spot, waiting to hear what the next word out of my mouth would be.

How had I let it get this far? Abigail was looking at me with a furrowed brow – she'd been right of course – I should have had the talk with Tim, should have made sure we were on the same page before I'd agreed to move in.

Why hadn't I talked to him?

I couldn't hurt him – or our friends and families. I just couldn't do it.

"I'm just so surprised." I laughed nervously then looked back at Tim and kept a wide smile fixed to my face. "I–I . . ."

But before I could get the next word out, a massive roll of thunder crashed out across the sky. There were screams from a few of the children, then another loud clatter of thunder and people began to dash up the steps past us towards the kitchen. Tim had jumped up and taken the ring out of the box. He slipped it onto my finger. Conor patted Tim's shoulder as he passed by holding Patrick but Tim never took his eyes off me. The ring stuck a bit on my knuckle, but Tim pushed it down and it slipped into place. We smiled at each other and he pulled me in towards him and gave me a long, passionate kiss.

Then he pulled back from me and held me at arms' length. "I'll make you happy, Chrissie. I promise." He kissed me gently on the lips again and just as the first raindrop fell, said: "Love you."

I smiled. "Love you too."

And I meant it. I did love him – Tim was one of the best.

"You *are* happy, Chrissie, aren't you?" Tim held my chin gently between his right thumb and first finger as he tried to read my face. "Sometimes I wonder . . ." His eyes searched mine for the truth, but it was buried down so deep inside me.

I should really have said something then. I wanted to but instead I took his hand in mine and smiled. "How could I not be?"

Tim looked instantly relieved. He smiled and squeezed

my hand then turned it around and, glancing at the ring, gently kissed my fingers just above my nails – as though I was a fair maiden he had just won in a duel.

That's when the rain really started to fall. Huge drops started to plop down on our heads and our shoulders.

"Coming through!"

We stood back as the one of the band grabbed the abandoned microphone stand, his instrument already packed away into its case.

Tim looked around. "We'd better get inside."

I hunched my shoulders to stop the rain going down my neck, but I was already very wet. People were scurrying around grabbing what they could – parents dragged protesting children away from the bouncy castle, the waiting staff gathered up empty plates and glasses. Tim ran to help them while I darted for the kitchen, picking up an abandoned jacket from the back of one of the chairs on the way.

Inside, the kitchen was already stuffed with people and I held the jacket draped over my arm as, one by one, our family and friends kissed and congratulated me.

"Fabulous news, darling!"

"Congratulations!"

"Mrs-Rogers-to-be, eh? Lucky ol' you. Tim's a great catch!"

"You guys should get married at Christmas. Best time of the year to get married."

And Rebecca: "Oh my God. That ring is incredible! The rock is *huge*!"

I tried hard to keep smiling as she examined the ring, but the air had grown very thick and I was beginning to find it hard to breathe. I could see Susan and Nicholas standing awkwardly on the other side of the room. I knew I should have gone over to them to try to smooth things over but it was all too much – I just wanted to yank my hand back from Rebecca and escape altogether.

Somebody squealed then at what sounded like a loud explosion. I whipped around just as lightning flashed out across the sky. Several people moved towards the open patio doors to gaze out at the lightning show while others backed away.

I edged backwards from the patio doors myself.

"Are you okay, Chrissie?"

I jumped.

Abigail was standing near the door from the kitchen to the hall, holding Mattie in her arms. The child looked terrified by the storm.

"Sorry, I didn't mean to give you a fright," Abigail said, all the while bouncing Mattie up and down and making reassuring noises.

"No, it's fine, you didn't," I lied. "I'm just going to put this jacket with the others."

Mattie let out a scream then as another flash of lightning lit up the sky. Abigail tried to comfort him, allowing me to escape out into the hall. I threw the jacket on the bannisters and ran up the two flights of stairs. I turned right at the top of the stairs on the third floor and went down the two steps into my small box room. I closed the door and stepped over my half-unpacked boxes to sit down on the stool at the desk by the window. The rain was pelting down outside. Through the steady stream of water running down the window pane I could just make out a couple of people dressed in shorts and T-shirts dashing across the heath, the woman holding a newspaper over her head. There was another roll of thunder then and a dramatic flash of lightning lit up the sky just as the couple reached the crowded bus shelter across the road from Tim's house. I could hear the communal screamed reaction to the lightning from the guests downstairs. I glanced up at the tall evergreens in front of the window and hoped my wood pigeons were okay up there. And though I couldn't see them, I was sure they were, knowing how much better animals are at anticipating the weather.

I turned back to the room and could avoid it no longer. I looked down at my left hand, then slowly splayed my fingers out in front of me. It was a beautiful ring, there was no doubt about that. The large square-set diamond was one of the brightest and sparkliest I'd ever seen. It must have cost Tim a fortune. I closed my eyes and tried to imagine what life might be like married to him.

It could be great. Of course it could. I'd have a beautiful home and an ever-attentive, loving, health-conscious, fit, successful husband. Okay, so I'd have to compromise on the travel – I probably wouldn't get to see too much more of the world, but I'd already seen so much.

Except Namibia, I thought. I'd love to go there. And Zambia – my mother wrote so descriptively about it in her travel memoir. God, how I loved that book! I sniffed, remembering her promise to go there with me 'some day'. But I never did get there with her. I sighed.

Oh, and I'd love to see the gorillas in Uganda, I thought. Mum said that was an incredible experience too. And of course I'd at least have to *try* to get to Antarctica while the ice is still there, before global warming does any more damage. And sure if I'm going to Antarctica, I should probably take the opportunity to tour South America – no point in going all that way and not visiting Peru, Argentina and the Galapagos Islands, I certainly couldn't miss the opportunity to see the blue-footed booby there – although I could give those giant reptiles a miss.

I sighed again. Maybe Tim and I could work something out on the travel.

And the children.

I knew Tim wanted them. And soon. I just wasn't ready and wasn't honestly sure if I ever would be.

And then there was the job.

Tim clearly wanted me to work towards the permanent job at Park View. Which of course made sense. But how was I to fit in everything else I wanted to do if I was to be tethered to the same job, in the same place for the rest of my life?

But if I didn't want all that – then what did I want?

I felt a shiver run down my back. My dress was damp from the rain. I looked around at the boxes on the floor, then stood up and rooted through a couple to try to find something to change into. There was nothing but underwear and pyjamas in the first one so I moved on to the second box, and as I opened the flaps a piece of newspaper fell from the top.

I picked it up – it was the article about Christine Thorpe that I'd torn out of the newspaper that day. I sat back on my heels and read through it, once again wishing that I had known the woman. From the small bit I'd read about her, it seemed to me that Mrs Thorpe had been the heroine of her own life. Here was a woman who wasn't afraid to live her life the way *she* wanted to live it. It wasn't clear from the article whether she'd had children –

but I guessed that she possibly hadn't as they hadn't been mentioned. So had Christine Thorpe managed to do what my mother hadn't? Had she found a way to be herself, to realise her dreams – without hurting or disappointing anyone along the way? Was there some way I could do that too?

"Damn it, I wish I could have met her," I said out loud.

I wanted to know more. I wanted to ask her if she had ever felt like I did right then – like the best supporting actress in the movie of your own life – feeling like you're living someone else's dreams, confused about what you want and where to go, frustrated as your hopes and dreams seem to be slipping away. I wanted to know about her life, her travels and her work in the music world. But most of all, I wanted to ask her about love and family.

And just then I was suddenly overcome with an overwhelming sense of loss for a woman I had never known. A couple of tears fell from my eyes, hit my cheeks and splashed down onto the article. I shook it dry, then put it back on top of the open box and wiped my eyes. But it was too late. I sank to my knees and began to really cry then – huge hiccupping tears of frustration, confusion and loss.

I have no idea how long I knelt there and cried.

It was Abigail's voice that stopped me in the end.

"Chrissie!" she called.

I sat up on my heels and wiped my tears away with the heel of my hand. Then I stood up and sat down on the bed.

I reached over to the box to pick up the article and read the last line again.

'. . . a wide range of international musicians will

perform at a special memorial service on Sunday 14th July at The Three Songbirds Inn just outside Harkston in Kent.'

I stared at the words for a few more seconds, but I already knew what I was going to do.

"Chrissie! Are you up here somewhere?" I heard Abigail's voice call again. I glanced at the door – she must have been looking for me in our bedroom on the next level down.

I snapped into action then, dropping the article on the bed and quickly going over to the desk. I picked up a pen and a piece of paper from the square paper-cube, scribbled a note, folded it over and wrote *'Tim'* on the fold. Then I turned and rifled through another box, finally finding a black cardigan. I grabbed it and pulled a couple of pairs of knickers out of the first box just as the bedroom door opened. I shoved the knickers and note into my deep dress pocket with the nightingale. The pocket bulged so I held the cardigan down by my side to cover it.

"Here you are!" Abigail came into the room. "I've been looking everywhere for you. Tim wants you to come cut the cake." She stopped suddenly when she saw my face. "Hey, are you okay, Chrissie? Have you been crying?"

But I couldn't stop to talk – not even to Abigail. *Especially* not to Abigail. I was afraid she might make me change my mind.

"Are you upset about what happened between your uncle and grandmother?" she was saying. "You shouldn't let all that upset you, Chrissie. It'll work itself out."

"Hmm? No, no, it's not that. I know that'll be okay. I'm fine, thanks, hon – probably just a bit of hay fever." I wiped my eyes. "I was just grabbing a cardigan, it's got a little chilly. I'm heading back down now." I slipped by her out the door, and flew down the stairs before she had a chance to stop me.

Mercifully, there was nobody in the hallway – the sound of people laughing and chatting rang out from the kitchen. I put the note on the hall table, put on the cardigan and grabbed my umbrella and shoulder bag from the coat-stand. I took the knickers out of my pocket and put them in the bag then stopped and touched the note for a moment before picking up the diamante C-shaped key-ring out of the bowl of keys on the hall table, and heading for the door.

I couldn't look back, not for a moment. I opened the front door, and a massive gust of wind blew in causing the kitchen door to slam. I didn't wait to see if it would alert anyone – instead I stepped outside and quickly pulled the front door closed behind me. I ran down the steps, struggling to hold the umbrella up over my head whilst I zig-zagged through all of the parked cars on the gravel driveway. The monster car was parked where Tim had promised earlier – by the gate facing out to the road. I pressed the button on the key and its lights flashed. Then I ran around to the driver door and climbed inside. I glanced back up at the house worried that Abigail or somebody else might have noticed me leaving, but was relieved to see that nobody appeared to be following me.

I knew I needed to hurry though. I turned the key in the engine, and just as I did a sudden, loud, rumble of thunder made me jump and hit my head off the top of the roof. I rubbed it, but I had no time to spare to steady myself. I found the switch for the windscreen wipers and turned them on before sending a shower of gravel flying into the air as I pressed my foot down hard on the accelerator. I took a deep breath to steady my nerves, lifted the handbrake and moved the car to the edge of the driveway just as a dramatic crack of lightning flashed across the sky. It cast a dazzling white light across the prematurely dark summer-afternoon sky. I closed my eyes for a moment, then pulled out of the driveway.

And finally, I was on my way.

Part two

The Red-capped Lark

Chapter 11

Leaving your own birthday party without explanation is certainly not the nicest thing to do. Screeching out of the driveway through a thunderstorm, less than half an hour after your boyfriend proposes to you, is a whole other level of low. In time I would come to feel really awful about it, but as I drove down the A2 all I could feel was an unequivocal sense of relief.

My scribbled note to Tim had just said: *'I have to go away for a night or so. I'm so sorry for leaving – just have to get away. Thanks so much for today – it was very special. xC'*

I hadn't taken my mobile phone with me. Nobody knew where I was going. I was free.

The storm had died down, and with it the sense of panic inside me. There was just a light sprinkling of rain as I drove down the motorway. It was strange driving such a big car at first, but after a short while the slow, repetitive movement of the windscreen wipers had an almost hypnotic, calming effect on me. I relaxed even more as I drove past the *'Welcome to Kent'* sign twenty minutes down the dual carriageway. The rain had stopped and, though it was still quite a dark afternoon, the storm seemed to have passed. I turned on the radio and found some mellow soul music to listen to, and it wasn't long before I was exiting the A2 in the direction of Chatham and Maidstone.

I took the first left off the roundabout at the exit, which was when I realised I had no map and no directions. From memory, I knew that The Three Songbirds was about a twenty-minute drive from Chatham, on the outskirts of the small, country village of Harkston, but I hadn't thought much further than that. It had been twenty-two years since I'd visited Harkston and even then I'd cycled there from Chatham train station – the route by car might be different. So I pulled into a petrol station to ask for directions and took the opportunity to use the bathroom. I bought a coffee and bottle of water too, and some nuts in case I got hungry later. I threw the large packet of nuts and bottle of water into my bag and drank the coffee as I looked over my new map and worked out the route.

I enjoyed the gradual shift from town to country as I drove from the garage along tree-lined secondary roads, then on through the busy town of Chatham and along by the historic Rochester village. I drove across the bridge over the Medway River, taking in the pretty riverboats moored below. Soon the roads grew narrower, the spaces beside them more remote and the houses more spread out as I drove deeper into the Kent countryside.

I was quite relieved to finally pass by the '*Welcome to Harkston Village*' sign. It was poised proudly in the centre of a roundabout of blue and white lupins, peach-coloured hollyhocks and orange dahlias. As I drove slowly through the village, I was relieved to find that it hadn't changed at all in twenty-two years – the row of pretty, brick cottages still lined the main road through the village, each one sporting decorative window boxes or hanging baskets of multi-coloured trailing petunias. It seemed very quiet – no doubt the storm had deterred the village's usual passing tourist and day-tripper trade. I passed by the small country churchyard and cemetery full of old granite gravestones and tall oak trees. At the end of the village the clock tower stood in the centre of the road, splitting it in two – it struck five just as I approached. Thankfully, road signs for Collinswood pointed me in the right direction and I drove slowly along the winding country road to my final destination.

I turned left at the sign for The Three Songbirds Centre. As I drove up the long, tree-lined avenue I wondered why they had changed the name of the place from '*inn*' to '*centre*'. The answer soon became apparent: at the top of the avenue a tall wooden sign stood at a fork in the road. Various arrows directed visitors to either *Collinswood and Cycle Tracks, Bike Shop, Bird Centre, The Venue* and the one I obediently followed: *Hotel and Car Park*.

I looked at the clock on my dashboard as I drove into the car park. It was about an hour and twenty minutes since I'd stolen out of my party. I felt a pang of guilt, but quickly put it to the back of my mind, glancing up at the old inn as I drove past. The place was so much bigger than when I'd last visited as a child. There appeared to be a couple of extra wings built on to either side of the building. The old Tudor frontage was now complemented

143

by the new extensions which had been built in the same style. The brickwork throughout was painted the bright white I remembered, with the black wooden exposed beams matching the black wooden window frames.

I drove right to the edge of the very full car park to a section where there were less cars. With some difficulty, I managed to manoeuvre my monster car into a spot that thankfully had an empty space on one side.

I turned off the engine and sat there, not quite knowing what to do next. I hadn't really thought any further than getting away from the party, about getting this far. I stared out at the white wooden fence and green meadow in front of me and watched a couple of bay-coloured horses graze on some luscious green grass beside a small stone cottage. I glanced in the rear-view mirror then and could see 'The Three Songbirds' sign swinging from two chains on a vertical post over the door. Though the whole entrance area was new, the sign looked like it might have been the same one that had hung over the inn door when I'd visited with my parents all those years ago. The familiarity was somewhat comforting.

I took the key out of the engine, got out of the car and took off my cardigan. Then I grabbed my shoulder bag from the passenger seat, folded the cardigan into it and locked the car.

A group of people emerged from the entrance just as I got to it. They seemed to be a family group – several elderly men and women, a few middle-aged people and a couple of teenagers and younger children. They were chatting amongst themselves and appeared to be quite familiar with the place.

I stood aside and smiled back at them as they passed,

then I went through the open glass double doors.

Inside, the lobby had a glass roof and the walls were painted olive green. The reception desk itself seemed to be made out of polished, exposed oak – it was really beautiful and looked to have come from a very old tree. You could see the narrow rings of the wood quite clearly in the front panel. Perched on top of the desk to the left was a large flower display of sunflowers and greenery and, between me and the desk, right in the middle of the lobby under the circular glass roof was a very wide tree stump. It was at least a metre and a half wide and about the same in height. Surrounding the stump were gravel stones, dotted here and there with small granite sculptures of woodland creatures – a squirrel, a rabbit and an oversized snail. The overall effect was earthy and modern.

"Can I help you, dearie?" the receptionist asked, capturing my attention.

She was an older woman – in her sixties or perhaps even seventies, quite small in stature but very buxom, with short, straight, dark-grey hair. From where I stood I could only see what she was wearing on her top half: a light mustard-coloured knitted jumper, with ornate pink, blue and green flower detail just below the high neckline.

"Oh yes, sorry." I walked over to the desk. "Can you tell me, is this where the Thorpe memorial service is being held tomorrow?"

The woman smiled sadly and tilted her head to one side. "Ah, did you know her then, dearie? Such a sad time for us all, but we mustn't feel too bad, she wouldn't have wanted that. Mrs Thorpe always said she wanted her memorial service to be a happy occasion, not a sad one. 'I'd like it to focus more on celebrating life than mourning

145

death,' she said to me once. It's such a nice way to look at it, isn't it?"

"Yes, yes, indeed." I instantly warmed to the friendly woman.

"So how did you know Mrs Thorpe?" she asked me.

It was a reasonable question really – just not one I'd prepared for. Confessing that I only knew Mrs Thorpe from a newspaper article probably wasn't the best idea though, so I fibbed.

"From the cycling?" I said the words as a question, not quite sure whether they would work.

The woman smiled and nodded her head. "Ah yes. She was great for the cycling, was our Mrs Thorpe – she founded the local cycling club here with her husband, you know? Every evening the two of them would cycle from their cottage beside the inn up through Collinswood behind us here before sunset. 'It's the best time of the day for birdsong, Mrs Gates,' she would say. My, but she loved those birds, and those trees."

The more I heard about Mrs Thorpe, the more I liked her. 'Was that why I read that she got into trouble with the police all those years back? Because of the birds and the woods?"

"Ho ho, yes, indeed!" Mrs Gates folded her arms under her bosom. "About twenty years ago, they wanted to knock down the inn and a huge section of the woods to make way for an apartment and hotel complex. The inn had just been sold and the place had been closed up for a short while. Mrs Thorpe read about the planned development in the newspaper apparently and was outraged at the harm that it would do to the trees and the bird life."

146

I put my shoulder bag down on the ground, leaned in on the desk and nodded to encourage her. I was enjoying learning more about the old lady's life and was already so glad I'd decided to come.

"So Mrs Thorpe came right here. Unfortunately she arrived half an hour after the diggers and demolition crew had started." Mrs Gates pointed behind me. "That poor oak tree behind you was their first victim." I turned to look at the tree stump. "It used to stand just in front of the old entrance to the inn – long before this lovely new reception area was built." Mrs Gates stroked the top of the reception desk lovingly then. "Of course, nothing ever went to waste when our Mrs Thorpe was around – she had Jimmy, the carpenter from Harkston, turn that lovely oak tree into this beautiful desk. Didn't he do a wonderful job?"

"He certainly did." I stroked the smooth top of the desk myself – it was as sleek as velvet. "But tell me what happened next? Did I read that Mrs Thorpe got arrested over it all?"

The woman chuckled and nodded. "Oh yes, indeedy. She was horrified to watch the oak tree fall, so what did she do? Only climbed up into one of the trees herself, all sixty-eight years of her! You'll see the eucalyptus tree she sat in behind the inn there – there were two trees and the new extension was built around them later, to protect them for all time." She pointed behind her, without turning around. "There was a big stand-off between the demolition crew, Mrs Thorpe, and of course dear Harvey, her husband, who followed her up into the other of the two trees. They were devoted to each other, those two. And he was sixty-five at the time himself – they were no spring chickens." Mrs Gates chuckled to herself.

I smiled. "So how long did they stay up the trees?"

"Oh, hours! We were able to get food and drink up to them, but they needed the facilities, and they got very tired of course. So the funniest thing happened next. My husband, Lawrence, the head barman here –"

"Lawrence?" I said. "I think I remember him. I came here once with my parents. Would he have worked here twenty-two years ago?"

"Oh yes, indeed, he would have. Aside from the short time it closed down, Lawrence has worked at The Three Songbirds for forty years now." Mrs Gates seemed to really be on a roll with her story. "Lawrence and I love this old inn – it's been the heart of our community for many, many decades. We were so upset when it had to close, and truly heartbroken to hear that they were going to tear the place down. So what does my foolish old goat of a husband do? Well, he ups and climbs Mrs Thorpe's tree himself, letting her come down for some rest and to use the facilities. That really was the beginning of the chaos – the very *nice* chaos, that is." Mrs Gates smiled. "One by one, more of the local lads and lassies got up into the trees – and not just the eucalyptus trees in the back, but lots of the trees around the inn and right on up into Collinswood itself. They guarded the trees in relay, in three-hour shifts before they would switch places. The demolition fellows couldn't knock down a single tree – it would have been too dangerous. Of course the environmentalists got involved. We had Greenpeace – Save Our Woods – you name it, they were here. So, yes, it was chaos in these parts those weeks with people living in the trees all around the place. We locals provided the sandwiches, and the flasks of coffee and buns. We had to hire Portaloos, there were so many people, and we even made the BBC news!"

I smiled. "That's amazing. So what happened?"

"Well, they arrested Mr and Mrs Thorpe as soon as they came down from the first tree. Poor old Ben, our local sergeant, had to do the job – the press loved that, of course! They made a big story about a sixty-eight-year-old woman and a sixty-five-year-old man being detained for the cause – it was marvellous publicity. Christine and Harvey became known around these parts as 'The Collinswood Two'." She giggled at that. "Well, after a couple of days, so much outrage and pressure built up about it all that the police decided to release the Thorpes without charge. The protest went on for months more though. It was marvellous for the village – revitalised the place, no end!" She threw both her hands in the air and chuckled. "We had to open up the inn again, stock up the bar and dust down some of the rooms to cater for all the visitors. It was a big job, but oodles of fun – all of the locals got involved – those of us too awkward or decrepit to climb trees." She laughed. "Sir David Attenborough even made an appearance to lend his support one of the days." She shook her head. "Och, it was a crazy time. But she won. Thanks to our Mrs Thorpe, they never did knock another tree here." She rubbed the polished top of the desk again. "And in time, she succeeded in getting Collinswood named as a protected woodland area. It would never have happened if it wasn't for her. I dread to think what this place would be like now. Probably high-rise apartments, supermarkets . . . it doesn't bear thinking about." Mrs Gates leaned her large bosom on the desk and put her head in her hand. "My, but we will miss her. Life will be a lot quieter without our Mrs Thorpe about the place."

"It certainly will from the sound of things," I said. "I haven't been here for years, myself. When was it all done up?"

Mrs Gates stood up straight again. "Well, after everything that happened, the Thorpes bought the place themselves. The previous owners were relieved, I think, when the deal with the developers fell through – they loved seeing the place back up and running and didn't want to see it levelled any more than we did, but they had been planning to move to Spain on the proceeds of the sale. So Mrs Thorpe thought it only fair to match the developer's offer, buying it herself. She and Mr Thorpe did the place up beautifully then, turning it into a cycling and nature centre and small concert venue. They even bought the little cottage on the grounds and moved into it themselves. It's very busy here. Lots of people come for the wooded cycle tracks, and we have concerts most weekends – a lot of local acts and new singers and groups, but we've had one or two big acts too – Boy George played last Christmas – he's such a lovely young man. And we even had a visit from Tom Jones for a long weekend a few years ago. He and Mrs Thorpe were friends."

"Wow, really?" I was just about to ask her how Mrs Thorpe knew the singing star when the front doors slid back and a noisy family group came in. I recognised them as the group I'd passed on the way in.

"Ah, that's Mr Thorpe and his family now," said Mrs Gates nodding at the white-haired man in the middle of the group. He'd picked up one of the young children who was now pulling at his white bushy beard. He gave the child a big smile and tickle as he led the group through a door to the right of the tree stump.

"He looks nice," I said.

"Oh, he's wonderful," said Mrs Gates. "What that man hasn't done for wild animals – here and all over the world." She leaned in over the desk to whisper to me and I had to lean in closer myself to hear her. "The Thorpes are a very old, wealthy family from these parts. Harvey's father, grandfather and no doubt many Thorpes before them hunted wildlife game in Africa. He told me that they hung the heads of beautiful lions and the tusks of rhinos and elephants on the walls of the big house on the family estate – he hated looking at them every day when he was a child. He said it made him so sad to think of the suffering the animals had been through. So much so that when Harvey's father died, many years ago now, he left the big estate to Harvey, his only child. Mr Thorpe promptly sold the place and dedicated his life and the family money to stopping wildlife hunting and poaching in Africa. Thankfully his own family support the work completely – they're a tight-knit group." She leaned in even closer. "All except the first wife, that was. She wasn't very happy about it apparently – we reckon that's why that relationship ended. But I wouldn't want to gossip."

She gave herself a shake and stood up straight.

"My, oh my, I'm forgetting myself. It's just so hard to believe she's gone." She looked at me and smiled. "Now, dearie, I assume you want to check in?"

I nodded. "Yes, please. I just need a room for one person, for one night. So I can pay my respects at the memorial service."

"Of course." Mrs Gates smiled. "I think we have one room left as it happens." She tapped away at the computer for a minute. "Bingo! It's just above the Green Room, but we don't have anything on tonight so it won't be noisy. Though the musicians may be practising at some stage for tomorrow morning's memorial."

I took the key card she handed me, relieved to have a room at all. "That sounds perfect. Thank you so much, Mrs Gates."

"Not at all. I think the wake will be starting in the bar a little later on too." She pointed to the door to the right of the tree stump where Harvey's family had gone. I could hear muffled voices and music coming from inside. "Some of the Cycle Club is there already," Mrs Gates said, "so you'll be in good company."

I nodded and smiled, but inside I was beginning to panic a little. I would know nobody at the wake. What if they got together and realised I was an intruder at their intimate, personal occasion?

"You'll be wanting to check into your room first though," Mrs Gates said, interrupting my thoughts. "It's on the first floor, just behind me here." She turned and pointed to a set of double doors behind to her left. "Follow the corridor all the way to the end and your room is one of three upstairs. The signs will direct you, and Lawrence can carry your things up to the room shortly if you need?" She leaned up on her tiptoes to look over the desk at the floor around me. "Have you left your luggage in the car, dearie?"

"Eh no, don't worry. I can manage. Thank you so much." I picked up my shoulder bag and walked quickly past the reception desk to the door to avoid having to give

152

an explanation about my lack of luggage. I needn't have worried though – Mrs Gates was immediately distracted by a couple emerging from the bar who she greeted like old friends.

I walked through the double swing doors, threw my shoulder bag over my shoulder and found myself in a long door-less corridor. Stepping inside was like stepping into a fairy tale – the corridor was a fusion of nature and clever lighting. I stopped just inside the door to take it all in. The corridor was lit by small spotlights along the side of the walls. It curved around to the left and the carpet underfoot was an earthy brown colour, spongy and soft. The wall on my left was all glass, the one on my right papered with a green foliage pattern. Along the papered wall hung wooden-framed images, about a metre apart. I looked at the first one inside the door: a sketch of a bird. I had to bend over slightly and squint to read the small print underneath: *The Red-capped Lark*. I stood back to take it in properly – an interesting-looking bird and not one I'd ever seen before.

I turned around to look through the glass then. I could see the white-washed sides of the inn building and what looked to be another long glass window on the other side of the atrium, but I couldn't quite make it out fully through the tall trees in the centre. I recognised the outdoor space as the beer garden of the old inn – the place where I had drunk lemonade with my mother and eaten fish and chips with my parents all those years ago. The tables had gone but there was a wooden bench just beneath the trees. Then I noticed a green-glass panel fixed to the glass wall a few feet away from me. I walked the few paces down the corridor towards it and as I got closer

153

I noticed that there was some black calligraphic writing etched onto the panel. I leaned in to read the heading which told me it was a verse from the poem 'Woodman, Spare that Tree' by George Pope Morris.

My heart strings round thee cling
Close as thy bark, old friend!
Here shall the wild bird sing,
And still thy branches bend.
Old tree! The storm still brave!
And, woodman, leave the spot;
While I've a hand to save,
Thy axe shall harm it not.

They must be the eucalyptus trees that Mrs Gates said Mr and Mrs Thorpe sat in, I thought. I looked back out at the trees and picked out a thick, wide overhanging branch about five metres up from the ground – I imagined Mrs Thorpe sitting resolute there for hours on end. I smiled to myself, then realised that I had unwittingly pressed my nose to the glass. I stood back and rubbed the smudges away with the sleeve of my dress, and as I did I heard the sound of a loud drum roll.

I looked around. The sound seemed to be coming from farther along the corridor. I wondered what it was but I couldn't take my eyes away from the trees for too long. I turned back to look at them again. They were like the prize exhibit in a gallery – majestic in their natural beauty, most definitely worth fighting for.

"Good ol' Mrs Thorpe," I said out loud.

The drumbeats started to build up then, becoming louder and richer in sound. I dragged myself away from the window and began walking along the corridor in the direction of the noise. I glanced at the other bird prints along the curved wall and, as I walked along, the drumbeats began to build in volume and pace – louder and quicker they pulsed through the corridor. I could make out several different beats – a tinny, almost metallic sound, and a deeper, lower thumping. There was no mistaking the African beat – I found my head nodding to the rhythm and a smile broke out across my face before I'd realised it. As I rounded the corridor and the glass wall ended, I came to a door on the left. The music was clearly coming from behind it.

All of a sudden the African drums stopped and a very familiar beat took over.

I stared at the door. "A bodhrán? No! Surely not?" I said out loud.

But there was no mistaking the familiar jig pattern. The player started gently, slowly at first, hitting the trebles effortlessly, melting them into louder rolls and eventually building up to a dramatic climax. It was a solo that only a very talented Irish bodhrán player could carry off. I could hear a couple of voices cry out their approval before the African beat joined in again and the Irish and African sounds fused effortlessly into the most unique, intriguing sound I'd ever heard. Not since I'd first heard the score to *Celtic Wings* had I felt such a thrilling beat – a sound so moving and powerful that I could feel it resonate deep within me. I wanted to burst through the door, grab a bodhrán and join in myself.

But then the drums stopped – suddenly, all together. A voice emerged from the silence – a beautiful, clear, woman's voice. She was singing in a foreign language – it sounded African but I wasn't sure what specific language. She sang a few lines of the song almost like a chant. Each line built in pace, until the originally slow, sweet tones had been transformed into a melodic tune. Then the drums came in again. Slowly at first – just the tinny sound – but as the song went on and the pace quickened, the woman's voice rang out louder, then the bodhrán and the deeper drums joined in too. Once again we were back to the uplifting melody, the sound becoming almost carnival-like.

I loved everything about it. I stood outside with my eyes closed and pretty soon my body had taken over from my head. My head, hips and arms swayed involuntarily to the beat – I couldn't have stopped them even if I'd wanted to. I only wished I knew the words to the song so I could sing along. I made an attempt anyway, copying the beat and substituting *la's* for the words.

"Are you okay, lady?"

I opened my eyes and swung around to see a young African boy of about five years of age grinning up at me. He was holding a small bodhrán and stick in one hand and was wearing a bright red Arsenal football jersey with jeans and white trainers. He put his hand out to try to reach past me to the door handle.

I stood aside. "Erm . . . sorry, yes, I'm fine."

The boy smiled, opened the door and went inside. He turned then and, still smiling, gestured to me to follow him. The music was pulsating inside, bouncing off the walls of the small room. I simply couldn't resist. So I pulled the strap of my bag up over my shoulder and followed the boy in.

Chapter 12

The boy crossed the small room to join the other
musicians who all had their backs to me. The sound they
were producing was wonderful. I walked inside and shut
the door quietly, then edged around the side. The room
was small and painted a very pale green colour. A thin
beige carpet lay on the floor and there was a single door
in the far corner of the room – I assumed that it led to
'The Venue'. There was just one small window, at the
back of the room – it faced out onto Collinswood and
outside I could just about make out the trees swaying in
the gentle early-evening breeze. Rows of stacked chairs
lined the four walls of the room and two large white sofas
were positioned facing each other just beside the window.
But other than the people and the musicians there was
very little else of note in the room – no pictures, no wall
hangings or other furniture – it was all very different to
the pretty, decorative corridor I had just left behind. I
walked a few steps to my left until I could just about see
some of the faces of the people playing. Five teenage boys
were standing up at the back of the group – a mixture of

heights, sizes and nationalities. I took another couple of steps and could see that two of the boys were playing round, African metallic drums. The other three were playing a mixture of tall wooden drums. Each of the boys was dressed similarly to the boy I'd followed in. He had gone to sit down at the front of the group in an empty chair beside an older red-haired girl dressed in shorts and a yellow vest T-shirt. She was the one who had been playing the bodhrán so proficiently. I could just see that her eyes were closed. The Celtic rhythm that she was belting out had somehow merged seamlessly with the African beat and the resulting music was deafeningly brilliant. I let my hips and head begin to sway again as I watched the boy I'd followed in place his own bodhrán on his lap, nod his head a few times to catch the beat, then join in himself.

Standing to the side of the group furthest away from me, holding her hand over her right ear was an older woman. She was singing the African tune, but very gently by that stage, I couldn't really make out any of the words over the sound of the drums. I was very surprised by her appearance though. I'd expected to see a large, soulful, black woman behind that big voice, but this woman was the complete opposite. Tall and lean, her hair was mostly grey with what looked like just a flash of auburn running through it. She wore it in a long fringeless layered-bob style just above her shoulders. Her eyes were closed and, as she sang, her whole body moved in tandem with the music – her free arm, her hips – everything. I loved her look – she appeared so comfortable and free. A brown crumpled scarf was wrapped loosely two or three times around her neck and she was wearing a long oversized cream T-shirt which exposed one bare shoulder and a dark string top or bra-strap underneath – I couldn't tell which, but the colour was very close to her scarf. The T-shirt was wide and angular, hanging right down over one knee, the other side just below her waistline. A large wooden cross-shaped pendant hung from a long black leather string around her neck and she had on tight red trousers that were splattered with a white pattern. She had no shoes on, but her toenails were painted a bright red and I spotted a discarded pair of tan-coloured open-toe sandals a few feet away by the wall.

As I took her in, I'd been moving gradually around the perimeter of the room until I was almost in line with the front of the group. As I walked, I continued to sway to the beat but as I did I tripped over an instrument case on the floor and stumbled sideways on top of a stack of chairs, causing them to topple over.

The music came to a sudden halt as the musicians swung around to see what had caused all the commotion.

"Oh my God. I'm so sorry. Please don't stop. That sounded wonderful." I tried to get up, but struggled to free myself from the chairs.

A couple of the older boys ran over to help me, but the woman came from behind, leaned over them and stretched her hand out to me.

I took it and let her help pull me up.

The woman put her hand on my back as I straightened up. "Are you all right?" She seemed genuinely concerned, but I was absolutely mortified. A few of the children were huddled around behind her, the rest standing back where they'd been playing. They were all staring at me. I felt like such an idiot.

"Thank you. I'm so sorry for interrupting your wonderful music. Please continue, I'll go." I picked up my bag and put it over my shoulder.

"It's okay – we were just finishing up anyway. Please –" The woman put her hand on my arm to stop me leaving.

I turned back and she looked at me for a moment longer than was entirely comfortable – almost as if she knew me from somewhere. Or perhaps she was just trying to decide what to say next to the lunatic woman who'd crashed her music session.

But instead of saying anything more to me she just gave me a warm smile before turning back to the children.

"Okay, everybody – that was wonderful. I think we're more than ready for tomorrow. Why don't we finish up now?" She leaned down to put an arm around the young boy I'd met at the door who was hovering beside her. "Your mother is going to be so proud of you, David." She kissed his forehead. The boy buried his head down as far as he could, but I could see from his smile that he was thrilled at the praise. I couldn't help but smile myself. "Keep practising, but don't let your mother hear you. This is to be a surprise for tomorrow, remember?" She looked back over at me then. "David and I have been planning this for a while. He's a natural – just like his mother was." She smiled at the young boy.

He looked chuffed. "Thank you, Red." He picked up the instrument case I'd just tripped over and put his bodhrán inside. Then he gave the woman a quick hug and skipped out the door.

The red-haired girl, who looked to be about thirteen or fourteen, tucked her own bodhrán case under her arm as she walked towards the door too.

"Keep an eye on David, will you, Fiona?" the woman shouted over to her. "Make sure his mother doesn't see the bodhrán before tomorrow."

"Sure thing," the girl said.

"Big day tomorrow, everyone." The woman clapped her hands. "Enjoy your supper, then make sure to get a good night's sleep."

The last of the children, who'd been piling the bigger drums into the far corner of the room, followed the others out – all of them laughing and singing as they went.

The woman and I stood and watched them go. As the last one closed the door she turned to me and smiled.

"They're lovely," I said. "And so talented."

"They are indeed." The woman gave herself a shake then and walked over to where they'd been playing. She started to stack the chairs they'd left behind and I walked over to help her.

"They're all children of friends and family," she said. "It's so wonderful to have them here together. We've been rehearsing all day for a wedding here tomorrow afternoon – young David's mother is getting married."

I was surprised. "There's a wedding here tomorrow?"

The woman nodded.

"That's funny. It's just that I'm here for a memorial service in the morning. It's going to be on in the function room next door –'The Venue' I think they call it?"

The woman stopped stacking the chairs for a moment and looked at me. "Function room? Gosh, I didn't even know they had one here." She started stacking the chairs again.

"Well, it's the concert venue really," I said. "I think it

doubles as a function room." But I wasn't sure if she'd heard me – she had her back to me at that stage.

I stepped in to help her move the small stack of three chairs and we lifted them over to the others that lined the wall.

She looked over at the small window after we'd put the chairs down. "It's cleared up quite a bit out there. I do hope the weather holds now – it was dreadful earlier on." She looked back to me. "We're having the wedding outdoors, you see – under the eucalyptus trees. It'll be lovely if the weather is good."

I wondered to myself how the staff at the inn were going to be able to cater for a wedding on the same day as a memorial service for the inn's owner. I didn't pursue the topic though – instead I wanted to ask her about the music.

She'd already gone back for the other chairs so I followed her over and we each picked up a side of the chair stack and started walking sideways towards the wall again.

"I was just on my way to my room when I heard your music," I said. "I couldn't believe it when I heard the bodhrán being played alongside the African drums. It sounded fantastic."

"Thanks – it's a piece I wrote many years ago. I love merging the different percussion sounds. Sometimes we add in some strings too. The piece we were just playing is, of course, one of my African-Celtic fusion songs."

We put the stack of chairs down.

"Yes, it sounded great," I said. "I loved the use of the bodhrán. I used to play a bit myself. A long time ago but I still use it a bit in my teaching now."

The woman looked surprised. "You do? Where are you from then? I assumed you were English. How did you end up playing the bodhrán?"

Where *was* I from? That was the question. I decided to avoid answering it. "I learnt to play in Dingle in the South of Ireland. They taught me the bodhrán there, but once they found out I could sing I barely got a chance to play it again. It's been a long time since I picked one up for anything other than teaching."

The woman put her hands on her hips and shook her head. "Gosh, I do love Dingle. I haven't been there in many years now. Do they still have that resident dolphin? What's his name again?"

"Fungie?" I laughed. "Oh yes, my grandma tells me Fungie's going strong. He's still a big attraction."

The woman smiled and pushed her hair out of her eyes. "So what kind of music do you sing? Traditional?"

I nodded. "I did sing a lot of traditional Irish music, but also soul, pop, folk. Anything really. I used to write some songs myself too, and I sang on tour with *Celtic Wings* for years."

The woman raised her eyebrows, seeming impressed. "Such a great show."

"You've seen it?"

"Of course. I've seen it several times in my sixty years."

"Are you sixty?" I didn't mean to sound rude, but I was surprised. Sure, her hair was mostly grey and she had some giveaway wrinkles around her eyes, hands and neck, but her brown eyes sparkled and she was in great shape. "I'm sorry. It's just that you don't look it. You look amazing."

The woman laughed. "Thank you. Regardless, it's true."

I found myself wishing I looked like her when I turned sixty.

"The kids all call me Red, by the way." The woman held out her hand. "You wouldn't know it now, but I once had long, flowing, red hair." She pushed a piece of her greying hair behind her ear.

I took her outstretched hand for the second time that day. "I'm Chrissie. It's lovely to meet you, Red."

"Chrissie . . ." She repeated my name slowly, then smiled at me. "Good name."

"Thanks," I smiled. "Do you mind me asking where you come from yourself, Red?" She had one of those difficult-to-place transatlantic accents.

Red laughed. "To be honest, Chrissie, I've given up trying to explain my background. I'm living in Devon at the moment, but over the years my music has taken me to countries over several continents. These days I just tell people that I'm a citizen of the world. I'm very susceptible to picking up accents – I've a tendency to pick up the inflection of the accent of the place I'm living in at the time. You should have heard me when I was in Dingle, begorrah!"

I laughed. "I know what you mean. I'm a bit the same myself. That must be great for your music though? To have lived in so many different places."

"That's it exactly." Red smiled and nodded. "I've been able to incorporate a lot of the different global sounds and influences into my compositions." She put her hands on her hips and tilted her head sideways. "But enough about me, Chrissie. Why don't you sing for me? I'd love to hear you." She knelt down on the floor and looked up at me, her hands on her knees.

"Oh gosh no. I couldn't." The thought horrified me. "You have such an incredible voice – I'd be too embarrassed to sing for you."

Red said nothing, just tilted her head, raised her eyebrows and looked at me sideways.

I sighed. "Honestly – I haven't been singing for years now. I'm going to sound awful."

"Come on, Chrissie." Red bounced on her knees as if she was trying to get me revved up. "Just sing me your favourite song. Something you know like the back of your hand. Maybe one of the *Celtic Wings* tunes? Come on, you've heard me sing. Fair's fair, girl."

I laughed. "All right, all right. But don't say I didn't warn you."

Red sat back and held her knees in front of her while I tried to think of what to sing. Then I took a deep breath in and sang the first line of 'Songbird.'

Red smiled and swayed her head slowly to the tune as I sang. "Beautiful," she whispered to herself.

I closed my eyes. Then I remembered my father's china figurine and tapped the pocket of my dress. I thought about my father, and as I sang his special song, the memories of the last time I'd been at The Three Songbirds came flooding back. That was back before any of us knew he was sick, back when I thought the only thing I needed to make me happy was to have my parents and me together always. I never imagined what it might be like not to have them in my life at all, for them both to be gone. I missed them so much.

I felt my throat constrict just as I sang the first line of

the chorus, remembering my father singing to my mother on her own thirtieth birthday. I tried so hard to hold it together, to stop my thoughts and to get lost in the words of the song instead, but that was worse. It was those words that finally broke me. As I tried to sing the last line of the chorus, I choked completely. The tears that had been hovering in my eyes escaped and I sank down to the floor in front of Red.

"I'm sorry – I-I can't."

"Oh sweetheart!" Red moved around to sit beside me. She put her arm around my shoulders and squeezed the top of my arm. Then she did the most amazing thing – she took up the song herself. And this time the familiar lyrics had a calming effect on me. I closed my eyes, wiped away my tears and listened to Red's sweet, melodic voice singing the song I knew and loved so well. By the time she'd got to the second chorus I was ready to join in again. I sang the tune and Red sang a harmony that I'd never heard before. It sounded absolutely gorgeous – so lovely, in fact, that we sang the last verse and chorus twice.

I turned to look at her on the last note and we smiled at each other as we sang it. Then, after we finished, we gave each other a hug.

"That was really lovely, Chrissie. You have such a beautiful voice."

I'd taken a tissue out of my pocket. I dabbed my eyes then blew my nose with it. "When I'm not blubbering, that is?"

Red smiled. "It's an emotional song – almost like an anthem to love. It's obviously very special to you. Does it remind you of someone in particular?"

We were both sitting cross-legged on the floor at that

stage. I tucked the tissue back into my pocket and nodded. "It reminds me of my parents. The last time I was here was with them. They're both dead now."

"I'm so sorry, sweetheart. Are you okay?"

Was I okay? It was a reasonable question. I examined the facts. It was my thirtieth birthday and I'd just got engaged. Was I enjoying the celebrations with friends and family? No, instead I'd darted halfway across the county to attend the memorial of a woman I'd never met, only to find myself sitting on the floor of an empty room singing with a complete stranger twice my age. Was I okay? I guess not so much. But I was afraid I'd burst into tears again so I didn't say anything in response, just shook my bowed head and drew circles on the carpet tile with my index finger.

"Why don't you tell me about it, Chrissie?" Red had leaned down slightly to try to catch my eye.

I glanced up at her. She seemed so kind, so genuinely concerned . . . and I needed to talk to someone . . . why not this woman? So I took a deep breath, and started to tell her my story. I surprised even myself by how much I told her – everything really – all about my birthday, Tim's proposal and my hesitation, and about how awful I'd begun to feel about leaving my own party without telling anyone. Red looked quite shocked at that so I tried to explain my actions by telling her how confused I'd been feeling lately and about how, after my mother's death a few years ago, I'd thought settling down would make me happy.

"Now I'm not so sure," I sighed. "I guess I'm just in a bit of a rut. The last time I felt like this I gave up singing and left *Celtic Wings* and my boyfriend of seven years." I sniffed. "Albeit my cheating toad of a boyfriend!"

Red raised her eyebrows.

I smiled. "Mmm, I know. It was just that when I found out about his cheating it made me question *all* of the choices I'd made up to that point of life. And it happened just after my mother died so I was a bit all over the place. That was when I decided that I needed to at least *try* to settle down. The thing is, now that I've done it, I'm beginning to wonder if it's the right thing for me." I sighed again. "These ruts can be very dangerous. I could end up messing up everything – all because of a rut – or a *thrisis* as my friend, Abigail, calls it."

"A *thrisis*?" Red raised her eyebrows.

"Oh yes, *thrisis* – it's a crisis that happens in your thirties, as opposed to a mid-life crisis." I smiled. "They're all the rage with people my age now apparently."

Red laughed. "*Sheesh!* Your generation have a term for everything!" She looked more thoughtful then. "Mind you, I wasn't much older than you when I left everything and everyone behind and went to Zambia to work as a volunteer. I guess that could have been my own *thrisis*."

"Wow, Zambia? You worked there?"

"Yes – in fact that song I was just singing was in Chitonga – it's one of the local dialects of Zambia."

I knelt up. "My mother wrote a travel memoir about Zambia. It was her best book by far – I've wanted to go to there ever since I read it. Then I met a couple from Zambia a couple of weeks ago and I've been thinking about it a lot since. I'd love to hear about your time there, Red – if you've time to tell me about it, that is?"

Red looked amused. "Well, Zambia is a wonderful country, that's for sure. And it's particularly special to me because that's where I met the love of my life."

My eyes widened. "Really? Oh, well, now you *have* to tell me all about it." I sat back down and crossed my legs. "Please, I want to hear everything. If I can't have my own overseas adventures at the moment, the least I can do is live vicariously through other people's!"

We both laughed. I could tell we shared a similar sense of humour. I liked Red and I was genuinely interested in her story. I think part of me even hoped it might help me to make some decisions in my own life – to put down roots or to branch out? That was the question. And at the very least, listening to someone else's story might distract me from my own problems for a while.

"Are you sure you want to listen to an old woman's ramblings, Chrissie? It could take a while."

I shuffled in a little closer to her. "Absolutely. And don't leave a single detail out." I closed my eyes and within seconds Red's story had transported me to Africa.

Chapter 13

Red was thirty-one and single with little or no responsibilities when she arrived in Zambia. It was Father Emmet Killeen who gave her the name she came to be known by. Apparently he took one look at his new teaching volunteer as she emerged from the arrivals hall of Lusaka airport and declared that he hadn't seen a mane of hair so fiery and striking since he'd seen his fellow Dubliner, the film star, Maureen O'Hara, up on the big screen. From then on he called her Red, and pretty soon it stuck.

For his part, the priest insisted she drop all formalities and call him Emmet. Red described him as a compassionate old bull of a man – well-built and hardened on the outside, but a warm-hearted old softie on the inside. He would "do anything for anyone", she told me, but he was especially kind to the vulnerable women and children of Zambia on whose behalf he worked tirelessly for over forty years. It was clear from the way Red spoke about Emmet and about her time working alongside him, that she held a very special place in her heart for the missionary priest and for the people of Zambia.

I listened enthralled as she told me all about her African adventure.

It was a mild, warm late afternoon at the end of March and coming towards the end of a particularly good rainy season when Red arrived in Zambia. To her, the country seemed to have a lush, green edge to it. Tall jacaranda trees lined the roads from the airport and Emmet told Red that she would have to try to stay on until at least September and October when the stunning purple flowers on the trees would be in full bloom. And even though the flowers hadn't yet fully blossomed, the grass verges along the roadsides were brimming with bright green grass.

Red rolled down the window of Emmet's beat-up old white truck a bit to listen to the sounds of the capital as they reached the city. Not dissimilar to any other big city, Lusaka was full of shopping centres, huge billboard signs, offices, imposing state buildings and heavy traffic. Discarded plastic bags and bottles littered the sides of the road and there were vendors at all of the main traffic lights – Red was offered football jerseys, leather belts and watches from the salesmen that worked their way along the line of cars stopped at the lights.

But it was when they finally left the city behind and set out on the two-and-a-half-hour journey south to Kamazuka, that Red really felt she was in Africa. The Zambian countryside was a positive assault on all of her senses – the sights, sounds and smells were all so alien to her, yet so interesting. She stared out the window, mesmerised by the small roadside villages of round circular huts with their straw roofs, and at the steady stream of people walking along the sides of the roads, and she knew she'd made the right decision to come. They drove past women wearing colourful wrap skirts and headscarves, many carrying huge loads balanced on their heads – large containers of water, sacks of grain and bundles of clothes. Men cycled by on overloaded ramshackle bicycles – how they were able to stay upright, let alone cycle them, was beyond Red. She and Emmet drove by lots of children too – young boys and girls walking on their own or in groups, most reasonably well-dressed with simple flip-flops or old shoes on their feet.

As they drove deeper into the countryside they passed by huge cattle and sugar plantations – Emmet told Red that the land in that part of Zambia was some of the best in the whole of Africa for agriculture, and that a number of individual businessmen had created large industries from it. Their companies gave mass employment to local people, he'd said, and they'd helped to build up the national economy through their export business. The sugar company had even made a donation towards the construction of Lankazi Community School where Red would be teaching. They'd contributed financially towards the construction of some new roads too – which explained to Red why the roads weren't too bad, save for the odd pothole which Emmet seemed to know in advance to avoid.

But of course it wasn't all good. As they crossed over the bridge of the wide Kafue River, Emmet launched into a monologue giving his impassioned views on the state of the country's education system. He went on to recount several anecdotes about the realities of life in Africa. He told Red about the local man who had cheated him out of thousands of kwachas by disappearing with the money he'd been given to repair the fence around the school perimeter. The priest had had to get a few volunteers to help him finish it off himself. Red thoroughly enjoyed listening to the old priest's anecdotes – good and bad – they were almost like a bonus extra to the main feature film that was playing outside the window of the truck.

The road to Kamazuka was long and dusty with very few turns, but at one corner at least twenty vendors sat along the roadside selling bananas to the passing traffic. Bananas of all sizes were laid out in piles on old sacks and baskets along the side of the street. Small minibuses which the local people used pulled up along the roadside and, as they did, the sellers would jump up from behind their piles of bananas, grab a basket and rush over to try to sell to the travellers. A row of small shacks behind the banana-sellers sold other goods such as drinks, clothes and maize. Emmet drove slowly by – through the cloud of dust that got shaken up as, one after another, the local buses pulled in and the sellers rushed over to vie for the custom.

Not long after they passed the turn in the road that Red named 'Banana Corner', the rain started – and it really pelted down. It was still warm, but the afternoon turned suddenly very dark and grey and the dust on the roads turned to muck, splattering up dirty rainwater over the windscreen and the truck's now firmly closed windows.

"The showers don't last too long at this time of the rainy season," Emmet said. "About an hour or two at most."

A few people were still braving the weather and walking along the sides of the road as they drove past.

Red felt very sorry for them as most had no coats or any protection from the rain. At one point, Emmet pulled over at a clump of trees where a group of women and children were huddled waiting for the rain to pass. He let the people climb into the back of the open truck – two women with babies wrapped tightly in colourful slings, an elderly woman and three teenage schoolboys who were wearing their, now very wet, school uniforms.

"They said they still had another eight miles to walk," Emmet said as he climbed back into the truck after helping the last woman and baby into the back. "Not pleasant in this weather."

Red turned around and smiled at them, feeling very guilty to be inside and dry while they had to deal with the elements in the back of the open truck.

A few miles further, Emmet had to swerve slightly to avoid a branch on Red's side of the road. She had to hold on to the dashboard to steady herself.

"Everybody okay?" Emmet slowed right down and shouted back through the window.

Red glanced behind – the women and young people were nodding and laughing as they steadied themselves again.

"Sorry about that!" Emmet shouted, then turned to Red. "They put the branches out on the road to tell us there's an accident or breakdown ahead. I didn't see them soon enough."

And sure enough, more branches had been placed along the side of the road at regular intervals. Emmet pulled out slightly to avoid them, and just around the bend a huge lorry was stuck sideways in a ditch. Loose boxes and crates were scattered all over the road around it and two men were standing in the driving rain, holding sticks and directing the traffic past.

"Happens all the time," Emmet said. "They overload the trucks, then hit a pothole or slip on the wet road and the whole thing topples over. It can take days to get them back on the road. Those fellas will be trying to make sure nobody steals their load – they're a prime target there now."

Red took it all in – every last detail of the everyday drama that was Africa.

They dropped the women and young people at their village and continued on for another half an hour. It was dark by the time Emmet drove through the gates of the house on the outskirts of Kamazuka village. The missionary priests' house had been built in the grounds of St Peter's School for children aged from twelve to eighteen and the adjacent Lankazi Community School for children aged from three to twelve. Emmet explained to Red that St Peter's was the first missionary school founded by his order in Zambia over forty years earlier – it was still going strong and had over seven hundred local boys and girls attending. A statue of Mary and Jesus at the entrance left nobody in any doubt of the Catholic faith of both schools, but Red couldn't see much more through the trees and the darkness that night.

The house was built within a secure compound. Emmet drove up to a tall metal gate at the top of the long driveway. He jumped out and put his arm through a hole in the gate for a few seconds. There was a loud clank and he pushed the gate open before getting back into the car.

Inside, the house was spread out over one level in a 'U' shape, wrapping around the driveway where Emmet parked the truck next to a white jeep.

"We'll have a full dinner table now that you're here," he said, unwrapping Red's suitcase and hold-all from the tarpaulin in the back of the truck. "You'll have heard of Father Joe, headmaster of St Peter's? He's an old rogue from Cork, but we try not to hold that against him. Ignatius and Samson, two of our Zambian trainees teach at St Peter's too and I mentioned the two other volunteers when we spoke on the telephone last week – good lads." He folded the tarpaulin up and squashed it in under the spare tyre in the back of the truck, then lifted the luggage out. "Cal, the Australian, finishes up in a few weeks' time – you're replacing him at Lankazi – but Julian will be here for another couple of months yet – he's from America – California or somewhere like that. He's volunteering with one of our charity partners on our water, sanitation and hygiene project – we're putting him up while he's here."

"Great, I can't wait to meet them."

Red tried to take the hold-all from Emmet, but he walked right past her, carrying the luggage up the step from the driveway. Clearly not a man for wasting time, Red had a job to keep up with him as he turned sharply right and strode along to the end of the long open corridor. He stopped outside the corner room, put down the luggage and unlocked the door with the key that was already in the lock. He picked the luggage back up then, strode inside and flicked on the light. Red followed him in.

The room was sparsely furnished, but quite big and surprisingly pretty. The closed curtains were bright yellow and patterned with red, green and orange birds and trees. A colourful African painting of a rural village scene

adorned the wall beside the window and a small plain
crucifix made out of reeds hung over the single bed. A
colourful bedspread with a pattern of the big five wild
animals was laid out over the bed, on top of which lay one
pillow and two blankets. An old beige spotlight lamp sat
on top of a small wooden bedside cabinet and beside the
lamp was a plug-type item and a number of wrapped
tablets.

Emmet unwrapped one of the tablets, put it inside the
plug and plugged it into the wall. "That should sort the
mosquitoes out, but use the net too." He pointed to the
mosquito net hanging from the ceiling. It was tied up in a
loose knot. "You can buy more tablets down in the town
as you need them – we have a few bicycles out back that
you can use any time to cycle around." He handed her the
room key then. "Make sure to lock the door at all times,
whether you're inside or out."

Red took the key, but she was less concerned about the
security than she was at the mention of the mosquitoes –
she knew they were one of the realities of Africa but she'd
always had an innate loathing of insects and creepy
crawlies. She looked up at a small open vent near the
ceiling – it was covered by just a wire mesh which was
torn on one side – the mosquitos and other small insects
would have no trouble getting in. She resolved to cover
herself in the extra-strong mosquito repellent she'd
brought as soon as possible.

Emmet pointed to a door in the corner of the room.
"There's a shower and toilet in there and a few towels –
you have the master suite of the house." He laughed.
"One of the perks of being the only woman at the
moment. Be careful with the water though. Use only what

you need and no more – that's our motto. We've had a good rainy season so we've got a healthy supply of water in the tanks now, but it gets a lot sparser in the dry season – use it wisely, please."

Red had prepared herself for much more primitive conditions and was pleasantly surprised. It was no suite at the Ritz of course, but her own shower room was not something she'd been expecting in Zambia. It was quite basic but nonetheless seemed almost palatial compared to some of the humble local dwellings she'd seen along the road.

"So have you everything you need?" Emmet asked.

"Yes, absolutely. More than that. Thank you," she said with a smile.

"Well, let me know if you need anything else – anything at all. We'll take you over to Lankazi tomorrow to meet the staff after you've had a good night's rest. Pop down for a bite to eat before you go to bed though – you must be hungry." He pointed behind him out the door of the room. "The living room and kitchen are just at the other end of the corridor. The others will have eaten by now but they should be down there watching television or reading so you'll get to meet them."

"Great thanks. I'll just take a quick shower and pop down then."

Red closed the door behind Emmet, then flopped down on the narrow bed. She moved the pillow up under her head and lay with her arms and legs spread out over the sides. Though the bed was quite hard and the pillow thin, she was exhausted from the journey and it felt so good to lie down. The ceiling above was covered in damp patches and peeling white paint, but Red didn't care. She was just delighted to have finally arrived. She did feel quite grubby from the long flight and the dusty, mucky road journey though, and she was keen to meet the other people in the house.

She jumped up and opened her hold-all, humming away to herself as she tried to pull out only her shower things and a fresh set of clothes, resolving to fully unpack the next day. She walked over and opened the door of the shower room and took a step inside but as she did, something scuttled across her open-toe sandal, tickling her toes. Red screamed and the small lizard-like creature scuttled under the shower curtain.

She stood there staring at the shower curtain for a few seconds, trying to collect herself. She knew she needed to toughen up if she was to survive in Africa and so she tried to shake her fear off. She walked tentatively over to the shower and moved the ripped plastic shower curtain aside to check that the creature was fully gone. But just as she moved the curtain another smaller lizard dashed out past her, scuttled up the wall and out a small grate near the ceiling.

That was the last straw – Red dropped her toilet bag and ran out of her room to find help, but there was nobody around. She walked quickly up the corridor, trying her hardest not to run. She tried a couple of doors towards the end of the corridor – one was locked, the other was a storeroom for towels and cleaning items. The last door was ajar though and she could hear the low noise of a television as she poked her head around it.

"Ah, here she is now. Come in, come in." Emmet struggled to stand up from his armchair.

Red was vaguely aware of four other men sitting on

the sofa and armchairs around Emmet, all of them watching the television. When she came into the room, they all got to their feet to greet her. Red smiled and said the hellos as Emmet introduced her to Father Joe and the two Zambians, Ignatius and Samson – both were from Kamazuka and were past pupils of St Peter's. Ignatius was the older of the two – in his mid-twenties, a large man with a firm handshake. Samson told Red he was a year younger than Ignatius – he was tall and fit and wore a Zambian football jersey. He also told Red that he and Ignatius were due to take their final vows the following year.

"And this is Julian." Emmet slapped a thin man on the back.

Julian looked to be in his mid-thirties. His black hair had almost fully receded and he was well dressed in a light-blue short-sleeved shirt, a navy sleeveless pullover and khaki Bermuda shorts.

"This man is a whizz-kid engineer." Emmet put his arm around Julian's shoulder. "What he doesn't know about boreholes and toilets is not worth knowing."

Julian gave Red a warm smile. "It's a dirty job, but someone's got to do it," he said.

Red returned his smile.

"Where's Cal?" asked Emmet, looking around.

"I think he's in your office making a phone call," said Julian.

"Ah, it's that time of day so," said Emmet, walking back over to his armchair. The rest of the men also went to resume their seats.

"Sit down there now with us, Miss, and tell us about yourself," said Joe. "Julian, go throw the soup on."

Julian went to get up again.

"No, no." Red gestured to him to stay sitting.

Normally she would have enjoyed nothing more than to have settled down and got to know everyone, and she was looking forward to some food, but right at that moment she had a mission to complete – and that mission was to rid her room of potentially deadly reptiles.

She smiled at Joe. "I was just going to freshen up first." She turned to Emmet then and, trying to not to make a fuss, said: "Eh . . . Father, I have a slight problem . . ." She said the words in little more than a whisper and gestured with her head to Emmet to try to encourage him back over to her at the door.

"What's that now?" he asked, staying firmly seated in his armchair across the room. "I can't hear a word you're saying, girl. Come in, I said – don't be hovering there at the door." He waved her over. "And didn't I tell you to call me Emmet?"

"Sorry, yes, Fath– I mean Emmet. It's just that . . ."

But Emmet had already turned his attention back to the television. He looked at Joe. "Did you hear that feckin' eejit talking about the elections? What the hell does he know about running a country? Sure he –"

"*Lizards!*" Red blurted out loudly – to herself as much as to the four faces that turned to stare at her. "There are lizards in my room. At least two of them running around the place!"

She expected Emmet, or perhaps one of the others to jump up and beat a swift path to her room to rid it of the reptiles. But nobody moved or said anything – until Samson burst out laughing.

"Those are geckos," he said. "Very common here in Zambia."

Ignatius started laughing too and Red felt very embarrassed.

Just then the door beside her opened unexpectedly and she jumped.

"Whoa! Sorry, mate." The man was standing there grinning, both his hands held up level with his head. "I didn't mean to scare you." He put his hands down then and held out one to Red. "I'm Cal. You must be my replacement – we've been expecting you."

Cal looked to be in his early thirties. He was tall with wavy, sandy blonde hair that he wore longish below his ears. He had a flurry of large freckles across his nose and his blue eyes were topped off by thick eyebrows. The light-brown stubble on his chin was so thick that it could probably have been considered a beard. Red thought he looked a bit like an ageing surfer but it was somehow a look that worked for him. In a shaggy, unkempt kind of way, he looked good.

"Nice to meet you, Cal." Red shook his hand, her other hand still on her chest. "Sorry for jumping – I'm just a little freaked out at the moment. I've got reptiles in my room, you see . . ." She looked over at the other men who seemed to have lost interest already. "Geckos, they're telling me."

Emmet shouted over to the door without taking his eyes off the television. "Cal, give Red a hand there, will you?"

"Red?" Cal looked over at Emmet and raised his eyebrows. He turned back to her then. "Is that you?"

Red nodded. "Guess so." She surprised even herself by what she said, and did, next. "It's the hair." She flicked her fingers through her hair and shook her head as if she were in a shampoo advertisement.

"Oh right," said Cal. "It's eh . . . very nice."

182

Red felt embarrassed again. What on earth am I doing, she asked herself. I didn't come to Zambia to flirt with men – quite the opposite. She looked down at the ground, wishing she could rewind the last few minutes.

"All right then," said Cal. "Let's go see what we can do about this unwanted wildlife situation of yours." He turned and walked out of the room.

Red hurried out and followed him down the outdoor corridor. She noticed his clothes more as he strode on ahead. You could tell he was Australian – he certainly wouldn't have looked out of place on Bondi Beach in the loose white T-shirt that covered his broad shoulders, and the long beige shorts and blue flip-flops that completed the look.

He turned when he got to her open bedroom door. "Ya gotta learn to lock up any time you leave the room, mate. There's a lot of thieving here and leaving your door open can bring in the snakes and stray dogs. T – I – A: This Is Africa."

"Oh dear God!" Red was horrified. "There are snakes as well as geckos?"

Cal laughed and stepped inside. "Come on, you'll get used to it."

"In the shower room," Red said, pointing to it from a safe distance just inside the door. "One went into the shower, the other scuttled up towards the grate at the top there."

Cal nodded. Red couldn't tell if he was smiling or if he just had one of those smiley faces. Either way, in that moment, she didn't feel he was taking the situation quite seriously enough. She followed him to the door of the shower room.

"The first one, the biggest one, attacked me. Right here." She pointed at the floor inside the door.

"Mm-hmm," said Cal, nodding and looking more serious. "Now when you say 'attacked' you, what do you mean exactly?"

"It ran right across my foot." She was relieved that he finally seemed to be taking the situation seriously. "It could very easily have bitten me."

Cal nodded slowly again, but he couldn't contain himself any longer – he burst out laughing.

Red frowned, but Cal had such a great laugh – one of those deep belly laughs . . . it was infectious. She couldn't help but smile, and before long she was even laughing along with him.

"I'm sorry," said Cal, holding up his hand.

"All right, all right. Laugh all you like at the newbie," Red said. "Just get in there and make sure that reptile has vacated my shower."

"You do know geckos are completely harmless, don't you? They wouldn't hurt a fly – well, actually no, that's what they're best at – they eat the mossies and other small insects. The geckos are our friends."

"Really?" Red was weighing up which was the lesser evil – slithery, wriggly reptiles or disease-carrying insects. "I never knew that."

Cal had walked the few steps towards the shower and Red followed him. Slowly, appearing to be acting with great care and caution, Cal pulled back the shower curtain. But as he did, he jumped suddenly, threw his arms in the air and chased Red out of the shower room, shouting as he went. She ran screaming back out to the door of the bedroom before she realised it was all a joke.

Cal collapsed on the bed – he was laughing so hard that he started to cough.

"Yeah, yeah, very funny," said Red. "Don't think I'm going to save your life if you choke. You're on your own, buster." She walked over and sat down on the chair by the desk opposite the bed.

Cal gathered himself and finally stopped coughing and laughing. Red took a tissue out of the small pack on the top of her handbag and handed it to him. He took it and blew his nose.

"Cheers," he said.

She handed him the bottle of water she'd taken from the plane then and he finished it off.

"Sorry, I'll get you another." He grinned at Red, and she couldn't help but smile back.

"Okay, so you've had your fun," she said. "Now can you please tell me what I can do to get rid of these bloomin' slithery things? I'm scared stiff of them."

Cal looked at Red for a few seconds, then he glanced over at the shower room. "Did you ever hear the story of Milarepa and the demons in the cave?"

"Who?"

"Milarepa – the eleventh-century Buddhist saint."

Red shook her head. "Eh, no. I can't say that I have."

"Well," Cal sat up straight, "Milarepa was living as a hermit in a cave and one evening he returned from collecting food to find the cave full of terrifying demons and monsters. He tried to chase them or force them out but they wouldn't budge, so he stopped that and instead told them he wasn't going to leave and as they didn't appear to be leaving either they might as well all just relax and live there together. At that point, all but one of the demons disappeared."

"There's always one demon that just won't leave you, eh?" said Red.

185

"Exactly!" Cal pointed at her. "You have it exactly. So Milarepa walks right up to that demon, puts his head in his mouth and says: 'All right, go on, eat me up if that's what you want, do your worst.' And wouldn't you know it? That demon disappears too."

Red laughed. "Are you suggesting I try to squash my big head into a gecko's mouth?"

"You could try." Cal smiled. "But no – the story teaches us that if we can change the way we think about our demons and not allow ourselves to be held captive by them, then we have the ability to transform their hold over us. Goes for the bigger issues as much as the geckos of life."

"So you're saying that by transforming how I think about something – like the geckos – that I might not be so afraid of them any more?"

"Yes, exactly. It's all in your mind. If you change your thinking, well then, you rob it of its power over you. It should be easy enough with the geckos– they're actually quite cute when you think of it."

"Hmm . . ." Red looked at Cal for a long moment. "I'm not sure about cute, but the idea of changing how I think of them is interesting." She began to think that there was a lot more to this ageing surfer that she'd first realised. "Are you Buddhist or something?"

Cal laughed. "God, no! I'd be a bit out of place in a Catholic missionary community for the last eleven months if I was, wouldn't I?"

"Not necessarily. From the research I did, it seems they're very open to other faiths here. It could be a good thing – mix things up a little!"

"True," said Cal. "But I'm definitely not Buddhist – I just like to read. I read a lot."

Red smiled. "Me too."

"Yeah?" Cal sat up straighter on the bed. "I can lend you some books if you like: I've started a library over in St Peter's for the older kids. It's only got a pitiful supply of books so far, but I roped Emmet and some of his woodwork students in to make some bookshelves, so it's at least looking like a library now."

"Yes, I heard about it," said Red. "Father Killeen, I mean *Emmet* told me all about it before I came out. It sounds great." She nodded to her large, as yet unopened, suitcase. "I actually brought a pile of books with me for the library – as many as I could carry in my luggage. They're mostly paperbacks – novels – but there's a few non-fiction books in there too. Emmet gave me an idea of what you were looking for. I hope they're useful."

"Aw yeah, that's awesome. Cheers, Red – we'll take a look at those tomorrow. I'll be showing you around the school in the morning. You'll be taking over my class soon – I go home in three weeks' time."

"Yes, I'd say you can't wait to get home now. Did you get back at all during the year?"

"Just once. I had to go home to look at wedding venues and suits. I'm getting married in six weeks' time."

Red couldn't help feeling a little disappointed, but she hid it well. "Oh that's great – lots to look forward to then?"

"Yeah, I guess." Cal looked around him. "I'm looking forward to seeing my fiancée, Lizzie, again of course, but I'm dreading leaving this place – especially the kids. They're awesome, Red– you're really gonna love them."

She smiled. "I can't wait to meet them."

"Well, you will tomorrow – you'll be shadowing me for the next few weeks in the classroom. It'll be great. I've always wanted an assistant." Cal grinned.

"At your service." Red saluted him.

Cal smiled, then slapped his hands on his bare knees. "Right, I'd best let you get organised." He stood up, went back over to the shower and pulled the curtain back. "I'm afraid this little guy has taken up residence in here," he shouted back to Red. "He's not budging from the corner of this shower."

Red closed her eyes and took a deep breath in. "Okay, I'll try to be brave and ignore him."

"Did you consider naming him?" Cal walked back out into the room.

"Huh?"

"Give the little fella a name – better than putting your head in his mouth?"

"And hers," said Red. "There's two of them, remember?"

Cal turned back to look at the shower room. "I'd call him something like . . . Gordo – short for Gordon."

"Gordo the Gecko," Red repeated the name. "I like it. And his girlfriend could be . . . Grace?"

"Gordo and Grace it is." Cal turned back to the shower room and saluted. "Glad to meet you guys. I reckon if you promise not to scuttle across this nice young lady's toes, maybe eat the odd mossie or two," he turned his head around to Red and raised an eyebrow, "then she might promise not to put either of you in a jam jar?"

Red laughed. "It's a deal!"

Cal turned back to the shower room. "Hear that, guys? You're all set." He walked over to the open bedroom door, then looked back. "Welcome to Africa, Red!" He gave her a wink before leaving her and Gordo alone to bond.

Chapter 14

I couldn't help but mirror Red's smile as she talked about meeting Cal in particular.

"It sounds like you made the right decision to go to Zambia?" I said to her. "It didn't take you long to start making friends."

Red shook her head. "Certainly not. Before the week was out I felt like I'd been in Kamazuka forever. The community really took me in as one of their own, the people were so wonderful, especially the children. Their families had so very little, yet they seemed so happy and the children were always eager to learn."

I thought about Park View Grammar School where I'd been working – it was such a privileged school. I couldn't imagine what Lankazi must have been like with so few materials and facilities.

"What was it like teaching there?" I asked Red.

"Challenging . . . wonderful . . . life-changing." Red laughed. "All at the same time."

I smiled but said nothing, hoping she would go on.

And she did. It was clear Red was enjoying reminiscing

about her time in Zambia.

"Until Emmet helped the local community to start Lankazi three years before I got there, many of the younger children had no schooling at all," she said. "The gap in early learning meant that teaching some of them was quite challenging, but the teachers were very patient and the children really responded. I think what really helped was the nutrition programme."

"What was that?" I asked.

"Well, the families of most of the children had barely enough money to feed and clothe themselves, so Emmet set up the nutrition programme so that all children attending school got a meal in the middle of the day. That way they got to eat at least once a day – usually chicken and vegetables in broth with maize, or *nshima* as it's called there – it looks for all the world liked mashed potato when it's cooked. If children are hungry they can't concentrate, so the nutrition programme was one of the most important aspects of life at Lankazi. The children took a long time to eat but by the end of each meal there was never so much as a morsel left on any plate."

I was reminded of my mother then who always frowned if I didn't eat every piece of food on my plate – now I knew why – her travels in Africa must have had an influence.

"The food helped encourage good attendance," Red went on, "and the local women, all mothers of Lankazi pupils, cooked, tended the school vegetable garden and looked after the chickens – they were paid a small salary for their work."

I nodded, impressed by the obvious sense of

community spirit at Lankazi. "So what was your normal teaching day like?" I asked her then.

"Well, I was woken early every morning by the birds. There was a big leafy tree just outside my bedroom window and hundreds of little sparrows slept in there every night. You wouldn't believe the noise they made every morning at six o'clock as they woke up and chattered to each other at the start of the day!" Red laughed. "After breakfast Cal and I would take the short stroll in the sunshine across the playing fields to the school. Or, if it rained, we ran across."

Red smiled again, and I just had to ask: "It was him, wasn't it? It was Cal you fell in love with?"

Red laughed. "That would be telling!"

"You don't have to tell me, I can see it in the way you smile every time you mention him," I smiled too. Then Tim came to my mind. I sighed. "I really wish I could feel like that about my boyfriend."

"How *do* you feel about him?" Red squinted as if she was trying to read my face.

"I'm not sure. I mean, I love Tim, he's a wonderful man. But it's never been exactly passionate between us. Tim sort of grew on me, slowly but surely. He makes me feel safe . . . loved."

"And is that how you want to feel?"

"Loved? Yes, of course."

"What about safe? Do you want to feel safe, Chrissie?" Red tilted her head sideways as she asked me the question.

I looked at her for a few seconds before answering.

"I don't know." I sighed. "I just don't know. I'm so confused about it all at the moment." I stood up and walked across the room to the small window.

Red got up and followed me over. She sat down on one of the sofas beside the window.

After a few seconds I sat down too – on the edge of the sofa opposite Red. I looked back at her. "How did you know, Red? You said you met the love of your life in Zambia, but how did you know he was the one for you?"

Red smiled. "It wasn't straightforward I can tell you that much. I came to expect the unexpected where he was concerned."

Chapter 15

Those first few days getting to know the children and the ways of Lankazi were quite magical for Red. She loved the school straight away and she thoroughly enjoyed her first week sitting at the side of the classrooms watching Cal take his classes. As English teachers, the volunteers moved around the school's classrooms, relieving the full-time teachers for a couple of hours at a time and taking lessons with children of all ages from four to twelve years. Twice a week they also taught some of the parents who came for adult literacy classes after school.

Red could soon see how challenging teaching in Zambia would be. The facilities were limited. Lankazi was just a small one-building school – four classrooms stretched in a line on one level – broken only by the headmaster's office and a staff room in the very middle. It was structurally very sound but funds had run out before the floors and windows could be finished off, so there was no glass in the window frames and the exposed concrete floors were usually covered in dust. With very few schoolbooks, as Cal taught, the pupils would repeat words and phrases back to him, diligently writing into their copy books everything he wrote on the blackboard. Their interest, joy and energy was infectious – they clearly loved to learn – but class sizes were enormous. Red couldn't imagine how she was going to keep a class of fifty children under control by herself. She had so much admiration for Cal who used just the right measure of discipline and control with them, the genuine warmth and concern he had for each child evident in everything he did.

He seemed to be very much in tune with the customs and ways of the local people too. The majority of Lankazi's children were from the local Tonga tribe and Cal introduced Red to the families in the villages, to the local teachers and to the Sisters who ran the orphanage where many of the orphaned pupils lived.

One afternoon as they were going back to school after lunch at the house, Cal had to call a young eight-year-old boy out of play. They had witnessed the boy shout at a girl his own age in the yard before pushing her to the ground and walking away. Red helped the little girl up while Cal called the young boy aside. Mapenzi, an opinionated little fellow, argued his case quite vehemently – he said that the girl wouldn't let him choose the next game and Teacher must know that boys are in charge?

Cal was furious – he wasted no time in clarifying Lankazi's equal gender rights – both for Mapenzi's benefit and also for the surrounding group of young onlookers that had gathered to listen in on the altercation.

Cal left Mapenzi to stand outside the classroom then for the duration of the next class. Afterwards, the boy, spirit broken, tearfully agreed to apologise to the young girl.

"Hopefully he's learned a valuable lesson today," Cal said to Red as they walked back over to the house after school that evening. "The young girl Mapenzi knocked over is called Lyliko. She's Tongan and lives with the Sisters in the orphanage now. She was born in one of the villages here near the school but her mother died in childbirth and her father abandoned her as a baby, so she was brought up by her grandmother. When the grandmother died last year, the Sisters took her in. Nice kid. She's eight years old, very quiet, but super bright – she's ahead of the class in maths in particular, not bad at English either. Some of the boys don't like that."

"Well, I was impressed at how you handled the situation," Red said. "I've no idea what I would have done."

"Ah, you'd have been fine, mate."

But Red wasn't sure. She was already nervous thinking about how she would deal with such situations after Cal was gone. She knew that the other teachers and Emmet would of course support her, but as each day went by she wished that Cal was going to be around a little longer than just her first few weeks.

The next morning when Cal and Red arrived at the school, Mapenzi was already seated in the front row of the classroom. A tall broad man stood beside him – hand on the boy's shoulder. He was wearing a beige-coloured open shirt and grey trousers. He looked angry – like he was ready for battle. His black eyes flared and his skin was already glistening in the warmth of the early morning.

"Oh fuck," Cal said under his breath as he registered the situation.

As they walked in, the man grunted a few words to Mapenzi in Chitonga, their own language. The boy nodded without looking up.

"You!" The man held out his arm and pointed a finger at Cal.

"What are you doing here, sir?" Cal asked.

"Out there!" The man nodded behind Red and Cal to the door, then pushed past them to stand outside.

Cal followed him out into the sunshine and Red hovered behind him at the classroom door. She glanced back at Mapenzi who couldn't meet her eye.

"Sir, it may be more appropriate for us to have this conversation in the office." Cal nodded towards the headmaster's office in the centre of the school.

"No! Here." The man pointed at the ground where he was standing. "You punish my son yesterday. For what? He say you make him say sorry to . . . a girl!" The man screwed up his nose as he said the last two words. He put his face inches from Cal's then, spitting as he spoke. "You people come here. You think you know how we live. But you do not know." He straightened up, took a step back from Cal and, with a clenched fist, thumped his chest. "I am the chief of my village. *Nobody shout at my son!* That is not our way."

Cal didn't so much as flinch, just nodded and let the man finish. "I appreciate your coming here, and your sentiment, sir," he said eventually.

"*No!*" the man shouted. "You no appreciate. This my son. He chief's son. He must have respect. He never say sorry to girl."

Red felt like battering the bully herself, but she said nothing. His fury and his flaring nostrils were intimidating.

But if Cal was intimidated, he wasn't showing it. In fact he seemed to have gone past that, appearing angry himself. Red noticed the tips of his ears turn red, his eyes narrow.

A circle of children had formed around the small group, curious about the commotion. Red spotted Emmet a few doors down then – his head leaning out of his office door. He looked poised and ready to come to Cal's defence, just not yet.

Cal stood up to his full height and stuck his chin out. "*Sir!*" He matched the man's volume. "I appreciate that you are chief of your village, and that *in* your village, you must be obeyed. But this –" He turned and pointed behind to the classroom, then back to the playground in front. "This is *my* village, and here –" he banged his fist on his chest, "here, *I* am chief!"

The man was about to interrupt but Cal held up his hand to stop him – the chief seemed so surprised that he said nothing.

"Mapenzi was rude," Cal went on. "And he was violent to a young girl. That is not acceptable to me. It is against the rules of my village. And –" another thump on the chest, "it is not *our* way!"

The man stared at Cal for a very long ten seconds. Red wasn't sure if he was going to lunge at Cal, pull a knife out or shout at him again. But then, the most surprising thing of all happened. The man grunted, nodded, then turned and strode away without another single word to anyone.

Cal glanced around at Red with widened eyes. He exhaled then and turned back to the children.

"All right, you lot – inside, please. The bell is about to

go!" He began to shepherd the children into class.

Red glanced down the corridor and caught Emmet's wink and wide smile before his head disappeared back into the office.

The bell went then and Red followed Cal into the classroom, knowing already that she was in big trouble. She might have only been in Kamazuka three days, but already she was unwittingly falling for one of the most unavailable, yet most desirable, men she had ever met.

For those first couple of weeks, Red spent all day with Cal in Lankazi. She would also see Emmet and the other teachers during the school day and Julian was often around with his workmen too – they were busy trying to finish off the snag list on the water, sanitation and hygiene project.

Before H20, the charity Julian was volunteering with, had come to Lankazi six months earlier, there had been no running water in the school. The staff had to transport buckets of water from the well over two hundred metres from the school building and the children had to use drop toilets – deep holes in the ground surrounded by very basic wooden cubicles. But just before Red arrived, the children had started to use the new boys' and girls' flushing toilets and sink basins with their clean running water. The new facilities were all housed in a new toilet block behind the school. Julian had ingeniously put the tank for the school's water supply up five metres high on an enormous anthill behind the school, saving H20 thousands of Zambian kwachas on the construction of a water tower. The borehole that Julian's workers had drilled deep into the soil below was working well too and, aside from installing the hand basins in the teachers' toilets, a bit of painting and a few other finishing touches, the project was almost complete. Everyone seemed delighted with the new facilities – they were the talk of Kamazuka. The project's success had helped H20 to secure significant funding for the roll-out of similar facilities across other schools, clinics and charities around Kamazuka, so the success at Lankazi was a major triumph.

Red saw more of Julian and the rest of her housemates in the evenings. Over dinner she enjoyed lively chats with Cal, Julian, Emmet, Joe, Ignatius and Samson, and she got to know their ways very quickly. Cal liked to read after dinner in the armchair in the far corner of the living room but he would join in the conversation whenever it got going. He never watched television, whereas Julian, Joe, Emmet and the Zambians were usually glued to it – anything would do – the news, a movie or their favourite: soccer. And if they weren't too tired, or if the mood was good, after their evening prayers Emmet would pick up his little concertina squeezebox and Joe his tin whistle and a music session would start up – always traditional Irish music. Cal hadn't a note in his head, but he and the Zambians enjoyed listening. Julian could never resist joining in though – when the music started he would fetch his guitar from his room and join in – he'd already picked up quite a few of the Irish tunes. Red would have happily sung a few songs herself, but Emmet loved to sing and rarely sat out a song. Red didn't mind – she enjoyed witnessing his and Joe's clear love of entertaining and she was happy just to join in on the choruses.

When Emmet realised Red had a musical ear, he threw her the old bodhrán that had been sitting idle on the side table in the sitting room – a gift from a visiting Irish volunteer some years earlier.

"Here, try playing that old thing," he said to her. "We could do with a bodhrán-player and this lot –" he pointed to Cal, Ignatius and Samson, "haven't a notion of how to keep a beat."

Cal made a mock sad face. "Sadly true. Not a musical bone in my body. It's up to you now, Red."

Red impressed the men by picking up the bodhrán very quickly. Soon, she, Emmet, Joe and Julian had become quite the traditional music quartet. Red loved their sessions and she took her bodhrán-playing very seriously, working out new beats and riffs in her room before dinner, or practising at break-time in the classroom while the children played outside.

Red was very nervous at first when she took over the teaching from Cal – she knew he would be a hard act to follow and she was very conscious of him sitting at the side of the classroom so she wanted to do everything right. Cal offered help whenever Red needed it but, as the days went on, she referred to him less and less, becoming more confident in teaching the Lankazi way.

Towards the end of her second week, she was practising the bodhrán in the classroom. It was break-time and most of the children were outside enjoying the sunshine. A couple of the older boys had stayed inside to finish off some homework and were scattered around desks at the back of the room. Cal was sitting at his small desk eating an apple and reading a book. The sound of the children playing in the yard was almost deafening – they used break-time to let off steam and they were shouting, playing football, running around and singing at the tops of their voices outside. Red's gentle bodhrán playing could really only just be heard over the noise from outside so it wasn't much of a distraction to the boys or to Cal.

As she played, Red noticed a small head pop around the classroom door. She smiled when she recognised Lyliko, the little girl who'd been pushed over in the playground by Mapenzi the previous week. She was peeking around the doorframe. Red could just see that she was wearing the school's dark-green uniform, but it was very big on her – the sleeves of her jumper hid her hands. She had no shoes, and her feet and legs were covered in the dust of Kamazuka – the traces of copper in the soil making the dust a reddish colour.

Cal had spotted her too. "Do you want to hear Teacher play the drum, Lyliko?" he asked her.

The girl nodded slowly and bit her bottom lip. Cal gestured to her to come in, and she stepped shyly inside. She kept her head down and, peeking up through her eyelashes, edged closer to Red.

"Would you like to try, Lyliko?" Red held the bodhrán out.

The little girl looked up. She glanced over at Cal who nodded, then she took a few steps closer to Red and, with a big smile, took the bodhrán.

The older boys down the back laughed and joked on seeing this, but Lyliko didn't seem to mind – she was too busy examining the strange drum.

"Sit down beside me here." Red patted the raised lectern she was sitting on and Lyliko sat down beside her

– copying Red by crossing her legs on the floor in front of her.

"So you hold it just like this." Red showed Lyliko how to place the bodhrán on her lap and hold the back of it. Then she gave the girl the stick and showed her how to hold it like a pencil, twisting her wrist around just enough to hit the skin of the bodhrán at a slight angle.

Lyliko missed the first time. She shook her head and looked up at Red. "I stop?"

"No, no. It's okay, Lyliko. Just try again. It takes a bit of getting used to. Here, try it like this."

By the time the bell rang twenty minutes later Lyliko had got the knack of hitting the bodhrán and she seemed to really enjoy it.

"Remember," said Red. "*KAM-a-zu-ka . . . KAM-a-zu-ka*. That's all there is to the beat." She looked up at Cal. "At least I think that's it anyway! I hope I'm teaching it right."

"Sounded pretty good from here," said Cal who had put his book aside altogether to watch the impromptu music lesson.

Lyliko repeated the words as she hit the bodhrán, and she wasn't at all bad. Red was impressed.

As the classroom filled up then, a small group of curious children gathered around Lyliko and Red. One boy tried to take the bodhrán from Lyliko to have a go.

Red shook her head. "No. Lyliko is playing. You can try later."

But Red needn't have worried: Lyliko wasn't relinquishing her instrument to any other child. She grasped on to it as if her life depended on it.

The little girl stood up then. "I go to my class now."

She held the bodhrán out for Red. "Thank you, Teacher. I love this."

Red smiled. She had enjoyed helping her discover the new instrument. "Why don't you keep it for the weekend, Lyliko?" she said. "It belongs to Father Killeen, but I'm sure he won't mind if you promise to take good care of it?"

Lyliko nodded eagerly. "I will, Teacher."

"All right then. Keep practising and come back to me at break-time on Monday," said Red. "We can have another lesson then if you like?"

Lyliko's wide smile lit the whole room. She gave Red a quick hug, then ran out of the classroom.

Red, tears welling up in her eyes, turned to Cal who smiled and mouthed the words: 'Nice one.'

"Lyliko really loved that drum of yours – wouldn't let it go." Cal gave Red a friendly nudge with his elbow as they walked back to the house after school that evening. "You'd make a pretty nifty music teacher, y'know. Ever think of teaching it?"

"What? Music?" Red laughed. "God, no! I've no training for that."

"Well, you've got a natural gift for it then – look how quickly you picked up all of those Irish tunes and ballads of Emmet and Joe's over the last couple of weeks? You're almost word and note perfect now." He opened the gate to the house and held it back for Red.

"Ah, that's nothing – they're easy to learn really and I knew some of them already – they're quite well-known songs."

"Maybe, but you're sounding pretty good on that

damned drum too." He followed Red inside the gate. "Can't say I was sorry to see it go to Lyliko for the weekend though – there's only so many *KAM-a-zu-ka* repetitions one man can listen to!"

"Oi!" Red poked him in the stomach. "That was just for Lyliko's benefit. I have a wider repertoire than that now – Emmet gave me an old teaching cassette he had so I've been learning some new rhythms and beats from that. Anyway, we musicians have to practise, y'know? Genius doesn't just happen."

Cal smiled. He stopped at the door of the kitchen before they went in to join the others for dinner. He turned and looked straight at Red then. "I'm serious though, Red. You're a natural musician . . . and music *teacher* – something these kids really need. They love singing and music. I reckon they'd really respond if you taught them."

Red nodded slowly. "Maybe. I'll think about it."

Cal patted the top of her arm, "Good on ya, mate. Now let's get in here and get some grub into us. Dunno about you, but I'm so hungry I could eat a roo off an elly's arse."

"A what? Off a what?"

"A roo – kangaroo? Off an elephant's arse?" Cal shook his head and grinned. "Jeez, you really need to work on that limited vocabulary of yours!"

Red laughed and followed him into the kitchen.

Chapter 16

"I knew it was going to be Cal!" I flopped back in the sofa and took a deep breath in. "He sounds fantastic. I love the way he defended Lyliko against the chief and his son." I looked around the Green Room then, almost surprised to be there. I'd been completely engrossed in Red's story and felt like I was right alongside her in Zambia.

Red smiled. "I haven't told you the end yet."

"Sorry, sorry. I shouldn't have interrupted. And I want to hear it. It's just that it all sounds so exciting." I stood up then and went over to look out the window.

"I miss all that so much." I twirled back to face her and leaned back against the window ledge. "The adventure of travelling, that is – the thrill of meeting new people. When I was with *Celtic Wings*, I got to meet so many interesting people, see so many great places."

"I know what you mean," Red said. "Travel can reawaken all your senses, jolt you out of your comfort zone. It can be both a good and a bad thing though – there's a time to travel and a time to stop in one place."

I nodded, but right then all I could really think about

was what I was missing. "The thing is though, that listening to you today, Red, makes me worry that life is passing me by. There's a whole world out there to explore and, aside from a couple of trips to Ireland and one to Malaga, I've barely left London in the last four years." I sniffed. "Tim says I suffer from FOMO."

Red raised her eyebrows. "Sounds nasty!"

"It's *Fear Of Missing Out*." I laughed. "He's right really. I hate the thought of missing any of the fun stuff. But how do you know whether you're missing out on something amazing, if you don't go there, don't try it. Like – if you hadn't gone to Zambia, Red, you would never have met Cal, and you would never been inspired to write your wonderful music." I walked over to the sofa she was sitting on and sat down beside her. "I mean, how do you know when it's time to move on, to get away . . . Or when it's time to risk missing out and staying put, sticking out the hard times?" I leaned back into the sofa. "It's so hard to know for sure."

Red pursed her lips and thought for a minute before speaking: "I don't think you can ever really know *for sure* as such, Chrissie. You just have to pay attention to the signs, go with your gut feeling. And I guess if all that fails, you can try a bit of both and see what works: get away for a short time, then see how it is when you get back?"

I sat forward again. "Yes! That's what I've done really – by coming here today." I felt a little better about my decision to leave the party then, but only for a second. "I dread to think how Tim will react when I go back though."

"It sounds like you may need to have a serious conversation with him, Chrissie. To tell him how you feel

– even if you are still confused about it. Just tell him that."

I nodded. "Yes, that's what my friend Abigail said too."

"Well, she's a wise woman. After all, there's little worse than being with the wrong person, is there? Even if that person is a good person. You have to speak up."

"I know." Red's words reminded me of the advice my father had given me all those years ago. I put my hand in my pocket then and pulled out the small package.

"What's that?" she asked.

I carefully unwrapped the bubble-wrap and handed her the china figurine.

"A nightingale!" Red's eyes lit up as she gently took the figurine from my hand.

"Yes. That's right." I was impressed at her bird knowledge.

Red placed the figurine on her outstretched palm then and held it up to the light. "They're one of my favourite birds."

"Mine too. My father gave me that little guy not long before he died."

Red said nothing for a few seconds, just stared at the bird. She turned it over then. "'*Use Your Voice*' . . ." She nodded slowly as she read. Then she looked up at me. "Wise words."

I could see that there were tears hovering in her eyes.

"I have very few regrets in this life, Chrissie, but if I had spoken up sooner . . . used my voice . . . I might have saved myself and other dear friends a lot of heartache. Not to mention many lost years."

Chapter 17

All too soon it was Cal's last weekend in Zambia. On Saturday morning the three volunteers got up early and borrowed the jeep for the four-and-a-half-hour drive down to Livingstone to see Victoria Falls.

"Last time I went to Livingstone was in the dry season," said Cal to Red, in the passenger seat beside him, as he pulled the jeep out of the driveway of the house. "It was pretty amazing then but I can't wait to see it now after all this rain we've been having. It's meant to be awesome in the rainy season."

Red couldn't wait either. She was excited about seeing the falls and the great Zambezi River, but she was most happy at the prospect of two whole days and nights ahead with Cal.

And Julian of course.

"Got all your equipment?" Cal asked Julian in the rear-view mirror.

"Hey, no need to ask such personal questions in front of the lady!" Julian said with a laugh. He patted the bag on the back seat beside him. "But yes, I think I've got everything I should need right here."

"What's all that?" asked Red. "It looks too big to be a camera bag?"

"Correct." Julian sat forward to talk to Red in the front. "It's sound-recording equipment. I just brought over some basic gear – as much as I could carry. I got into it a few years ago when I was on a safari trip in Kenya. I like to record animal sounds – *big* animal sounds like rhino, elephant and lions . . . but also birdsong."

"Wow, really?" Red turned around in her seat to look directly at him. "Why do you do that?"

Julian scrunched his eyebrows and thought for a moment, before answering: "I guess to me the sounds are one of the most thrilling things about spotting animals in the wild." As he spoke, he began to look more animated than Red had noticed him look in all her time at Kamazuka. "You know, when you hear a lion roar and you can almost feel the vibrations inside you? Or when you happen to notice the delicate trill of a bird calling to its mate in the bush? Well, I wanted to try to capture those sounds, those experiences." He was sitting up straight in the seat, his eyes positively sparkling. "Each vivid sound celebrates the fact that these animals are alive and free where they're meant to be, and each recording tells us a story of the animal behind it. When I hear my sound recordings again, no matter where in the world I am – be it at home in LA or wherever, I'm instantly transported back to Africa – to the Serengeti or the Masai Mara or to here in Zambia where we have some beautiful songbirds. To me, those sounds are more unique, more personal and much more interesting than photographs. I seem to have started to collect them. I've got thousands of sound recordings now."

"Gosh, that's so interesting. I didn't realise you were into all that." Red looked at Cal. "Have you heard any of them?"

"What? The recordings?" Cal laughed. "No, but I was wondering what all those grunts and whistles coming from the room next door were all right. I thought you were having a wild time in there with a secret girlfriend, Jules mate!"

Red rolled her eyes and sat back in her seat.

"Nah! Course I knew," said Cal, looking right and left as he pulled out onto Kamazuka's main street. It was very early so there wasn't a car on the road, just a few people walking along and the odd cyclist. "In fact, I keep telling Jules here he's wasted as a civil engineer – he should look into that sound-recording game more – maybe take it up proper."

"Well, he's a pretty good civil engineer, by all accounts," said Red. "He's done some incredible work at Lankazi – the new water system is fantastic."

"Thanks, Red," said Julian, sitting back in his seat.

"Yeah, but is engineering what you're really passionate about, mate?" Cal looked in the rear-view mirror. "I mean, I know you like being out here, and you're doing very valuable work, but what about when this charity placement's finished? Are you gonna be happy to go back to building those concrete flyover bridges and highways again?"

Julian sighed. "Don't remind me."

Red glanced at Cal in the seat beside her. "You've missed your calling, Cal. You're like a career-guidance counsellor." She laughed. "I should be teaching music . . . Julian should be a sound engineer . . ."

Cal shrugged his shoulders, then glanced up into the rear-view mirror again. "I'm just saying you seem to love this sound business, Jules mate. There could be something in it. Would be worth exploring at least?"

"Yeah, maybe," said Julian. "It'd be great if it paid the bills. There's only so long I can work for nothing."

Cal looked around at Red. "See?"

She smiled. "Hmm . . . maybe you're right." She paused for a moment. "About both of us, actually. While I'm here I really need to think about what I'm going to do after this placement. I've been a bit all over the place in recent times, trying to work out what I need to be doing with my life. It's been quite stressful really. Getting away from it all has been such a relief."

Cal nodded as they pulled out onto the long straight main road to Livingstone. "Yeah, I've been reading a lot on this subject lately as it happens." He put his elbow up on the window ledge. "And I reckon that a bit of stress or tension is important at certain times in life. If you've been feeling stressed about where you're going, Red, it might be because there's a gap between where you are now and where you need to go, between what you've done to date and what you need to do."

"Jeez – that's all very deep for this early in the morning," said Julian with a laugh. He wound down his window then, not seeming too interested in Cal's theory.

But Red was very interested. "So do you think our lives are predestined then? That they're all mapped out for us before we even get here?"

"I'm not sure," said Cal, going quiet for a moment while he thought about it. "But I do think that if we're lucky enough to have our freedom, if we can follow our

211

own path, and if we pay attention to the clues we're given, life can be pretty damn great. It's like these road signs –" He pointed at the sign for Livingstone as they passed by it. "They appear at intervals along the side of the road to reassure motorists that they're headed in the right direction, or if they've gone off-course to redirect them back on track. It's the same with life – our interests and passions, the things that inspire and move us – they're like the road signs, trying to direct us along in a particular direction – gently at times, more forcefully at others."

Red nodded. "I get that, but where does the tension and stress come from then?"

"Well, I think if you've veered off the right path, then you probably begin to feel that tension, and if you don't pay attention to it yourself you might get a mighty shove from the Universe to get you back on track. Either way, it's important to pay attention to the road signs – if we follow them we shouldn't go too far wrong."

"Hmm . . ." Red looked out the window. "I'm just not quite sure what my road signs *are*."

"Well, what are your passions? Your interests?" asked Cal. "Those things you do, or even the people you spend time with, that make your heart sing, your spirit soar? So much so that when you're occupied with them time vanishes into thin air?"

The first thing that sprang to Red's mind right then was Cal – but she put the thought to the back of her mind and tried to come up with something else: "I don't know – music, I guess? And teaching is great too. I'm really loving working with the children here."

"See? That's exactly what I meant yesterday," said Cal. "You're naturally gifted at both things, Red. You should follow them and see where they lead you." He smiled at her. "Either way, something tells me you're on the right path at the moment. I can't say I've noticed any stress or tension in you while you've been here."

Red smiled as she realised that was true. She'd been feeling so happy over the two weeks since she'd arrived in Kamazuka – her best self.

"And what about you, Jules, mate?" said Cal into the rear-view mirror.

"What's that?" asked Julian sitting forward. "I can't hear too well from back here with the window open."

"I just wondered if you'd consider following the sound recording thing a bit?" said Cal, speaking a bit louder. "See where it leads you?"

Red only half-listened to the men as they talked, instead getting lost in her thoughts. Yes, she loved music and teaching at Kamazuka, but unfortunately the one thing she was growing more passionate about by the day . . . the hour . . . the minute, was Cal. Was he the reason she was feeling so relaxed and happy in Africa? Could her path lead to him? She was too scared to let herself believe that might be possible, and she knew that indulging herself by thinking about it too much was a bad idea. The more she allowed herself to entertain such thoughts, the more miserable she would be in a few days' time when Cal left to go home to marry Lizzie. She knew she needed to snap out of it so she gave herself a tough mental shake and tuned back into the conversation.

They arrived in Livingstone by noon and wasted no time dumping their bags at the two private rooms they'd rented in the hostel. They'd stopped for morning coffee along the road so they drove on to Victoria Falls before lunch. The hostel owner advised them not to take anything that they weren't happy to get wet. Red expected Julian to leave his sound equipment behind with the hostel owner for safe-keeping, but instead he wrapped the microphone in a special waterproof cover he'd brought with him and packed the rest of the equipment in his backpack which went into another waterproof cover.

The weather was beautiful when they got to the entrance of the park – the sun was already shining and inside by the car park the local people were selling craft items and souvenirs to the tourists from stalls. Cal parked the car and they bought their tickets from the kiosk. Just inside the main entrance to the falls, they were given white plastic waterproof ponchos to wear.

Cal laughed as he got his stuck while putting it on.

"Here, let me help you," said Red, laughing at the mess he'd got himself into. "I take it you don't get much rain in Australia then?"

"Thanks," said Cal. "It rains at home all right, but when it does we stay indoors – none of this business." He got a mischievous look in his eyes then, waved his poncho-covered arms in the air as if he were a ghost and chased a screaming Red down the path. Julian had already gone on and was standing at a gap in the trees where visitors got their first glimpse of the view.

Red stopped dead in front of the gap. She had never seen anything quite so spectacular as Victoria Falls in full flow. She took a couple of photographs – one of Julian and Cal in front of the falls and one of Cal on his own. Then she handed the camera to Julian. "Can you take one of us?"

Cal moved in close to Red, putting his arm around her waist. She in turn put both arms around him and smiled. It took Julian quite some time to work out how to use Red's old camera and she wished it could have taken longer – she could have stood like that all day. Julian finally worked out the camera though and soon they were moving again.

As they crossed over a wooden drawbridge which straddled a deep ravine below, they felt the first droplets of water.

Red looked up and held out her palm. "It must be raining?"

Cal laughed. "Or it could be something to do with the tons of water falling over a height of three hundred and fifty feet, hitting the bottom and causing a spray of up to one thousand three hundred feet – a sight that's visible for up to thirty miles. That might justify us feeling a few droplets, would ya think?"

"Yeah, yeah." Red rolled her eyes. "You and your facts and figures!"

Julian, who'd been leading the way, turned back to them at the end of the bridge. "Awesome, isn't it?"

"Sure is!" shouted Cal back up to him. "Much better than the last time I was here."

"Yeah, me too," said Julian. "I don't even remember having to wear one of these things before." He lifted his poncho. Then he pointed ahead. "I think I'm going to go on to find a good spot to do some recording. If I can do it without getting the equipment wet – that is."

"All right, mate," said Cal. "Take it handy." He turned to Red then. "Looks like it's just you and me?"

Red smiled.

"Wait until you see around the corner," he said, leading the way.

They strolled around the side of the hill and the sight that met Red on the other side almost took her breath away. The top of the falls were just in front of them, not twenty metres away on the other side of the narrow ravine. She got wetter and wetter with every step as the splash-back from the thundering water filled the space all around them. They both pulled up the hoods of their ponchos but it was a pointless exercise – the light ponchos were no match for the might of the full-flowing falls. The wetter the two volunteers got, the funnier it seemed and by the time they got to the edge, Red and Cal were giggling like teenagers. Cal took Red's camera and tried to take a photograph of her in front of the falls, but his arms kept getting caught in the poncho and before long he was tied up in knots again.

"For Chrissake, this damn thing! What's the point? I'm soaked anyway." He tore the plastic poncho off his chest with a loud roar.

Red was laughing so much she was quite sure she must have been crying, but she couldn't distinguish the tears of laughter from the rest of the water streaming down her face.

Cal tried again to take the photograph then but the camera lens was covered in water. "I think we'll have to give up on it," he said.

Red took the camera back and put it into her backpack. Thankfully, everything was still dry within.

She turned back to the view then. From where she stood she could see a small rainbow had formed through the spray – it was one of the prettiest sights she had ever seen.

Cal had bounded ahead, right down to the railing to look over the edge. He turned back to Red and pointed over at the rainbow.

She nodded and smiled. "It's absolutely stunning."

Cal nodded too, then turned back and leaned over the railing again.

Red began to walk slowly down towards him. They were both soaked to the skin by then – Cal's beige safari shorts and his pale blue T-shirt were stuck to him and, as she walked towards him, Red could make out every contour of his body – his broad shoulders, his narrow waist and his tanned, athletic legs. She would have given anything right then to have been able to walk up behind him, put her arms around his waist, and her head on his shoulder. There they could stand and gaze together at the kaleidoscope of colour over the majestic falls. But instead she stopped walking – the drops of water that continued to spray over her felt like a gentle, warm shower as she stood there rooted to the spot.

Cal turned around. "All right, let's keep going." He walked back up to her. "There are heaps of different viewing spots – you gotta see it from every angle. We'll find Julian at the best one, I'm sure. On we go!"

He put his hand on the small of Red's back as they walked – she felt each of his five fingers, sensed the gentle pressure of his palm against her skin, and she knew she was in trouble. Big trouble.

After seeing the falls, they leaned back against the jeep in the car park, finishing off ice creams from the small park shop and drying off in the midday sun. Julian played them back some of the sounds he'd recorded. He'd captured the drama of the roar of the falls and had even managed to record the song of a couple of thrushes from the quieter side of the falls, from down by the bank of the Zambezi River.

"The birdlife here is awesome," he said as he packed his sound recorder away. "I think I'm going to try to capture some more after lunch. I saw a notice about bird-watching in the hostel earlier. You guys interested?"

"Yeah, I'm game," said Cal, licking the melting ice cream off the side of his hand. "Have to admit to being a bit of a bird nerd myself." He raised his eyebrows at Red.

She smiled. "Sounds good. I was actually thinking we might even hire some bikes at the hostel and explore down by the Zambezi River later. Maybe we could combine the two – bird-watching and cycling?"

"Good idea," said Julian. "I'm sure we can cycle to one of the bird-watching spots."

"Sounds like a plan," said Cal, finishing his ice cream and opening up the jeep.

After a change of clothes and lunch in the small café at the hostel, the three volunteers set about organising their bird-watching and cycling expedition. While Red organised the bike hire and discussed the cycle route with the hostel owner, Cal and Julian studied the reference list of birds he'd given them.

"Okay, so the guy tells me there's a good spot not too far from here," said Red when she joined the two men by the door of the hostel. "It should be a very manageable cycle." She handed them each a set of binoculars and put the strap of her own over her shoulder. "It's a grassland area quite near to the Zambezi. We have the binoculars and bikes rented until tomorrow morning, so we could even fit in the twilight river cruise after the bird-watching if we fancied it?"

"Sounds good," said Julian, handing the bird list back to Cal. "There's quite a few species here I haven't recorded before."

"Great." Cal put the list in the back pocket of his trousers. "So how did it go with the bikes?" he asked Red.

"Yes, we're all set," she said. "It wasn't easy getting them without having to hire a local bird expert too, but I told him we didn't need a guide and he let it go eventually. The good thing was, though, I negotiated us three bikes for the price of two." She handed them each a voucher. "We pick them up at the bike store next door."

"That's my girl!" said Cal, putting his ticket in the pocket of his shorts and throwing an arm around each of the other two.

Red couldn't help the wide smile that spread across her face.

"All right, you two," said Cal as they walked out the door. "Let's go get us some bird action."

After about ten minutes' cycling they turned off the main road and onto a side dirt road. It had rained heavily at lunchtime so the rust-coloured dust had turned quite mucky and their trouser legs and the bikes soon became covered in dark-red clay-like mud. But the weather was warm as the sun had reappeared. Red was at the front of the group, navigating. She was loving the feeling of the warm breeze on her face and the solitude of the African bush. Save for one or two people walking along the sides of the road, it was just them on the small secondary road

– no cars or traffic at all. The hostel-owner had given her good directions and she found the turn-off for the grasslands with no difficulty. She recognised the signs and small village he'd given her as landmarks and soon they were off the bikes and wheeling them up a narrow pathway.

"I can already hear the birds," said Julian as they got to the end of the footpath. Ahead lay an expanse of African bush, sheltered on one side by a thick copse of trees. The whole area looked green and flush after the rains.

"Yep, if I were a bird, this is probably where I'd hang out too," said Cal as they pushed their bikes through the tall, damp grass.

"I'm glad we thought to change into long trousers," said Red, stopping to tuck hers into her socks. "God knows how many creepy crawlies are lurking in this grass."

"Probably a few snakes too," said Cal with a grin. "Watch where you stand."

"Ugh, stop!" She shuddered. "I was bad enough just thinking about the insects!"

"Hey, look, isn't that a lourie, Cal?" Julian dropped his bike suddenly and grabbed his binoculars. "There – it's flying towards the trees."

Cal leaned his bike against his body and looked into his own binoculars for a few seconds before resting them down again. "Sorry, mate, didn't see it." He put his bike down on the ground. "Why don't we just leave the bikes here? They should be quite safe. We can head closer to the trees over there on foot then."

They left the bikes and spent the next half hour happily

spotting a wide variety of Zambian birds – waxbills, thrushes, starlings, parrots and turtle doves – the selection was impressive. Julian was in his element with his sound recordings, while Cal seemed to have memorised the bird list, hardly needing to refer to it at all before identifying the breeds.

"You're unbelievable," said Red as Cal pointed out a pretty hoopoe in flight. "How do you do that?"

"Ah, I think I'm just programmed to retain lots of useless information," he said, hunching down in the tall grass to watch the glamorous hoopoe come in to land. He put his binoculars down, allowing them to dangle around his neck. "I rarely forget something I've read or seen. It drives Lizzie mad."

Red had hardly heard Cal mention his fiancée's name in the two weeks they'd known each other. She knew that he called Lizzie several times a week from the telephone in Emmet's office, usually after dinner. But Cal never discussed the calls with Red or talked about Lizzie much at all – which, all considered, was fine with Red. She couldn't help but wonder if there was a reason he didn't talk about her so much though. Maybe things weren't so good between them . . . maybe she had a chance.

Julian was about twenty metres ahead of them. He was close to the trees, recording a couple of diederik cuckoos calling to each other. He was completely engrossed in his subject – the furry microphone was pointed up at the branches of a tree and he was holding the end of the microphone stick in one hand, the small recording box in the other.

Red dropped the jacket she was holding and sat down on it beside where Cal was hunkered down. "Let's stop for a few minutes," she said. "We've a great view of both the clearing and the trees from here."

"Good idea," said Cal. "Move over there in the bed." He sat down on the edge of the jacket and nudged her over with his full body, causing her to giggle.

They sat there for a minute or so in relative silence, watching the hoopoe hop around on the low-lying branches of the bushes until he flew off.

"Nice little fella," said Cal, resting his binoculars down.

Red smiled. "Mmm . . ."

Neither of them made any move to get up so Red decided to ask the question she'd been wanting to ask for so long.

"So, Lizzie?" she said, letting her binoculars go and tilting her head around to Cal.

"Mmm?" Cal looked at her "What about Lizzie?"

"Well, if you don't mind my saying, you don't really talk about her that much?" She said the sentence like a question.

"What do you want to know?" Cal took his binoculars off over his head and leaned back on his elbows.

"How you met?" Red felt a little brazen, but she needed to know. "When you got engaged?"

Cal screwed up his face and nodded it from side to side a couple of times. "Ah, Lizzie's a great girl. We've been together a long time – since uni. We got engaged before I came out here – she'd been wanting to get married for years, and I did too, so it made sense."

"*Made* sense?" asked Red. "Has something changed?" She couldn't help hoping.

"What?" Cal sat back up, seeming surprised at the

question. "No – no, of course not. It's just . . ." He sighed.

Red said nothing, allowing him to go on in his own time.

"I dunno. Maybe it's me . . . or maybe it's Africa . . . I'll have been here almost a year by the time I go back. Lizzie didn't want to come over to visit while I was here, so I had to go back to Sydney to see her and look at all the wedding stuff." He picked up a blade of grass and started twirling it around the ring finger of his left hand. "I'd been in Africa six months when I last went home, for two weeks. It was great to see Lizzie again at first, but much of the time we were together was spent looking at wedding rings and flower arrangements or tasting cakes and discussing guest lists. After six months apart, I'd been dying to get home to see her, but after two weeks together I couldn't wait to get back to Kamazuka. I missed the kids, Emmet, Joe and all of the people here." Cal smiled. "And Sydney . . ." he put his hand on Red's arm, "don't get me wrong, I love my home town, but it felt almost alien to me after Zambia. The time people spend worrying about meaningless things, the lifestyle we live there – I kept equating the money we were spending to how far it might go in Zambia. Like, if we went out for dinner with a few mates to a nice restaurant, I'd be thinking: that woulda bought enough books for a classroom of kids at Lankazi or St Peter's." He gave a half-hearted laugh. "Sad, eh?"

"No, not at all," said Red. "How could you do otherwise when you see such poverty and need every day in Kamazuka? It must be such a shock to the system when you go back home – it'd be unusual *not* to feel the way you felt."

"Hmm, well, Lizzie didn't see it that way." Cal screwed up his nose. "I made the mistake of sharing my thoughts with her just before I left to come back. She wasn't impressed and she said that she doesn't want me coming back to Africa again after we marry – she reckons it's changed me."

Red raised her eyebrows. "Well, I didn't know you before but, if that's true," she looked right at Cal, "I can only imagine that it was a change for the better."

He smiled and held her gaze for a few seconds.

At that moment Red wanted so badly to reach out to him. The thought flashed through her mind in those few long seconds, but something stopped her doing anything, saying any more. Perhaps it was respect for a faraway fiancée, fear of rejection or perhaps she just wanted him to come to her.

Cal turned around suddenly, squinting at the bushes in front of them. "Do you hear that?"

"Hear what?" She followed his gaze.

"Sssh, we should keep our voices low." Cal snatched up his binoculars and knelt up high on the jacket.

Red picked up her binoculars from around her neck, but half-heartedly, disappointed the moment between them had passed. She became conscious of a bird calling quite close to where they were sitting. It was a lovely, melodious song – a jumble of longish trills each followed by a series of shorter tweets and tchwerps – sung at full voice by a little guy clearly working very hard to garner the full attention of the mate he was calling.

Cal pointed. "Over there, hopping along in the clearing beside those small bushes!"

Red knelt up high beside him and pointed her

binoculars in that direction, but she couldn't see the bird.

"It's a red-capped lark, I think." Cal kept looking through the binoculars, holding them with one hand, using the other to take the bird-identification card from his back pocket. He glanced down at it and turned it over before looking back into his binoculars. "Yep, that's it. I've never seen one of these before. The card says they're relatively common in Southern Africa in particular, but you can also see them here in Zambia."

"Mmm . . ." said Red. "I see that."

Cal turned and pretended to look cross. "We'll have less of the sarcasm now, young lady."

She smiled.

He looked back through his binoculars. "You wouldn't know it was a lark except for the song, would you? Larks are usually quite dull in appearance but they have these very extravagant songs and mating rituals."

"A bit like Australians then?" said Red, though she wasn't sure why she'd said it. There was no mating ritual in play between this Australian and herself. She just had a strong feeling that there was something between them. Or was there? She wasn't sure – it was all so confusing.

"Yeah, exactly!" Cal laughed. "You should hear my mates down the pub at the weekend!"

Red smiled. "Well, I can certainly hear this little songbird. He's singing his heart out, but I still can't see him."

Cal hung his binoculars around his neck, then he put his arm around Red's back and, reaching for her right arm, he moved her slightly around to the right. "Just over a bit . . . and down. There. You should see him now."

Red did see the bird – a small little fellow hopping

around on the ground. The red-crested plumage stood up on his little head, his brown dark-spotted chest was all puffed out, his shoulders upright. Red waited a while longer before she admitted she'd seen him though. She needed a few more seconds to process the thoughts and feelings she was experiencing – she loved the feel of Cal's body pressed against hers, the touch of his hand on her arm . . . More than anything at that moment, she wanted to turn around in his arms, to look deep into his eyes and tell him how she felt.

But she knew to do so would be ridiculous – she'd only known him for a few weeks, and he'd just been talking about getting married to his long-time love. But Red felt she'd known Cal before ever she'd met him – she'd recognised him the moment she'd set eyes on him and she'd been gradually falling for him over the days and hours they'd been together since. Did he know how she felt? She wasn't sure. One move now, one sentence from her lips, and he would know. He might not feel the same, most likely wouldn't, but at least he would know.

Red opened her mouth to speak, not knowing what she would say until the words came out: "Oh yes, I see him now, nice little tuft of red on his head."

"Yes, a bit like you." Cal put his hand gently through the back of her hair, then down her back to rest on her shoulder blade.

She closed her eyes without putting down her binoculars. She hardly dared move.

"Hey, guys! Whaddya got here?" Julian knelt down beside them.

Cal dropped his hand away from Red. "Shhh!" He put his finger up to his lip, then whispered, "It's a red-capped lark. He's singing up a storm over there in the clearing."

"No way? Awesome! I don't have a lark recording yet." Julian pulled up his headphones, squeezed in between Cal and Red, pointed his microphone over the long grass and began adjusting the buttons around on the recording machine.

Cal stood up to give him more space and Red turned to look back through her binoculars at the lark who was still hopping around in the clearing and singing at the top of his voice. She was more confused than ever. Had she just shared an intimate moment with Cal? Or was it nothing more than just two good friends hanging out? It was all so damned confusing.

Julian was with them every moment for the rest of the weekend in Livingstone.

After the bird-watching, the three enjoyed the twilight river cruise down the Zambezi, along the way spotting crocodiles, hippopotamus and many more exotic birds as they began to settle down for the night, but the boat didn't quite stop long enough or get close enough for Julian to record the sounds.

Afterwards, they treated themselves to drinks while they watched the sun go down over the Zambezi from the deck of a local hotel. They could just about make out the misty spray of Victoria Falls in the distance as the sun cast its parting shots at the sky – the sunset a dazzling array of red and orange hues.

They returned the bikes the next morning after breakfast at the hostel and hit the road back to Kamazuka early. The hostel-owner had said the forecast was for a lot of rain and Julian had decided he'd quite like to get back early to sort through his new sound recordings. Cal was happy to go early too – he said he'd make a start on his packing that evening. Red had been very quiet over breakfast. It had been such a magical weekend and she didn't want it to end at all, let alone end early. She cursed the rain.

"I was thinking about what you were saying on the way here, Cal," Julian said as they left Livingstone behind and the jeep pulled out onto the main road in the direction of Kamazuka. "I have a friend back home in LA – good guy. He works for one of the film studios – in production. I might send him over some of my recordings – see if they might interest anyone there."

"Good idea," said Cal. "I'm sure they always need good sound engineers in Hollywood."

"Yeah, probably," said Julian. "What was that you said? Follow where the road signs lead you?"

"Yeah, that's it, mate," said Cal. "Go for it – you only get one crack at life."

Julian sat back in the rear seat just as the rain started to dot the windscreen. Cal flicked on the wipers.

"And what about you, Cal?" Red sat up straight in the front seat. "What about *your* passions?"

Cal looked surprised at the question – he glanced sideways at her and Red panicked for a moment, wondering why the hell she'd spoken in such a snippy voice. She tried to salvage the situation: "I mean, your love for Africa, for teaching here – are you really going to be happy to leave it all behind? *Forever*?"

Cal frowned. "I don't know, Red." He took a deep breath in. "All I do know is that I've made a promise and

I'm going to keep that promise. I know that means giving up some of the things I love." He looked around at her for a moment before turning back to the road ahead. "But that's life. We move on. We all move on."

His words were like a dagger – any vague hope of a fairy-tale ending that Red might have been clinging on to evaporated at that moment.

She somehow managed to feign a smile. "Right, well . . . that's good then." She turned around and stared out the window at the rain falling outside, and the three travelled back to Kamazuka in relative silence, lost in their own thoughts.

Chapter 18

"Cal left Kamazuka that week and a few weeks later he married Lizzie in Australia. He wrote and sent us some of the wedding photos." Red took a deep breath, then tried to smile.

But I couldn't pretend. I was utterly dismayed. I'd felt sure she and Cal would end up together and in many ways I'd hoped Red's story would help me to make some decisions about my own next steps. I'd expected the moral of the story to be to take more chances, to see more of the world. But the way things had turned out, I was beginning to wonder if there was going to be any moral to her story at all.

"I don't believe it," I said, trying to mask my disappointment. "So if Cal wasn't the love of your life, then who was?"

Red, still smiling, patted my hand. She looked at her watch then. "Goodness, it's getting late, Chrissie. We've been talking for hours. Don't you have things you need to do? Dinner perhaps?"

I shook my head. "No way. I want to hear how this

story ends. Unless of course you need to go? I'm sure you're hungry."

Red smiled. "I'm not that busy and I had a big lunch so I'm not really that hungry. Though I guess I could eat something small."

I had a thought then. I jumped up and went back over to the middle of the Green Room to where we'd been sitting earlier. I picked up my shoulder bag and rummaged inside, pulling out the bag of nuts I'd bought at the garage on my drive down. I held them up and turned back to Red with a smile.

"Did someone call for dinner?"

Red laughed. "My favourite!"

She stood up then and looked out the window. "Why don't we go outside, Chrissie? It's turned into such a beautiful evening. I know a lovely spot for taking the evening sun."

"Great idea." I put my bag over my shoulder and followed Red out the side door. We walked along a short dark corridor and through a set of double wooden doors before we came to a glass exit. Red pushed the bar to open it and we stepped outside into the sunshine.

The sun had broken through the bad weather of the afternoon and a cheerful, optimistic glow had spread over the evening – it made the pretty, landscaped grounds look very inviting.

"Come on, let's sit over here on this bench," said Red, leading me over to a wooden bench underneath some trees. I recognised the spot from earlier as the centre of the atrium that lay behind the glass corridor.

We sat down on the bench and I opened the bag of nuts, offering them to Red. She took some and started to pop them in her mouth, one by one.

"So tell me, what happened next?" I took a handful of nuts myself and stretched out my legs in the warm sun.

"Well, after Cal left, I threw myself into life at Lankazi," said Red. "I tried to forget about him, kept telling myself I'd only known him a few weeks – that it was no more than a holiday crush, not even as much as a fling." She finished off the nuts in her hand and I offered her the bag again but she shook her head. "In hindsight I think Emmet knew how I felt. He kept a very close eye on me in those weeks, often checking in with me, asking me how I was and making sure I was kept busy. Not long after Cal left he encouraged me to do what Cal had suggested, to start teaching music to the children. I was so nervous about the idea – I loved to sing and I'd written a few songs but I'd never learned to actually *teach* music. But Emmet was relentless. Cal had told him about the lesson I'd given Lyliko on the bodhrán, so he got some of the children to make their own instruments in woodwork classes. You should have seen them, Chrissie – they were ingenious."

I was intrigued. "What kind of instruments?"

"Mainly drums, but they also made these wonderful small guitars. They were no bigger than a large shoebox really – they fixed a few nails to each end of the wooden box and stretched old guitar strings between the nails. Each instrument had a small, thick triangular piece of wood under the strings on one end and a circular hole cut out of the centre of the top of the box. They sounded pretty good actually, especially with the drums and the bodhrán."

"Wow, it's amazing what you can do with so little," I

said. "Emmet and the children sound very creative."

Red nodded. "They really were. And when they all showed up with Lyliko at the door of my classroom, holding their makeshift instruments, how could I say no?"

I smiled. "So did you teach them?"

"Not only that. We started a little band. We called it Zuka – short for Kamazuka. Thandi, Lankazi's deputy head teacher, got involved. To this day she's still one of my dearest friends. Her three children were grown up by then so she was able to stay behind after school to help me with the large numbers of children who wanted to join the band. Thandi is an amazing singer in Chitonga – she taught me many of the traditional songs of the people. In time, I began to write pieces for the children to play and Thandi helped me to translate the lyrics into Chitonga. The songs were mostly about Kamazuka and about the animals and the country of Zambia. Lyliko and I shared the singing – Lyliko singing most of the Chitonga songs, me the ones in English, with the rest of the children joining in for the choruses."

"It sounds wonderful," I said, shaking a few more nuts out of the bag and offering them to Red again. She took a few more. "Good for you teaching them guitar too without any training. I'd never be able to do that."

"Well . . . actually, I did get training." Red raised her eyebrows. "It wasn't until after Cal had left that I really got to know Julian. When he heard about the music classes, he offered to teach me guitar and to take the children for lessons himself when he could. He dropped in to band practice most afternoons after school for an hour or so and he'd take Mapenzi and a small group of children to one side to teach them guitar. They had to pass Julian's guitar around so each got a turn but they also had five or six of Emmet's homemade guitars for practice. I would take the singers and drummers for the first half of the class and, for the second half, we would bring the guitarists, singers and the drummers together to play a couple of my arrangements. In the evenings after dinner, Julian would give me guitar lessons in the house. We got quite close and before long Lankazi was awash with music. It was a wonderful time. Within a couple of months, Zuka performed in front of the whole school –"

I didn't want to interrupt her story, but I suspected I knew where it was going. Red had ended up with Julian. He sounded like a nice enough guy, but I couldn't help feeling a little disappointed.

"Then we were asked to play at the opening of the new church building in Kamazuka town," Red was saying.

I had to ask . . . "Mmm. So you and Julian? You say you grew close. Did something happen between you then?"

Red smiled and looked away from me for a second. "We did have a kiss in Kamazuka. Just one. It took me quite by surprise, to be honest. After Julian kissed me, he admitted he was in love with me and had been since we'd met." She turned back to face me. "I was honestly so shocked, Chrissie. I'd never thought of Julian that way. He didn't expect anything from me, he said – he just wanted me to know how he felt. And y'know, I appreciated that. The funny thing was, though, once he'd told me how he felt, I began to think of him differently."

"Hmm, well, he is beginning to sound a little more interesting, I must admit."

"Yes, I thought so too," Red said, wiping her hands

together after the nuts. "In fact I found myself thinking more and more about Julian after that kiss." She touched her lips. "It wasn't a bad kiss, now that I think about it." She giggled. "Not earth-shattering, but it was nice."

I smiled – it was funny to see an older lady like Red acting so girlish – funny, and quite sweet.

"I mean, I didn't ever really have the same kind of feelings for Julian that I had for Cal," she was saying. "But I'd grown quite fond of him and I had a lot of admiration for him for having the courage in the moment to tell me how he felt. In so many ways I wished I'd done the same with Cal before he married Lizzie."

"Really?" I swallowed the last of the nuts. "Don't you think Cal *knew* how you felt? After what he said to you in the car as you left Livingstone. What was it again? Something about you all having to move on?"

Red nodded. "Yes, he definitely knew. But I guess there was something about actually *hearing* Julian say it out loud that made me . . . I don't know . . . think about it . . . think about him. After the kiss, and especially after Julian went back to America, I started to think about him more. I knew there was no chance for me and Cal – he was married and he'd never let Lizzie down. But there was Julian – a good man who'd said he loved me. A girl could do a lot worse than that, couldn't she?"

I thought about Tim. "Sure." I said it but I really *wasn't* sure. If Red liked Cal more, was it really fair to encourage Julian?

"Hmm . . ." Red looked out into the distance for a moment. "That's what I thought at the time anyway."

"Did you say Julian went back to America?" I asked.

Red looked back at me and nodded. "Yes – the day

after that kiss, he got a letter that changed all our lives forever."

I sat forward on the bench. "Really? What was in it?"

"Well, do you remember I mentioned that he'd been thinking of sending off some of his sound recordings to a friend of his in LA?"

"Ermm . . . Oh yes. I remember – wasn't that after Cal gave him the advice that day in Livingstone?"

"Yes, exactly. Well, to cut a very long story short, that letter was an invitation to Julian to come to Hollywood to meet the producers of a new big-budget animated movie, set in Zambia. They were interested in using Julian's recordings. He had to leave Kamazuka quite quickly to make the meeting, but thankfully not before our concert for the church opening."

"Did he get into the movie?" I opened the bottle of water I'd fished out from the bottom of my bag and offered it to Red.

She accepted it with a smile, took a mouthful then handed it back to me. I took a long mouthful myself then put it back in my bag.

"He sure did," she said. "And his work on it was so wonderful." She bent her head down a little and looked up at me through her eyelashes. "I actually ended up co-writing a couple of the songs for the movie too – with Zuka. The movie was *Ringo*."

"*What!* The kids' movie *Ringo*?" I couldn't believe it. "That movie was huge! Didn't it get nominated for a couple of Oscars?"

Red nodded. "It certainly did – 'Best Sound' and 'Best Original Song'. That little gold statuette is one of my most treasured possessions."

236

"No way! You have an Academy Award?" I jumped up from the bench and stared down at her. "What song did you win it for?"

Red laughed, seeming to be quite used to people reacting like I just had. "You know the backing track for *Ringo* and the song 'There Is Another Way'?"

I nodded. "Of course."

Red raised her eyebrows. "Well, I wrote that song and performed it with Lyliko and Zuka on the movie's backing track."

"Of course . . . the drumming . . . the African singing. I'll have to watch it again now." I sat back down on the edge of the bench and turned to face her. "Tell me everything. I want to hear all about it, Red, please. Don't leave a single thing out. I've never met anyone who won an Academy Award before. Wow!" I shook my head and put my hands to my cheeks. "I still can't believe it."

Red laughed. "Where to start? Well, okay . . . true to his word, Julian recorded Zuka's concert at the opening of the new church building before he left Kamazuka. It went so great – the children were marvellous, they were so proud of themselves. Do you remember the chief I told you about earlier?"

"Yes – Mapenzi's father. The man who tried to bully Cal that time?"

"The very man," said Red. "Well, he was in tears watching young Mapenzi perform his solo piece on the little box guitar at the concert. He gave me a huge hug afterwards – it was very touching."

I smiled thinking about the tough chief getting so emotional. Music really did have the power to reach everyone.

"So Julian left for America just after the concert," Red went on. "And we all really missed him. Just like Cal had before him, Julian left a big gap behind in Kamazuka. The charity sent another project manager over to finish off the orphanage water project. He was an older man though and he stayed with the nuns at the convent. I only really met him once."

"Did Julian stay in touch with you?" I asked.

Red smiled. "Yes, he was very good about that. He called a couple of times and I got a few cards and letters from him – he let us know he'd been signed to the movie. He was so excited to be working on such a great project and with one of Hollywood's best production teams. And then, on one very ordinary day in Kamazuka, a few weeks before my placement was due to end, I got the phone call that changed not only my life, but Thandi's, Lyliko's, Mapenzi's and the lives of pretty much all of the Zuka kids and their families forever."

"They wanted you guys to work on the movie, too."

Red nodded. "You've seen the movie so you know that Ringo, the young orphaned rhino, loves his music? Especially the sound of the drums he hears from the local village. He copies the sound by stamping his feet to the rhythm, and his friend, a young elephant, Ella, plays an old guitar that they find – using her tusks. The producers wanted a unique, fresh African sound for the soundtrack, so Julian played them the recording of Zuka's school concert, and they loved it!" Her eyes widened as she recounted the story. "Of course we had a *lot* of work to do – the next year was a bit of a whirlwind. I went over to Los Angeles first to work with their music team. I spent three months with the guys there working on the score,

238

and I loved every minute of it – especially learning the ins and outs of composing for film from the professionals. When the score was ready, we went back to Kamazuka with a team from the studio to rehearse with the children. They loved it, though it took Emmet and Thandi a long time to explain everything to the local people. They were suspicious of it all at first – especially the village elders, but they came round eventually. Mapenzi's father really helped."

"What about Julian?" I asked. "Did you see much of him in LA?"

Red bit her lip and nodded. "You could say that. In fact we became an item not long after I arrived. Julian and I spent a lot of time together when we were making *Ringo*. The whole experience . . . that whole time . . . it was all so exciting. We experienced it all together and I suppose I got swept along in it all, Chrissie. After a week or so in LA, I moved in with Julian – into his small apartment near the beach in Santa Monica. I don't remember planning any of it to be honest. It all just seemed to happen very quickly – one minute we were working together on the movie, the next we were dating, then we were living together. We just sort of fell into a relationship."

Red's words sounded so familiar to me. Her experience with Julian, so similar to mine with Tim.

Red took a deep breath in, then slowly exhaled before going on: "Half of Kamazuka came over to Hollywood to record the soundtrack for *Ringo* – forty-two children and ten adults – it was nuts! Emmet, Ignatius, Samson all came – only Joe stayed behind to run the schools. Two of the Sisters from the orphanage came too – no way were they missing out on a trip to America! And of course Thandi was there throughout. We had four Kamazuka parents along too – including Mapenzi's father, the chief. It was wonderful to have them all in America but it was also one of the most surreal experiences of my life."

I laughed. "I can only imagine! Did they enjoy it?"

"Did they what?" said Red. "They had a ball! So much so that they all came back again when the movie premiered, and again for the Oscars ceremony. It was an amazing experience for us all. Zuka went from strength to strength and they kept going as a band afterwards. Thandi became artistic director and producer, we got them a management team and for years they toured around America, Europe and most of Africa. Some of the kids are still playing together – they're adults now of course – you met some of their children here earlier."

"Wow, really? They were the family of the original Zuka kids? How come they're here today?"

"Remember Lyliko?" said Red. "My little bodhrán and singing protégée?"

"Of course."

"Well, when she grew up she was able to pay her own secondary school fees in Kamazuka with her money from *Ringo*, and she went on from there to university here in England, in London. She's lived here ever since. I'm so proud of everything she's achieved in her life – especially given the rough start she had. She's a social worker now and she sings and plays percussion with a popular club band – they're fantastic and they get a lot of weddings and corporate gigs. Then five years ago, she got pregnant by a man she hadn't been seeing very long – David, who you met earlier, is her little boy. She's such a wonderful mother to him and I often look after him when Lyliko is playing with the band. Sadly, her relationship with his father didn't last but tomorrow she will be marrying Oscar – the love of her life. He's such a lovely, gentle man – plays violin with the London Symphony Orchestra. They're getting married right here at The Three Songbirds. In this very spot under the eucalyptus trees." Red turned and looked up at the trees just behind us. "I'm giving her away."

I glanced up at the trees, then looked back at Red. "It's so lovely to hear that everything turned out so well for Lyliko, but what about you, Red? What did you do after *Ringo*?"

She smiled. "Oh, I had a lot of fun, Chrissie. The Oscar opened up so many doors for me. The whole *Ringo* experience took up the best part of two years, then once things calmed down a bit I started studying film scoring and composition at UCLA. At the same time I got lots of amazing freelance work with established film composers and studios so I studied part time and worked the rest of the time. I loved it and I've worked in the area for almost three decades now – I built up quite a portfolio. I still do a small bit of composition work now, but I've wound down a lot in recent years."

"And Julian?" I was dying to know. "Are you still together?" I glanced down at the thin gold wedding band on her left hand.

Red laughed. "Heavens, no! That was all a long, long time ago. Julian and I split up around about the same time that the whole *Ringo* bubble ended. We were never really right together – probably let it drag on for longer than we should have, but we had so many friends in common by

241

then and we worked on several more movies together – our lives were intertwined in so many ways. In the end I had to finish it – Julian wanted us to buy a house together in LA but I just couldn't bring myself to do it. I'd never really put down roots anywhere or with anyone, and I wasn't sure Julian was the man for me." She scrunched up her nose and shook her head. "And LA certainly wasn't the place. It took me a bit too long to realise what I wanted though. Julian was very upset when we did break up. It was horrible hurting him." She took a deep breath. "We managed to stay friends though and I still visit him in LA any time I'm over. He always looked us up too – whenever he was visiting England."

"Us?" I raised my eyebrows.

Red smiled. "Oh yes, I haven't told you the best bit yet."

Chapter 19

After five and a half years in LA, Red decided she needed a change of town and moved to San Francisco to rent a small house in Sausalito near the northern end of the Golden Gate Bridge. It made sense to make the move away from Julian who still socialised in the same circles as her. And the at-times exciting, but more often quite surreal, Hollywood lifestyle had begun to lose its appeal. Red much preferred the bohemian vibe of San Francisco. She adopted a scruffy mongrel from a local rescue centre, named him Fran after her new home city and quickly made a new group of San Franciscan friends – many of them also frequent users of the local dog park. She had a couple of brief affairs – one with a Labrador-owning local Sausalito artist who'd never left the state of California – his limited world view eventually began to grate on Red. The other relationship – with a divorced book publisher – was slightly longer-lived. But when Red eventually discovered just how dependent on alcohol he was – the reason for the break-up of his marriage – the relationship began to crumble.

The series of failed relationships put her off men for a while and as Red settled into her late thirties, she resigned herself to living the single life – happy for it to be just her and Fran. She never stopped working though. Setting up a studio in her house she was able to continue her freelance work from San Francisco, needing only to travel to Los Angeles or New York every couple of months for meetings.

She'd been living in California for seven and a half years when the call came from Ignatius. It wasn't that unusual for her to get a call from Kamazuka. Since *Ringo*, Red had stayed in close contact with her friends there, in particular with Thandi who kept her up to date on Zuka's bookings around the world. Their tours were always timed to coincide with school holidays so that the children could continue to go to school at home in Kamazuka. Red had travelled to see them several times in America and around Europe. Never one for the phone, Emmet exchanged letters with Red a couple of times a year and she enjoyed hearing from him even though he always kept the news frustratingly short. He hadn't even told her Joe had died – Thandi had been the one to tell her. In Red's letters back to Emmet, she almost always promised to go visit Kamazuka soon. But though she longed to go back to visit the rest of the children and to see how the new building phase of Lankazi had turned out, she'd never quite had the chance to go back to Zambia. Emmet had sent her lots of photographs but she wanted to see everyone and everything in person again. It had proved impossible to get there though, work was so busy.

When the call came from Ignatius on an idle Tuesday, she wished she had somehow found time to get to

Kamazuka sooner. Ignatius was calling to tell Red that Emmet was sick, and it was bad. He'd been diagnosed with pancreatic cancer a few months earlier and had refused treatment. He didn't want to leave Kamazuka to go home to Ireland or to hospital in Lusaka. They had thought he might have had several months but in the last couple of weeks he'd caught pneumonia and, at seventy-eight years of age, Emmet had been given only a matter of weeks to live.

Red was devastated at the news. "He's always seemed such a strong man," she said to Ignatius on the telephone. "And so healthy. I've never known him to be sick a day."

"I know," said Ignatius. "But I think Joe's death last year really affected him. He seemed to get very old very quickly after that – at least that's what we thought at the time – we now realise it was the cancer. When the infection came he just didn't have the strength to fight it. He retired altogether from Lankazi earlier this year, did you know?"

"No, I didn't know that," said Red. "He was well overdue retirement of course, but I know how much he loved teaching there – that place was his whole world. I can't imagine it without him, or him without it."

"I know," said Ignatius. "But Samson took over from him as headmaster – he's doing very well and I'm enjoying running St Peter's now. Things have changed a lot since you were here, Red. But we hope Joe would be proud – Emmet is always telling us he would be anyway."

"That's good, Ignatius. I'm sure Joe is resting in peace knowing the schools are in such good hands. And being overseen by local men too – it's wonderful."

"Thank you." Ignatius paused for a moment, then

245

said: "Red, he's been asking for you." She could hear him take a deep breath on the other end before going on: "It's too much to ask for you to come here of course, but maybe you could talk to him on the telephone? I could bring it to his bedside. He's very weak and he refuses to go to the hospital for treatment, but the Sisters are taking good care of him here – they take it in turns to care for him, to sit with him. I know he would like to talk to you though, Red – he's been saying so every day for the past week."

"Say no more, Ignatius." Red's mind was flooded with so many different emotions, but there was one thing she was very clear about. "Emmet hates the telephone. Tell him to hold on, tell him to wait for me. I'm coming to see him. It's been a long time, Ignatius, but I'm coming back to Kamazuka."

Over seven years might have passed since Red had first been driven up the driveway of the house in Kamazuka, but from the looks of things very little had changed there in all that time. It was getting dark by the time she arrived. Ignatius turned off the engine of the jeep and jumped out to close the gate behind them.

Red got out and took a deep breath as she looked around the familiar setting.

"Would you like to see him straight away?" Ignatius asked as he came up behind her.

She smiled and nodded. "Yes, please. Thanks, Ignatius."

They left the bags in the back of the jeep while Ignatius put his arm on Red's shoulder and led her over to Emmet's room.

He had his eyes closed when they got to the open door of the bedroom. The curtains were drawn but a small bedside lamp had been left on. It threw a dim light into the otherwise darkened room. A simple wooden crucifix hung over the single bed and the only other picture was hanging on the wall beside it – a scene from Emmet's native Dublin: Sandymount Beach in the sunshine, the red-and-white Poolbeg incinerators in the background. Red hardly recognised the frail old man in the bed in front of her. It was quite a shock. He was very thin and pale and seemed to have shrunk to half his size.

Ignatius walked into the room behind her and quietly greeted the Sister who had been dozing in the armchair in the corner of the room. She was quite a young nun – Red didn't recognise her. She nodded at Red as she walked past her out the door.

Ignatius turned to Red then. "Come in, come in."

As Ignatius spoke, Emmet slowly opened his eyes. "Is it yourself, Ignatius?" he asked in a muffled voice.

"It is, Emmet. I am here. And your good friend is here also. See who it is . . ."

Emmet's head barely moved but his eyes looked behind Ignatius to Red. "Ah, you came." He closed his eyes and nodded with a slight smile. "I thank God that you came."

Ignatius stood back and Red sat down on the side of the bed.

Emmet opened his eyes and Red took his limp hand – her heart was almost breaking at the sight of him. "Of course I came, Emmet, my friend. What's all this about you being sick now?"

Emmet rolled his eyes. "Ach! Damn body's failing me, Red. I've not long to go now."

Red had to swallow deep. "Is there anything you need? Anything you want me to do for you?"

Emmet squeezed her hand as best he could. "You're here. It's done now. The rest is up to you, girl." It seemed like he winked at her then – but it may just have been a problem with one of his eyes – Red wasn't sure.

Red glanced up at Ignatius but he was folding some blankets on a chair in the corner of the room, not listening to the conversation.

"What do you mean, Emmet? What's up to me?"

Emmet let go her hand and patted it. "I'm tired now. We'll talk more later. Will you sing me a song? Sing me to sleep, girl." He closed his eyes.

Red sat up straight. Ignatius had come over to her – he put his hand on her left shoulder and Red covered it with her right hand. She took a deep breath and started to sing Emmet's favourite song, 'Dublin in the Rare Ould Times'.

"He likes it," said Ignatius. "Look at that." A faint smile had slowly spread across Emmet's tired face.

"It's one of my favourites too," said someone from the door.

Red looked behind her at the open door without missing a beat of the song. She could just about make out the silhouette of a man in the darkness outside. She turned back to Emmet to try to focus on the words she was singing then suddenly realised who that voice belonged to. She kept singing but turned to look back at the door just as Cal took a step inside.

She stopped singing and looked up at Ignatius, who smiled nervously at her. "Emmet made me promise not to tell you," he whispered. "Forgive me?"

Red smiled and nodded at him. As she did, Cal took up

singing the song where Red had left off. The years had done nothing to improve his voice and Red smiled as Cal made every effort to sing in tune the chorus of the song he had come to know so well from his time with the Irish missionaries.

Red joined in the singing, then stood up and went over to Cal. She'd never been so glad to see anyone in her life. Years had passed since she'd so much as spoken to him, but she'd have known him anywhere. He'd filled out a bit and in the dim light she could just about make out some tell-tale wrinkles around his eyes, but they were the same kind, smiling eyes. She put her hand out to touch his bristly cheek. Then she turned back around to Emmet. Cal put his arm around her shoulder and they stood together overlooking the bed singing, until the words finally ran out.

Ignatius walked over and touched Red's arm. "Go now. He is sleeping. Sister and I will take turns to sit with him tonight. You could see him again in the morning."

Red glanced up at Cal. He nodded, then led Red out of the room.

She turned to look at him in the corridor outside. "Cal! It's so good to see you." She glanced back at Emmet's open bedroom door, afraid to speak too loud. "It's so hard to see him like this. He –" but she wasn't able to say any more before she had to give in to the emotion that had been building up inside her since she'd got the call from Ignatius. Seeing Emmet so frail, so close to the end, reminded her of every other loss in her life – and in that moment, all of the sorrow . . . all of the pain . . . came spilling out.

Cal enfolded her in his arms and just held her for a

long time, letting her cry. Eventually he gently patted her back. "Come on, you – let's get you settled in your room. You must be exhausted."

They walked in silence down to Red's old room. Cal leaned in front of her to unlock the key in the door and pushed it open for her.

"Go on in. I'll get your bags from the jeep."

Red smiled her gratitude. Inside her old room the patchy white walls were gone – replaced with a pale yellow colour. There were now two sets of bunk beds and a single bed all squashed into the room. The same painting of the African village scene hung on the wall by the window and a new brass St Brigid's Cross – a replica of a traditional woven-reed Irish cross – hung over the single bed. Red walked slowly around the room, touching the pieces of furniture she did remember – the single bed, the wooden chest of drawers, and the patterned curtains – very old and worn but still fit for purpose. She thought about how little a person truly needs to be comfortable – about how, if you're lucky in Africa, those basic needs can be met, but not that much more. There would be very few changes of curtains or furniture in this room's lifetime. It was worlds away from the life Red had just left behind in America and was a humbling realisation.

Red walked into the little shower room then. Slowly, gently, she pulled back the shower curtain and as she did a gecko scuttled up the wall of the shower. Unwittingly, even though she had been looking for Gordo or Grace, she jumped, then held her chest and laughed.

"Everything okay in there?" Cal's head popped around the door. He was holding Red's small suitcase.

"Oh Cal, look!" Red gestured to him to come over to

the shower. He put the suitcase down and stepped inside. "Look, it's Gordo!" She pointed to the gecko resting nervously on the ceiling in the corner of the shower. "Or it could be Grace. They're still here anyway. Isn't that's amazing? After all these years!"

Cal laughed. "Jeez, I've got a serious case of déjà vu! Pity geckos only live a maximum of about five years. I'd say this is a new tenant you got here – Gordo or Grace the Second."

Red laughed and rolled her eyes. "You and your useless facts!" She pulled the shower curtain back. "Well, whoever it is, I'm very glad to see them." She smiled and turned around to face Cal. "There's nothing quite like seeing an old friend again. How the hell are you, Cal?"

"I'm okay. Thanks, Red." He went back into the bedroom and sat down on the single bed.

Red walked over and sat down beside him. "You look great." She nodded at his chest. "I see you're still wearing your University of Sydney sweatshirt?"

Cal pulled at his old grey sweatshirt and nodded. "Ha, yeah – warmest and most comfortable thing I own, this ol' thing." He looked up at Red for a moment and smiled. "You haven't changed a bit, y'know – you're like a feast for starving eyes."

Red rubbed his arm. "Thanks, Cal – that's sweet of you to say even if it's not true – I feel I've aged several decades since I was here – a lot has happened."

"It sure has," he said.

Red sighed. "I only wish I'd come back sooner – when Emmet was fit and well. It's so hard to see him like this, isn't it?" Her voice cracked a little as she said the last few words.

"Yes, it's the worst. I'm here just over a month now myself," said Cal. "I brought a group of the kids from my school over on an immersion trip in the middle of November." He nodded to the bunk beds. "I'm afraid those are my fault." He laughed. "We managed to squash twelve extra young people into this house."

Red raised her eyebrows. "Wow, impressive! How did the trip go?"

"It went really great," said Cal. "Emmet seemed to really enjoy their visit anyway. He'd been sick for a while when we arrived, but he didn't say anything before we came over. I felt terrible landing in on top of him with a big group when I realised he wasn't well, but he insisted he wouldn't have it any other way. I could see he was getting weaker by the day though, he'd lost a lot of weight. For the first week he wasn't so bad, but then he got the pneumonia and he started to go downhill very fast. The immersion trip finished up two weeks ago but I couldn't leave him when he was so sick. So I stayed on."

"I'm sure he appreciated that." Red smiled. "What did you do about work though?"

"Well, my school's headmaster was with me on the immersion trip – his mother was originally from Dublin so he got on great with Emmet. And as we're not long from school holidays, he said he'd find cover for my classes and gave me compassionate leave until after summer break in Australia. So I'm on unpaid leave for a few weeks and off until the end of January. Decent guy, Mike."

"That's great that you could stay on," said Red. "I'm sure it's been a great comfort to Emmet to have you here. Not to mention to Ignatius and Samson."

Cal nodded. "Samson's done such a great job at

Lankazi, Red. He's really built on Emmet's work. You won't recognise the place. They've finished all three building phases now. My kids painted the newest building while they were here. They can take up to six hundred pupils there now, can you believe it? Emmet is so proud of the place – when he was well the first week he came over to the school every day when my kids were there. He kept a close eye on the painting project and introduced us to the children, teaching staff and the local people."

Red smiled. "I really can't wait to see it and to meet everybody – and of course I'll have to inspect this paint job of yours." She looked right at Cal then. "It sounds like you're still loving the teaching anyway?" She sighed. "I haven't been in a classroom in years myself – not since my placement here at Lankazi in fact."

"Yes, I've been following your dazzling musical success. Good on ya! An Oscar-winner no less?" Cal poked Red's arm. "Zuka are still quite the celebrities around here, y'know? And you – well – people here have a lot of respect for you, Red – and for Thandi – she's done so well in ensuring the children's education comes first. And of course *Ringo* brought a lot of money to a lot of people in Kamazuka. The members of Zuka have been taking very good care of their families and their communities ever since. Some of the money even part-funded the building work at Lankazi . . . and I hear you made a big donation too?"

Red was embarrassed that news of her contribution had got out. "Oh stop – that was the least I could do. Lankazi changed my life. I still keep in close contact with Thandi and with some of the children – Lyliko especially. She's fifteen now and doing so great in school – she writes to me all the time. I'm dying to see her, to see them all again – hopefully in the morning depending on how Emmet is."

Cal smiled and nodded and neither of them said anything for a few moments.

"So have you seen much of Julian, lately?" Cal asked eventually.

"Eh . . . a bit," said Red. "Julian's still in LA. I'm living in San Francisco now though. Did Emmet tell you I'd moved?"

Cal raised his eyebrows. "No, he didn't. Emmet is pretty bad at relaying news."

"Isn't he though?" said Red, with a laugh. "I never knew you were coming back here for example."

Cal nodded. "And nobody told me you were coming until today. Samson just mentioned it in passing at dinner tonight when I asked where Ignatius was. I would have borrowed the jeep and come up to collect you at the airport myself had I known."

Red smiled. She thought about asking him about Lizzie then and about how she felt about him coming back to Zambia, and especially about him staying on for the extra few weeks – she'd been dead set against him spending time in Africa before. Perhaps she'd mellowed with time though, she thought. Red knew she should ask him about his life back home but, given her own single status, she wasn't sure that she wanted to hear all about his perfect marriage, and about the young family he most likely had waiting for him at home in Australia.

"It was a pity you couldn't come over for the *Ringo* opening," she said in the end. "It was you who encouraged me to follow my interest in music, Cal.

Without you, I don't think I would ever have had the confidence to start Zuka and *Ringo* would never have happened for me, or for the kids. I would really have loved for you to have been there for the celebration. Why didn't you answer the invitation?"

Cal shuffled away from her a bit. "It's very kind of you to say that I played a part in Zuka, Red. I don't think it's true though – you guys would have been successful with or without me. And I would've just cramped your style." He got up then and walked over to the window, leaned on the sill and looked out. "I saw you on TV – on the red carpet." He turned back to face her. "You and Julian looked great together."

"Ah, all that's just an illusion, really." Red leaned back on her hands on the bed. "All that Hollywood stuff. I think we did get a bit swept away by it a bit at the time, but it's not real. The cracks in my relationship with Julian started to show soon after *Ringo* came out. We should have broken up sooner than we did to be honest – we let it drift on a bit too long."

"I'm sorry," said Cal.

"That's okay." Red smiled. "We gave it a go. We had a good time for a few years and we're still friends – can't ask for more than that, can you?"

"No, indeed. You're lucky to be able to stay friends. Julian's a decent guy."

Red nodded. "Yes, he is. He's getting married soon – to Sandrine. She's lovely – they've both become good friends of mine. I visit them in LA any time I'm over that way.

"That's great." Cal leaned back against the window and smiled.

Red could no longer avoid the topic. "So what about

you? How have you been?"

Cal sighed and rubbed his chin. "It's a long story, Red. Let's just say things didn't quite go as I'd hoped they would after my time here in Zambia."

"Oh?" She walked over and put her hand on his arm. "Do you want to talk about it?"

Cal smiled. "Aren't you tired? You've had a long journey."

"I'm not too bad. I have this God-given ability to sleep on airplanes. I pretty much slept the entire flight from San Francisco to London and I had a stopover there. My body clock's all over the place with the time zones and I could do with a shower but I haven't seen you in so long, I can't go to sleep yet."

He smiled. "Well, have your shower at least. I'll go make us a sandwich and some tea – I take it you still love your tea? You haven't gone all-American on me yet and prefer *cawfee* now, have you?"

Red laughed. "No, no. And I'd absolutely love a cup of tea right now."

"Great, see you down in the kitchen in ten minutes then." He turned around from the door. "And don't go washing poor Gordo-the-Second away. His family must have squatter's rights to that shower by now – there's probably a whole heap of little Gordo and Graces living in it!"

"Aaah – don't!" Red laughed and shoved him out the door. "Get out. Now!"

Red touched the old dresser in the dining room, and smiled to herself at the row of old mugs, many of them chipped or cracked. They hung from the hooks on the shelf as they always had. She picked two of the better ones and set them down on the oilcloth-covered round kitchen table next to the plate of sandwiches Cal had produced.

"Is this the same table cover they had when we were here?" she asked Cal as she sat down on the opposite side of the table to him.

"Probably." Cal smiled and poured out the two mugs of tea. "Not much changes around this place, eh?"

"No, indeed." Red poured the milk.

"Cheers!" Cal picked up his mug and chinked it against hers.

"I saw the wedding photographs you sent Emmet after you and Lizzie got married," said Red. "You looked great. Lizzie is really beautiful." She feigned a smile.

But Cal's face fell.

"Is everything okay?" Red sat forward. "Did something happen to Lizzie?"

Cal put his mug down and looked at her for a moment. "Y'know, I think I might need something a bit stronger than tea." He pushed his chair back and left the room.

Red stared at the door and within half a minute he was back.

"Bingo!" He held up a bottle of Paddy Irish whiskey then walked back to the table. "I'd say this was probably Joe's – Emmet wouldn't touch the stuff. You'd miss ol' Joe about the place, wouldn't you?"

Red nodded.

Cal got a couple of glasses out of the sideboard. "Emmet said he went peacefully in his sleep." He poured himself a small glass of whiskey, then paused with the bottle poised over the second glass and raised his eyebrows questioningly at Red.

She shook her head. "I think that would finish me off altogether! Tea is fine for me."

Cal rested the bottle on the table and took a large swig out of his glass.

She said nothing. He needed to tell her whatever was bothering him in her own time, she knew that. So she took a sandwich and waited.

Cal took another large swig of whiskey, then he leaned into the table.

"I found it very bloody hard to settle back in Australia after this place, Red. A year is a long time and Africa gets under your skin in a way that's hard to understand. Well, it was hard for Lizzie to understand anyway. I wanted to book us a trip back here or to Kenya or South Africa for our honeymoon, but she refused. Instead we went to Fiji. We didn't leave the resort once – five-star place, completely over the top – not to mention out of our price range."

"Well, the wedding looked great from the pictures anyway." Red tried to ease his obvious tension.

"Yeah, it was a great day and Lizzie and I even got on okay on the honeymoon. It was when we got home that things changed." Cal sighed. "And it went on for two years – two, long, frenzied baby-making years. Lizzie wanted us to start right away, so that's what we did. I remember lots of calendar-watching, functional sex at peak times, strict alcohol-free regimes – we even became vegan for a while – and you know how I like my meat!"

Though she was a bit taken aback by what Cal was saying, Red managed a laugh. "I sure do. I've never seen a man devour a roast beef dinner as quickly as you."

Cal smiled but only for a moment, the tense look soon

returned. "After a year, when nothing happened, Lizzie and I went to see various specialists and to cut a very long and painful story short – it turned out that *I* was the problem." He raised his eyebrows and finished off the whiskey in his glass. "Yep, my swimmers were underperforming – down, but not strictly out, they said. The docs told us to keep trying though and another year went swiftly by. Problem was that all the while things between Lizzie and me were getting worse – pretty much by the day. It got to the point where I didn't want sex at all – it felt like a job – all the fun and the intimacy had gone out of it."

Red didn't quite know what to say, or why Cal was telling her all this.

"It was during all this that your movie came out," said Cal. "Looking back I think I was in quite a deep depression by that time. I'd withdrawn from Lizzie almost entirely. I was still teaching at the school – functioning, but only just. So when I saw *Ringo* it was like it reawakened something inside me. I loved the scenes of the Zambian countryside and, even though it was just an animation, every time I turned on that movie, I was back in Africa – I could almost smell the smells – hear the sounds – picture my friends there. I watched it over and over, and every time one of Zuka's songs started, I could see you – you and the children from Lankazi singing and playing your hearts out. And as for that daft rhino and his guitar-playing elephant mate!" Cal laughed. "I could probably still recite every last line of that bloody movie." He imitated the accent of the young American actor who voiced the part of Ringo: "'*Come on, Ella. We'll show them that there is a different way. Let's show the world what can be done when we believe in ourselves and do what we really love.'"* He laughed. "Shit. No wonder my wife had an affair."

"Lizzie had an affair?" Red sat forward.

"Yeah." Cal sniffed. Then he poured himself another glass of whiskey. "Got pregnant, didn't she? Thing is, at first she told me it was mine. I was a bit stunned by the news of course. Almost two years we'd been trying, and finally, when we'd all but stopped, it happened. But it didn't even occur to me to question it. I just started to get my shit together. I lost some weight, did up our spare room for the baby, even gave up the booze again. And for a while Lizzie and I seemed to be getting on better, or so I thought." He took a large swig of whiskey, then wiped his mouth. "It was all an illusion." He went to top up his glass but changed his mind. He put down the bottle. "Turned out Lizzie had been having an affair with Jack, one of my friends since childhood, my groomsman in fact – what a cliché." He laughed. "They'd been at it for years apparently – started when I was first here in Kamazuka."

"Oh my God, Cal. Are you serious? And you never knew?"

"Never suspected a thing! I mean, I knew she struggled with me being away for so long, but we'd agreed it was the last time I'd do it. I was going back to get married, to settle down." He sighed. "Y'know, I don't think Lizzie ever would have told me about it at all if it hadn't been for the baby. I have to be thankful for that at least. Jack was married with a couple of kids of his own and by all accounts wasn't keen to mess that up. But it seems that when Lizzie got pregnant and we looked to be getting on better, Jack couldn't take it. He finally found the balls to

260

leave poor ol' Kate and, as soon as he did, Lizzie ditched me – and that was that – end of marriage, end of baby. For me anyway. They're still together and the kid is five now. Ah, to hell with 'em!" He shoved his chair back from the table.

Red flinched.

"I'm done thinking about it," said Cal. "I'm well shot of them both."

"Did you see her much after that?"

"Lizzie?" Cal's eyes widened. "Are you kidding me? I saw her practically every day – we were teaching at the same school!"

"Oh no, that's awful. How did you manage?"

"With difficulty," said Cal, pulling his chair back in to the table. "The first few months of the break-up were very hard. I got very down – it was around the time that you guys were at the Oscars."

"Ah!" Red leaned back in her seat. No wonder Cal hadn't responded to their invitation.

"You seemed to be doing so well," Cal went on. "I was proud of you all, of your achievements, but it made my miserable life seem so damn pathetic. Then I saw you and all the kids from Lankazi on television singing during the ceremony and I was surprised when it stoked up a lot of *good* feelings in me – lots of good memories. It was exactly what I needed right then. And the funniest thing happened: I picked up a notebook and a pen after watching the Oscars that night, and I started writing. And to be honest, Red, I haven't stopped since. It took me almost four years, but I finally finished the manuscript of my first novel, and I'm working on my second now. Oh, and I eventually got sick of seeing my ex in the corridors, so I changed schools. The place I teach in now is a state school – not quite as good facilities or as affluent as the one I taught in before, but it suits me a lot better as a result – the kids are really great. We'd been fundraising to come on this trip for a long time. Seeing Zambia and Kamazuka again and seeing it all through my students' eyes – most of them seeing the place, meeting the Zambian people, the children, for the first time – well, it's just stoked up my deep love for this country, for Africa."

Red smiled. "That's great, Cal. It sounds like you all got a lot from the immersion trip. And hey, a novelist now too? That's amazing!"

"Ah, it's not that amazing really. I haven't been published yet. I've discovered that writing a novel is one thing, finding a publisher is another altogether."

"It's only a matter of time, I'm sure. What was your first novel about?"

Cal looked at Red for a few seconds without saying anything, then he got up and moved his chair around the table so it was just beside hers. She didn't know what he was doing, but instinctively she turned her chair outwards to face his.

"It's about my time here, Red. I mean, it's fiction, but it's about a young man full of hopes and dreams. Then out of some sense of misguided loyalty he gives up two of his great loves . . . Africa and . . . well . . . you. He gave up you, Red."

"Me?" Red was stunned.

"Red, this might sound crazy, but just hear me out." Cal avoided her eyes for a moment. He took a deep breath in, then looked straight at her again. "I'm sure you won't remember that weekend in Livingstone all those years ago? The day we went to Victoria Falls, then afterwards for a cycle down to the grasslands near the Zambezi?"

Red looked at him. "Of course I remember that day. It was one of the highlights of my time in Africa."

Cal smiled. "And do you remember that moment when we were bird-watching and we spotted the red-capped lark?" He sat back. "I was actually quite surprised to see him there because that breed is much more common in South Africa and –"

"Cal!" Red gently touched his hand on the table. "I'm thinking that this may not be the best time for your always very interesting facts?"

He smiled and nodded. "Mmm, you could be right." He moved his chair a few inches closer to hers and turned his hand over on the table.

Red put her hand in his and looked sideways at him, not daring to imagine what was coming.

"Y'know, it was all I could do not to pull you into my arms that day in Livingstone," he said, "not to kiss you . . . If Julian hadn't arrived when he did, I probably would have. I was completely and utterly besotted by you, Red."

All she could do was stare at him.

"Of course I knew Julian had fallen for you too," Cal went on. "We never discussed it, but I knew. He'd never shown the slightest interest in taking a weekend away with me before then. And I'm not sure if you noticed, but he rarely left the two of us alone together in Kamazuka if he could help it."

Red eyes widened. "Gosh, that's true actually."

Cal shook his head. "Yeah. Before you came I didn't see too much of Julian at all really. He was usually glued to the television in the evenings or in his room playing around with his sound recordings. We didn't really connect too well. I'm more of a book man and, as you know, I like to talk! Julian's not so much of a talker."

Red smiled. It was one of the things she'd loved most about Cal and one of the things that disappointed her most about her relationship with Julian – their conversations had always been about practical things – work, the movie. When all that died down, the cracks had really started to show.

"Cal, why on earth didn't you say something?" Red squeezed his hand. "We talked all the time, you and I. Why didn't you ever tell me how you felt?"

Cal sighed. "Well, partly because I thought it was just a crush – you know, one of those travel things? And also of course because of Lizzie. I didn't want to let her down." He squinted at Red then. "And even though you and I did talk all the time, we never talked about us. I wasn't fully sure if you felt the same way."

Red looked up at the ceiling and took a deep breath before looking back at him. "Yes, I'm told I'm notoriously bad at talking about things that matter. I so wish I'd said something now."

"Don't apologise," said Cal, sitting back but holding on to her hand. "It wasn't a straightforward thing – I was engaged to Lizzie and I reckoned you and Julian would get together when I was out of the way." He raised his eyebrows. "And I was right, wasn't I? You did get together."

Red took her hand back. "Well . . . we had one kiss here in Africa . . . But, Cal, why didn't you get back in touch?" She sat forward. "You must have known Julian and I didn't work out. You could have got my contact details through Emmet or Thandi. If you felt like this why didn't you contact me?"

Cal shifted in his seat. "It's going to sound stupid now but I had this idea that I had to get my book published first. You've had so much success, done so much with your life that I wanted to at least have achieved that much before I saw you."

"Oh Cal, you don't need to prove anything to me," Red said. "You've already achieved so much – taught and inspired so many children."

"You're being kind, but thank you for saying so." Cal heaved a deep sigh. "And I suppose in many ways you're right – I just didn't see it that way. In fact my grand plan was to invite you to a dazzling book launch party and surprise you with the book's storyline. I just never expected it to take so long! When I started writing in earnest I expected it to take about six months, instead it took four years. And I still can't find a publisher for the damn thing! I should have given up and just contacted you anyway but it's turned into a bit of an obsession now – I have to get this book published."

Red laughed. "You shouldn't have to publish a book to be able to tell me how you feel, Cal. From the moment I met you I thought you were wonderful." She leaned over and touched his cheek. "And I still do." It was more than she had intended to admit, but she was glad she'd finally said it. "I was really devastated when you left Kamazuka." She sat back again. "And I'll be honest now – I know I didn't ever know her, and I don't dislike many people, but I never liked the sound of that Lizzie. The very mention of her stupid name always set my teeth on edge. 'Lizzie' sounds like lizard, and you know how I feel about reptiles – except geckos of course!"

Cal laughed. "Ha, now you find your voice!"

Red started to laugh too – laughing and crying at the same time – so much so that her nose started to run so she dabbed at it with one of the paper napkins from the table before going on. "All of those damn phone calls – all of those bloody nights you'd be gone off to talk to her. I hated the thought of you telling her about our day together, or the idea of the two of you discussing your wedding plans."

"Red –" Cal rubbed her arm, looking more serious.

"And don't get me started on those wedding photographs – why did she have to be so damn pretty?

"Red –"

"So flippin' *blonde*?" Red screwed up her nose. "And petite too? I mean –"

"*Red!*" Cal finally got her attention. She stared at him as he leaned in close to her and with a softened voice said, "For pity's sake, girl – would you please just shut the heck up for one minute so that I can kiss you." He leaned right in then so that his nose was just inches from hers. "I've waited over seven years, after all!"

Red was still staring at him, her mouth wide open. Cal reached out and gently lifted her chin to close it. Then they smiled at each other and, finally, over seven years on from the moment they'd first met, Cal and Red had their first kiss.

Chapter 20

"It might have taken years, but it was a kiss worth waiting for, Chrissie." Red sighed and touched her lips. "A person could wait a whole lifetime to get kissed like that." Her eyes were closed and she was smiling to herself – she looked almost completely lost in her memories.

As I looked at her, I realised with surprise that I was a little jealous. I looked up at the branches of the trees swaying in the evening breeze above us. I wasn't sure why I was feeling envious of Red and Cal's kiss – I'd had lots of first kisses myself – some good, some not so much. Tim had kissed me first after he drove me and Conor home from the airport on our return from Zanzibar. We'd dropped Conor off first, then we'd chatted in the car for some time after we reached my flat. I'd been expecting the kiss – I knew Tim liked me and I'd been thinking about whether we should get together for a while. Tim had been so good to me around the time of my mother's death and I felt he could give me the stability, the security, the roots I so desperately craved at the time. Our first kiss in the car that day was nice, nothing earth-shattering, but I thought there was more to a relationship than just passion – my at-times-passionate, but ultimately disastrous, relationship with Brian had taught me that.

I looked back at Red and realised then why I was feeling jealous – no man had ever made me feel the way Cal had clearly made her feel that night.

"You two sound perfect for each other," I said after a few minutes. "Please tell me it all worked out for you?"

Red opened her eyes. "Oh yes." She smiled. "After that night in Kamazuka, I went from being this independent, single woman to being one half of an unbreakable whole. Cal brought out the best in me in every way, encouraging me to continue to be myself. It was all I could ever have asked for from a relationship."

I smiled. Even though I was feeling a little envious, I was genuinely happy for Red and Cal. "So tell me what happened after the kiss," I said.

"Well, sadly, Emmet died a couple of days after I arrived at Kamazuka. Cal and I were both there at the end – it was very special. Over those couple of days we cried with him, sang for him, and surprisingly even laughed a few times. We both felt so privileged to be able to share his last days with him, and to have been there with such a wonderful man as he breathed his last breaths on this earth." Red's voice cracked a bit and a couple of tears sprang to her eyes. She wiped them away with one finger of each hand. "We buried him beside Joe in the priests' burial ground beside the house. It was what he wanted – to be laid to rest in Kamazuka close to the people he loved so much. Some members of his family came over from Ireland, the Sisters sang and Zuka played so beautifully at his funeral Mass – it was very much a celebration of his life – a life dedicated to other people."

I was very touched, almost wishing I'd known Emmet myself.

"After everything that had happened," Red went on, "Cal and I agreed that we weren't ready to go back to the real world just yet, so we threw caution to the wind and spent the next six weeks travelling around Africa. Cal's school was about to start their summer holidays so he was okay for time, but I had to pull out of a film project I'd been due to work on – it didn't go down very well with my agent, but I didn't care. My friends were very sweet and kept my dog, Fran, for longer than the original week they'd agreed. So Cal and I were free to be together. We acquired a tent and two bikes and we travelled all over Zambia, then South Africa. It was a magical time – finally being able to be together – it was so easy, like we'd always been together. That was the happiest time of my life, I think. But the six weeks went by very fast and Cal's school was due to start again at the end of January. I had to go back to San Francisco and Cal went back to Sydney. We lasted a couple of months with the long-distance relationship, then as soon as Cal got his mid-term break we agreed to meet up halfway in London for the week. One of the days we were there we hired a car and drove out here to Kent – it was such a beautiful spring day – I remember it like it was yesterday. We stopped off right here at The Three Songbirds for lunch and afterwards we went for a stroll outside in the sunshine. We were so happy to be back together again and the setting was lovely . . . the birds were singing their hearts out in the trees all around us, the sun was beaming down . . . And right here," she pointed behind her at roots of the trees, "is the exact spot where Cal got down on one knee and proposed to me. The eucalyptus trees weren't there then, but where they stand now is the exact spot where it happened."

"Oh, that's so romantic," I said. "What a gorgeous setting!"

"Yes, it was lovely. *So* lovely in fact that, as soon as Cal's divorce finally came through later that year, we started to make plans to come back and get married here. Cal smuggled those two little eucalyptus saplings out of Australia and the owners here were kind enough to allow us to plant them the morning of our wedding at the very spot where we'd got engaged." She smiled.

We both instinctively turned to look up at the trees and that's when I noticed their branches were intertwined at the top.

"When we were planting them," Red was saying, "Cal and I stood beside each other facing Collinswood with the inn behind us. Then we stepped apart sideways until my right arm and his left arm were fully stretched out and just our fingertips were touching. Then we each dug our right heel into the spot directly in front of us and that's where we each planted our tree. We got married between them later that day – just Cal and me and a local registrar, with the hotel owners as our witnesses. Lyliko and Oscar are getting married in the same spot tomorrow under the arch made by our trees." She walked behind the bench and touched the trunk of one of the trees. "Over the years they grew together and became intertwined." She smiled and put her arms around the trunk. "Just like me and Cal."

I gazed up at the trees which stood right in the middle of the wide atrium, filling the area almost completely. Their trunks were half-covered in ivy, but I could make out the smooth, yellowish-white bark beneath. They stood tall and proud, each one almost the same height as the two-storey inn. The branches of each tree snaked out above us, spreading out to form a thick canopy of green foliage. One distinctive branch of each tree had grown at an angle to the trunk, reaching out towards its neighbour, their intertwining branches forming an arch over our bench below. I noticed three nests at the top of the trees then and spotted a couple of starlings flying into them. There was certainly something magical . . . almost mystical . . . about the trees. I was intrigued by their interconnected mystery.

I looked back at Red. "Tell me, Red, what is it about Cal that you love? What is it that makes you two work so well together?"

Red stood back from the tree, took a deep breath in then slowly let it out. "I think when you're with the right person it's all just very easy, Chrissie. That sounds very simplistic, but it's the best way I can describe it. I mean there can be other clues – the person who's right for you will probably have some of the qualities you lack, and I think they should really draw out the best in you – allow you to grow, to be yourself. And ideally you'll share some interests. Cal enhanced my life in those ways, in every way really. When we got together a lot changed for me – I moved to Australia with him and for some time I really loved it. We lived very near Bondi Beach and I loved the walk along the cliffs from Bondi to Coogee – looking out at the blows of the migrating whales on the horizon. In the summers I would swim in the open-air sea-pools along the coast, and I loved mooching around the markets in Bondi. Cal and I worked together too – we made a couple of independent movies together – he wrote the scripts and I composed the scores – they weren't bad actually. We set up our own little production company and travelled over to Africa to make them – it was enormous fun. And we holidayed there too – every year at least we would go back – either to some much-loved place like Kamazuka or Livingstone, or we'd discover a new country, a new adventure."

"Oh, that sounds really great! So good to have someone who shares your interest in travel." I thought about Tim's Malaga travel brochure with a heavy heart.

"Yes, indeed. Mind you, all of that was after Cal got published. It mightn't have been so easy otherwise with his teacher's salary and school schedule." She smiled. "I was able to introduce him to Barry – the book publisher I dated for a while when I lived in San Francisco. He loved Cal's writing and gave him a deal. Cal's books did very well indeed – *Birds of a Feather* was published first and it became a *New York Times* bestseller."

"Wow, really?" I was surprised I'd never heard of it. "I must make sure to read it."

Red smiled. "I'll send you a copy – it's a wonderful book, and its success meant that Cal had to give up teaching to write full-time. He was sad about leaving teaching behind, but he loved to write and he'd been struggling to do both. After a few years in Australia then, we eventually we moved to England. I found the Australian summers a struggle – it was even hotter there than it was in LA – stiflingly so at the height of the summer. So we bought a beautiful cottage by the coast in Devon and became country folk. It was quite a simple life really, but we were very *very* happy." She laughed. "It's funny, before Cal came along I never thought I'd have been able to settle down in one place for so long but I've been living there fourteen years now. I learnt from Cal that when you find the right person even the world's greatest wanderer can finally be happy to put down roots."

I smiled, but something she'd said had bothered me. "Red, you said you *were* very happy. Why past tense? Did something go wrong between you and Cal?"

Red's face changed. She walked back over to me on the bench but didn't sit down. Instead she took a few paces forward. She stood there just staring at the woods for a few seconds before turning back to face me.

"I mentioned I have very few regrets in life, Chrissie. The biggest is those wasted years that Cal and I could have had together. If I'd spoken up that day in Livingstone, pushed things a little, might we have got together sooner? Perhaps yes, perhaps no – I'll never know of course." She came back over to the bench and sat down. "Promise me, you'll never be afraid to tell someone how you feel about them, Chrissie. Even if nothing can happen between you, don't ever suppress your feelings. Take that leap of faith – you never know where it might lead you. Do you have that nightingale?"

I nodded and took the figurine out of my pocket. I took it out of the loose bubble wrap and handed it to her.

She turned the base around to me. "As your wise father said: '*Use Your Voice*'."

She handed the figurine back to me then and I turned it over to read the words myself. I looked back at her. "I'll try, Red. But I think my dilemma at the moment is quite different to what yours was. It's not that I can't find the

273

words to tell someone that I love them, it's almost the opposite. I can't find the words to tell him that –" I stopped.

Red nodded and put her hand on my arm. "You have to talk to Tim, Chrissie – to tell him how you feel. That way you can try to work it out together – or not, if that's what you decide. Whether it's telling someone you love them, or telling them you don't love them enough, it's much the same thing – you have to be honest. And think of it – if Tim is not the man for you, you could be missing out on the one that is. It's like me and Julian. We were never right together – in many ways I always knew that – I should have known from that first kiss. But we drifted on, and years went by – years when I could have been with my love."

"But you and Cal got there in the end, didn't you? I know you lost seven years or so, but you're together now?"

Red looked down at her hands for a moment, then back up at me. She had tears in her eyes. "Cal died three and a half years ago, Chrissie. One minute he was here, large as life, writing his beautiful books, spouting his useless facts, laughing at my daft jokes, sharing his life with me – the next he was just gone. He died of a heart attack while writing at home one day. It was such a shock." She stared ahead as a stray tear rolled down her cheek. "I remember it as a stifling hot day. I had to go to London on the train for a meeting with my UK agent. I wasn't happy to have to be going. I would've much preferred to have been able to stay at home in the garden that day - it was so hot. When I got home late that night I found Cal slumped on the floor beside his writing desk.

If I'd been at home that day, he might have been saved. He was only fifty-eight years of age."

"Oh no, Red, I'm so sorry. That's awful. He was so young. You must have been devastated."

Red looked around at me. She wiped her eyes and took a deep breath. "I was, and still am to be honest. After he died I fantasised about being one of those couples that you hear of – where the spouse dies from a broken heart within days of their loved one. I almost envied the dead, that they could be with him and I was left behind on my own. I still feel a little like that to be honest – almost looking forward to my own death, to the moment when I finally get to see him again, feel his arms around me." Her eyes had filled up with tears again.

I was quite taken aback to hear her speak of her own death in such a way when she still seemed so full of life.

"I miss him every second of every day," Red went on, managing to hold back the tears, "but I feel so blessed to have had those years with him – they were, without a doubt, eighteen of the happiest years of my life. And I think, in many ways, that Cal prepared me for this time of my life all along."

"What do you mean?"

"Well, he always advised me to follow my passions, you see?" Red sat forward. "'You have to follow your own path,' he'd say. 'The only person who is with you for your entire life is yourself, so you have to make damn sure to make yourself happy – or you could be in for one very long, very miserable, life.' I remember laughing when he said that – I never imagined being in this life again without him. But he was right – even though his death broke my heart and I miss him every moment of every day, and with every fibre of my being, I know I'm going to be okay."

It was sad but somewhat consoling to hear her words, but there was one more thing I felt I needed to ask her.

"Red, do you mind me asking – did you and Cal ever have children?"

Red shook her head. "No – we didn't get married until we were both into our forties and Cal had had such a bad experience trying to have a family with Lizzie . . . it wasn't really something that was ever on the cards for us."

"And do you ever feel sad about that? I mean, was there ever a time when you wished you'd had children? It's just that I'm worried that might happen to me – if I do decide not to settle down, not to have children myself."

Red looked at me for a few seconds. "Well yes, if I'm honest, every now and then I wonder what it might have been like to have had my own children – to have seen my own or Cal's eyes looking back at us from little faces, to have watched them grow up. But that said, neither Cal nor I ever really had a burning desire to have children of our own so we soon accepted it wasn't going to be our lot in life to be parents. In the early years, when we first got together and most of our friends had young children – then, it was a little difficult. I think what saved us was making friends with people who were in the same situation, other couples and friends without children. I do think that no matter what stage in life you're at, it's so important to be around others who are at that same stage, experiencing similar things. You would always feel yourself to be the consummate outsider if you only surrounded yourself with people who are in a different place in life." She put her hand over mine on my knee.

"And I now realise that the key to happiness is to be grateful and content with what you do have. That was Cal's and my philosophy anyway – we weren't *always* successful in following it, but most of the time we managed."

I nodded slowly. "That all seems to make a lot of sense. And it sounds like the way everything worked out suited both you and Cal?"

"Yes, I firmly believe it was the right thing for us, but it didn't end there. Cal insisted that if we weren't going to have children that we needed to find some other meaning in our lives. He said that meaning is almost always derived from our relationship to other people – whether it's by loving another person or by helping or influencing people in some way. We loved each other, I reminded him, wasn't that enough?" She shook her head. "But no – he thought we could do better than that, so after Cal's second book did so well we decided to start a small foundation to support Lankazi school, the orphanage and other children's projects in Kamazuka, and eventually all over Zambia. From then on we always donated a percentage of any royalties we made to the Foundation – Cal from his books, me from my music and film work – and we used our contacts in the film and literary worlds to support the various fundraising events we held. As a result, our little foundation raised millions of pounds over the years." Red smiled and leaned in to me. "So I suppose what I've learned from it all, Chrissie, is that there are so many different ways to live – life cannot simply be a case of one-size-fits-all."

Her words made me think of my mother. She'd never been able to conform, to give up her passions.

"There are lots of different roles to be filled in the world, in society," Red was saying. "We just need to find the one that best suits the person we are. Cal and I wouldn't have fitted half as much into our lives as we did if we'd had children, and yet we were lucky enough to have worked with, and helped so *many* children and young people. We got to do the work we loved and we had so many adventures – and thankfully we had the time, freedom and money to do it all. I mean, sure – parenthood is wonderful – everybody who does it says so, so it must be true. All I'm saying is that if, for whatever reason, it turns out not to be for you, Chrissie, well, the alternative is pretty damn good too. Life is what you make of it – how you play the cards life deals you."

I smiled at her. "Well, it sounds like you're still enjoying life, Red? Despite everything that's happened."

She nodded. "It's the music that has kept me going, Chrissie. Through everything, music has been my passion. That's why it worries me when I hear you say you don't sing any more. I've heard other musicians describe music as something they can't live without, something that not only allows them to be, but enables them to enter into new realms. One singer once told me that music breathes life into her soul, another musician said that his fiddle was like a fifth limb to him. But for me . . . well, I always thought of my music like the wheels of a bike – it keeps me moving, propels me forward, often at a greater speed than I intended – at times even like I'm free-wheeling down a steep hill! But it's what's kept me going through the good times and the bad. When I have music in my life those wheels keep on turning, when I don't, they slow down or grind to a halt, like a needle stuck on a record."

She tapped my hand. "I think you and I may be alike in that way? If you're feeling stuck and can somehow find your way back to the music, Chrissie, it could just be what you need to help you move forward again."

I nodded slowly as I thought about her words. "You could be right," I said eventually. "I'll think about it, Red. I certainly would like to do something musical again. I was never very comfortable performing, but you seem to have had such a fulfilling musical career in other ways. You've really made me think today." I gave her a smile, feeling more at ease about my life than I had done in a long time. Almost excited about it again.

But there was still one thing bothering me, one question I wanted to ask her.

"Red, are you worried about living alone now or worried that you'll be alone at the end?"

I expected her to look sad and to explain how she dealt with loneliness but instead she smiled. "Goodness me, no. I've always had heaps of people around me – friends, family – from the very young to the very old, and everything in between. I've a big family and I've never had trouble making friends. Cal and I grew very close to Lyliko over the years too – especially since she moved to England to go to college. She became like a daughter to us and young David is like my grandson now. We're all so close." She smiled. "I'll be just fine."

"What about love, though?" I asked. "Do you think you'll ever marry again?"

"Oh no!" Red shook her head. "I could never find a man to match my Cal. He wasn't just a man – to me he was a giant of a man."

"But you might find another good man?" I said.

"Surely there can be more than one person for each of us in this life?"

"Ah, the optimism of youth!" Red smiled at me. "No, no, I was lucky enough to have had one great love in my life – that's more than enough for me." She looked wistful for a moment. "Do you know Cal and I never spent a single night apart after we married? One time when we were travelling through Canada by train and our cabin only had bunk beds, we squashed into one bunk rather than sleep apart. My but that was a steamy night!" She laughed, then looked a little embarrassed. She patted my hand then, stood up and put her hands on her hips. "I'm afraid I've been rambling on far too long, Chrissie."

I stood up too and stretched. "You never know though – you could meet someone at any time, Red."

She smiled. "No, this old bird is resigned to being without her mate. It's not the worst – I mean, of course I get lonely. It's the small things I miss really, like when something good, or something bad happens, and I instinctively go to tell Cal then realise once again that he's not here. But I do talk to him. On our wedding anniversary each year, and any other time I get particularly lonely for him, I come to visit this place where we got married. I sit here under our eucalyptus trees and have long chats with him." She looked up at the branches over the bench. "I feel closest to him here, in this place. And in my head, he's talking back to me and still boring me rigid with all his useless facts." She smiled and looked back at me. "And I wouldn't have it any other way."

And even though she'd lost the love of her life, she certainly did look at peace.

Red looked at her watch then. "Heavens, it's ten past

eight already! I have a wedding tomorrow to get ready for – I'd best get moving." She took a step towards me, put a hand on each of my shoulders and kissed me on the forehead. "It's been so lovely to chat with you, Chrissie – thank you for listening to my stories. I've enjoyed reminiscing."

I smiled at her and wished she didn't have to go, I would have liked to have gone on talking to her for longer. "No – thank *you*, Red. It's been so wonderful to have met you and to have been able to think about something . . . someone . . . else for a few hours. I've so enjoyed hearing your story – it's given me lots to think about."

"Well, you're welcome, sweetheart. I've loved meeting you too." She pulled me into a big hug then. "I might see you about the place tomorrow," she said after pulling back. "But if not, best of luck with Tim and with everything else. I've no doubt you'll make the right decisions and all will be as it should be in the end." She patted my right shoulder, then smiled at me as she left.

I watched her disappear off around the side of the inn, then sat back down on the bench and stared at the woods ahead, almost in a daze.

Red had indeed given me a lot to think about. Her story had got me thinking about my own path, my passions in life. Perhaps it was time I worked out what they really were and began to follow where they led me?

But could I do that while married to Tim? And if I did say no to Tim's proposal, would I be no better than my mother? Would refusing to marry Tim just delay the time when I would have to settle down anyway? Might I be throwing away my one chance of security, my chance to finally put down roots with a good, solid, dependable man?

So many questions spiralled around and around my head.

I thought of Red and Cal then. After so many years, they had firmly planted their roots together in England. I looked up at the eucalyptus trees, a symbol of their commitment. Should I be doing the same, committing to Tim? Or if I did that would I just be doing so to prove something to my mother, to prove that the way she acted wasn't right? To prove that I wasn't like her.

The thing was, I was beginning to understand her choices a little better. I still couldn't agree with her decisions, but I was beginning to understand better why she'd felt the need to carry on travelling.

I sat there for a few more minutes staring above at the intertwined trees. I knew I needed to try to clear my head. I checked my watch – it had just gone twenty past eight. I wasn't tired enough to go to sleep and I didn't particularly want to spend the night of my birthday alone in a hotel bedroom. I thought that a short walk around the grounds might be just what I needed so I grabbed my bag and left the eucalyptus trees behind.

Part three

The Starling

Chapter 21

I walked around by the side of the inn, turned the corner and got a shock when a bicycle seemed to come from nowhere, almost running me over. I jumped back just in time to avoid it.

"Oh my goodness, I'm so sorry!"

The man stopped a few feet past me. He jumped off his bicycle then and I recognised him as old Mr Thorpe. He was dressed in cycling gear – a short-sleeved, navy-blue cycling shirt and tight black cycling shorts. A red cycling helmet covered his wild white hair which was sticking out from underneath. He quickly unstrapped the helmet from under his beard, put his bike on its stand and came back to me.

"Are you all right, my dear? I'm most dreadfully sorry for almost running you over there."

Up close, Mr Thorpe's looked more like his eighty-six years. A tall man, though he seemed quite fit, he had deep wrinkles around his kind brown eyes and his wild white hair and beard betrayed his advanced age.

I held up both my hands. "I'm absolutely fine. Please

don't worry. I'm the one who should be apologising – for not looking where I was going."

But Mr Thorpe wasn't letting me take the blame. "Not at all. It was wholly my fault. I was trying to get a quick cycle in before dusk – it's such a good time to see the birds as they come in to bed down for the night. This was always my wife's favourite time – and daybreak too." He sighed then smiled sadly. "We rarely missed them."

I was instantly intrigued at the mention of the old woman again. "It sounds like Mrs Thorpe really loved the birds and these woods?"

The man's eyes lit up and he stood up straighter. "Yes, indeed." He looked behind me at the inn then. "I suppose I should really be inside welcoming our friends and family for the wake." He looked back at me then. "Did you know my wife? I'm sorry, perhaps I should recognise you? There's just so many people around today, I can't remember who everyone is. Christine was the one who remembered how we knew everyone, remembered all the names – she never forgot a single person." He looked lost in thought for a moment before he remembered me. "Sorry . . . yes, now how did you know my Christine?"

I decided it was time to come clean – whatever about Mrs Gates, I couldn't fib to an old man in mourning for his wife.

"I didn't actually know her personally," I said, "but I saw the piece about her death in the paper last weekend. To be honest, it caught my eye at first because we share the same first name. Well . . . my name is Chrissie, but it's short for Christine." I felt my cheeks redden – the more I spoke, the dafter the whole thing sounded. "And then when I read the article," I went on, "I thought she

286

sounded like such an interesting, inspiring lady. So much so, that I wanted to come along this weekend to pay my respects."

"Now there's a thing." Mr Thorpe shook his head slowly, all the while rubbing his bushy white beard with the tips of the fingers of his right hand. "There's a thing."

I wasn't sure if he was referring to mine and his wife's shared first name or to my deciding to come to her memorial. A moment's silence passed between us and I felt very awkward – an intruder at a very private, personal time for this man and his family. "I'm so sorry for your loss, Mr Thorpe," I said. "I'll leave you to your cycle now."

I turned to go but he reached out to stop me, catching my arm. "Please."

I turned back around and he smiled.

"Call me Harvey, dear."

I smiled back at him and felt a lot more at ease.

"You see, Chrissie . . . the thing is, I'm not sure I can do this cycle tonight." He looked back up at the entrance to the woods. "I've been trying to find the courage to go up there every evening since Christine died, but I just can't do it – I haven't had the heart. I get as far as the start of The Songbird's Way," he pointed to the entrance of the woods ahead, "before I have to turn back." He looked back at me. "It's just that I've never cycled this path on my own before. We always did it together – Christine and me – right up to the evening before she died. Always together." His voice cracked then and he looked away from me back up at the woods. "The Songbird's Way is her path, you see – her way. She had it laid out some years back to run along under the trees, giving the cyclists and

287

walkers that come here shelter from the sun in the summer and from the rain and wind in winter." He looked back at me. "It snakes up past so many beautiful spots for birdwatching. Did you know, for example, that Collinswood is one of the best places in the country to hear nightingales?"

I nodded. "Actually I did know that. I was here many years ago with my parents – back when it was just a crumbling old inn and an overgrown woodland. My folks have both since passed away but we heard a nightingale sing that day. I have a very vivid memory of it." I put my hand in my pocket and pulled out the figurine, undoing the bubble wrap. "My father gave me this shortly after that day – not long before he died."

Mr Thorpe took the china bird from me and inspected it. "It's an extraordinarily good likeness of a nightingale," he said, glancing up at me for an instant before looking back at the figurine. "They're really quite ordinary, dull-looking birds I suppose, but I find them strangely beautiful, and their song is like no other – just mesmerising. My Christine loved them."

He went to hand the figurine back to me, but seemed to change his mind then and pulled his hand back. "Chrissie, this might sound quite odd . . ." he looked back up at the woods, "but I wonder if I might be able to interest you in a short cycle this evening? The Songbird's Way is a lovely cycle path – and it leads up to the clearing where the birds put on quite a show as they settle down for the night."

I was a bit surprised. "Are you sure you want me to join you, Harvey? I mean this must be a very difficult time for you – wouldn't you rather go with someone you know?" I gestured behind me with my thumb. "I could pop in and fetch a friend or one of your family?"

Harvey shook his head. "I don't think there's anyone here who would fully appreciate the magic of this place at dusk – not like she did. But, you –" he looked at me through squinted eyes, "I have a hunch that you just might, Chrissie." He stood up straighter and glanced to his left away from the woods. Then he handed me back my nightingale and held up the palm of his hand. "Please. Wait here. Don't go – I'll be back in just a jiffy."

I put the figurine back in the bubble wrap and into my pocket, then watched him run off around the corner. For an old man he certainly was fit. I looked back up at the woods then. It was starting to get darker – was I prepared to cycle in there with a total stranger? I shook my head. Of course not. I was just about to try to find Harvey to tell him that unfortunately there was somewhere else I needed to be when he walked back around the corner towards me with another bicycle. I stared at it, mouth open, as he wheeled it up in front of me.

"My child, are you quite all right?" He looked at me with concern. "You look like you've just seen a ghost."

I glanced up at him, then looked back at the bike he was holding. "Yes, I'm sorry, I'm fine." I took a couple of steps forward and ran my fingers along the bike's frame. I didn't recognise the make – it wasn't a Raleigh, and it wasn't old or rusted. But otherwise it looked so much like Sky that it almost took my breath away. It was the exact same light blue colour, had a classic, sturdy frame and a large wicker basket at the front.

"Isn't she a beauty?" Harvey said. "This was my Christine's bike. She had it custom-made last year – she had a very clear idea of what she wanted – eighteen gears, easy to handle yet sturdy enough to make light work of our woodland tracks." He touched the handlebars. "It's an upright model though – she didn't want to have to lean too far forward – Christine's back got a bit stiff in recent years so she liked to sit upright. Otherwise, though, she was fit as a fiddle until the day she died."

He proudly held the bike out for me to take. I put one hand on the handle furthest from me and one leg over the frame. I sat up on the saddle then, my right foot still on the ground. The bike was indeed a beauty – it didn't just look good, even the saddle seemed to mould perfectly to my shape.

"Better make sure to stay safe." Harvey took a white helmet out of the wicker basket and handed it to me. I put my handbag into the empty basket and the helmet on my head as Harvey walked back over to his own bike. And then before I knew what I was doing, I'd cast aside all sense, reason and logic and, as dusk approached, I found myself cycling behind a perfect stranger up into the woods.

Harvey glanced around for me as he passed the entrance. I cycled up alongside him as the path started to incline slightly. The setting sun was already quite low behind us, shining dimly through the trees, warming our backs as if to encourage us along the way.

Harvey gave me a thumbs-up sign. "I did it this time – I made it this far. I had a feeling you would be my lucky charm, Chrissie!"

I smiled and waved at him, already glad I'd taken the leap of faith and joined him on the cycle. It felt good to be on a bike and such a beauty too – it made light work of the incline and I hardly felt the uneven ground beneath. In fact I felt very much at ease as we followed the path up through the canopy of trees. The birds were still singing around us and the wild roses, foxgloves and other wild flowers dotted around the woodland bed provided a pretty splash of colour in contrast to the greenery of the trees and the moss.

Harvey was cycling a little ahead at one point. "There's your nightingale," he shouted back to me, holding up one finger to point into the woods to our left. He kept cycling on and, sure enough, as I passed by the spot where he'd pointed I recognised the sweet birdsong that had so enchanted my parents all those years ago. I remembered my father singing to my mother, his heartfelt proposal and her refusal.

"The trees get very tall up here!" Harvey shouted, jolting me away from my memories.

"Yes, they're huge." I had to stop my bike for a moment to put my head right back to see the tops of the tall birch trees. "Very impressive!" I shouted up to him, but he'd already cycled on.

I started to fall a little behind then and my breathing grew more laboured as our bikes weaved along the winding path and climbed higher up into the woods. I was very relieved when the path finally unwound before us and opened up into a clearing. Harvey stopped and stood, one foot either side of his bicycle. I cycled up behind him and instantly recognised it as the place where I had picnicked with my parents all those years earlier. The trees gave way to a wide open space – a patchy grassland area dotted with red poppies. The clearing stretched out ahead of us as far as the eye could see. We could just make out the silhouette of the mountains in the hazy disappearing light.

I'd grown quite hot from the cycle so I welcomed the cool evening breeze that gently tousled my hair when I took off my helmet. Harvey had already taken his own helmet off and had balanced it by its strap across the saddle. He put the stand of his bicycle down, then strode out into the clearing. When he got out into the last fading patch of sunlight, he pushed his chest out and held his arms back before inhaling a very long, deep breath.

He spun around to me. "Isn't it beautiful?" he said. But before I could answer, he'd turned away from me again, and though I couldn't quite make out all the words, I think he said something like: "It's good to be back, my dear. I'm sorry I was away so long."

I rested my helmet on top of my handbag in the wicker basket, got off my bike and leaned it on its stand. I looked to my left and saw the big tree trunk nestling alongside the edge of the wood – exactly where it had been when I'd picnicked there with my parents on my mother's thirtieth birthday.

I closed my eyes and I was back twenty-two years – I could see our old green-and-purple-checked picnic rug spread out in front of the tree trunk, our Tupperware containers full of sandwiches, the red apples, and the clashing red tartan flask of tea. I could see my father standing in front of the fallen trunk, his arms wrapped around my mother who was leaning back against him as she listened to him sing. And as the many birds continued to sing in the woods around us, I was sure I could pick out the lone song of the nightingale – chirping, trilling and whistling confidently – sounding determined and clear in the darkening woods.

I opened my eyes and walked over towards the tree trunk. It was as big as I remembered – lying on its side it was as high as my shoulder. I closed my eyes again and walked the length of the fallen tree, feeling the contrast of its rough, coarse bark against the smooth skin of my fingertips. And before I knew what I was doing, I was humming the tune of 'Songbird' under my breath.

"What's that song you're singing, Chrissie?"

My eyes opened. I was almost surprised to see Harvey standing beside me at the tree trunk. In the moment I'd almost forgotten he was with me.

"It's just a song my father used to sing. This place . . . right here," I tapped the trunk, "this is where we came that day I mentioned earlier, Harvey – just before we found out how sick my father was. It was such a beautiful day – a perfect day really – well – until my mother spoiled it, that is."

Harvey raised his eyebrows "Oh dear. I'm sorry to hear that. How did she spoil it?"

And so I told Harvey about my mother's birthday and about her refusing to marry my father.

"I think that in many ways that moment was one of the saddest of my childhood – up there with the days my parents died or when my mother left me behind as a child to live with my grandmother in Ireland."

I turned and leaned my back against the trunk, Harvey did the same and we looked out through the haze at the faded shapes of the mountain in the distance.

"When we were here together that day," I went on, "everything I could have possibly dreamed of was there – right in front of me, but just slightly out of reach. Until my mother said no I'd always believed that someday it would all just work out, that my parents would get married and live together all the time – that I could finally know where I belonged and could feel safe, secure. I don't feel so angry any more and I think I may even be beginning to understand her better, but thinking about it all still makes me sad to this day."

Harvey said nothing for a few minutes, then turned and looked at the tree trunk we'd been leaning against.

"Come on," he said, gesturing to me to follow him.

I let him lead me around to a large rock that was leaning up against the middle of the back of the trunk. Harvey put his hand on the tree and a foot on the rock and pulled himself up on top of the trunk. He turned to look out at the clearing for a second before leaning back down and holding out his hand for me. I took it and hauled myself up onto the rock, then onto the trunk. Harvey sat down then and I sat beside him. I looked out at the clearing – the rolling hills in the distance had become ever more obscure in the fading orangey-grey glow. Speckled lights had started to come on across the distant countryside – clusters of them together indicating the small Kentish towns and villages.

"This place has many good memories for me," Harvey said. "It's the very spot where I proposed to Christine – so many years ago now."

"Really? Gosh, I didn't realise. I'm sorry if I sounded negative about it, Harvey – I didn't mean to put a dampener on your memories."

"Not at all," he said, patting my hand. "Your memories are important too." He looked out into the distance. "I was just fifty-six when Christine and I met at my son's wedding at The Three Songbirds. A year to the day later, we came back up here for a walk." He looked around at me. "You couldn't cycle up here in those days – these landscaped tracks are all new. Christine and I had them done after we bought the place almost twenty years ago."

I nodded. "You did such a wonderful job."

"Thank you. We were very happy with it." Harvey smiled. "It was this sort of time of day – just before sundown that we first walked up here together. It was so beautiful then," he waved his hand around in front of us, "wild and rugged, just as it is now. And even though I hadn't planned it, I asked Christine to marry me that day." Harvey laughed. "Thankfully she said yes!" He looked more serious then. "She was like an angel sent to save me, you know? By the time we got together we'd each been through so much in our lives – painful divorces, separations, deaths of loved ones. But we were lucky – love took us both by surprise and we had three blissfully happy decades together – I couldn't have asked for more." He looked around at me again. "I always thought I'd go before her, you know? Even though she was a few years older than me. She was so fit and healthy – always raring to go – right up to the end." He tilted his head sideways. "I mean, she slowed down a bit over the last few years, and her back gave her some problems, but otherwise she was in good health and we enjoyed our life together – the ups and the downs – right up until the end." He smiled and turned to me again. "Did they tell you that we were due to have a big concert at the centre for her ninetieth birthday this year?"

I shook my head. "No, I didn't know that. I mean, I knew there would be music at the memorial but I hadn't heard about a concert . . ."

Harvey nodded. "Yes – lots of old friends were due to fly in for it from all over the world – but she didn't quite make it to ninety in the end. They all still came – but for her wake and memorial instead. There'll be lots of music tomorrow." He sighed. "Sad to think my lovely girl won't be here to enjoy it – she always did love a good music session."

My heart really went out to him. I was trying to think of some words of comfort when I became distracted by some movement in the sky above. I looked up just as an enormous swarm of birds swooped down, then back up through the sky. They moved together almost as a single organism, perfectly synchronised, swirling and rolling through the sky at a breakneck speed. Their movement made a loud swooshing noise each time they passed by overhead.

"Oh my, it's a murmuration! What luck!" Harvey stood up on the tree trunk and I jumped up beside him. "It's a group of starlings," he said. "They do this sometimes just before darkness descends – just as they come in to roost for the night. We're very lucky to see it."

I looked back up at the sky and became entranced by the graceful aerial ballet unfolding before my eyes. For over five minutes, the birds kept perfect pace together, the flock appearing like a beautiful, black wave, rippling and tumbling across the sky. Our heads bopped up and down as we watched them rise and fall, twist and turn.

"There must be well over two hundred of them," Harvey said. "More perhaps. See how more fly in to join the flock."

"It's incredible!" I stood with my hands on my hips, barely able to take in the sight. "Why do they fly like that, Harvey?"

"Nobody is quite sure," he said. "It could be to protect these small birds against larger birds of prey, or it could be to act as a beacon to smaller flocks commuting back to the main one. It's thought that they move together in formation in groups of seven – each bird tracks the movements of six other birds – to keep them all from colliding. Their reflexes are about thirteen times as fast as ours."

I was quite overcome by the spectacle but I tried my best to take it all in. The birds moved together in perfect harmony, synchronising their movements so closely that they seemed to move together as one. And as I watched them my own spirit joined them and soared to their height. I was right there with them – dipping and weaving, rising and twirling. It was such a glorious sight that it felt like there had to be meaning to it, a reason why Harvey and I had been right there at the right moment to witness it. I wondered if it could even be a message – sent from above to lift my spirit, to lift me.

Harvey touched the top of my arm. "Watch now, they're starting to settle down into the trees to rest for the night," he said, "ready to awaken with the sunrise, to go their own way again. They'll have all day to be themselves then, to go out foraging for food, to build their nests or seek out a mate. And that's when you'll hear these starlings really sing – and my, are they noisy! Interesting little fellows though – their song is a series of clear whistles followed by a variety of sequences that they have often copied from other species of bird – sometimes they even repeat man-made noises. After that comes a number of types of repeated clicks followed by a final burst of high-frequency song. Each bird has its own repertoire with more proficient birds having a very wide range of variable song types and clicks." He folded his arms and bounced up and down on his toes. "You know you're feeling good yourself when you notice a bird's song, don't you?"

The starlings were chattering, clicking and tweeting loudly as they settled down on the tops of the trees. The noise was quite chaotic, but beautiful.

I turned around to Harvey. "That's true actually. I never thought of that."

"Oh yes." Harvey nodded. "This is where Christine and I were happiest – in the morning we listened to the birds sing, and most evenings she would sing to me herself, right here in this very spot, with the birds as her backing singers."

I looked at him for a moment. "So is this where you feel most at home, Harvey? At The Three Songbirds? Collinswood? Is this the place where you feel you really belong?"

"Heavens, no!" Harvey looked at me almost in surprise. "I've travelled all over the world and the one thing I do know is that home is nothing to do with a place, Chrissie dear." He shook his head. "No, no, no. The place is nothing without the people. You see, it's wherever your heart is, wherever the people you love and care for are – *that's* where your home is. And that can be anywhere – we can choose to put roots down anywhere, anytime." He put his hand on my shoulder. "In any one lifetime, many different places can conjure up deep emotions within a person – but that's just because those places are a tangible, physical reminder of the people we loved, and of the happy times we shared when we were there. Places are just landmarks to the memories we share with the people we loved." He turned to look directly at me. "The thing is, Chrissie – we don't really need a place for that. We can keep those people, those memories, right here." He touched his heart and smiled. "I'm glad I was able to come back here one more time. Thank you, my dear, for coming with me." He took a deep breath in then. "I'm ready now. I'm ready to say goodbye to my love." Tears started to roll down the crevices of his craggy cheeks as, still holding his hand on his heart, he turned and stared out across the clearing. I put my hand on his elbow, but he didn't react. It was as if I wasn't there at all. Instinctively, I turned to go, touching him gently on the shoulder to let him know I was leaving. He put his hand over mine for a moment to acknowledge my touch. Then I climbed down onto the rock to give an old man the space to say goodbye to his love.

I walked back over to my bike, stepping over the fresh white carpet of droppings on the ground beneath the trees. It had grown darker but the starlings were still chattering noisily above as if delighted to be back together for the night and busy exchanging the news of the day. I put my helmet back on then glanced back at the tree trunk at Harvey who was still staring out into the distance.

I thought about his words. For so long I'd been yearning to find my roots, regretting that there wasn't one place in the world where I felt I belonged above all others – that all-elusive home. When all along it had been right there in front of my eyes, in the *multitude* of places where I had loved and been loved. Whether my mother was in Dingle or London, Nairobi or Amsterdam – wherever she was, that was my home. The same with my father and

Uncle Donal and Aunt Gem in Greenwich, and my grandmother in Dingle. I didn't need a single place and I didn't need one person to give me the singular sense of identity I'd craved for so long. It had been inside me all the time – nestling safely within my memories of times spent with people I'd loved, people I'd always love.

The realisation made me feel more at ease than I ever remember feeling in my whole life and I smiled as I watched Harvey climb down from the tree trunk a couple of minutes later. He strolled slowly towards me then, his hands on his hips as he walked. He smiled sadly when he reached me, then he turned and looked back out at the clearing again. The sun had almost completely vanished down behind the distant mountains and was now casting a hazy red glow over the clearing, and the lights of the towns and villages were twinkling in the distance. It was such a beautiful sight, very difficult to look away from.

"I wish she could have been here tonight," Harvey said. "Just to see all this one last time."

"I think she is here, Harvey." I looked out at the night sky. "In fact, I reckon she's up there with my mother and father smiling down on us right now. How else could you explain all this?" I waved my hand around me. "The starlings, the nightingales, this beautiful evening? I think it's their gift to us this night."

Harvey turned to me and smiled. "You could be right, my dear." He took one last look around before walking over to his bike and putting his helmet on. We cycled back to the centre in silence, free-wheeling most of the way down the winding cycle path, the dim summer evening just bright enough to light our way.

When we got back to the centre I wheeled my bike into

the bike shop behind Harvey. The shop was already locked up but he had his own set of keys.

"Do come and join us in the bar for a drink," Harvey said after we put the bikes away and were walking towards the entrance of the inn. "We're having a bit of a wake for Christine tonight. You should come."

There were lots of people milling around inside the inn and I could hear some lovely folk music coming from the direction of the bar. I was tempted to stay, but I was absolutely exhausted. It had been quite a day – I couldn't really believe that just that morning I'd been working in the market and worrying about the party later that afternoon. Seeing my grandparents at the birthday party, then Tim's proposal and my dramatic escape through the thunderstorm to Kent was a lot to handle in one day. And it had been very emotional being back in Collinswood, by the tree trunk in the clearing. The memory of my parents was so vivid, and the stunning images of the murmuration so fresh in my mind. I was absolutely drained and needed some time alone to process it all. But I was very glad I'd come – meeting Red and Harvey had made me think about my life . . . my thrisis . . . in a new way. I felt lighter, perhaps even closer to the point where I would be able to make some decisions.

"Thank you so much, Harvey, but I'm exhausted. I'd best check into my room and get some sleep." I gave him a big hug and wished him well for the morning.

There was nobody at the reception desk so I walked past it and along the corridor enclosing the eucalyptus trees. They were all lit up, the little spotlights in the ground creating an almost magical, fairy-tale effect. I walked on and passed by the hushed door of the Green

Room, following the signs for Room 103. I climbed the short flight of stairs and turned right at the top as the sign directed, and that's when I noticed that there was a man sitting on the floor at the end of the short corridor. He was crouched over, his head down on the folded arms that were resting on his knees. He looked up when he heard me approach – then he jumped up.

"Chrissie, where the hell have you been?" he shouted as he strode up the corridor towards me.

I stopped dead in my tracks when I realised who it was.

Chapter 22

Tim looked awful. His eyes were bloodshot, his face looked pained and he was clearly furious with me.

"I'm so sorry, Tim." I reached out to touch his arm as he got to me, but he yanked it back.

"Sorry? You're sorry?" he sneered. "Oh well, that's okay then. You walk out of a house full of people there for your birthday, less than ten minutes after we get engaged . . . and all you can say is you're sorry? Jesus, Chrissie, what the hell is going on with you? What are you trying to do to me?"

I kept my head bent as he spoke – I couldn't look him in the eye. When he finished I took in a deep breath – it was shaky as I exhaled. I dared to look up then and he really did look distraught. I felt so awful.

"I'll try and explain." I nodded behind him down the corridor. "Let's go on down to the room."

Tim closed his eyes for a few seconds as if trying to stay calm. Then he stood aside to let me pass.

I walked down the short corridor until I got to the end to Room 103. I slipped the key-card into the door.

Tim followed me inside. It was quite a big room for a country inn. There was a king-size bed on the left-hand side by the wall, flanked by two small bedside lockers. A built-in wardrobe stood across from it. No television, but a kettle and tea and coffee were laid out on a dressing table beside the wardrobe. The walls were white and hung with abstract forest and leaf pictures. A lovely big cream-coloured armchair sat facing double glass doors on the other side of the room. A small balcony lay just behind the doors – it overlooked the trees of Collinswood at the back of the inn. For a moment I wished I could have been there on my own – to just have been able to curl up in the armchair with the balcony doors open to listen to the heartbeat of the woods as they bedded down for the night.

I tossed my handbag on the bed and turned around to face Tim. He closed the door, and took a few steps inside.

"So?" He stared at me.

But I had no idea what to say. How could I give a satisfactory explanation for what I'd done?

I sat down on the bed. Tim stayed standing.

"How did you know where to find me?" was all I could think of to say.

Tim reached into his pocket and threw a piece of paper at me. "I got your note."

I caught it and opened it up, recognising my writing.

"I had to press Abigail to tell me where you'd gone. She said she didn't know, but she gave me this –" He handed me a second piece of paper.

I unfolded it and recognised the newspaper article about Christine Thorpe's memorial that I'd cut out.

"I put two and two together then," he said. "The woman at the front desk confirmed it for me from the register. I've been sitting outside this damned room for almost three hours now. *Fuuuck!*" He turned away from me and pounded the wall behind him with the palm of his hand.

I jumped up and put my hand on his back. "Tim, don't. I'm so sorry. I never meant to hurt you, I just had to get away."

He spun around to face me. "Why, Chrissie?" He took both my arms and looked at me with such intensity. "Why did you have to get away from a party of all your friends and family? And why come here? You didn't even know this woman."

"I-I think I just felt a connection to her." I took a step away from him and picked up the newspaper clipping from the bed. "I noticed the article about her death in the paper at first mainly because we shared the same first name but then, as I read about her, I became more interested in her. I thought if I came to her memorial service I could find out more about her. And this was a place I came to with my parents not long before Daddy died. I almost felt like I had to come."

But Tim wasn't buying my story about Mrs Thorpe or about my parents. "I've been planning today for months, Chrissie. It was all for you, everything was for you. Why in God's name would you have to jump in the car that I just gave you and drive halfway across Kent to get away? Do you despise me that much?"

"No, no – of course not." I closed my eyes for a few seconds, then opened them and looked at him. "Tim, please, can't we sit down?"

"Why? So you can change the subject? Avoid the issue somehow." He took a step towards me. "You never deal with what's really bothering you, Chrissie. This memorial thing – coming here – it's all classic Chrissie avoidance. You seem to have this disassociated approach to life – never talking about what's really bothering you, ignoring your own needs and problems while idealising other people – your father – that damned Brian – Abigail – and now this old dead woman." He raised his hands in frustration. "Why won't you tell me what it is that's really wrong with you? Why you walked out today? We can't fix whatever it is unless we talk about it."

"I'm sorry, Tim." It sounded so lame. I knew I had to do better. I had to try to make him understand that he couldn't fix everything – that there were some things I had to work out for myself. "I just didn't want to hurt you," I said eventually, "or cause an argument."

Tim grabbed one of my elbows. "My God, Chrissie. I long for an argument! Something . . . anything . . . that will help me to understand what you're feeling . . . what you want."

I pulled my arm away. "But what if you can't give me what I want?"

Tim flinched. Then he nodded slowly and looked down at his feet. "Well, then, I'll have to deal with that." He looked back up at me then. "Whatever the situation, refusing to deal with problems doesn't make them go away, Chrissie. Quite the opposite."

I bit my bottom lip and nodded my agreement.

Tim sighed, then walked past me, turned the armchair around to face the room and sat down. "All right. I'm sitting down now. I'm sitting and listening. The floor is yours. Talk, Chrissie."

I went over, sat down on the edge of the bed facing him and took a deep breath in.

"I think I just felt overwhelmed by everything," I said eventually. "It was all too much – the car, the party . . . And it felt like everyone wanted to claim me – my mother's family, my father's family . . . you." I looked right at him. "I was beginning to feel that I, the real me, was disappearing. I felt like I was suffocating in the middle of it all."

Tim squinted at me. "It was just a party, Chrissie. We were all there to celebrate your birthday, that's all. Nobody wanted to claim you."

I pursed my lips together for a moment and with all the courage I could muster said: "Tim, you asked me to tell you how I feel. I'm trying to explain. It may not make sense to you, but it's how I felt, how I feel. I-I've always struggled to work out where I fit in – where I belong – and today everyone else seemed to be deciding for me."

Tim sat forward in the chair. "You belong with me, Chrissie. We're living together now. We'll be getting married soon. We're a unit. There's no need for you to worry about any of this, don't you see? Everything is going to be fine."

His voice sounded much softer which was a relief, and for a moment I thought about just nodding and begging his forgiveness. Letting the whole sorry day become little more than a bad memory – something to be forgotten as we proceeded with his plan to get married. But then Red's words flashed into my mind: 'You have to talk to him . . . to tell him how you feel. . . Whether it's telling someone you love them, or telling them you don't love them enough, it's much the same thing – you have to be honest.'

I knew Red was right. Suppressing my feelings had been slowly killing me, taking away my spirit. Meeting

307

her, and then Harvey, had reawakened something in me and I wasn't prepared to let it lie dormant again. No matter how difficult it would be, I had to at least try to help Tim to understand what I was feeling.

"See? You're doing it again," I said. "Telling me what I should be doing, where I belong – when right now the only place I want to be is right here." I sat up straighter. "The party was wonderful, Tim. You've been amazing and kind and the most thoughtful boyfriend a girl could ask for." I took a deep breath in. "And you were a wonderful support after my mother died and after I broke up with Brian. I couldn't have got through it without you. You were there for me throughout all of it and I'll always be grateful to you for that."

He sat forward more and reached out for my hand. "I don't want your gratitude, Chrissie. We're a team, you and I – I'll always be there for you."

I squeezed his hand in mine and said nothing for a moment. I knew I had to stay strong, had to say what needed to be said. "You really saved me back then, Tim." I said eventually. "You were my rock." That was when it all started to get a bit too much for me – tears had welled up in my eyes and I felt as though my voice was going to crack. But I had to finish what I wanted to say. I let go of his hand, got up and walked over to the window to collect myself. I looked out of it for a few minutes.

Tim got up then too. He stood behind me, put his hands on my shoulders and gently rubbed them. "Look, it's okay, Chrissie. We'll sort this out. I was angry that you left the party without telling me, but I understand now that it was a very emotional day for you. Obviously your mother must have been on your mind on your birthday and I'm sure having your father's parents there brought up lots of difficult memories for you too." He turned me around to face him. "Let's forget about this for now. Go back to how we were yesterday – before the party."

"No." I shook my head. "I can't go back now, Tim." I moved away and sat back down on the bed, facing the window.

Tim looked surprised at my reaction, but he came over and sat down beside me on the bed.

I stared out the window at the darkening night sky. "I think by being with you, Tim, I've been trying to prove that I'm not like my mother. I've been trying to put down roots, to settle down. But the truth is . . ." I turned around to face him, "I realise now that I'm more like her than I've ever wanted to admit. I mean, I still think she was very wrong to have left me behind for so long when she went away, and I still wish I'd had a mother who was there for me all the time, but I understand her better now. I'm beginning to understand why she had to do it – it was just who she was really." I turned back to face the window. "But that's no reason for me to try to be something I'm not."

"What are you saying, Chrissie?" Tim sounded very worried.

I stared at the shadows of the swaying trees outside. "I met a woman here earlier today. She was twice my age and she's had such an interesting life, full of ups and downs, but packed with lots of amazing people, experiences and adventures. And I got the sense that she still has a few more adventures in store for her yet." I turned to face Tim. "I realise now that that's what I really want. Much as I thought I wanted to settle down, the truth is I don't want everything in my life to be decided already. I don't want to know that at thirty years of age the story of my life is more or less already written – the interesting part of it anyway." I turned around on the bed, leaned across it and picked up the newspaper article. I handed it to him. "Tomorrow is Christine Thorpe's memorial service – she was another woman who lived deliberately – right up to the last. I want to be like these women, Tim. I want to follow my passions, to live life my way – I don't want to die and realise that I haven't yet lived. So I'm going to go back to singing, to my music. And I want to travel some more. I want to see the world, to follow my own path and see where it leads me."

Tim glanced at the article then dropped it down on the bed beside him. "All right, I hear what you're saying, Chrissie, and I think it will be fine. With all your singing experience, I'm sure that you'd be able to get a job teaching music – with some training perhaps. And we can take more long-haul holidays. I'll get used to them in time, I'm sure."

I shook my head slowly, then took Tim's hand in both of mine. "I need to do this alone, Tim. You and I, we want different things. You want a wife, children, a happy home life – and you deserve all that."

"Yes, but I don't have to have it all right away – we have plenty of time. I can wait until you're ready for it too." He put his other hand on top of both of mine. "I love you, Chrissie. I want to be with you, no matter what. Don't you want to be with me? Don't you love me?"

I closed my eyes. When I opened them again they began to brim over with tears. "Tim, I-I . . ."

He read my face in a panic. "Oh fuck . . ." He let go

of my hands and pulled back from me. "What are you saying?"

I reached out to touch his arm but I couldn't reach him. "I do love you, Tim. I love you so much, but it's not the kind of love that you need, or deserve, from me." I brushed away my tears with my fingers. "I think I love you like a dear friend."

Tim stood up and stared down at me. "Are you serious? You love me like a friend? That's it? A friend? We just got engaged for fuck's sake!"

"No." I shook my head up at him. "No, we didn't."

"What are you talking about?"

"I didn't say yes, Tim. If you remember, I couldn't say it."

Tim's eyes widened. He rubbed his hand on the back of his neck, then walked away from me – over to the other side of the room.

"How long?" he asked.

I turned around to face him and I could see then he had tears in his eyes too.

"How long have you felt like this, Chrissie?"

I tried to wipe my own tears away with the back of my hand. "I don't know. Perhaps in some way I've always felt it? I've just never been able to say." I stood up. "I'm so sorry, Tim. I never meant to hurt you like this. Please believe me."

He looked away from me and dried his eyes with his sleeve. Then he turned and walked into the bathroom, shutting the door behind him.

I turned to stare out the glass doors at the darkness. I could scarcely take in what had just happened. I felt numb and have no idea how long I stood there. When Tim eventually came back into the room, he came over and stood beside me. We both stared together out at the night. After a minute or so, he handed me the box of tissues he was holding. I took one and wiped my eyes, then blew my nose. Tim did the same.

"I knew, you know?" he said after a while. "I knew all along that you didn't love me."

I turned and looked at him in surprise.

"Not enough anyway." He stayed staring ahead out the window. "I knew you were scared after your mother died. I knew how angry you'd been at her over the years, and then how alone you felt after she died. I thought that if I gave you the security you seemed to crave, gave you a nice home, a good lifestyle, a partner that loved you . . ." He sniffed. "Well, I guess I thought that we might be able to overlook the small fact that you weren't all that much in love with me." He sighed and turned to me. "Daft, eh?"

I put my hand on his arm. "The only daft thing about it is that you deserve so much more, Tim. You're an amazing man. You deserve to be with someone who loves you passionately, unconditionally. I haven't been fair to you, letting our relationship go on so long, letting it all get this far."

He sniffed again. "There's a pair of us in it."

I just squeezed his arm and smiled sadly.

"So what do we do now?" Tim raised his eyebrows and put his hands down into his back pockets.

I looked at my left hand and touched the ring he'd given me. I twirled it around on my ring finger a couple of times before taking it off.

"No, Chrissie." Tim held his hand up to stop me. He'd started to cry again. "You keep it."

I clasped the ring in my right hand, stepped towards him and held him. He wrapped himself around me then, burying his head in my shoulder and weeping openly into my hair. We stood there for quite some time just holding each other and crying.

Eventually I pulled back and we kissed one last time, then I put the ring into his front pocket and he didn't protest.

"You look exhausted," I said then.

"You're not looking so hot yourself." He made an attempt at a smile.

I managed a weak smile myself. "I'm absolutely shattered." I glanced at the bed.

"You go on to sleep," said Tim. "I'll go."

I took his arm. "Why don't you stay, Tim? It's late now and you're upset. I'd hate to think of you driving home on those country roads tonight."

It didn't take much to persuade him. It wasn't how either of us had expected my birthday night to end, but we were both exhausted in every way.

Tim and I fell asleep together for the last time that night. I knew breaking up was the right thing, but it was such a sad night and I clung to him, terrified to finally let him go. He did the same and we fell asleep like that, wrapped around each other.

I woke up very early the next morning to the sound of the room door closing. I looked around – Tim was gone. It was all over. I felt an overwhelming sense of sadness, but also of relief. I sank back down onto the pillow, and even though I thought I had no tears left in me, I cried myself back to sleep.

Chapter 23

I woke up with a start as a booming drumbeat came pounding up through the floorboards from below. I looked at my watch on the bedside table. It was just after ten. I couldn't believe it. I must have fallen back into a deep sleep after Tim had left. I sat up in bed – we'd left the curtains open the night before and the sun was streaming in the balcony doors.

That was when I recognised the music – it sounded like the African-Celtic fusion music of Red's group. The Green Room was just below my bedroom and I assumed they were down there rehearsing for the wedding again. This time I couldn't stop to listen to it though – the memorial service was due to start at eleven and I had to get ready.

I got up and jumped into the shower. I was very glad I'd remembered to pack clean underwear and, as I pulled my party dress back on over my head, I wished I'd had time to grab a fresh set of clothes too. It wasn't too bad though – I wouldn't look too out of place at a memorial service in a dark grey dress.

I patted the pocket of my dress as I straightened it out

– the china nightingale figurine was still there, safe and sound. I smiled to myself, then gathered my things and left the room to make my way down to Reception.

I was so tempted to pop my head around the door of the Green Room to say hello to Red as I passed by. I would have liked to have talked to her about the rest of my night – my cycle with Harvey, the break-up with Tim – but I didn't have enough time. So I passed it by, nodding my head to the rhythm of the music as I walked down the corridor. I passed a couple and their young child and smiled at them and, as I walked along past the atrium, I could just about see people moving around in The Venue on the other side of the eucalyptus trees. I assumed they were setting up for the memorial service so I quickened my step.

Mrs Gates was in her element presiding over the reception desk when I got there. The foyer was very busy with lots of adults and children milling around and Mrs Gates had just finished dealing with a group of well-dressed teenagers when I got to the desk. I wasn't quite sure where to go for breakfast, so I waited to ask her.

"Ah, there you are now, dearie!" She clapped her hands, tented her fingers together and held them up to her lips. She was wearing a lime-green long shirt with a contrasting emerald silk scarf draped around her neck. The scarf was patterned with life-size canary-yellow-and-scarlet bird silhouettes. "Did your young man find you last night?" She looked worried. "I wasn't sure if I should have given him your room number, but he said you'd left your mobile phone at home and there was no answer when I called your room. We had no way of reaching you and he said it was extremely urgent."

"That's okay, Mrs Gates." I smiled to reassure her. "I did see Tim and everything is fine. Thank you for directing him to me."

Mrs Gates heaved a dramatic sigh of relief. "Oh, thank goodness." She released her hands and waved them in the air.

I looked around. "I just wondered where I should go for breakfast."

Mrs Gates turned and looked at the clock on the wall behind her. "Oh dear – it's almost twenty past ten, and breakfast stops at ten o'clock on a Sunday." She turned to me. "The kitchen is very busy today too, so I fear they may be determined to stick to the rules." She must have seen my face fall. I was absolutely starving. "But no need to worry. Why don't you take a seat over there in the corner," she nodded to a coffee table and couple of armchairs over by the door, "and I'll see what I can do."

She left the reception desk and I dutifully sat over at the large round coffee table just beside the revolving entrance door. It kept turning with a steady flow of people, young and old, streaming into the centre. Most of them went straight through to the bar – probably on their way to The Venue, I thought. Everybody was dressed well, in bright colours, and some of the people were carrying instrument cases. I was particularly taken by a small group of African people who went up to the desk – the women and young girls in the group were wearing beautiful patterned, colourful skirts and very dramatic traditional African headdresses. I wondered if they were there for Lyliko's wedding later on, or perhaps they were friends of Mr and Mrs Thorpe. A few other people queued up at the empty reception desk behind the African group then and I felt quite guilty for taking Mrs Gates away from her station when it was so busy.

But I was so *very* hungry.

Mrs Gates reappeared after a few minutes carrying a big tray. On it was a tall silver coffee pot and a green earthenware mug, with matching milk jug and sugar bowl. There was a container full of small jam pots and an enormous basket of breads, scones and croissants. On a smaller green side plate was a selection of cheeses, and a pile of ripe, juicy strawberries and blueberries sat in a matching green bowl. It all looked divine – my dream breakfast.

"There you are now." Mrs Gates set the tray down in front of me on the low coffee table. "We can't have you going hungry."

"Oh my, this is wonderful! Thank you *so* much, Mrs Gates." I smiled up at her. "I'm so sorry for being late down and making you go to all this trouble."

"No trouble at all, dearie. Now eat up – the service starts at eleven and we'll be shutting everything up a few minutes before that so we can all be there."

I nodded and wasted no time picking out a warm, flaky croissant while Mrs Gates hurried over to the reception desk to deal with the newly formed queue.

I spread a piece of the croissant with the homemade strawberry jam and poured myself a cup of steaming coffee. I took a sip from my cup, then a bite of croissant just as a voice from over my shoulder said: "That looks awesome. Care to share?"

Still chewing the delicious buttery pastry, I wiped the stray flakes from my mouth with my napkin as I turned around.

"*Holy shit!*" I almost choked on my food when I saw who it was.

The man laughed. "I've been called some things in my life – often 'shit' but never 'holy'!" He rested the guitar case he'd been carrying up against a chair, then went around and pulled up the seat opposite me.

"I'm so sorry," I managed to say through a spray of crumbs. "It's just that . . ." I wiped my mouth again and remembered to breathe. "You . . . well . . . y-you're Ethan Harding, aren't you?" I gazed at my all-time favourite singer-songwriter who by then was sitting in the armchair opposite me, stealing a strawberry. I'd met some famous people in my life – especially during my time with *Celtic Wings* when they'd pop backstage to say hello to the cast after a performance. But I was always ready for them – I hadn't been expecting to bump into England's biggest-ever male solo artist over breakfast. Ethan Harding had the most incredible vocal range – better than any other contemporary rock or pop performer I knew. He could go from a very deep baritone to a high falsetto in one phrase of a song. To me he was a musical genius – each album he'd turned out over the years was better than the one before, and I had every single one of them. I'd loved him since I was a teenager and had even hung posters of him on the wall of my bedroom in my grandmother's cottage.

Ethan swallowed the stolen strawberry. "Yes, indeed, I am he." He reached out for another strawberry, but this time he paused, raising his eyebrows at me for permission.

"Oh yes. Absolutely." I nodded several times and pushed the bowl closer towards him. "Please, help yourself."

"Cheers!" He saluted me with a strawberry before

popping it into his mouth, speaking as he chewed: "I was up till the early hours at last night's wake – completely slept it out." He swallowed, then gazed at the spread in front of me. "I must admit I'm very envious of your food – the breakfasts here are legendary. I can't believe I missed it."

"I actually did too." I grinned inanely at him. I knew I must have looked like a complete idiot, but I couldn't help it. It was *Ethan Harding* after all! "Mrs Gates was kind enough to organise a tray for me," I somehow managed to say.

"Was she indeed?" Ethan glanced up at the reception desk where Mrs Gates was busy dealing with the African group. He pursed his lips, then turned back around and looked me up and down. "I see I wasn't alone in my struggle with the dress code."

I glanced down at my dark grey dress but didn't quite know what he meant. He picked up another strawberry then reclined back sideways in the armchair to eat it, his long, thin legs dangling over the arm of the chair, almost touching the floor.

"When practically every garment you own is black, what do you wear to a service where they insist you wear bright colours?" He popped the strawberry in his mouth and ate it quickly. "Mrs T was adamant she didn't want a sad funeral though," he went on. "She always said she wanted a wake and a memorial service – nothing too formally religious, though she wanted God to be there." He smiled to himself. "She was clear that she wanted it to be full of music where people remembered her life with laughter and colour though, and that was about the hardest part for me – the colour." He pulled at the long navy-blue shirt he was wearing over dark-green skin-tight jeans. The jeans were tucked into super-cool black boots with extra-long pointed toes. "This was about the best I could do – my wife found this shirt at the back of my wardrobe – behind all the black!"

I just nodded, and I kept nodding, all the while smiling like an idiot. It was all a bit too much – I suddenly didn't know what to say any more. I was quite overcome. Ethan Harding was just as beautiful in real life as he was on television. He still looked well for his forty-plus years. His hair was dark brown and long, covering his ears and neck, and he had a short stubble on his chin. As far as I knew he was at least ten, if not eleven years older than me, but I wasn't disappointed at meeting my idol – he was still the coolest, sexiest being I had ever laid eyes on.

Just then Mrs Gates arrived at our table. "Ethan! Sit up straight when you're eating." She slapped at his knees.

Ethan winked across at me then straightened up in his chair. "Hey there, gorgeous!" He pulled back to look at Mrs Gates and gave her a low wolf whistle. "*Hooo-eee*, are you lookin' hot to trot this morning, Maud, old girl! How *do* you stay looking so young and lovely?"

Mrs Gates couldn't help but smile. "One must make an effort for Mrs Thorpe." She patted her poker-straight grey bobbed hairdo and straightened her colourful scarf.

"Too true." Ethan smiled at me. "Too true." He took Mrs Gates' hand then and wrapped it in both of his. "In fact, I was just telling this nice young lady about how I missed your sensational breakfast this morning because I was up very late playing at Mrs T's wake. They kept requesting more songs – I just couldn't get away."

"I see," said Mrs Gates, pretending to look stern when

I could tell she was loving every moment of the interaction. "I expect you'll be wanting the star treatment now then? You know that you're still just plain old Ethan Harding to us – local lad, former lounge boy . . ." She laughed to herself. "You weren't even a very good lounge boy at that."

"I was a god-*awful* lounge boy!" Ethan rolled his eyes.

Lounge boy? Ethan Harding had been a lounge boy here? I never knew that and I thought I knew everything there was to know about him.

"Still," he went on, "surely that's enough sway to get me a cup of green tea and a morsel of food for ma poor, empty belly?" He poked at his stomach and made doe-eyes at Mrs Gates.

She rolled her eyes, but giggled nonetheless. It was a very amusing dynamic to watch.

"You're welcome to share this." I nodded to the feast of food in front of me. "It's far too much for just me and the memorial will be starting soon – we don't have that much time."

"Sweet! Thanks, doll." Ethan grinned at me and leaned over to grab the other croissant. He looked back at Mrs Gates then. "I'll get the tea from the kitchen myself, don't worry, Maud."

"No, no, you stay there and eat up. Reception's gone quiet for a minute. I'll get it."

Maud scurried off and I watched Ethan devour the croissant in three quick bites.

I picked up some bread. "So you knew Mrs Thorpe then?" I asked, trying to appear calm and collected as I reached for a piece of cheese.

Ethan had just reached over to my plate to borrow my knife. He stopped when I asked the question. "Yeah, I

321

knew Mrs T very well. In fact . . ." his voice grew a little shaky, "that woman made me. Christine Thorpe is an absolute bloody legend as far as I'm concerned."

Just then a group of three middle-aged women came over. They'd spotted Ethan as they were walking out the door and asked if they could take a photo with him. And even though they were disturbing his breakfast, Ethan got up and patiently posed with them for photographs. He chatted and laughed with the women as they each took it in turns to pose with him. I finished my piece of bread and cheese while watching, fascinated, silently thankful that I could eat in peace.

While it was all going on Mrs Gates came over and put a pot of tea and an extra mug on Ethan's side of the table. "The price of fame!" she said to me, just before she got roped in to take a group shot of all four.

When Ethan finally got a chance to sit down again he pulled a pair of dark shades out of his shirt top pocket and put them on. He spotted the tea then. "Ah, sweet! Good ol' Maud." He shuffled forward in his chair and poured himself a cup.

I folded up my napkin and took a sip of coffee before leaning forward myself. "Do you mind me asking, Ethan – how did you know Mrs Thorpe?"

He swallowed his mouthful of tea, then proceeded to tuck into the food, chatting between bites. "I used to work here – long time ago now. I come from Cobham, the next village over from Harkston, and I worked here as a lounge boy – started straight from school."

I had heard Ethan had done bar work near his home in Cobham before he became famous, but it was funny to think of the musical legend starting out at the bottom of the scale as a lounge boy.

"My father died a few years earlier," Ethan went on, "and then not long after I started to work here my mother died too."

"I'm so sorry," I said. "My parents have both passed too."

Ethan scrunched up his nose. "Sorry to hear that, sweetheart. It sucks, eh?"

I just nodded.

"My folks left me and my younger sister our small terraced house so we had a roof over our heads at least," Ethan said. "But I had to work to pay the bills. I was afraid social services would take Sarah into care if I didn't look after her properly so I couldn't leave home until she was finished school. I was still working here when Mr and Mrs T took over the place." He lowered his voice then and leaned in further. "It had turned into a bit of a kip by then really and the previous owners had just sold out. I was really worried when that happened – there were no other jobs going locally and it was going to be very bloody tight for both Sarah and me to live off my meagre dole payment. My sister was smart you see, very smart – she wanted to go to college. So we had all those worries, then The Three Songbirds closed and, soon after, all that stuff went down with the trees."

"Oh yes, Mrs Gates told me about that earlier. It sounded quite dramatic?"

Ethan smiled. "Yeah, the hype and the media attention were pretty exciting – it all livened the place up no end. In fact that was when I first saw the Thorpes in action. I didn't really get involved myself – I was just a disengaged, naïve kid back then – but I watched as they fought off those developer guys and made sure this place stayed intact. I was pretty impressed by them – the whole village was really. We were all psyched when they bought the inn afterwards – we expected things to pick up straight away. But the truth was, other than a few small renovations at the beginning, life pretty much went back to normal after the purchase, and soon we were back to the humdrum, sleepy pace of a country village. I got my old job back which was a relief but I was nineteen years of age and bored stiff – it felt like my life was going nowhere. The only thing that really interested me back then was music. Any spare time I had, I spent playing my guitar – singing – writing songs. One night Mrs T heard me playing in the cellar during a break – I was messing about with a song I'd been working on. It wasn't long after they'd taken over the place and the Thorpes were working here themselves – 'to get to know the ropes', Mrs T said." He put on a woman's voice to imitate Mrs Thorpe. "Anyway, she made me play her the song she'd overheard and she said she really liked it. I was stoked by that – other than my own family who'd heard me through my bedroom walls over the years, and Lawrence, Maud's old man and my boss, who let me practise in the cellar, Mrs T was the first person I'd ever properly played for. She encouraged me to practise and helped me to polish off a few of my songs, then a few months later when she felt I was ready, she gave me my first gig." He pointed his thumb over his shoulder without looking around. "Right out there in the bar."

"No way? *This* was the bar you were playing in when you were discovered?" I looked over his shoulder at the entrance to the bar with a newfound interest.

He nodded his head. "The very place. Man – that was

an awesome night! I was terrified beforehand – I was so insecure about my music at the time, but knowing that Mrs T believed in me and thought I was good enough really helped build my confidence. The gig went really well. I couldn't believe people liked my music. I will never, as long as I live, forget the feeling of first playing my own songs for a room full of people – it was positively terrifying and exhilarating all at the same time."

"I can only imagine," I said.

"The best feeling ever," Ethan smiled. "What I didn't realise before I went on, though, was that Mrs T had arranged for a couple of music producers to be in the inn that night. I don't know how she knew those guys or how she got them to come out to this one-horse town, but they were here. One of them approached me when I finished my set and offered me a record deal there and then. And the rest is history – I haven't stopped playing since."

"Wow! That's such an amazing story."

"Yeah, and it's not finished yet. Mrs T really stood by me. She and Mr T came to all my early gigs and they kept an eye on Sarah whenever I was away. To be honest, we consider Harvey and Christine to be our surrogate grandparents. They're awesome. And with their support, I got lucky – fame came pretty quickly. My first song went to number two in the charts."

"'Love on the Inside'," I said, proudly showing off my in-depth knowledge of the Ethan Harding repertoire. "It's one of my favourites."

"Yeah, that's the one." Ethan smiled. "That song opened the floodgates. And it was awesome for the first couple of years – bit of a whirlwind of concerts, TV shows, publicity tours and record launches, I loved it. But it was damn hard work – I was working fifteen to eighteen hours a day, seven days a week. I got a bit swept up in the party scene and even lost touch with the Thorpes for a few years. Sarah was in college – she's a doctor in Edinburgh now, married a Scot five years ago. Anyway, back then I was touring most of the time and when I wasn't working I was partying and getting deeper and deeper into the drug scene – it wasn't pretty. At the rate I was going, it was probably inevitable that I would hit rock bottom."

My idol's fall from grace had been well-reported. He'd been dating a beautiful, famous actress and by all accounts had fallen apart quite publicly when he discovered she was cheating on him with her co-star.

"I remember you disappeared for a couple of years all right. After your second album, wasn't it?"

Ethan nodded. "Yeah. My manager checked me into rehab in the States after a particularly nasty overdose episode. I was there for a month or so and I managed to get off the booze and the drugs – it was one of the hardest things I've ever done – in many ways, it still is. While I was there I got a call from Mrs T who'd managed to track me down through my manager. We hadn't seen each other in some years but she insisted I come back to The Three Songbirds after rehab – or 'back home' as she said. And that's what I did. I came back here to put my life back together. It wasn't easy, but the long break away from the music and party scene was exactly what I needed. For the first couple of months I was here, I actually did very little else other than sleep. The Thorpes gave me a room in the new wing they'd just had built. Room 103 – it's just above the Green Room at the back."

"No way!" I sat up straighter. "That's the room I

stayed in last night."

"Cool." Ethan smiled. "By the time I came back here, Mr and Mrs T had finished that whole part of the new wing and they were working on renovating the entrance and the old inn building at the front. The Green Room area at the back was one of the quieter parts of the centre as a result. I stayed here almost a year and a half in total – writing and getting myself back on track. The centre was coming together nicely and when it came to building the final part of the project – The Venue – Mrs T got me involved. Have you been inside it?"

I shook my head. "Not yet."

"It's small enough really for a music venue, but it's a wicked place for gigs – the acoustics are awesome. We spent a lot of time getting it right. When the new centre finally opened in full we used The Venue to give a platform to new musicians. I mean we got a few well-known names in too – to pay for its upkeep, but for the most part The Venue was built to give new younger groups and musicians a stage – somewhere to perform. We held summer camps during the holidays then for younger kids from disadvantaged backgrounds, using music to help them access their creative side. I helped Mrs T get it all going and, any time I visited, I taught the kids during the camps, or played a set or two with the up-and-coming bands and musicians in The Venue. And if ever Mrs T and I saw someone with real promise, we would invite some of our music contacts to come in." He looked around and smiled. "A lot of new acts got their first break right here. Mrs T encouraged us all to follow our dreams."

"She sounds like quite an inspirational lady," I said.

"She certainly was." Ethan smiled, then looked off into the distance behind me. "I'll never forget a conversation I had with her not long after I arrived back at The Three Songbirds. I was still a bit of a mess then." He focused back on me. "I mean I was clean – rehab had helped me to give up the booze and drugs – but my last two singles had both flopped. I was gutted when I heard my ex was getting married to that prat she'd cheated on me with and, all in all, I was pretty shaky. It was Mrs T who helped me get my groove back – she reminded me that neither the success, the money nor the fame were what had attracted me into the music business in the first place. It was the music. Nothing else mattered except the music." He smiled and tilted his head. "Sounds obvious, but I think I'd forgotten that. And so, while I was here, I was able to get away from that whole toxic scene – from the false friends, the dealers, the gutter press, the girls, the critics. In fact I forgot about everything except the music and I got stuck back into writing and composing. While I was here I spent hours locked up in my room, composing. Mrs T would bring me meals and if I got stir crazy I would take my guitar up into the woods and carry on there. I wrote my entire third album at The Three Songbirds – most of it from my room."

I almost fell off my chair. "Are you serious? You wrote *Roots and Wings* from Room 103?"

"Sure did." Ethan grinned. "You've heard of it then?"

"Of course – everybody's heard of it! I absolutely *love* that album – it's one of my favourites. I used to be part of a singing group and we would often sing the title song at our after-show music sessions or on the tour bus. We put some nice harmonies to it."

"So you're a singer?" asked Ethan.

"Used to be. I sang with the *Celtic Wings* show. I haven't been doing too much lately, but I've been thinking of getting back into music. I miss it. To be honest I've only recently realised just how stuck I've been without music in my life."

"Of course you have," said Ethan. "Music is like oxygen to people like us. Mrs T reminded me of that."

I was trying so hard to act cool but I couldn't help myself from grinning. I was beyond chuffed to be the other half of Ethan Harding's *us* reference – especially when it came to music. I looked around. "I still can't believe you wrote *Roots and Wings* right here in The Three Songbirds. And in my room too." I blushed then. "Well, your room, but you know what I mean . . ."

Ethan smiled. "Thanks, sweetheart. It's a pretty special record for me too. I met the love of my life while I was promoting it in the States – she was a presenter on a music show I was performing on. She's at home in New York now with our kids – our second is just three weeks old." He pulled his phone out of his shirt top pocket and went through it to find the picture to show me.

"Oh, they're adorable." I smiled at the new baby and her cute toddler brother looking over the top of the cradle. "Congratulations."

"Cheers!" Ethan took another look at the picture himself and smiled before putting his phone back into his top pocket. "They say that a new life often starts just as one finishes, don't they? I wish Mrs T had had a chance to meet our little Aimee. She was so happy to hear the baby had arrived safe and well – at least we got to tell her over the phone anyway. Mrs T would have loved Aimee –

she got on great with our son, Craig. We were all due to come over and stay here this Christmas." Ethan looked down at his hands – he seemed so sad.

I really felt for him. "She meant a lot to you, didn't she?"

"Yeah, Mrs T meant the world to us." He looked up at me. "Did I tell you I wrote the title song from *Roots and Wings* for her? I'll be singing it for her at the memorial shortly. The world sure as heck lost one amazing lady last week. I'm really going to miss her."

I nodded. I was only beginning to realise just how important this woman had been to so many different people. To hear people speak so well of someone after they are gone is the sign of a life well lived. She made me want to be a better woman myself.

We finished up our breakfast and Ethan got up, brushed the crumbs off his clothes and grabbed his guitar case. "Thanks again for sharing your food, Chrissie. It was a lifesaver. See you inside?"

I smiled. "Yes, see you in there."

I stopped off at the reception desk to check out and had another quick request to make of Mrs Gates before I made my way into The Venue.

Chapter 24

I arrived into The Venue just before eleven with a couple of minutes to spare. I looked around, half expecting to see Red there. The African-Celtic fusion music that was playing was so similar to her band's sound and to the music I'd woken up to that morning – but this time it was being played quite low, in the background. I couldn't quite see the band from where I stood inside the door at the back of the room so I edged my way slowly up the side aisle towards the platform at the front. As I got closer I could see that, although there was a similar mixture of children in the band, this group were completely different children, and neither young David nor Red were anywhere to be seen. The children were playing similar instruments though and the familiar beat put me at my ease. I leaned back against the side wall to listen to them play.

In the centre of the platform a single lectern was standing beside a couple of chairs. Just in front of the lectern was a huge spray of sunflowers and greenery, and a few feet in front of that down from the platform stood Mrs Thorpe's dark walnut coffin. I looked back up at the platform – behind which was the glass wall to the atrium where the two eucalyptus trees stood. A couple of starlings flew down then to one of the nests that I could just about make out at the top of one of the trees.

I glanced back at the room. The front three rows were completely empty, no doubt waiting for the family's arrival. Behind them all of the rows in the rest of the room were packed – The Venue was almost completely full and people had started to stand around at the back of the room. Young children were being ushered into the few remaining seats towards the front and several small groups of adults stood chatting at the ends of a couple of the rows. There was a low murmur of chatter throughout the room and a few people were still moving about greeting others they knew. Everybody was wearing bright, summer colours and the chairs along the centre aisle were decorated with lots of greenery and large yellow sunflowers similar to the ones on the platform and in the foyer. It was an unusual choice for a funeral but the place looked so happy and joyful that I decided I liked it. And, even though the flowers and dress code were very different, there was still a solemn air of respect in the room as befitting a memorial service. Those that were chatting did so in hushed tones and the joyful music was being played very low. The overall effect was very calming, respectful and strangely upbeat.

"I like the scarf – big improvement." I swung around. Ethan Harding had walked through one of the open side doors – the one just behind me. He put his left hand on my shoulder and stood back to take me in. "Yeah, Mrs T would have approved of that look."

I smiled and patted my newly borrowed, somewhat

garish, coloured scarf. "Thank you for the tip-off. Mrs Gates very kindly loaned it to me."

"Good ol' Maud." Ethan smiled, then looked around. "Hey, I don't think you're going to get a seat at this stage." He looked back at me and raised his eyebrows. "That's what you get for sharing your breakfast with an ageing musician."

"Oh, that's okay," I said. "I'm just up here to listen to the music. I'll move down to stand at the back of the room once the service starts." I was quite happy to melt into the small crowd that was forming down the back.

"I think we can do better than that – follow me." And with that, Ethan Harding, my teenage idol, legendary musician, and all-round megastar, took me by the hand and led me right up to the platform and across to the musicians on the other side. I was embarrassed to be up at the front when I hadn't even known Mrs Thorpe but I didn't want to make a fuss so I went with him without protest. He led me to a couple of empty chairs near the African-Celtic fusion band who were still playing. Beside them and right beside the two empty chairs was a small group of three musicians – one holding a fiddle, another a tin whistle and the other a bodhrán.

Ethan nodded at the bodhrán player, then he sat down and started to open his guitar case. I stood hovering beside him, waiting for him to finish, intending to say a quick goodbye and dash down the back.

Ethan looked up at me as he rested his guitar on his lap. "Do you remember the words to 'Roots and Wings'?" he asked me in a low voice.

I looked at him in surprise. "Of course. Why do you ask?"

"Right. Stand there for a second."

He got up and I stared at him as I stood in front of one of the chairs and he adjusted the height of the microphone in front of me.

He sat down, then looked up at me. "Come on. I won't bite." He patted the chair beside him.

I was so conscious that most people in the front few rows were looking at us, many whispering to each other. Of course I knew it was Ethan they were interested in, not me, but it still made me feel very awkward. Regardless, I did as I was told and sat down on the edge of the chair beside Ethan.

He plucked at a few strings, and set about tuning the guitar before strumming a few chords – very quietly so that he didn't interrupt the group that were playing. He leaned sideways in to me then. "So if you can come in on the chorus – for the line: '*You gave me wings . . .*'"

"Oh no, no, I couldn't!" I swivelled around to look him right in the eye, the terror rising quickly within me. "Really, Ethan. I couldn't possibly."

"Why not? You said you were a singer, right?" He raised his eyebrows. "And you know a few harmonies to this?"

"Yes, but I haven't sung in public in some years now." I looked around at the packed room in panic. There must have been at least three or four hundred people there – all people who actually knew Mrs Thorpe. I was an outsider, a stranger. I wanted to stay inconspicuous, to melt into the background. I hadn't intended to sit up at the front and I certainly hadn't planned on singing – even if it was with Ethan Harding.

"What was that you said about wanting to get back

into music?" Ethan grinned at me. "Well, now's your chance."

I was about to answer him when, out of the corner of my eye, I noticed Harvey walk in through the side door to our left. The room started to quieten down. Harvey was flanked either side by a middle-aged man and woman – his children, I assumed. The man put his arm around Harvey's shoulders and the woman looped her arm through Harvey's. Behind them filed a large group of adults, young people and children of all different ages – they included the women and girls in the colourful African head-dresses and skirts that I'd seen earlier at the reception desk and a couple of African men were with them too. A priest and a vicar came in just behind the group then and, as they walked into the room, a gong sounded and everybody stood up.

Harvey noticed Ethan as he passed by us on his way to the front seats – Harvey nodded to him and gave him a sad smile. Then he glanced at me. I was so embarrassed – Harvey knew I hadn't known his wife. But if he was wondering what I was doing with the musicians up at the top of the room he didn't show it. Instead, he stood a bit taller when he saw me and he gave me a little smile too, putting me more at ease. I smiled back at him just as he wiped a stray tear away. He turned back to his daughter then and she and his son led him to his seat, the rest of the group following behind.

The music began to fade out as the family sat down and everyone else in the room did the same. The priest explained then that the memorial service was for all of Mrs Thorpe's family and friends and that it would be followed by a removal to the local church in Harkston where a private funeral service would be held for the family, followed by a burial in the churchyard. The priest and the vicar took it in turns to say a few words of welcome. Then, just as the vicar was saying an opening prayer, Ethan gave me a nudge with his elbow.

"We're up next. Your mic's on. Up you get."

I looked at the microphone stand in front of me. I was terrified but I didn't want to let Ethan or Mrs Thorpe down, so I stood up, adjusted the microphone stand and held onto it for dear life. I could see the people in the front rows already turning to look at us with interest.

I closed my eyes, and as soon as the vicar stopped speaking Ethan strummed the familiar opening chords of 'Roots and Wings'. My heart was pounding fast. Eyes still firmly shut, I tried to calm myself down by nodding along to the tune until Ethan reached the last line of the verse. I opened my eyes then and glanced around at him. He nodded to me just as he got to the last word. I turned back to the hundreds of faces that were staring up at us. For a split second I thought I wouldn't be able to make a sound, but then my father's words came back to me.

'Use your voice, Chrissie.'

I put my hand in my pocket and clenched onto the china figurine in its bubble-wrap. Then I took a deep breath and joined Ethan:

> *"You gave me wings to soar into the blue,*
> *Solid roots to always come back to,*
> *I never knew I could fly so high, so free,*
> *Those demons of mine, didn't expect to see,*
> *But with you behind me, I survived,*
> *With you beside me, learned to thrive,*
> *You gave me roots and wings and I, I, I*

I love you."

I don't remember breathing until we'd finished singing the last word of the chorus and Ethan had started into the next verse. That's when I had time to think again, when I realised that we actually sounded pretty good together – it was really beautiful. I noticed some people dab at their eyes with handkerchiefs and, though I'd been so scared at first, I realised that I'd actually started to enjoy the music. As I listened to Ethan sing the moving words of the second verse I felt so blessed to be a part of his beautiful song – even if only for a few minutes. It was such a privilege to be able to witness other people accessing such deep feelings and emotions through the music. This, I knew, was one of the greatest joys of performing, and at that moment I couldn't quite believe that I'd forgotten how good it felt.

As Ethan and I sang the second chorus, I put in the couple of extra harmonies I knew. It sounded so lovely and I was quite sad when we reached the end of the song. I sat down then and glanced around at him. He had tears in his eyes and couldn't speak but he grabbed me into a big hug and I had to wipe away my own tears.

"Thank you for letting me sing with you, Ethan," I whispered. "That meant so much to me."

He pulled back. "Not a bother." He smiled. "You're awesome."

I smiled too, then I took a long, deep breath and sat back in my chair just as Harvey walked up onto the platform.

He stood there for a few moments – holding onto the sides of the lectern for support. He looked around the whole room, then up at the front rows where his family sat. He smiled at the few small children who had come to sit cross-legged at the front of the platform a couple of metres in front of the lectern. His eyes moved to the coffin then and he closed them for a moment. He took a deep breath, opened his eyes again, drew himself up to his full height and spoke into the microphone.

"Thank you all for coming today. It truly is so heart-warming to see so many friends here and in such numbers. My only regret is that my darling Christine could not be here to see you all – how she would have loved to have caught up with all your news and to have met the new arrivals." He smiled at the children again. "Or to have shared a tune or two in the bar last night." He paused for a minute and looked down at the coffin before looking back up at the room. He took a deep breath, then went on. "Christine loved music. She said the best times of her musical career were those early days before success came her way – discovering new sounds, new traditions in music. She loved to make music with others and to infuse young people with her passion for it." He glanced over our way then. "So my sincere thanks to all of the musicians who have given us such heart-warming performances this morning. I'm delighted to see so many of Christine's protégés present."

Ethan saluted Harvey and I glanced behind me at the drummers who were leaning back against the wall – they smiled and nodded back up at Harvey too.

"Thanks also to those who will be playing later in the service." The traditional music trio beside us nodded. "And of course to all those who played for us last night in the bar, thank you all. I wish we had been gathering for her ninetieth birthday weekend as we had been planning for so long, but the wake was a very fitting send-off. Christine would have loved every min–"

But it all seemed to get too much for Harvey then, his voice cracked and he stopped talking. His head sank down into his chest as he held on to the sides of the lectern – it seemed to be the only thing holding him up at that stage and it looked for a moment as though he wouldn't be able to go on. I noticed the man who I'd assumed was his son start to rise in the front row. But just as he did, Harvey took a deep breath and stood up tall. He held his hand up to the man and smiled. The man sat down and Harvey went on.

"And of course it is so comforting to have all of our family around at this sad time. My own children, Eva and Oscar – you shared a close bond with your stepmother, I know." He smiled down at them. "And of course there are so many of us now – Christine and I have five grandchildren and seven great-grandchildren – not bad, eh?" There was a ripple of laughter and a few people clapped. "Thank you." Harvey smiled. "Christine was the great love of my life," he went on. "After my first wife and I split, I thought that was it for me. I felt ancient – at the ripe old age of fifty-three." He raised his eyebrows and there was a low ripple of laughter in the room. "I never expected to meet anyone else and had quite given up hope of finding love. I threw myself into my work and was quite reconciled to the idea of living alone by the time I met Christine. She told me that she too had thought her chance of love was over after the death of her first husband. But when we met, right here in fact –" Harvey turned around and pointed out the window at the eucalyptus trees, then turned back to face the room, "– we realised just how wrong we had been. Thankfully, I now know that there can be more than one person for us in this life – we both felt very blessed to have found love for a second time. As many of you know, Christine and I met when my son Oscar married her protégée – well, in fact I think it might be fair to say that she considered you more like a daughter, Lyliko?"

My eyes darted to the front row where a woman held up her hand. She was nodding and wiping away heavy tears. Was this the Lyliko Red had told me about? She was wearing beautiful African clothing, but it couldn't be Lyliko – this woman looked to be too old. Red had said that her Lyliko was thirty-five – this woman looked to be in her sixties at least. And Red's Lyliko was only due to be getting married that day. No – it must be a different person, I thought. But what a coincidence to have the same name . . .

"And of course we can all see the trouble that got us into," Harvey was saying. "Three wonderful grandchildren from that union, each of you a blessing in our lives." He paused, took a deep breath and smiled at his family in the front, before going on. "I am especially delighted that Lyliko's eldest son could make it here today too – all the way from his hometown in Zambia – he and his wife Choolwe have just had their third child, young Harvey junior – our seventh great-grandchild. He's bound to be a fine young man with a great name like that." Harvey chuckled and everyone in the room laughed at the joke.

I looked at the young children at the front of the platform and could imagine how Mrs Thorpe must have enjoyed them.

"Life with Christine was never dull," Harvey went on. "She and I spent most of our winters in Africa. From the day we met, Christine embraced my work with The Tuskhorn Trust and soon became our top volunteer. She worked hard with us to stop the poaching of elephants and rhino, mainly through advocacy work and regular campaigning. We also had many an adventure taking groups over to work at the Trust's rehabilitation centres in Kenya – Christine almost always managed to persuade me to visit her beloved Zambia while we were there."

I'd read in the article that Mrs Thorpe had spent time in Africa, but I wondered what her specific connection to Zambia had been. Perhaps it was something to do with her family – I looked over at Lyliko and her family in the front row, but I was getting quite confused.

Just then I thought I heard someone behind me whisper my name. I turned around, but the band members were all looking over my head at Harvey. I thought I must have imagined it and turned back around.

"Christine always rose to a challenge," Harvey was saying. "When I met her The Trust was struggling, but as soon as I shared with her the problems of poaching in Kenya, she didn't hesitate in calling in her old Hollywood friends to help us. The success of the Julian Harris documentary in particular really turned the charity's fortunes around – that was all down to Christine – she had met Julian when they collaborated on the Oscar-winning movie *Ringo*."

"*Ringo*? But she couldn't have," I said quietly to myself, but loud enough for Ethan to hear.

"Everything okay?" he whispered to me.

I swivelled around to him. "Did Mrs Thorpe win an

Oscar for *Ringo*?"

Ethan nodded. "Great movie, eh?" He put his finger up to his lip then. "We should listen."

I turned back to look at Harvey but I couldn't understand it. Were Christine Thorpe and Red somehow connected? I stared at Harvey as a bizarre thought suddenly hit me: were they the same person? But how could they be? How could that be possible?

"Chrissie."

It was the same voice behind me – this time it sounded familiar, but I couldn't quite place it. I turned around but nobody was looking at me. I started to think I must be coming down with something. I turned back around and looked at Ethan, but he didn't seem to notice anything – he was leaning on his guitar and looking straight over at Harvey. I looked out at the rest of the people but the room had begun to grow quite blurry. I rubbed my eyes and looked back up at Harvey who also seemed out of focus. I put my hand to my forehead – but it felt fine, no temperature. I tried to calm down and tune back into what Harvey was saying.

". . . and of course I didn't hesitate in following her up that tree all those years ago. Christine was determined to save her eucalyptus trees and every other tree in Collinswood for that matter – there was no way she was going to give them up. It wasn't always easy following my Christine wherever she wanted to go but, with her, life was never dull. When she announced to me after we won the battle for the trees that she wanted to buy this place, I thought she was crazy at first. She had all these wild notions about building cycle tracks and developing bird-watching trails in Collinswood." Harvey turned and looked behind him out the window before turning back to the microphone. "She did an amazing job, didn't she?" There was a murmur of agreement. "But this was where she said she wanted us to put down roots and I had already grown quite fond of the place, so we moved here and spent two very happy decades living together with our menagerie of cats, dogs and horses in our little cottage in the grounds. I have to give Christine the credit for discovering the place though – she came here first many years earlier with her parents on her mother's thirtieth birthday."

I stared at Harvey, barely able to comprehend what he was saying. It was all too much to be a coincidence – he must be mistaken.

"She always felt a deep connection to them here," he was saying. "She said buying the place and moving here made her feel close to her parents too."

"Come back to us, Chrissie."

I stood up and turned around. The people, the musicians, they were no more than a blur by that stage.

"Who's saying that? Who's calling me?" I shouted out.

But nobody responded. I spun back around – not even Harvey seemed to have noticed my outburst. I found myself walking slowly towards him as he kept on speaking.

"Christine said that until she met her first husband Cal, she'd struggled all her life to feel at home in any one place. She was born in Dingle in Kerry and moved to Greenwich in London when she was a year old. She lived there until her father's untimely death when she was just nine. It was he who inspired her to follow her musical pathway – she went on to sing with *Celtic Wings*, and when she left the show she reopened his music stall in Greenwich market."

"*Stop it!*" Before I knew what I was doing, I'd run the remaining few metres over to the lectern. But Harvey just kept talking, not seeming to notice me. I stood frozen to the spot as I listened to him.

"When I met her, Christine was still grieving for her first husband, Cal, who had died a few years earlier. She always said that here, at The Three Songbirds and behind us, up in Collinswood, was where she felt closest to him, and closest to her parents. This was where she finally learned to accept Cal's death and it's where we too met and soon afterwards fell in love. So this is a very special place to us for so many reasons. Christine said that she learned that it is possible to mourn someone, to go on loving their memory, while allowing yourself to love again. I always knew that she was someone else's before she was mine – and that was okay – the people she loved before made her the woman I fell in love with."

"Stop it, Harvey!" I sank to my knees and looked up at him until I could only see the top of his head and his eyes over the lectern. "Please – I don't know what this is all about, but it's too cruel a joke."

But neither Harvey nor anyone else seemed to see or hear me.

"I'm sure Christine and her loved ones are all so happy to be back together again up there now," he was saying.

"Why won't you stop this? Please, somebody –" I looked behind me out to the room but it had all but disappeared into a hazy blur of colour. I turned back, closed my eyes and buried my head in my hands.

"*She's waking up. Her eyes are moving.*"

I opened my eyes again to try to see who was speaking. The room was still very blurry and my body felt leaden. I couldn't move my head at all.

"She's awake. Thanks be to God! She's awake."

I closed my eyes, which was when I realised that I was lying down. I slowly opened them again and a blurry face, then another, started to come into focus. It was my Uncle Donal and my Aunt Gemma. Beside them Tim's face also peered down at me and behind him I could just about make out my grandfather and grandmother.

Chapter 25

I don't remember too much from those first few minutes after I came round in the hospital. The familiar faces vanished very quickly until it was just a blur of doctors and nurses – unfamiliar hands touching me, unknown but concerned voices asking me questions. I just remember hearing a few random words like 'accident' and 'lucky to be alive' before closing my eyes again. I've no idea how long I was asleep, but when I woke up again Tim was sitting alone beside my hospital bed.

He'd obviously been watching me for some time. He sat forward in his chair and took my hand as I opened my eyes. "Chrissie, darling – how are you feeling?"

I tried to speak, but only just about managed to croak a noise in return.

He kissed me gently on my forehead. "It's all right, don't try to talk. Everything's going to be okay, my love. The doctors say you'll make a full recovery. You just need to get lots of rest. I'm going to take good care of you, don't worry."

"Wh-what happened?" I managed to ask.

"Your car was in a collision with a truck after you left the party yesterday. It hit you just as you drove out of our driveway through the storm. It was a bad accident, Chrissie. You were unconscious and they had to cut you out of the car. That damned car – I wish I'd never bought it." Tim's voice cracked and he buried his head in my hand. "My God, Chrissie, we thought you were . . ." He couldn't seem to go on but after a few seconds he kissed my hand gently and cleared his throat. "They took you here in the ambulance and they operated straight away. You lost a lot of blood and were in surgery for hours – they fixed a broken leg and a crushed ankle. You have three broken ribs and a lot of superficial cuts and bruises too, but they said it was remarkable you sustained no major internal injuries. You're going to be just fine, my love."

I closed my eyes. I tried to remember, but I had no recollection whatsoever of the accident, of leaving the party or of the time before that.

"Was the truck driver okay?" I asked.

Tim's face tightened. "Yes, he walked away from it, the bloody idiot."

I managed a weak smile. "Thank God for that."

"He said he didn't see you pull out." Tim looked so angry. "That you seemed to come from nowhere. He just wasn't bloody well paying attention – that was the problem."

I felt my eyes start to close over again. I was so tired.

"Go back to sleep now, my love," said Tim. "You're going to need lots of rest to get better. We've got so much to look forward to." I felt him squeeze my hand and I flinched – it was just a gentle squeeze but it hurt a little.

347

"I thought I'd lost you, Chrissie, but thank God you're still here. We can get married as soon as you're well enough – no need to delay it. I'll plan everything – you just concentrate on getting better."

I didn't have the strength to reply so I just closed my eyes and slowly fell back asleep.

My first conscious day in hospital went by in a daze. I was groggy and weak and I slept – a lot. Ever the dutiful fiancé, Tim stayed by my bedside the entire time. It was a comfort to have him there, but he looked shattered the whole time.

On my third day awake, I overheard the nurse persuade him to go home for a couple of hours at least to get some rest – he'd been sleeping and showering in the hospital for days by that stage. He only agreed to go when Abigail came in to sit with me.

I was beginning to feel a little better by then and I was delighted to see my friend. Bit by bit my memory had started to come back. I still couldn't remember the accident but I was beginning to remember more about the time before it. And there was something about it all that didn't add up.

After a while I decided to ask her about it.

"Abigail, I remember Tim's proposal now, and the thunderstorm . . . and talking to you upstairs. I remember feeling a bit all over the place after the proposal . . . it came as a complete surprise. I felt like I was suffocating . . . I needed to get away. Abigail . . ." I touched her hand as she sat on the side of my bed, "I wrote a note. I remember it quite clearly now. I wrote a short note and I left it by the door before I went out to the car."

Abigail nodded but said nothing.

"The thing is . . . I can't understand why Tim hasn't mentioned it. I said in the note that I was going away for a few days. I mean that's not good, is it? To go away without telling anybody? During the party they've thrown for you? Why hasn't Tim mentioned it? He hasn't even asked me where I was going – he just keeps talking about us getting married as soon as possible."

Abigail took a deep breath in. "Oh Chrissie. I hope I did the right thing." She got up and leaned over to the bedside chair to get her bag. She opened it up and took out a folded piece of paper. "I took the note, Chrissie. Tim has never seen it." She handed it to me. "I'm sorry. It's just that we didn't know what was going to happen, whether you would pull through." She started to cry and pulled a tissue out of her bag to wipe her tears. "I found the note by the door after Tim had gone with you in the ambulance to the hospital. I knew you were having doubts about the relationship and, if anything happened to you, I didn't want him to think . . . Well, I just thought that if you weren't going to be around to explain why you'd left, it might be better he not know at all – that it would be fairer to him that way. People seemed to agree that you were just popping out to get something for the party. Someone said that you'd been running low on white wine. I think they all just assumed you must have been going to get more – and trying out your new car. I'm sorry, Chrissie – did I mess everything up?"

I read my note again: '*I have to go away for a night or so. I'm so sorry for leaving – just have to get away. Thanks so much for today – it was very special. xC*'

I looked back up at Abigail who was blowing her nose.

"No, you did the right thing." I scrunched the note up, put it on the bedside locker and took her free hand. "That wasn't right. Tim deserves more than that. Thank you so much for the save, O Wise One." I smiled.

Abigail looked so relieved and, though it took all of what little strength I had, I managed to sit forward to give her a hug.

"So where *were* you going, Chrissie?" Abigail asked when I lay back down.

"I'm embarrassed to say, to be honest." I took a deep breath, then decided to open up to my good friend. "I had a dream before I woke up after the accident, Abigail. It's still quite vivid in my memory. I mean I can't remember all the details, but I do remember that I'd gone to Christine Thorpe's memorial. Do you remember me mentioning her to you?"

"The old woman who died a few weeks back?" Abigail asked. "The crackpot who sat up in a tree with her husband?"

I laughed, but it hurt my ribs and I resolved not to do it again. "Yes, that's the one. I thought about her a lot last week for some reason. She was interested in cycling and travel and so I think in some ways she reminded me of my mother. With my thirtieth birthday approaching, she and my father were on my mind a lot so when I saw Christine Thorpe's story, it almost made me wonder how my parents' lives might have turned out if they'd lived and if they hadn't had me by accident."

"Oh Chrissie!" Abigail put her hand on my arm. "I'm quite sure your parents loved you very much. Their lives might have been different without you, but I'm sure they wouldn't have changed them for the world."

I smiled. "Thanks, Abigail. I know that is true, and I feel a lot better about everything now I must admit. I think the dream helped me a lot. I met myself in it, y'know?" I paused to gauge her reaction. Abigail raised her eyebrows slightly but she said nothing so I went on. "That is, me in thirty years' time, and me in sixty years' time. In my dream I turned out to *be* Mrs Thorpe, Abigail – she was me in sixty years' time!"

Abigail squinted at me. "Well, unless you're a Japanese woman, married to a British property developer, I don't think you could be the real Christine Thorpe. I read her full obituary in the Sunday newspaper while we were waiting for you to come out of surgery."

"She was Japanese?" I was surprised. But why not? I'd only read a short article about the woman and I'd never seen her picture. I knew very little at all about the real Christine Thorpe. I shook my head. "Gosh, the imagination is a powerful thing, eh?"

"Was it your imagination? Or . . ." Abigail edged a little closer up the bed to me, "your subconscious? This dream sounds very interesting, Chrissie. Very important. Tell me more about it – you're saying you met your older self?"

I nodded. "Yes, I met my sixty-year-old self – and I met her at my own memorial service!" We both laughed at the absurdity of what I was saying – I held my ribs again to try to stop the pain. "Okay, I know it sounds nuts now, but it did all feel so real."

"It must have been very revealing, to talk to your older self. What did she have to say?" asked Abigail. "Did she tell you lots of profound things?"

"Sort of. I didn't know who she was when I met her

though. If I had, I would have had more questions." I thought hard to remember Red's story but it had all become so hazy. "I can't remember too many of the details, but I do recall thinking her quite a cool, older woman, if a little sad. Someone close to her I think had died. I remember being quite fascinated by her anyway – she had a great romance story. She'd ended up in the wrong relationship . . ." I sat forward. "Yes, that was it! She was with the wrong man so she missed out on being with the right one for years – and all because she didn't speak up for what she wanted. She seemed very sad about that – I felt quite sorry for her."

Abigail sucked in her breath. "Interesting . . ."

"And then there was Christine Thorpe. Me in sixty years' time." I raised my eyebrows and Abigail smiled. "She wasn't afraid to stand up for what she believed in – she and her husband sat up in those trees for weeks until they won the battle to conserve them and the woods around them. I have a very vivid recollection of the trees – they were two intertwined eucalyptus trees. I didn't meet Mrs Thorpe of course, but I did meet her second husband. I really liked him and I remember feeling very much at home in his company."

Abigail nodded a few times, all the while squinting at me. I could almost see her brain working. "You know, I did an article for the magazine about dreams a few years ago," she said. "I really enjoyed researching it in fact. Freud believed that during sleep our forbidden wishes are released from their normal daytime reserve so that they can become part of our waking consciousness – he said that dreams are codes to be decoded, that their images and symbols need to be fully interpreted to work out their full meaning."

"Really? That's interesting." I sat up a bit in the bed. "I do remember that there were lots of birds . . . songbirds . . . in the dream. At one point there was even a full flock – a murmuration of starlings – it was very dramatic."

Abigail nodded. "Well, you do love your birds, don't you? I've never known anyone able to recall so many species – even ones you've only read about. And you have an incredible ear – you can recognise them from their calls too." She squinted at me for a minute, seeming to be thinking again, analysing. Then she sat up straight. "The bird must symbolise freedom or travel." She scrunched up her eyebrows. "Interesting that they were all songbirds though. I guess it could even symbolise your music too in some way?"

"Yes!" I sat forward more. "In fact I remember that Red, my sixty-year-old self, had been successful in music somehow – there were certainly lots of different types of music at the memorial. Ooh!" I pointed at Abigail. "There was African music . . . drums . . . I remember lots of drums, even a couple of bodhráns. Yes, that's it! It was a sort of African-Celtic fusion sound."

"There could be something in that, Chrissie. Maybe you need to think how you can bring more music into your life? Aside from selling the second-hand albums on the stall now, you don't really do much of it any more, do you?"

"No. I lost the heart for music after Mum died." I lay back down. "I do quite miss it though. A lot actually. Not so much the performing in public. I was never all that keen on that. I think I only stuck with *Celtic Wings* so long because I got to travel with the show and because it was what Brian wanted to do. But I do love to sing in small groups, and I used to write music too – I might try to get back into that."

"Well, you know Carl Jung felt that dreams are meant to guide us back to ourselves, back to wholeness. He said that they can even help us solve a problem in our waking life and, when we've strayed too far from our foundations, they can help to point us back the right way."

I closed my eyes. "The Songbird's Way," I said under my breath.

"You know, now that I think of it," Abigail was saying, "it's perhaps not that surprising to meet yourself in your dream. In fact, isn't everybody in our dreams a reflection of ourselves, our own subconscious, in some way? In a dream we imagine everyone else into being, so they are all a part of us even if they seem like someone else?"

Abigail seemed to be enjoying teasing out her hypothesis but she was losing me a bit along the way. I just nodded along.

"And very interesting also that it was African-Celtic fusion music that you remember. That's quite specific," she said.

I opened my eyes. "Yes, I definitely remember that a part of the dream took place in Africa. I can't recall too much of the detail but it could have been Zambia? Which makes sense – I met a couple a few weeks ago who volunteered over there – maybe that's how I got that idea?"

Abigail nodded. "Could be – either that or your mother's travel memoir?"

"True, I absolutely loved that one," I said. "And listening to Isaac and Joan talking about Zambia a few weeks ago stirred up my interest again. It sounds wonderful – I'd so love to go there, maybe do some volunteer work for a few months myself."

"You should get on to CAL," said Abigail.

"What did you say?" I sat bolt upright, then instantly regretted it when my ribs reminded me of their broken state. I flinched and held my side.

"Are you okay?" Abigail asked.

I nodded. "Yes, I'm fine. Go on . . . Who's Cal?"

"CAL – the Christian African Legion," said Abigail. "Now don't be put off by the name, Chrissie. I know you're not really religious but this group is very accepting of all faiths and none, and the missionaries you'd be volunteering with are very inspiring people by all accounts. Penny volunteered with them just before we got together. She raves about her time teaching in Kenya."

"CAL!" I nodded slowly, remembering my conversation with Isaac and Joan. "That's the organisation that those people I met a few weeks ago used." That must have been where I got his name, I thought, and smiled to myself as I lay back down – slowly this time.

Just then my mobile buzzed on the side table. I rolled my eyes. "Sorry, Tim insists I keep it with me and on at all times now." I picked it up and checked the text message. "He's back – he's on his way up and wants to know if I need anything in the shop."

"That was quick." Abigail stood up. "Well, I'll leave you guys in peace."

"Did I mention that Tim was in the dream too, Abigail?" I looked up at her when I finished texting Tim back.

She shook her head then sat down again.

"He'd followed me to the place where the memorial was being held, we had a long conversation and in the end we broke up. I remember that part quite clearly – it was awful."

Abigail nodded and squinted at me. "And how did you feel about that afterwards?"

I took a deep breath in. "Honestly?"

Abigail nodded. 'Honestly. Think hard, Chrissie. It's how you feel in a dream that is the most telling."

But I didn't have to think too hard. I remembered exactly how I'd felt. "I was very sad about it, but also relieved. I knew it was the right thing." A single tear fell down my cheek.

"Oh Chrissie!" Abigail came over to me and gently brushed the tear away with her thumb just as Tim walked into the room.

She stood up straight then and I slowly pulled myself up on my pillows.

"There's my favourite patient!" said Tim.

He looked a lot better. He was wearing fresh clothes and he looked refreshed, if not fully rested.

"Hi, Tim." Abigail picked up her handbag then reached over to the locker and took the scrunched-up note too. "I was just about to go." She turned back to me. "I'll be back to see you tomorrow, Chrissie. Is there anything you need?"

I shook my head. "I'm fine, thanks. Sorry for all the fuss – do say hi to Penny and the kids for me." I leaned out and grabbed her hand. "And thank you, Abigail. Thanks for everything."

She put her hand over mine and smiled.

Tim came over and sat down where Abigail had been sitting on the side of my bed. I nodded goodbye to my friend, then turned to face him.

"Tim . . ." I took a deep breath and reached for his hand. "I need to talk to you."

Epilogue

I smiled to myself as I tied my long red hair back and put my cycling helmet on. I'd gone back to my natural colour since the accident and was feeling more myself than ever. It was the day that I finally got to ride Sky again, twelve months on from the accident that changed my life. Abigail was just beside me outside Chatham Train Station. She was quicker than me saddling up her bike after the train journey, and was already ready and raring to go. I quickly strapped my helmet on and gave her a thumbs-up.

It was so lovely to feel the sun on my face and the warm breeze billowing around me as we cycled through the Kent towns and countryside. I felt so blessed to be alive and feeling so well again. I thought back over the last twelve months as we cycled. The doctors said I'd been very lucky to have recovered so fast. I knew there had been a lot of luck involved, but I also put my swift recovery down to my grandma. When she'd heard about the accident, she insisted I come to stay with her in Dingle to recuperate, and as soon as I arrived she went into overdrive on the faith healing and baking. I'd never had so many prayers said over me or apple pies put in front of me!

As I got better, I began to join in on her Saturday-night music sessions again. I thoroughly enjoyed the music and catching up with all the locals, and I loved the time that Grandma and I had together. We talked about my mother quite a bit during those months. She told me a lot more about my mother's childhood and about what she was like as a teenager – she said that my mother had always wanted to explore the world. Apparently she used to insist her father tell her every detail about his voyages with the British navy. She also read about the great explorers and collected old maps and travel books for as long as Grandma could remember. It all helped me to better understand the choices my mother had made, helped me to understand her better.

By the day Abigail and I went cycling in Kent, I'd been back in London just a couple of weeks, staying with Donal and Gem. I'd even spent the previous weekend with my English grandparents. It was a very pleasant stay in Hampstead – Susan seemed to have mellowed quite a bit since the accident. I'd mentioned my grandma's apple pies to her in passing and the next day she'd baked scones for my tea. I smiled as I remembered how my grandfather and I had had to secretly lather them with butter and jam to make them in any way edible.

Tim hadn't been quite so happy to see me though. I'd met him for lunch in Greenwich not long after I arrived in Donal and Gem's. He was perfectly polite as always but the lunch was quite awkward. I could tell that he was still very hurt at the break-up and still upset with me for moving out so quickly after the accident. He'd still wanted to take care of me when I came out of hospital, but I couldn't live with him. I couldn't expect Tim to look after me after I'd ended things with him, and every time I saw Jasper I burst into tears, knowing how much I was going to miss that goofy dog. All in all, it made most sense to go stay with my grandma in Dingle. So the lunch with Tim was quite awkward and short, but my cousin Conor had told me that he'd started dating again recently, so I was happy to hear that. I understood that Tim would probably never be able to fully forgive me, and that was okay. I just wanted him to be as happy as I was. I was so excited about my trip to Africa the following week. I was finally going to Zambia, having volunteered with the CAL organisation. They'd placed me in a small primary school not far out of Lusaka in Zambia and I was going to be teaching English there. I'd been collecting some small second-hand instruments to carry out too – just in case they might come in useful.

I smiled to myself, careful to avoid the potholes as I cycled Sky up the uneven avenue. I glanced back to check on how Abigail was doing – she was just a short distance behind me. She waved at me, then quickly put her hand back on the handlebar as she avoided a pothole herself. I smiled and turned back around. I was so grateful to my friend for offering to spend my thirty-first birthday with me – and to Penny for minding the kids so we could put our bikes on the train and cycle out to The Three Songbirds for the day. It was such a beautiful sunny afternoon in July and the birds were in full voice in the tall elm trees that lined the driveway.

We cycled past the inn and over to a broken fence across from the entrance. I'd just started to lock Sky to it when Abigail reached me. I stood back and shaded my eyes to take a long look up at the old inn while she locked her bike to mine.

"How long is it since you've been here?" she asked me when she'd finished.

"Twenty-three years." I said. "It's hard to believe it's been that long. A lot has happened since then."

"Sure has." Abigail put her arm around my shoulders and gave me a gentle squeeze. "Come on. Let's go do what we came here to do, eh?"

She nodded behind us to Sky's carrier bag. I turned back around and started to lift the two tall black bags out. I handed one of them to Abigail and carried the other through the near-empty car park myself.

"It looks quite small now," I said as we approached the entrance of the inn. "And it's got quite run-down over the years really." I felt a little disappointed. "I'd expected the place to be old, maybe a bit run-down, but I hadn't expected it to look quite so shabby."

"Bit like ourselves!" said Abigail.

"Hey – speak for yourself!" I poked her in the side. "I've never felt better."

Abigail jumped, then laughed. "Yes, I must say, all jokes aside, you do look amazing, Chrissie. For someone who we'd almost given up for dead just a year ago today, it's such a relief to see you so fit and well again."

I smiled. "Thanks, hon. I know I've been very lucky." I linked my free arm through hers and we went inside.

It was a Sunday afternoon but the bar was as quiet inside as the car park was outside – only three tables were full. We walked over to the counter and I asked the barman if we could speak to the manager. He made a quick phone call then turned back to us and said: "He'll be down in a second. Would you like a drink, ladies?"

"Sure." I put down my black bag and sat up onto a tall bar stool. "I'll have a soda and lime."

"Make that two," said Abigail, sitting up on the stool beside me.

"So how's business?" I asked him as he made our drinks. I was almost afraid to hear the answer.

The barman scanned the bar, probably to see if anyone was listening, but there wasn't really anyone nearby at all.

"It's not good," he said. "I'd be surprised if the place stays open much longer to be honest."

"That's a pity. It's in such a great location." I looked out the window. "With the beautiful woods and being so close to London. You get nightingales here in the summer too, don't you? It's one of the few places in England where they come in such numbers."

The barman shrugged his shoulders. "I can't imagine too many nightingales around with those noisy quad bikes ripping up and down through the woods. It's a pity. Like you say, the woods are actually very pretty, but they're a no-go area for walkers and other visitors."

My heart sank as he handed us our drinks but I tried to stay positive.

"Why do you want to talk to the manager anyway?" he asked as he took my money.

"I just want to ask his permission for something," I said.

The barman just nodded then turned back to pick up his mobile phone. We sipped our drinks in silence for the next few minutes while we waited for the manager to arrive.

We were almost blinded by the sun when we walked back

outside. Abigail was holding one black bag and I had the other one. In my other hand I had the shovel that the manager had just loaned us.

"This way!" I strode off around the side of the inn and Abigail followed. We had to avoid the empty beer kegs that were piled against the side wall and the old broken chairs and benches that were rusting in a pile beside the kegs, but things improved once we got around to the back of the building.

Behind the inn the sun shone down on a bright, wide grassy area. Poppies were scattered all over the long grass, and wild roses and buttercups grew along by the old stone wall bordering the woods.

I waded through the tall grass for a bit, turned around a couple of times, looked up at the woods, then back around at the inn. "Yes, this is it. This is the spot."

"Okay then," Abigail put down her black bag. "Let's do this!"

She opened the tie at the top of the bag and knelt down on one knee to gently lift out the small sapling in its plant pot. "Which one is this?" she asked.

"That's the oak from Dingle. I grew that one in Grandma's garden from acorns I found in Garfinny." I put down the shovel I'd been carrying then and opened up my black bag. "And this is from my grandparent's garden in Hampstead. It's grown from a seed of the oak tree my father played in when he was a child." I pushed back the plastic bag and lifted the sapling out, holding the light plastic pot underneath. "They started growing it for me a few months ago as I asked – so sweet of them. Apparently Susan took the project very seriously – Nicholas said she was out watering it in its pot every day."

Abigail smiled. "So where exactly do you want them?"

I stood up. "Come over here." She picked up the sapling and came over to stand beside me. "Now let's take a few steps apart."

We faced the woods and took a few sideways steps away from each other.

"Here?" asked Abigail.

"Wait a second." I held my pot in one hand and stretched out my arm towards her. Abigail did the same and we touched the tips of our fingers.

"Yes, this is perfect." I placed the sapling down right in front of me and Abigail did the same. "Time to dig now," I said, leaving the tree there and going to fetch the shovel.

I stood back from the Dingle sapling after patting the fresh soil down around its roots.

Abigail stood a respectful distance back.

"There you go now, Mum. You're here with Daddy, back in the place where we spent your birthday all those years ago. I'm ready now to let you rest in peace, Mum. It's taken me some time and I may never agree with all of your choices, but I understand now that you had to follow your own path. It's time now for me now to follow mine again, to go my own way. Thank you for giving me my wings and for sharing your roots with me. I love you, Mum, and I miss you every day."

I stared at the sapling for a minute or so, then I turned around to Abigail and she smiled at me. I took a deep breath and walked over to the tree that she'd planted. I picked up the shovel from the ground and put a few last pieces of soil around its base, then I knelt down and patted the soil firmly into place.

I reached into my pocket then and pulled out the last few broken pieces of the china nightingale figurine that they had found in my dress pocket when they'd cut it off me after the accident. Both of the wings had survived and a small piece of one of the bird's feet. I turned the pieces over in my hand a few times, feeling the ridges of the wings, the indentations on the claw of the foot.

Then I looked up at the sky and closed my eyes. "I don't need this any more, Daddy. You helped me to find my voice and I promise you I'm never going to lose it again. Music has been one of the greatest passions of my life and I have you to thank for that. I love you so much."

I looked back down and could just about see the fresh soil through the tears that were brimming in my eyes. I made a small hole with my fingers and placed the pieces of china in, covered the hole back over and patted the soil back into place.

Abigail came up behind me then. She put her hand on my shoulder. "Are you okay, Chrissie?"

I wiped a few stray tears away with the back of my hand, then turned and shaded them to look up at her. I nodded and smiled. "Yes, I'm good – thanks, Abigail."

I got to my feet and we stood there for a time, just gazing at the two young trees swaying in the gentle breeze.

"It's such a beautiful spot here," Abigail said, looking past the saplings over at the woods, then back to the inn. "It's so sad to think it may not be able to stay open much longer. Sounds like business isn't great."

I sighed. "I know. I do hope they can keep it going for a few more years at least though. I need to see a bit more of the world, meet new people and hopefully make a bit of money somehow." I looked down at the saplings in front of us. "These trees are just the start. Now that I've put roots down here I know I'll be back."

"Really?" Abigail linked her arm through mine as we walked over towards the opening of Collinswood. "Why would you come back? To do what?"

"Oh, I have a few ideas." I glanced back at the inn, then over at the two saplings in their new home and I heard the songbirds singing from the woods behind us – a beautiful medley. They sang to each other . . .

"As if they know . . ."

"What's that you said?" asked Abigail just as we reached the entrance to Collinswood.

I turned back around and just smiled at her before we stepped onto The Songbird's Way.

If you enjoyed
The Songbird's Way by Jennifer Barrett
why not try Chapter One
of the previously published

Look into the Eye

Here's a sneak preview

Look into the Eye

Jennifer Barrett

Chapter 1

MELANIE

May 2007

I couldn't wait to be out of the stuffy function room. I stood there on the edge of the outdoor terrace, desperately trying to breathe in enough of the delicious, tobacco-filled air to ease the pain of the fundraising lunch.

Ah, that's better – at least I can breathe again, I said to myself. Which was when I noticed I was getting some strange looks from the glamorous, fully fledged smokers on the terrace.

I left the second-hand smoke and walked down the few steps to the lawn.

Whatever about the dull event, there was no denying the beauty of the setting of the Wicklow Landon Hotel – it was breathtaking. Freshly cut grass lay green and proud as it swept down the hill towards a running stream and copse of trees. I stared out at the sea in the distance, then kicked off my high heels and took a sip of my gin and tonic. The cool grass felt wonderful beneath my bare feet.

"There you are, Mel!" I turned around to see my best friend Katy walking towards me down the hotel steps.

"Isn't the weather glorious?" She linked her arm through mine when she reached me. "So are you enjoying the day?"

Katy and her boyfriend Frank had invited me along to the fundraiser for a new youth café and counselling service, so I didn't want to seem ungrateful. "Eh . . . yes, thanks, hon. And it's such a great cause." I looked away from her, back out at the view.

Katy touched my elbow. "Come on, Mel, this is me you're talking to."

I turned back. Katy's usually smiling face was sporting a furrowed brow. The game was up. "I suppose it's just not really my kind of thing, that's all."

"What? It certainly used to be your kind of thing, Mel – you used to love going to events like these when we were in college. Why don't you let your hair down a little and enjoy yourself today?"

"It's not the same, Katy. College was a long time ago. We're grown up now, and everyone's all coupled up and sensible these days – most of them anyway."

"Well, the music's just started and Frank has some nice single friends – why don't you come in and talk to a few of them? Maybe have a dance with one? You never know, Mr Right could be waiting for you just inside . . ."

I smiled at her determination. "Sure where would I have time for any man, let alone Mr Right? I've more than enough to cope with, trying to stay on top of my new promotion at work and saving up the money I need to renovate the new house. I want to make sure my future is secure – with or without a man."

"Fair enough," said Katy. "But remember, your dazzling career won't keep you warm at night."

"No, but the new fully insulated roof it puts over my head will!"

"All right, all right, I give up," Katy sighed. "You win."

She went to sit down on the grass, holding up her lovely, long, sea-green chiffon dress that went so beautifully with her wavy auburn hair.

I eased my own tight black dress up slightly and sat down beside her.

"I wish I'd worn something a bit lighter," I said to change the subject. "I'm roasted in this thing. I should have realised that everyone would be wearing bright colours and pastels at a lunch in May."

"Sure you look great in whatever you wear, Mel," Katy said, but she sounded a little distant. I knew she was disappointed in me, and I started to feel a bit bad then. It was nice of her and Frank to invite me along to the lunch. I needed to try to pick myself up and get into it.

"Ah sorry, Katy. Don't mind me. Why don't you go in and find Frank for a dance? I'll follow you when I've finished this." I held up my glass. "I'll even come and talk to some of his friends."

"Right – I'll hold you to that." She gave me a smile, scrambled to her feet, shook her dress out and went back inside.

I rested my head on my knees and just sat there for a few minutes, staring down over the rolling green hill out at the Irish Sea in the distance, enjoying the peace.

"Nice quiet spot you've got here."

I turned and shaded my eyes to look up at the man standing over me, pint glass in one hand, fat smoking cigar in the other. He was tall and broad and looked a little familiar, but the sun was shining directly above him, making it difficult to see him properly.

"Mind if I join you?" He sat down beside me and took a long puff of his cigar.

I stole a brief glance at his face – late thirties, I reckoned, good-looking but not in an obvious kind of way, just something about him. He had sandy-coloured hair, cut short at the sides but already starting to curl on top. Who was he, though? How did I know this guy?

I turned back to the view, and I couldn't help myself breathing in some of the cigar smoke. For the first few seconds it was divine, but either the smoke was very strong or I breathed it in too deeply – either way, I started to cough.

"Sorry, is the cigar bothering you?" The guy flapped his hand around but just ended up blowing more smoke in my direction.

I swallowed the last of my drink and thankfully it seemed to work – the coughing finally stopped.

"Sorry about that – me and my evil cigar can go away if you like?" he said.

It took me a few seconds to get my voice back enough to speak. "Yes, that's probably a good idea." I was already missing the tranquillity of a few moments earlier.

"Ah, you don't mean that really?" He looked at me sideways and grinned.

I just sighed loudly, willing him to leave. But he didn't take the hint – just stayed sitting beside me, alternating between taking a swig of his pint, and a puff of his cigar.

"I haven't smoked one of these in years," he said after a while. "Somebody bought it for me earlier, though, so I thought why not? I need something to get me through – just one of those days, y'know?"

"Yep, I hear you," I said – referring to both the lunch *and* my growing need for a proper nicotine fix.

He must have read my mind. "Sounds like you might need a drag yourself there?" He offered me the cigar.

"No, thanks, I don't smoke," I said, feeling like such a phony. Though there were days like today when I really missed it, I hadn't smoked a cigarette in almost seven years. My ex-fiancé Ian had hated my smoking habit – it was one of the first things he pressured me to change about myself when we got together.

"Dead right too, filthy habit," said the man, stubbing the cigar out in the grass. He parked the pint glass precariously on the grass beside him and looked at me. "I noticed you earlier at the lunch. Did you have somewhere else you needed to be?"

"Sorry?"

"Just that you were checking your watch all through lunch – you seemed pretty uptight, that's all."

He'd hit a raw nerve. "Uptight?" I put my knees down and turned to face him. "Who are you calling uptight? You don't even know me."

"All right, steady on!" He pulled his head back and opened his eyes wide to feign shock at my reaction.

I turned back around to the view.

"You just seemed on edge, that's all," he said. "You couldn't sit still – must have got up from the table at least four or five times during the meal. Either you had somewhere else to be, or you have an overactive bladder!" He raised his eyebrows and smirked at me.

More than anything in the world at that moment I wanted to wipe that irritating smirk right off his face.

"So you were watching me then, were you?" I flicked

my hair behind my shoulder. "I'm afraid I'm not interested." I looked straight ahead at the view, delighted with myself.

He laughed. "You're all right – me neither, darling."

Right, that's it, I thought.

I went to stand up. "Time I was going."

"No, wait, don't." He put his hand out to stop me. "Where are my manners? I'm sorry about the comments. I'm not that bad really when you get to know me. I just can't ever seem to resist stirring things up. It's a personal failing – has got me in a lot of trouble over the years. Please sit back down – you looked happy there."

I settled back down with some reluctance.

He held his hand out. "The name is Richard Blake – pleased to meet you."

"Richard Blake . . . I'm sure I've heard your name before, and you look familiar – have we met?"

"Could have done, I guess. I'm a journalist for the *Irish Chronicle*. You?"

Of course. That was it!

"You're the guy who wrote that article about the Dublin Millennium Centre for the Arts last week, aren't you?"

"Yes, the very man," he said, looking pleased with himself. "Not a bad article that, though it should have been better. I tried to spice it up a bit by throwing in a flavour of my theory about an imminent Irish property crash, but my editor was having none of it – she and I hold vastly differing opinions on this country's economic outlook. In the end, that compromise report I filed was pretty bland – just like the subject matter. I did like my headline though." He leant back on one arm and sketched it out in the sky: "*Another Run-of-The-Mill Development Project* – most excellent, even if I do say so myself. Edith just about let me away with that one – after a struggle."

"Indeed. Well, let *me* introduce *my*self," I said, turning towards him and holding out my hand. "I'm Melanie McQuaid, director of marketing and development at The Mill. I'm responsible for marketing the venue, all public relations and fundraising for any new development at the centre. You'll find that that was my newest building project you were trashing."

"Ah," he said, sitting up straight, looking suitably chastened.

"Yes – 'Ah' is right. Do you have any idea of the hassle your article caused me? I spent all week fielding media queries after it went out – and as for my boss . . ."

I closed my eyes, remembering my boss's reaction – one I would have preferred to have been able to forget. Marcus Boydell, The Mill's CEO and artistic director went nuts when he read the scathing article about his pet project – which wasn't good for me. I'd only recently been promoted to director level and I knew I still had a lot to prove to Marcus, and to all the others who felt that at the age of thirty-four I was still too young and inexperienced to be taking over as second-in-command at Dublin's fastest-growing arts venue. After the article went out, it was all I could do to keep the press at bay and to convince Marcus that the piece wouldn't affect the forthcoming major fundraising campaign for the new wing.

"Correct me if I'm wrong, but didn't The Mill issue a press release on this project?" Richard said. "And isn't the whole point of a press release to get the media interested? You should be thanking me really."

Wise-ass!

"Anyway, you can just be glad I didn't get to file the copy I really wanted to file," he said.

I just stared ahead, almost afraid of what I might say.

"Oh, come on! You have to admit it was a fair piece, Miss McQuaid. There's no way you're ever going to raise all that money – fifteen million euro of private funding to co-fund the twenty-million government grant? No chance! No matter how successful The Mill has become, or how wealthy your clientele, it's completely off-the-scale stuff for a relatively new arts centre."

I sat up straight. "I admit nothing, Mister Blake. This project is sure to be a massive success."

I tried to sound confident but the truth was I'd never really been convinced about the scale of the new project myself. It was a highly ambitious plan, arguably *overly* ambitious. I'd tried to persuade Marcus at least to put off briefing the press until we had the majority of the funding in place, but he didn't want to hear it. My boss was nearing retirement, and now that the dream of running a venue with facilities large enough to stage full-scale opera and ballet productions was finally within his grasp, there was no way he was going to stay quiet about it. In the end it seemed my opinion didn't matter. I had to toe the company line.

"You'll see," I went on, in an effort to convince myself as much as Richard Blake. "In less than three years' time, you'll be standing in a queue along the quays of the River Liffey trying to get in to see a full-scale ballet production in our new state-of-the-art auditorium."

"I wouldn't bank on it." He laughed.

But when he saw I wasn't coming around, he looked

down and nodded slowly in defeat. "Right, I'll just go now then, shall I?" He took a long swig of his pint then went to get up.

"No, you're all right." If I was being honest I'd actually agreed with most of what he'd written – even if I would never admit it to him. "Whatever about the rest of the article, I did quite enjoy the bit you wrote about our chairwoman." I couldn't help but smile.

"Ah yes – the infamous, spoiled Fenella Wright," he said. "That bit was an added bonus." He smiled, then tilted his head down and looked sideways at me. "Any chance we could start again? My friends call me Richie." He held out his hand. "Peace?"

I paused for a second to think about it, then gave in and smiled. "Oh all right, go on then." I took his hand. "Nice to meet you, Richie. I'm Mel."

I scanned his face properly as I shook his hand. It was one of those friendly faces – he looked tired and his eyes were a bit bloodshot, but he had a cheeky smile. I imagined nobody was able to stay annoyed at Richie Blake for too long.

I turned back to face the view and we both just sat there for a minute in silence.

"So what drove you to the cigars?" I asked him after a while.

"Women! What else?" He gestured behind us towards the hotel. "I'm avoiding one, and supposed to be in there celebrating my engagement to the other."

"I thought you said you were at the lunch?"

"Yes, but we only got engaged yesterday, so we just told our friends and families about it at the lunch today. My future father-in-law and fiancée are in there now organising champagne for everyone. Which is a bonus, I guess – she's been trying her best lately to turn me teetotal – reckons I drink too much." He took a large swig of stout from his pint glass.

"Do you?"

He wiped the froth from his mouth.

"What?"

"Do you drink too much?"

He looked at the pint glass. "Ah, I suppose. But I need something to get through. I mean, why is it we all have to conform anyway?"

"What do you mean?" I asked. "Conform to what?"

"Marriage. Why do we all have to get married anyway?" he said. "What's wrong with just staying as we are and enjoying one another's company? Why do we have to give in to convention – to marriage, kids and the like?"

"I couldn't agree more," I said. "I, for one, am never going back there."

"Back? Were you married before, then?"

"Nearly – it's a long story." I changed the subject quickly: "So why are you getting engaged if you don't want to get married?"

"Shagged if I know." He shook his head slowly. "Sometimes I think I must be on some kind of white-knuckle ride that I got led onto – now I'm being carried along on it and I have no idea how to get off – don't even know if I want to. It's all pretty damned confusing." He took another swig of his pint. "The trouble is, I've never been very good at relationships. Sooner or later every one that I've ever been in comes crashing down around my ears."

There's nothing like a fellow-sufferer to make you feel better about your own situation.

"I hear you," I said, warming to the topic. "I'm a bit of a disaster in that department too. In fact, I find it easier these days to just keep life simple and stay single."

"Sounds like I should have spoken to you last week then – before I popped the question. Everyone else kept telling me to make an honest woman of her – herself included. I guess I just caved in, in the end."

"Well, I hope it all works out for you."

"Thanks." He looked at me. "So you're really single then? No boyfriends? Fiancés?" He took my left hand and turned it around, looking for an invisible ring.

I pulled my hand back. "No. I've more important things on my mind at the moment." I flicked my hair behind my shoulders.

"Like what? Fundraising for that daft ego-driven development project?"

I shot him a sideways look. "Yes, actually, that is one thing. But there's more than just that – in fact I've got a five-year plan."

"Oh, you have, have you?" he said, raising an eyebrow. "Now why doesn't that surprise me? Go on then, let's hear it."

I knew he was mocking me, and my five-year plan was one thing I didn't joke about.

"Why would I tell you my secrets?" I said. "You're a total stranger."

"Stranger?" he said, feigning hurt. "Sure you know more about me already than most of my closest friends do."

I smiled – he had a way about him, despite all the talk.

"Why is it that it's always easier to talk to a stranger, d'you think?" I asked. "Is it because there's no baggage there? No past?"

"Maybe," he said. "Or maybe it's because you know you're never going to see them again, so whatever you say can't be used in evidence against you in the future."

"You never know!" I said. "I could turn up at your newspaper some day to sue the pants off you for another of those libellous articles of yours."

"Ah, it'd be worth it to see you again." He gave me a cheeky smile.

I tried very hard not to smile back. "I thought you said you weren't interested?"

"That was before I got hooked by your magnetic personality, and now that I know you're available, well . . ."

I caught him looking down at my legs, and pulled the hem of my dress down to cover my knees. "Eh, you're engaged, remember?"

"So I am. I keep forgetting." He glanced back at the hotel. "Ah, I'm just kidding around." He turned back to me. "Come on, I want to hear about this five-year plan. Tell the nice stranger your innermost secrets."

"No chance. I'd probably end up reading about it next week in the gossip column on the back page of that rag you write for."

"Touché," he laughed. "Go on – our discerning readership wouldn't have the slightest interest in a lowly arts-centre director, so you're safe on that score."

Oh, what the hell, I thought. I'll never see him again anyway . . .

I turned around to face him. "All right then, I'm almost four years into the plan now and I just bought my dream house – or at least the best one I could afford given Dublin property prices these days. I've had some work done to it, but there's still a bit to do. I also now have an

382

MBA to my name, and I recently got the promotion in work that I wanted. So it's going well so far. In a year or so, when I've finished refurbishing the house and have replenished my savings a bit, I'd like to travel some more, maybe visit a few of the top dive locations around the world."

"So you dive then?" He seemed impressed. "Where would you go?"

"Red Sea, Great Barrier Reef, those kind of places." I started to get into the conversation, warming to one of my favourite topics. "But the trip I really can't wait to do is one I read about in a water-sports magazine last year – it's to the Norwegian fjords to see the killer whales. You wear a drysuit, mask and snorkel and then float on top of the water to watch them swim underneath."

"Killer whales, eh? Wouldn't it be dangerous getting in the water with them? They've killed people in the past, haven't they?"

"In theme parks and aquariums, yes – they can become quite dangerous in captivity. But it's not the whales' fault – they can go a bit crazy after being kept cooped up in swimming pools no bigger than bathtubs to them, away from their family pods, made to perform inane tricks for food. It's so sad." I sighed. "But there's no record of a killer whale hurting a human being in the wild."

Richie raised his eyebrows. "That's good to know, should I ever happen upon one."

"The company running the trip in Norway is fully licensed too," I went on. "They have to follow very strict regulations and safety precautions – to protect both the whales and the people going in the water with them. And anyway," I smiled, "I like a challenge – keeps life interesting."

"I bet you do." Richie smiled back at me. "It's an impressive plan, I'll grant you that, and I get the sense you'll do it all too."

"I most certainly will." I leant back on my elbows.

He took another swig of his stout, finishing it off. "Thing is," he said, interrupting my daydream of sailing through the snow-capped Norwegian fjords, "the good stuff is all a bit of a way off, isn't it? I mean, what do you do for fun nowadays?"

I sat back up straight. "I have fun. I'm bloomin' great fun, in fact."

Richie sucked his cheeks in. "I'm not sure I believe you, girl. That master plan of yours is all about work, doing up houses and saving. The interesting bit – the travel – doesn't come into play for another couple of years."

Why was everyone on my case about this lately? I sighed. Maybe they were right. I had been a bit dull of late.

Then I had an idea. I jumped up.

"What's up?" he asked.

"I'm going to prove I know how to have fun. Now give me those glasses." I took the slim gin glass I'd been holding and the empty pint glass he handed me, then turned and dropped them both down beside the nearest bush.

"*Woah!*" Richie looked shocked.

"Ah, I'm sure they're bio-degradable." I knew he thought I was dumping them but I quite liked the idea of shocking him.

I walked in my bare feet over to the edge of the lawn without a backward glance. Then I knelt down and stretched out so that I was lying flat, face-down at the top of the grassy hill.

"What are you doing now?" Richie shouted over. "You're going to wreck your clothes!"

"That's one of the advantages of wearing black – no grass stains." I laughed and rolled myself over until I was lying flat just on the brow of the hill. "My brothers and I used to do this all the time when we were young – it's great fun. Come on – get over here. Or are you all talk?"

Richie stayed sitting where he was. "Most definitely all talk." He looked back up at the terrace. "People are looking at us, y'know? And I'm trying to keep a low profile here today."

"That's fine, Richie!" I shouted back. "Stay there. Be boring. But don't accuse me of not knowing how to have fun!"

"You're cracked!" He got up and walked slowly over towards me.

"Yeah, maybe . . . *wheeeeeee*!" I pushed myself off the side of the hill, and I was off, quickly picking up speed. I was rolling so fast down the soft, downy grass, and laughing so much, that I could only just about make out the blurry shape of the man rolling down behind me.

"This is *craaaaaaz-y*!" Richie shouted, just before bumping into me at the bottom.

We lay there beside each other for a while. I was laughing so hard that tears were streaming down my face.

He sat up then and leant back on his hands to look at me. "All right, I'll hand it to you, Miss McQuaid – that was great *craic*."

"Thank you, Mister Blake. So I'm not so uptight then after all?" I said, wiping the tears away.

"Definitely not. It seems first impressions can be

deceiving. You're not one bit uptight, Miss – you're completely stark raving bonkers!"

I laughed.

He shook his head, then started to get up. "All right, that's enough fun and frolics for one day. I'd best get back to the lads, not to mention the fiancée and future in-laws – they'll be sending out a search party for me at this rate."

He held out his hand and pulled me up, and we walked slowly back up the steep hill, stopping every now and then to pick up the loose change that had escaped from his pockets.

"You go on ahead," I said as we got to the top and I sat down to strap my shoes back on. "You might just want to tidy yourself up before you present yourself to the future in-laws though." I nodded at the back of his trousers.

Richie looked over his shoulder at his rear. He grinned, then wiggled his backside from side to side as he brushed the dirt and a few loose pieces of grass away.

I shook my head and smiled.

He turned to go.

"Hey, Mister Blake, any chance you could drop those two not-so-biodegradable glasses back to the bar?"

He grinned and picked up the glasses.

"Catchya again so," he said as he strode off indoors.

If you enjoyed this book from
Poolbeg why not visit our website:

www.poolbeg.com

and get another book delivered straight
to your home or to a friend's home.

All books despatched within 24 hours.

POOLBEG

Why not join our mailing list at
www.poolbeg.com and get some
fantastic offers, competitions,
author interviews and much more?